LAMIA

A WITCH

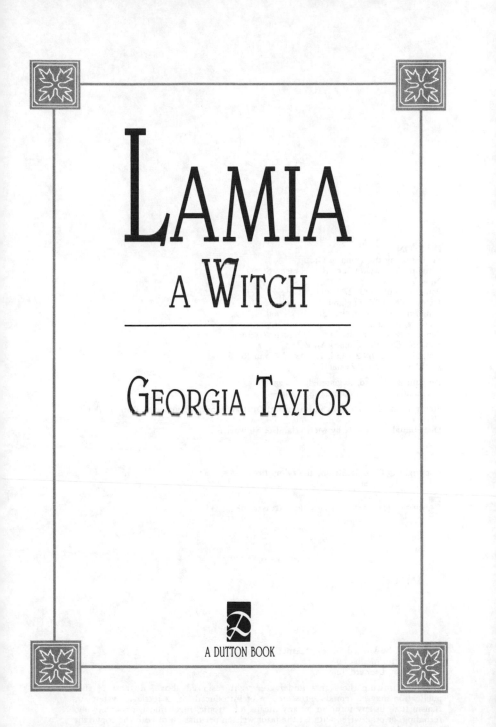

LAMIA
A WITCH

GEORGIA TAYLOR

A DUTTON BOOK

DUTTON
Published by the Penguin Group
Penguin Books USA Inc., 375 Hudson Street,
New York, New York 10014, U.S.A.
Penguin Books Ltd, 27 Wrights Lane,
London W8 5TZ, England
Penguin Books Australia Ltd, Ringwood,
Victoria, Australia
Penguin Books Canada Ltd, 10 Alcorn Avenue,
Toronto, Ontario, Canada M4V 3B2
Penguin Books (N.Z.) Ltd, 182–190 Wairau Road,
Auckland 10, New Zealand

Penguin Books Ltd, Registered Offices:
Harmondsworth, Middlesex, England

First published by Dutton, an imprint of Dutton Signet, a division of Penguin Books
USA Inc.
Distributed in Canada by McClelland & Stewart Inc.

ISBN 0-525-93745-5

Printed in the United States of America
Set in Trump Mediaeval
Designed by Leonard Telesca

For my daughter, Diana—
"So rainbow-sided . . .
And full of silver moons . . ."

She was a gordian shape of dazzling hue,
Vermilion-spotted, golden, green, and blue;
Striped like a zebra, freckled like a pard,
Eyed like a peacock, and all crimson barr'd;
And full of silver moons, that, as she breathed,
Dissolv'd, or brighter shone, or interwreathed
Their lustres with the gloomier tapestries—
So rainbow-sided, touch'd with miseries,
She seem'd, at once, some penanced lady elf,
Some demon's mistress, or the demon's self.
Upon her crest she wore a wannish fire
Sprinkled with stars, like Ariadne's tiar;
Her head was serpent, but ah, bitter-sweet!
She had a woman's mouth with all its pearls complete . . .

John Keats, *Lamia*

PART ONE

THE CHILD

Chapter 1

THE LOIRE VALLEY SEEMED to sigh, its whispering breath shivering a ground-hugging mist into whirling, spectral forms. The sun was not yet visible in the sky, lingering behind distant hills, but its light had painted streaks of pink and gold upon the gray, calmly moving surface of the river.

Curled up underneath a tent of intertwined, rustling trees, Lamia slowly awoke. She stretched, yawned, and rolled over on her back, rubbing her eyes with grimy fists. A rabbit scampered out of the undergrowth and hesitated before her, curiously sniffing the air, then vanished in a flurry of disturbed dry leaves.

Suddenly filled with energy, Lamia leaped to her feet, alert, dancing in circles on the flat of her toes, eyes darting into every shadow of the heath. Her filthy arms and legs goose-fleshed in the chill dawn breeze. When she was certain that no danger lurked, she dashed to the river's edge and jumped into the icy water, wading up to her knees. Crouching low over the clear water she searched with keen eyes for any fleeting, silver movement. Swiftly she lunged, her arm a blur of motion, a struggling fish quickly defeated by the bite of her sharp teeth.

Smiling triumphantly, Lamia sat back on the bank and casually gnawed at her breakfast, chewing and swallowing resignedly, her ear constantly tuned to catch the slightest disturbance in the surrounding woodland, her eyes casting around about her in agitated watchfulness.

Lamia abruptly sprang to her feet, her head snapping sideways that her ear might better capture the sound of approaching, plodding hooves. She scampered into the brush, brambles tearing at her ragged clothing and exposed flesh. Breathing rapidly, she skulked out of sight, clinging to the thick branch of a tree that grew close to and overhung the river.

Bishop Geoffroi halted his ass and dismounted, taking himself to the riverbank, where he splashed water up to his parched lips. The sun was in full sight over the hills now, slicing through the trees in warming shafts of light. Just before dawn he had departed from the parish of Pevele for the castle of Nevers and its parish, which would be the last call on his monthly visitation schedule.

Dropping his scrawny frame to the grassy slope, he lifted his skirts and slipped off his soft leather shoes, then stretched out his legs to drop his aching feet into the water, sighing with pleasure.

The forest rose silent and shadowed all around the bishop and he felt momentarily at peace with a chaotic world. An occasional shout echoed from a distance, the castle of Nevers only a few leagues south of this small, open heath. The sharp cry of a falcon spoke of Count Jacques' occupation this morning. He thought that it was a good and prosperous time in France, Louis XII having forsaken his Italian aspirations, the Hundred Years War at an end, all France enjoying, in this year of our Lord fifteen hundred and nine, a delightful moment of peace and contentment. King Louis was called Father of the People. Indeed, Louis was the protector of the poor, but just as his recent predecessors had been, he was the enemy of the Church and of the landed nobles. Louis' ambition was to swallow up both land and churches in order to form what he envisioned as a "nation" under his absolute authority; a vision smacking of Godless avarice and pretension. Burgundy, Armagnac, Brittany—so many of the great provinces had already been absorbed into this so-called nation, as well as uncountable millions in revenues that by divine right belonged to the Pope.

To remain loyal to Holy Church would force him to align himself with the nobility, the barons and counts, Charles Duke de Bourbon, all of whom were firmly on the side of Holy Church against King Louis. These oppressors of an already wretched populace had vowed to fight to the death rather than bow to Louis' inclination to vastly enlarge his kingdom. Though he agreed with King Louis' benevolent attitude toward the peasantry, the bishop could not give the king his allegiance, because he pressed Rome harder each year for further concessions, for larger percentages of the Catholic revenues, and arrogantly assumed authority over the clergy of France to which he had no right whatsoever.

Suddenly the bishop's eye caught a flash of red to his right and his gaunt face blanched. That sense of tranquility he had been enjoying was gone and would not return this day. He was not calmed by the fact that the menace was now invisible behind brush that rose fifteen feet in a clump and fell to touch the river. He crossed himself and whispered a prayer. He knew what was lurking only yards from his vulnerable soul—it was the Devil incarnate.

A horse and rider crashed out of the forest twenty yards behind the bishop and he jumped to his feet, hands clasping together over his quaking lips, so shaken by the unexpected intrusion he had nearly fainted.

"Greetings to you, good friar." Giles de Sade grinned down at the bishop from his mount, after reining in sharply before the startled priest. "Could you direct me to the Castle de Nevers? I have wandered this forest for an hour and am lost, I fear. I am cursed by too little knowledge of this countryside. Pray, is the castle north or south of this heath?"

Gathering himself up and taking hold of his shattered wits, the bishop stared rudely at the comely stranger, distrustfully noting the foreign cut of his attire, the glint of his dagger, and the white plume arrogantly stabbed into his velvet cap. He wore soft leather riding boots of the finest quality that rose to the middle of his muscular thighs. The accompanying heavy-laden mule spoke of the lad's intention to remain for some time at his destination. Odd, but from a distance one would think him to be Rainulf, son of the count; he had the de Nevers cut of the head and amber eyes that matched his hair and beard. But his height was far greater than any member of the house of Nevers, and his features were more regular, with a slightly feminine delicacy of bone structure.

"Bless you, my son," the bishop said peaceably. "I can indeed direct you to the castle, for I also travel there. I will personally escort you, if you please."

Murmuring his gratitude, Giles stiffly threw a leg and slipped from the saddle. When he had cupped water into his hands at the riverbank, to wet his tongue and cool his face, he said curiously to the bishop, "Tell me about this place called Nevers, Father. Are there sufficient sins here to occupy you? Or do I enter a valley of Godliness?"

Taken aback by the youth's disrespectful words and tone, the bishop faltered an instant, then snapped, "I would hardly discuss with a brash and impious stranger the private affairs of my diocese."

Giles lifted himself to his feet and smiled at the priest. "You wear friar's robes, Father," he said goodnaturedly, "but I suspect you enjoy a higher rank."

"*Bishop* Geoffroi de Nevers. And, pray, indicate your own rank, my son, which appears to be Lord of Insolence. May God forgive you such excessive pride."

Giles stared coldly at the bishop for long moments, then said roughly, "It was you who performed the sacrament that bound Francesca de Sade of Florence to Count Jacques de Nevers for eternity, was it not, Bishop Geoffroi?"

"It was."

"Well, I am the single issue of that connection. It was you who baptised me Giles. And now you name me Lord of Insolence. I am deeply offended, Bishop."

Bishop Geoffroi's mouth had dropped open in amazement, and a coldness had formed behind his eyes. "You have returned." He stated the obvious in the somber voice he might have used to pronounce penance upon a confessed sinner. "Is your mother well, my son?"

Giles averted his eyes and said emotionally, "She died a fortnight past." Clearing his throat, he added, "She is in Heaven."

"Indeed . . ." was the bishop's response, his tone suggesting there was some doubt in his mind on the matter.

Giles' eyes sparked and he shouted defensively, "What is the meaning behind your most peculiar tone of voice, Sir?"

"How can any of us know, for certain, my son, which of the dead ascends to Heaven, which descends into Hell? Only God, in His merciful wisdom, can know."

"I! I can assure you my mother found Heaven, for, in this instance, we are speaking of a saint, who lacked only the habit and investiture, living otherwise as virtuous and divine an existence as the virgin nun herself!"

The bishop stepped toward Giles, his face flushed with indignation, but before he could say a word, a high-pitched screech issued from the brush, then a splash and further wails of distress.

Both men whipped their heads around in surprise.

"No!" the bishop warned, as Giles instinctively began a dash for the brush. "You must not interfere."

"But someone is—Bishop! Let loose of my arm!" Giles stared dumbfoundedly into the priest's panic-filled eyes; his arm was being stabbed by the man's fingernails. "Bishop! I said, let loose of me!"

Bewildered, Giles hesitated. A chill ran up his spine. It was as if the priest had seen a demon that was invisible to himself. But when another screech, more urgent now, emerged from the brush, Giles wrenched his arm free and rushed to rescue whoever it was thrashing out of sight in the bramble.

"Saint Mary!" Giles exclaimed, as his eyes fell upon a ragged urchin caught in the branches of a fallen tree. Her legs were held by branches from which she hung down with her head half under water. She was fighting like a wild thing to keep her head above water and to release her fastened legs. When he reached down and pulled her head and shoulders up, she whirled on him, baring her teeth and fighting desperately, as if he were attempting to drown her, rather than save her.

Swearing and cursing her, Giles struggled to free her legs from the tangle of branches while she scratched at his face and yanked at his beard. When he finally succeeded in releasing her, he clutched her up under one arm and shouldered his way out of the bramble to the clearing.

Giles planted the creature on her feet before the cowering man of God, keeping a firm grip on her frail arms. He snapped at the bishop exasperatedly, "What ails you, man? You continue to tremble before what turned out to be only a slip of a girl, not more than eleven years breathing on this earth! It is only a hapless babe."

The child eyed the bishop hatefully, her thin chest heaving as she fought to catch her breath. Water ran in muddy rivulets down her forehead and over her cheeks, dripping off her chin. Her long hair clung to her face, nearly blinding her. She lifted a trembling hand to wipe her eyes clear, then whipped her hair back from her face. "Swine," she hissed, and spat at the bishop's feet.

"Here, now," Giles protested paternally, "that is no way to behave, hmm? The bishop will not like you if you spit at him, and if he does not like you, God will not like you. So be good, Fiametta, for Heaven awaits the virtuous."

In reply, the wretch spat at the priest again. At the bishop's puffing, speechless distress, Giles found it difficult to hide his amusement. Returning his attention to the wretch, he inspected her closely. Rags hung over her protruding bones, only a semblance of clothing. Her fingernails were so long that they curved over into claws and were as crusted and infested as the rest of her. Twigs and burrs were tangled in her mass of red hair. Mud had formed a grim mask on her face. Her feet were bare and bruised. Behind the savage defiance in her eyes, Giles thought to glimpse a special, unreadable kind of agony. He had looked into the eyes of many unfortunates, but never into a pair such as these, full of a loathing so volatile that it unsettled him. He knelt down so that his face was level with hers and softly asked her to tell him her name. She gaped at him an instant, seeming uncertain, then she spat on him with a stubborn ferocity.

"Do not *touch* her!" the bishop commanded, as Giles lifted a hand to strike the wretch for spitting on him. "She is lamia! That name speaks for itself!"

"A witch—a demon?" Giles stared at the priest in disbelief. "This damp and ragged orphan? You are mad, priest, simply bereft of your senses." But the bishop's expression indicated total conviction, his horror as genuine as it was foolish. "You frighten the child with such talk," Giles said softly. "A witch? Absurd."

"Absurd!" the bishop echoed vehemently. "Look to your soul, Giles de Nevers. It is Satan you would protect from my accusation. Not merely a witch. She"—jabbing a convicting finger toward the iron-jawed little girl—"she is not merely a *witch*, she is the daughter of Satan, the child of incubus, conceived upon Midsummer's Eve at the Witches' Sabbat. The blessed saints protect you, do not touch that child again."

Lamia suddenly lunged forward, growling as fiercely as a lion cub, baring her teeth in an effort to further intimidate the terrified prelate.

The bishop backed away from her approach. When she halted, laughing at him, he cried out, "I will see you burned, loathsome wretch! Soul of Satan, I will see you *burned!* Seize her. Seize her, I say, in the Lord's name. God forgive me the negligence that has kept my judicial hand from her these many years. Giles de Sade-Nevers, I have commanded you to seize her!"

First he was commanded not to touch her for fear of his immortal soul, then he was ordered to seize her. Giles drew himself up to his full height, transfixed before a phenomenon he did not quite comprehend. Witches were everywhere, even in enlightened Florence, and they were being burned everywhere, but none that he had ever heard of were *children*. Surely this priest would not put a child to the stake. But the man's continuing agitation offered no assurance of that. The child was leering at the priest with a profound fearlessness, the twist of her mouth and light in her eyes suggesting at the least insolence but certainly not fiendishness. Giles thought that in these times, with Holy Church on an Inquisitorial rampage in Europe, it was decidedly foolish of this child to defy a bishop so brazenly. A child witch. Ridiculous.

Giles' mind lingered on the subject of witches. Self-styled sorcerers and witches did indeed exist and were said to be performing at all levels of European society, even within the framework of Holy Church. Claiming liaison with the Devil, they defied the Church with obscene rituals. Giles was uncertain whether it was Satan that motivated them or some mysterious disease of the mind. Undeniably, there existed a festering evil in the world, rampant and increasingly virulent. Though its impetus might be questionable to Giles, it was distinctly manifest to this clergyman, who saw the living Devil in a grimy, disrespectful urchin.

"Forgive me, Bishop," Giles said firmly. "I will not seize this child so that you can burn her. It was a barbarous suggestion, which I am certain you already regret."

He had rendered the bishop speechless with indignation, but Giles, raised in a city where disdain for the clergy was the capricious enthusiasm of a new age, the light of which did not yet shine upon Nevers Province, fearlessly ignored the threats of priests. He disclaimed none of the tenets of the Faith. It had never occurred to him to deny what had to be considered fact. He merely no longer practiced his religion. In Italy it was *popular* to criticize the clergy. He found this French bishop's fury somewhat irritating. Defiantly he took one of the child's dirty hands in his, which she allowed to rest there, her wide and curious green eyes fixed upon him.

"I shall call you Fiametta from here on," Giles said warmly to her. "The name means 'little flame.' Lamia is not a good name for so pretty and innocent a child. My name is Giles de Sade. I have traveled far, from the city of Florence, and plan to dwell at Nevers castle for some time." He leaned to place his mouth close to her attentive if wary ear, and whispered confidentially, "In seven days I will return to this heath, Fiametta. If you will meet me on that day, I will have new clothing for you; shoes perhaps."

The expression on Lamia's face did not alter. She stood with her feet set wide apart, meeting his eyes unfalteringly. She nodded her head slightly in agreement.

"Bon," Giles murmured, patting her on the shoulder. He turned back to the bishop and said, "Now, you may guide me to monseignor's castle. As you can see, lightning has not struck us down, though we have been half of an hour in the Devil's presence."

"You have invited Satan's hand to touch yours, Giles de Sade. May God have mercy on you and forgive your sinful deference to the fiend." The bishop vowed further that a wound would begin to fester from that satanic touch. Soon

Giles' very soul would be consumed by a raging fire of damnation that would set his blood boiling.

Lamia ran behind Giles and the bishop as they spurred their mounts, shrieking every curse she knew and devising originals to strike terror in them. "Satan! I call thee. Merciless spirit who sits in the cemetery, go and place a knot in the bishop's head, in his eyes, in his mouth, his tongue, his throat—put poisonous water in his belly that will kill him. Kill him! Satan, kill him!"

When the two men had vanished into the wood, Lamia bounded to the riverbank and clutched up the bishop's shoes, which he had forgotten in his haste to escape her presence, hiding them inside her shirtwaist. Scampering away, like a fox with a stolen chicken, she followed the curve of the river, then turned onto her own well-worn footpath. She never hesitated long in any one place, fluttering like a restless hummingbird to the river and back again, by one of a dozen such paths, a hundred times a day.

To Lamia the world was one square mile of woodland that was surrounded by an ocean of malevolence. She roamed this seemingly vast wilderness alone. In summer she ran naked. In winter she stole into the village, snatching torches that she might have a fire, and food that she would not starve. In spring, flowers fairly exploded into miraculous life in a thousand secret places, and she would wriggle under a fallen, dead branch, or into the brush, to gasp in awed delight at the sight of a minute and perfect thing of beauty.

Lamia plunged breathlessly into the cave, dropping upon a heap of dry leaves and branches. Sunlight sliced down from a crack in the rock over her head, a yellowish beam that caressed her still mud-masked face. Quickly she hid the leather shoes in a crevice behind her. She smiled triumphantly, for they might bring her coppers with which to buy bread from the baker's son, who was more greedy than fearful of her. Her mouth watered, her tongue flicking out over her lips in anticipation. Sighing contentedly, she wiggled down to stretch out full length, fascinated by the dancing fairies in that beam of light entering from above. How tiny they were, she thought in wonder, her innocent eye able to see their sparkling wings. Some had laughing faces, others impish grins, and one or two were of a more sour disposition—but they all had come upon the sunbeam just to cheer her lonely heart. She did not know what she would do if the fairies ever ceased to appear. When the sun did not shine, they came upon the flames of her night fires and gave her added warmth. Eliza had said that every little-creature had a mother, but no father, and that the fairies' world was lovely and happy, because they had a good God who loved them and would not allow them to suffer or ever be lonely, and they did not know pain, nor did they die, but lived forever dancing on sunbeams and firelight. Eliza had taught her so many things. But Eliza was dead.

Lamia shivered and rolled over on her stomach, burying her head in her arms. She did not like to think about her mother, for when she did she would see her there, in the flames, Eliza thrashing, the fat boiling under her crackling flesh, screaming horribly as they slowly roasted her before all Nevers Town. She tried, but she could not block out the memory; it shimmered grotesquely before her mind's eye and tore her heart to shreds, knotted her stomach into a hot ball and tossed it up to her throat. She beat the damp earth of the cave floor with her fists, wailing, "Ma mère—ma mère," but her eyes remained dry. A witch could not weep, and she was a witch. The Devil, her father in Hell, would ascend and beat her soundly, if she loosed a single tear.

Chapter 2

 THIRTY-ONE YEARS BEFORE GILES de Sade rode into France from Italy to claim his inheritance, Lamia's ill-starred existence was designed by persons she would never know. It was the year 1477. Louis XI was king of France and Count Henri, Giles' paternal grandfather, was the despised overlord of Nevers province. The Catholic God was enthroned in the minds of the peasantry as monarch over all men, even over the Spider King, who, occasionally, appeared to think himself more almighty than the Almighty. The one monarch was of this earth, the other of Heaven and of the spirit, but, in actuality, the Devil reigned, King Louis said to have made a pact with Him. In vain a wretched populace had raised its gaze to Heaven; then, in despair, it turned its gaze elsewhere, in search of a better God, and the Prince of Darkness rose from Hades to heed their cries and to rule immutable.

On Midsummer's Eve of that year—it was a black and moonless night—Satan's demons seemed to yowl hideously on the winds outside the hovel of the widow, Jeanne. The woman lay alone on her rude bed, filthy rag coverlets pulled up fearfully to her trembling chin. She was not old, only thirty and nine, but field labor, malnutrition, and the bearing of twelve children had fashioned a mask of old age that enshrouded her from straggling, gray-streaked hair to wrinkled face, bent shoulders, warped and varicosed legs, broken and bunioned feet. All Jeanne's children had been sons. Only two lived of the twelve. Three had died at birth, two of mysterious causes before they were one year, four of the pox eight years past, and one son had been hung at the age of twelve for petty thievery on the well-used gallows of Count Henri de Nevers.

Only the eldest of Jeanne's two living sons had been allowed to marry, gone now to the fief of Baron Louis de Pevele. Count Henri had refused permission for Georges, the younger, to wed from another fief as his brother had, and the Church forbade his entering into marriage with any cousin less than six times removed. Georges was one and twenty, and connected by blood to almost the entire fief. There was not a single young female whom he could take as wife, and unsanctioned intercourse was God-despised. Georges did not dare to sin openly, for Heaven was the only compensation offered to him. He had no sisters to ravish secretly within the privacy of the hovel as would other lads facing the same predicament. All the sunlit hours of each day were consumed in brutal field labor, yet at night Georges' energies were such that the unsatisfied hunger within him often erupted in violent explosions of temper. His dirty, sallow flesh was forever pocked with festering boils and scabs that drove him mad with pain. He bitterly held rein on his sexual appetite and prayed to God for a miracle, which he was still young and naive enough to hope for.

Returning from the village festival of Midsummer's Eve that night, so drunk he could barely stand and only dimly aware of what he so desperately required, Georges entered the foul-smelling hut, viciously kicking aside chickens and a pig, to find his way to the one bed in which the entire family had always slept, now shared only with his mother. He fell to his knees and stared open-mouthed and drooling at the woman drawing the coverlets further up to hide her face.

Jeanne's mind froze in terror under the threatening stare of her son. She prayed to God for deliverance, but, once again, He did not hear her. Georges' hands were upon her in the dark. She cried out in protest, but he did not have to beat her into submission, as many another son had and would again.

Pure despair prevented the mother from resisting any of the multitude of evil forces pitted against her daily. With a stiff resignation she succumbed to the inevitable. Thus was Eliza conceived on the Devil's night, the night of the Witches' Sabbat.

Jeanne gave birth to Eliza one week after Georges died of dysentery. There was no one left to till the soil and the tiny plot was given to another family to work. Jeanne was driven out of the hut with her infant. Father Jean, the young parish priest, condemned and excommunicated her for the sin of incest, and none would give charity to the hapless widow or to her squalling infant. Jeanne called out for alms at the castle gate for six days, but was again and again driven off as unworthy of charity.

On the seventh night, starving and in a state of hysterical desperation, Jeanne took herself into the forest. She lay flat on her back on the damp earth of the small open heath, the babe tucked into her bodice for warmth. Gazing up at a black sky, she cursed God for his everlasting punishments, his brutal, loathsome silence and neglect. She accused Him of deafness, of fiendish joy in her endless sorrow. Then she screamed out a plea to Satan for charity. In her delirium, the Devil came to Jeanne, stood before her hideous but benevolent, and she promised him her soul, anything, everything, if he would give her aid, save her infant from death, which the fiend gallantly promised.

Thus armed with the conviction that now she would survive—no longer limited by the laws of God, all the devious, malfeasant powers of Satan at her disposal, Heaven irretrievable—Jeanne set upon the villagers and peasants with a fearful vengeance, proclaiming her pact with the fiend. With brutal threats, trickery, and contrived witchcraft, she obtained food enough and sufficient monies to sustain herself and Eliza.

Soon the townspeople and serfs, each with their own sorrow and grudge against a denying God, and ever credulous, began secretly coming to Jeanne for potions and charms, cures and hope, which she concocted imaginatively and with amazing success. The unimpeachable instinct to survive had transformed the widow Jeanne into a witch. Loathed and dreaded, she nonetheless was the one person sought after by the desperate, whether noble or peasant, when all else failed. She attended the Witches' Sabbat the first year, where she met the witches of Pevele and Bourges, and from every village and town of Nevers Province, some having traveled from as far as Bourbon and Sancerre. Following that Black Mass, Jeanne was in constant association with others of her kind, and her techniques were refined, her degradation consummated.

Count Henri de Nevers died of a heart seizure in the summer of 1481, and his son, Jacques, fell heir to the great castle, the town of Nevers, and a few thousand wretched souls. Fewer corpses hung from the gallows now, the castle dungeons were not quite so densely populated, and peasant wenches were less often ravaged by drunken hordes of bored knights sweeping down from the castle hill, but the young count quickly earned as much disrespect and loathing as had been heaped upon his father.

When Eliza was seven years old, Jeanne The Witch ill-advisedly sold Count Jacques a potion to cure his ailing wife of the falling sickness. After swallowing the potion, the frail countess, wed to the count less than a year, fell dead rather than into one of her usual comas. The old witch was hunted down, captured, and brought before the secular court of Nevers on accusation of witchcraft, murder, and heresy. When she refused to speak in confession, Jeanne was sentenced to the supreme test. She was stuffed into a sack that was weighted with stones and tossed into the river Allier. If she floated, she was proven to be a witch, since water was the holy fluid of baptism and refused to swallow anyone who had made a pact with the fiend. In that event she would be released from the sack and immediately burned at the stake. But if she sank, drowned, she was proven innocent.

To the dismay of the clergy and nobility looking on, Jeanne sank to the bottom of the river. She had been innocent. How could that be? But no matter. God knew his own. Either He would take her up to Heaven, or condemn her to Hell; it was in His hands now and, satisfied, they departed from the scene.

Eliza was taken into the household of young Father Jean, where her soul was put to exacting tests in order to determine whether the sins of Jeanne had irreparably contaminated her. The Devil was exorcised from her flesh again and again, but the Father was never certain enough of his success to put her in a state of Grace. He withheld the sacraments and Heaven from the pathetic child, while he at the same time explained, with diligence to detail, every horror of the Hell to which she would undoubtedly descend after death. He also described to Eliza, as was his duty, the more lurid aspects of the deterioration of the flesh after death, once having a corpse that had hung from the gallows two weeks brought to the rectory as concrete evidence of the inflictions suffered by the damned. He used that same corpse the next morning at Mass, as a reminder to his entire flock.

Eliza had been sapped of emotional strength by the deprivations of her short existence, had been of unsound mind when she entered the house of Father Jean, thus she could not withstand his pious harangues. One night, six months after the death of her mother, Eliza lay gasping in terror as the priest hovered over her, vehemently cursing the putrid, abominable, loathsome, hideous, scaled, slimy demon that was alive somewhere inside her. The light of Eliza's mind snapped out. After that, she no longer heard the priest's voice. She lay smiling simply, unable to offer reply of any kind to his insistent, repetitious queries and condemnations.

It finally became apparent to Father Jean that Eliza was indeed possessed and incurably so. He confined her in a cell deep under the church, to be kept there until she was of an age to burn.

In the grossest squalor, barely alive, Eliza languished in that cell, entirely unaware of the punishment in store for her.

In the year 1487, Geoffroi de la Tremoille was appointed Bishop, accepted by Charles VIII, son and successor of the dead Spider King, and investitured in Rome. That winter he made his first ecclesiastical call on the parish of Father Jean, during the course of which he demanded a look at the prisoners in the dungeons. Subsequently, a young man blinked at him from out of a black hole, his crime that of fornication, having been apprehended in the act of carnally possessing a willing peasant wench on the hallowed ground of the church cemetery. He had been in prison one year. The bishop motioned to the guards to close the iron door, satisfied that another year would do much to purify the lad's soul and prevent another such blasphemy.

However, when the bishop beheld the child, Eliza crouched in the far back corner of her five-foot-square cubicle, he was appalled. Though she was now nine, her appearance was that of a girl of six or seven years. She weighed no more than forty pounds. Her flesh was horribly infected, her toes and fingers scabious and oozing where rats had chewed at her. It was a miracle that she lived.

"In the name of the Blessed Virgin, Father Jean! What is the meaning of this violation of innocence?"

Father Jean's hasty explanation of demonic possession did nothing to salve the bishop's indignation. The book that was to thoroughly clarify Holy Church's methods of detection, that would correct errors, instruct against ignorance and direct action, had not yet been printed in Germany by His Holiness, Inquisitor General Jacob Sprenger. At this time Bishop Geoffroi was unable to accept that a child was capable of effecting the works of the Devil. Therefore, he demanded Eliza's immediate release, and the next day she was put into the hands of the parish charwoman.

Eliza was allowed to survive to womanhood, even grew lovely, with long and waving auburn hair, the physical scars of her imprisonment quickly healing. But her height at full growth was no more than four feet and five, and her mind remained infantile. Eliza's body, however, diminutive as it was, developed as voluptuously as any normal wench's.

In 1495, seven days prior to All Hallow's Eve, one year following the publication of the Malleus Maleficarum, the Inquisitor General's Hammer Against Witches, Eliza vanished from the charwoman's house. The witch of Claire, in need of a virgin priestess for the coming Sabbat, had chosen the daughter of Jeanne, who dumbly allowed herself to be taught the simple, obscene rituals.

On the night of the Black Mass, men and women of Nevers slipped stealthily away from their narrow confines and trudged expectantly toward the predetermined meeting place. Whispering invitations had been delivered by the witches; only a select few knew the sternly guarded secret— the precise location.

In silence they entered the chosen field from worn footpaths, ragged serfs each with a woman, nobles disguised by tattered cloaks and face masks, that same pious Father Jean in his black-skirted soutane and a fiendish mask, until more than one thousand were amassed before the idol erected at the edge of the wood. Carved in human form, with a grotesque and prominent phallus, the figure of Satan loomed before the credulous and trembling assemblage. His goatlike face was twisted into an expression of fierce lust and mockery.

A hush fell upon the thousand, as a torch was lighted and flamed between the horns of the idol. Then the witches and sorcerers appeared in ceremonial parade from the black wall of trees; at their head, Eliza de Nevers, whose bright hair gleamed supernaturally in the torch and moonlit darkness. The procession halted before the forbiddingly shadowed statue, forming a line before it, while Eliza knelt with her hands folded reverently.

Four youthful, intent witches stripped Eliza naked, then removed their own apparel, whereupon they knelt with Eliza for suspenseful moments in silent prayer. They then rose and lit their torches from the flame burning between the idol's horns, stepping back and surrounding the young priestess. Eliza rose unsteadily to her feet and fearfully moved to the deity, careful not to look upon his face, for to her eye he was not wood and plaster but the living Devil. She did as she had been instructed and leaned forward to put her lips upon his buttocks in a symbolic gesture of obscene mockery to God, each witch following her lead. "It is not a backside," she had been told, "but a second face he has under his tail."

A chalice of blood, urine, and moss water was put into Eliza's hands. She raised it to her lips, letting the vile fluid spill over her chin, down the length of her to the ground. Thus confirmed as priestess, two witches aiding her by holding her under the arms, Eliza impaled herself on the erect phallus of the idol, a sharp cry exploding from her throat.

Eliza had given her virginity to Satan, and the crowd fell to its knees and prayed to Satan as Chief of the Serfs and God of Liberty. Wine, beer, and hard cider laced with belladonna was served to the thousand. Soon they rose intoxicated to dance, whirling back to back in dizzying circles, building to a frenzy. The Mass could now be resumed.

The naked, now drugged priestess was placed outstretched upon the stone altar at the feet of the idol. The witches sang in chorus, "*Adonai, Elohim, El, Eheieh, Asher Eheieh;* King of Kings, Existence of all Existences, be merciful to us and look upon Thy servants who call Thee with humility, and beg by Thy most Holy Name Tetragrammaton to be benefitted. Order Thy angels and planetary spirits to come and be here; o angels and planetary spirits! O all of you spirits! We conjure you; we the deputed of God! Let God order you to come, that we ask most fervently and humbly. Amen."

The crowd gasped in delicious terror and cowered back like a wave from the shore, when the Devil ascended from Hell in an explosion of flame and smoke from out of the bowels of the giant idol. The fiend stood masked and naked before his own likeness. Almost immediately, out of further explosions, he was surrounded by a host of masked demons. The Devil moved slowly to the altar and deposited upon the belly of the priestess the offerings of the faithful—a black cat with its blood drained. He spoke the Catholic Credo backward in a loud, resounding voice, and pieces of human flesh, representing the last dead and the latest born of Nevers, he laid beside the cat. The morsels were devoured ravenously by the attendant demons. In effect, the priestess had given her own flesh to be eaten in sacrifice. A witch came forward and broke off the head of a live toad over Eliza's belly, reciting, "Ah Phillip! If I had you in my hands, I would do the same to you," referring to Phillip de Valois, who led thousands of serfs, and France, to the slaughter at the Battle of Crécy, and into the agonies of the Hundred Years War that still raged.

The rites having reached their climax, Satan threw himself upon the priestess and ravaged her, which was the signal for a mass orgy, each man falling upon the nearest woman, no matter which, mother, sister, another's wife, all identities lost in the storm of their hysteria.

Eliza, having been released by her satanic lover, eyes fired by rekindled insanity, leaped from the stone altar and threw her arms to the black heavens, but she could not recall the lines she had been taught. She stood open-mouthed and immobile, blood running in thin rivulets down her inner thighs.

An elderly witch rushed forward and cried Eliza's words

for her, in a terrible, shattering voice, "God! Bring down your lightning upon us—if you can!"

The silence was profound. No lightning struck. God had been vanquished. The Sabbat was concluded.

The congregation was slow to disperse, but finally began to wander off, the serfs staggering back along their well-worn footpaths to the everlasting circles of their hopeless existences; Father Jean to his parish, where he would continue in callous veneration of the God he had just insulted; and the noblemen to their empty, aimless lives. Eliza de Nevers, possessed by Satan, drugged and insane, stumbled not back to the charwoman's house, but remained in the wilds. Not one who trembled in dread of her believed more thoroughly in her evil taint than Eliza herself.

Eliza gave birth in naive conviction that the infant emerging from within herself was flesh of the Devil, daughter of Satan, and she named the infant Lamia. All those who had seen the demon ravage Eliza believed this also, and all those who heard tell of it, which made Eliza a very special witch, her child even more remarkable.

The faithful were instructed that the Lord God could manifest Himself to mankind in various forms, including human, and so could the Devil. No doubt was permitted on this point. Thus Lamia was considered to be the offspring of Satan, entering the world from the loins of Eliza, just as the Christ had emerged from the loins of the Virgin Mary. Villagers and townspeople became so enthusiastic about this phenomenon, exaggerated it to such an extent, that soon not one of them dared set foot near the cave where the witch, Eliza, dwelt with her diabolical infant. That daughter of Satan possessed hair of fire and eyes green as a cat's, it was said, and even the witches were in dread of this incarnation and they too avoided the cave. But the peasants dared not totally desert Satan's offspring; he might crack the earth and swallow them down into hellfire in retribution. So each day they sent their terrified children into the woods with offerings of food and clothing.

Lamia indeed seemed to possess the Devil's own strength, managing to survive the putrid dampness of the cave, growing fat on witch's milk. Her perfectly formed head had sprouted hair the color of hellfire, and her flesh was pale as autumn moonlight, resisting almost entirely the common skin eruptions following upon filth and malnutrition. She lived untouched, when a thousand children died of pox. She spoke words at an age when normal infants still gurgled moronically, and she never wept, the truest evidence of possession. The Devil's own arrogance lighted her intelligent cat's eyes, and Eliza came to live in as much dread of her child as the villagers.

Plagued by the heretic priest whom he had years past reprimanded for Eliza's imprisonment, Bishop Geoffroi at last succumbed to the pressure put upon him by the entire clergy of Nevers. The book of Jacob Sprenger was now his Bible, second only to that containing the Word of God, and he ordered Count Jacques to send his guards into the forest to seize the witch, Eliza. But her child was to be left unmolested. It was written, "—if a father has compelled his young son to go to the Sabbat and give himself to the Devil, then I should judge the son worthy of the lash or banishment, but if the child has been there repeatedly, then he is worthy of being punished by death, for such repetition shows a consent and evil intent of ill-doing." An eleven-year-old child had recently been burned at Basle—but the bishop could not yet bring himself to accept this edict, suffering enormous degrees of mental anguish due to this heretical lack of faith in the Inquisitor General's edicts. A child of nine years; he could not burn her alive and continue to live with himself.

Eliza readily and innocently admitted to her pact with Satan, her part in the Sabbat, without benefit of torture. How could she deny what was unquestionable truth? Lamia was brought from the wood so that the sight of her mother's agonizing punishment would discourage any propensity in her to evil ways—then was returned to the cave. Offerings from the peasants stopped at Eliza's death, for the bishop had proclaimed it mortal sin to give alms to the child of Satan, thereby giving authority to what he did not himself entirely believe.

Lamia was left to survive as best she could, but she was nine years old, and the daughter of a daughter of a witch, as much at home in the forest as the scampering rabbits. That she would be allowed to reach womanhood was doubtful. The bishop's weakening mind had already brought down the age of reason from sixteen years to fourteen—tomorrow he would say twelve. Tomorrow his terror of Satan, his frantic hunt for witches and demons that existed everywhere, visible and invisible, upon the winds, in the air, in the screech of a lusting cat of a dark night . . . a room, a street, a field, now suddenly unsure . . . a door untouched might close, a picture might walk, a tree might speak, an animal might not be an animal, a man might not be a man but a devil—these waking nightmares wrought by his absolute conviction of the truths outlined by his faith, would by tomorrow have driven him to the point of madness.

As Lamia lay envisioning fairies in the sunlight that brightened her dreary rock hovel, but a few days before her twelfth birthday, miles away the bishop strode red-faced into the church of Father Jean and ordered an immediate force of men to take the child of Satan into custody; he would see her vile flesh turned to ashes within a fortnight.

Giles de Sade-Nevers also thought of the flame-haired child, as he approached Nevers Castle. What a strange little waif, he mused, unable to erase the image of her from his mind's eye. He glanced down to his hands that held the reins, looking at the places where she had touched him. He smiled contemptuously, for his skin was as free of abcess as it had been before. What fools, these Frenchmen, these illiterate barbarians, living in an age that passed away half a century ago. Superstitious children, the lot. Criticism of the clergy was definitely *not* a diversion in Nevers but sheer folly, punishable by death at the stake, so Giles warned himself to mend his Florentine ways and show more respect to the priests.

Giles expected his father to be no less archaic, a man whose face he could not possibly recall, last viewed when he was only one year of age, a face he dreaded looking upon this day. It would be all he could do to control a murderous impulse to cut the brute's throat.

Damn him, why had he come to this place, to grovel before such a man as Count Jacques de Nevers? How he detested his uncle Cinto for his lustful affair with the siren *money*, but it had to be admitted that gold had enslaved himself as well or he would not have allowed Cinto his way, would not be riding thus toward an inheritance that he held in utter contempt. Suddenly he must become a Frenchman, become heir to the petty throne of Nevers, while in his heart he was Italian, only his mother's child. Ah, but it was only for today. Tomorrow, when this land was his, he would give it all to Cinto and return to Florence, his City of Flowers— return to graceful living, a life of ease and merriment, according to the promise made him. The thought that his father was only forty and nine chilled his hope slightly, but he quickly reassured himself and entered the castle gate smiling confidently.

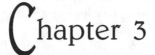

Chapter 3

ON A NARROW LEDGE above the floor, at the far back of the cave where the darkness was complete, Lamia slept curled into a ball. Outside, the night sounds of the woods whispered a familiar lullaby.

Suddenly Lamia reared up, her heart slamming against her ribs. She flattened her back against the rock wall and listened with breath held. No unusual sounds had reached her finely tuned ear; it was instinct alone that had alerted her.

Someone approached the cave; she sensed the foreign presence, even if she could not hear the steps. She sucked in air, holding it until her chest pained her. Still she heard nothing. She was certain the bishop had come—God had sent him to capture her. God could not wait until women died, to roast them in hellfire, sending his soldiers after them while yet they lived—He did so enjoy the screams and groans of his suffering children. She saw Eliza burning, her meat cracking and separating from her bones, a memory that caused Lamia to tremble so violently her teeth clacked together noisily. It was not fear that wracked her; it was hatred.

"Bring lightning, Father," she hissed under her breath to the Devil. "Burn him where he stands. *Burn* him as he burned Eliza. Burn—him!" In her quaking urgency Lamia's face had twisted into lines of fierce and brutal resolve.

Her mind sharpened and her vision cleared, so that her eye seemed to pass through the rock dividing her from the approaching enemy. She saw a woman hesitating only yards from the cave opening. Often she affected such images, which she accepted as perfectly natural, never once doubting the authenticity of what she beheld in this way. Her tension immediately relaxed. It was a woman and not the bishop, or the count's guards, so she slid from the ledge and crept toward the cave opening, to observe the intruder and ascertain her purpose, for good or ill.

The woman was not young, or old, but her face in the shadows was unusually fair to the eye. Her hair was hidden by a drab woolen scarf. Her skirt was of rough cotton, her bodice worn and patched, and over her shoulders she wore a brown, knitted shawl.

Lamia watched silently from her hiding place, asking herself if this woman was friend or enemy. The voice in her head answered, *Friend.* Confidently, she stepped out of the cave into the open and waited for the woman to notice her.

The woman did not at once see Lamia. She felt the child's presence even as her own had been sensed. She turned her head slowly and smiled across the space that divided them. Walking smoothly toward Lamia, she said in a pleasant voice, "Greetings to you, ma petite."

"Greetings, woman," Lamia replied civilly. The voice in her head had said friend, and she did not doubt it for an instant. Of a certainty, then, this woman was also a friend of the Devil, or she would be no friend to his daughter.

The woman studied Lamia's face closely with pitying eyes, then she reached out a graceful hand to touch Lamia's cheek in maternal affection. "I have come for you, little witch. You realize, of course, that you must leave this place. You are no longer safe here."

Lamia's mind scampered uneasily over the woman's words. Leave her woods? This was the world. Venture out into that sea of evil beyond? Surely she was safer in her cave. "I thought you the bishop, at first," she offered lamely.

"Will you come with me?"

"I wish to stay here, good woman. But, if my father has sent you, then—"

"Your father?"

"Satan is my father."

"Oh, I see." The woman frowned, then said urgently, "Let me speak to you of why I have traveled to this place in search of you, child. But come, let us seat ourselves, for I am quite tired. I walked from Bourges, which is some distance to the west."

Fascinated, Lamia moved backward to drop her rump to a soft pad of leaves under a tree. The woman sat down beside her, leaning back with a sigh against the tree's trunk.

"What is your given name, child?"

"Lamia."

"Lamia! That is the name your mother gave to you at birth?"

"Oui. Why does everyone gawk so when they hear my name? Yesterday the bishop told it to a stranger and he quickly cried out, 'witch.' How did he know that I was a witch, only from the speaking of my name?"

The woman hesitated, leaning forward uncertainly. "It . . . it is actually a well-known name, but . . . it is the name of an ancient queen of Libya, who was loved by a god named Zeus. The goddess, Hera, was jealous and had Lamia's children slain. Lamia, in spite and malice, robbed other mothers of their children and tore them to pieces, sucking their blood. Presently, her beauty, which Zeus had loved, altered to bestiality. It is a name spoken in the Bible as the word for witch, or evil woman. It is a dangerous name to inflict upon a child in these times. You must have a new name, ma petite."

Dumbfounded, Lamia stared at the woman, amazed at the lurid tale attached to her name. But she could not imagine herself as anyone else; a different name implied a different self. She thought upon the ancient, dead queen, then said flatly, "I would not kill a child."

"Indeed . . . why not?"

The woman's eyes revealed a strange attitude behind the question. Again Lamia found herself gaping at the woman in confusion. Finally, she snapped, "Because I have enough to eat; I do not need to kill children."

"God has said that it is sinful to kill anyone—ever," the woman persisted softly.

Lamia gasped, eyes rounding. "Did you hear him say such a thing?" she asked incredulously.

"It is written. In the Bible."

"Oh, God's book," Lamia muttered in disgust, recalling the enormous volume held in the bishop's hands as Eliza burned. She added emphatically, "I do not believe God does not want us to kill. God said no such thing."

"No?"

"No. God puts everybody to death, sooner or later. Eliza said that he made us in his own likeness and there is nothing he enjoys more than killing. I don't know why he would be angry. All we would do is kill someone before he could? *My* father does not kill people; he only takes to Hell the ones God kills and does not want in his Heaven."

The woman laughed admiringly at Lamia's logic, gained from a short lifetime in the forest, only God knew how many years utterly alone—judgments made with an intelligence that was obviously inordinate and precocious powers of observation.

"Back to why I have come for you," the woman said warmly, still smiling. "It is strange, sometimes frightening, yet wonderful that we experience these—what can we call them but messages? Eight nights past, as I lay wakeful upon my bed, my mind not concentrated upon anything in particular, a sudden awareness overcame me. 'The Red Witch of Nevers,' my mind said clearly to me, over and over again. Then I heard a voice say, 'Men will seize her, men of God; the child must be saved.' I could not comprehend the meaning. I knew of no child; no Red Witch. I was haunted by the voices for two days, until I could do naught but strike forth toward Nevers. You must come to Bourges with me, or these men who are to come will kill you. Do you believe what I am saying, Lamia? If you do, then you must follow me."

Lamia met the woman's eyes squarely, searching for truth behind her soul-hiding features. Then she saw the face of Giles de Sade clear before her inner eye, the kindness it wore that had melted her armor against him. He had promised her clothing and shoes. She had agreed to meet him seven days hence. With a small sigh of regret, she abruptly jumped to her feet, running into the cave. She returned moments later with the shoes of Bishop Geoffroi in a hand.

"I will take only these," Lamia said intensely, raising them to show the woman. "I thought to sell them, but now

I think I will cast a spell upon him through this stuff that has touched his flesh. You are a witch. You must teach me how to kill him. He will never burn me. Never! I cannot be burned."

At that, Lamia struck out determinedly, leaving the place where she had been born without looking back to see if the woman followed, without emotion.

"Wait," the woman called after her. When she caught up to Lamia, she said, "Here, ma petite. Put on this scarf to cover your hair." She drew the cloth from her shirtwaist and wrapped it around Lamia's head so that not a red hair showed to the eye. "Now, little witch, we will walk to Bourges, but only at night. During the day hours we will hide and sleep."

Two nights later the woman and the child entered the city of Bourges, a rambling cesspool of filth, ramshackle wooden structures, and crowds of clustering, yammering people.

"What is—*this!* What is it you have here, Peronnette? Is this to what your vision led you? I fear you have wasted five days."

The man was dressed as handsomely as a nobleman, Lamia noted, as she gazed cautiously up at him. She had never been within the walls of a house before. The carpet was soft as moss under her bare feet, and the piece-glass in the windows of the room, now reflecting the flames of a dozen candles, was the Devil's own miracle. Upon the wall behind the man who examined her so arrogantly hung a shimmering object which appeared to be a room, or part of one, dead center of the wall. But within that curious room stood the woman who had come for her—now standing exactly behind her at the door.

Ignoring the low words passing between the man and the woman, Lamia moved closer to the mirror, and as she did so the top of a red head appeared, then a grimy forehead, two green, inquisitive eyes. Reflected in the river she had seen a wiggly-wavy image that she knew to be herself, but this was true and lifelike. She backed away in dread, for it was a demon most certainly.

Noticing what Lamia was doing, Marco Cellini laughed roughly. "Peronnette, she is one part human and four parts puppy dog. I expect she will bat a paw at the glass any moment now."

"Teach her, Marco. She has a will of iron. We walked twenty miles in a night, and not once did she falter or complain."

"Its name?"

"Believe it or not—it is Lamia. She is called The Red Witch."

"Ah hah! The Red Witch, eh? I am aware of her terrible reputation. The scourge of Nevers, I have been told." He laughed to indicate his contempt for such hysterical nonsense. "Child, step here to me. Come. Do not lag back; I will not eat you. I have had my evening meal."

Lamia glanced once more into her own eyes, then obeyed the command, moving to stand directly before Marco, whose broad, ruddy face scowled down upon her contemptuously.

"It is true, eh? You are a *witch!*"

"Oui," she replied questioningly.

"Ah. Then you can fly, eh? Eh?"

Lamia hesitated, but did not take her confident gaze from his, finally admitting in a whisper, "Not yet, Sire."

"But you are a *witch!*"

"Oui, but—"

"But you are a fool. A very stupid witch. How can you know that I am not of the kind to accuse, eh? Tomorrow I could point my finger at you and say that you admitted to being in league with Satan! You would be burned. Stupid!"

"No!" Lamia barked at him. "They cannot burn me. I will not *burn.*"

"Ah, so? And why not, pray?"

"I—I am the flesh of Satan, his child. My flesh will not—not burn."

Marco stared at her in astonishment. Then he swiftly strode to a table where candles burned. He lifted one from its base and moved back to face Lamia. "Here, then," he said, "hold out your filthy paw, and we will see how invulnerable you are."

"Marco!" Peronnette protested, moving quickly to stand beside Lamia defensively.

"Hush, woman," he snapped in annoyance, never taking his dark eyes from Lamia's grimacing face.

"I will not feel it," Lamia insisted, but did not offer her hand.

"Well, *prove* it, then. I say you lie. You are not so divine a witch that you can resist fire. You cannot delude Marco Cellini as easily as you have intimidated an entire province."

Lamia set her jaw in a furious resolve, and her hand shot outward. The man seemed taken aback for an instant, but recovered quickly and set the candle flame a foot below her palm, slowly raising it.

Lamia felt the warmth turn to heat, then to agonizing pain, but she did not flinch. She held the man's eyes and refused to so much as blink, as smoke curled up a fine thread around her hand. "It—it does—not hurt me," she said between clenched teeth.

"Stop it!" Peronnette cried out, lunging to dash the candle from Marco's hand. "Must you torture her so to determine her strength? I have told you; let it suffice!"

Marco's expression immediately softened. "Look at your palm, child," he said in far gentler tones. "Look at it, ma petite witch."

Dumbly Lamia turned over her hand and stared at the watery blister and blackened flesh. "It hurts me," she confessed, her confidence shattered. She was not invulnerable. She could burn as Eliza had. A shiver began at her toes and moved up to wrack her entire body.

Marco glanced at Peronnette's accusing eyes and said, "I will teach her, my love. I will teach her. Strong innards, eh? Amazing stamina. She has the spirit of a tigress."

"Marco?" Peronnette raised her brows to form an expression that indicated she was about to say something very significant but much would be left unsaid. "It is common knowledge that thirteen years past the child's mother was priestess at the Black Mass, this child conceived in her ceremonial union with Satan." She raised her eyebrows pointedly.

Marco's eyes shot to Lamia's face, his mouth falling open in surprise. He examined every feature for a resemblance to himself, but there was no single line drawn by nature that would assure him of the seed from whence she had sprung. He could not be expected to recall a face probably not even glanced upon during a ceremony.

"Lamia," Marco asked kindly, "do you understand how children come to be?"

"Oui. They are born, entering the world from here," she said, pointing to that place on herself. "Eliza told me of that night when I came out of her. The Devil stood beside her all the while, and when I cried out a loud voice, he laughed and a hundred demons came and danced and gave me gifts."

"How interesting. And how did you get inside of her, eh? How did the Devil manage to become your father?"

"I have crept up to watch the Sabbats. I have seen men and women rolling together in the woods, just like the dogs and cats who are not afraid of me and come to play with me. That is the way, I think."

"Correct. But the Devil is a demon, not a human; he is not a man."

"Oui . . ." she agreed hesitantly.

"If he is not a man, he cannot *act* as a man. Just as the cat cannot connect with the dog and produce infants. Therefore, you are the child of a *man*, not that of the Devil."

"No! I am the child of Satan!"

"What do you mean 'no'? Smug and stubborn wretch! You are *not* the daughter of Satan!"

Lamia argued confidently, "God is not human, either. Why can *he* have a child, but the Devil not? Satan rolled with Eliza. I am his child!"

Peronnette laughed at the consternation flushing Marco's face. "Explain it to the child, Marco—do."

Ignoring the jab, he shouted, "God is God. He allows the Devil only a limited power, begetting children not included. I swear, wretch, you have the mind of a priest, illogical logic coming to your simple tongue by instinct; a congenital irrationality."

"But Marco," Peronnette argued sweetly, "is it not remarkable, considering she has never lived among people, that she can think at all, even illogically?"

"No, not particularly," he growled, sullenly staring down at Lamia. "Living divided from people I consider the greatest gift a human being could receive from the Most High. But she is tainted nonetheless, eh? Society seeped into the forest and spoiled what I might have received in a pure state. What I have here is just another deluded, opinionated, self-styled

God that I will have to melt down, pound, and remold into something resembling what God intended her to be."

Lamia twisted her mouth contemptuously, staring up at the man as if he were an idiot; not a word he had said had she understood. She determined not to bother with him further and let her eye wander around the room, thinking she would as quickly as possible take leave of this house and return to her cave in the wood.

Marco, thoroughly annoyed by the child's arrogance, and by Peronnette's insinuation of paternity, turned away from Lamia and drew Peronnette aside to the window. "The scourge of Nevers, eh?" He smiled and affectionately rested a hand upon the woman's arm.

"Ah, yes," Peronnette replied, carefully drawing her arm away from his touch. "What she believes about herself, every person from the count to his shepherds believes. It would have been only a matter of days. In the village there was talk that the bishop had ordered her to be taken. Do you think it possible to completely disguise her identity?"

Marco bit at his lower lip thoughtfully. "Perhaps. But she possesses very pronounced features; that red hair, for one thing. Those cat's eyes of hers. Remember you what the good book of Jacob Sprenger says regarding hair—that the Devil is attracted to a woman with lovely tresses, for such a woman must give her hair excessive attention, following that she is vain, thus vulnerable to the fiend's wiles. Red hair is unique, thus suspect. She is fair of feature, and time will give to her the curves of a woman. Ah, the stake looms grimly probable—unless she becomes a nun, and that, my dearest Peronnette, is as inconceivable as a bitch having kittens! And let us remind ourselves how many nuns have been burned of late, eh?" He sighed despairingly. "All are suspect, even God's own. It is said ten thousand have burned in Europe during this year. Hell has risen. Risen."

"Could we not send her away to some safer place, Marco?" Peronnette asked, looking around to where Lamia made faces at herself in the mirror.

"What place is safe? England? She would starve. And the accusing finger points wherever a church stands, wherever men live their depressed lives. Any stranger is suspect and must explain himself. She speaks only French. If asked of her parents, she would no doubt say, 'My father is Satan,' and, *ppft*, she is ashes. No. I will teach her what I can, and perhaps she will be more fortunate than her mother."

Peronnette met Marco's eyes, a light of guarded affection for him in her own. She said worriedly, "The rumor was correct. Giles de Sade has arrived and resides now within the castle. He was welcomed cheerfully, I was told, by the entire de Nevers pack."

Marco's face flushed and he began snapping his fingers in a tense, rhythmic fury. "And why not, eh? Has not Cinto de Sade—the Devil rot his string of guts—paid a king's ransom each year to de Nevers, to keep that castle door open to his nephew? He stole back the bride, his sister, when she could bear the count's barbarities no longer, after she supposedly shamed herself. It mattered not that she carried the child off with her—Cinto merely increased the dowry agreement to placate the count's wrath. . . . Damn him to hell, what sort *is* this pick of the litter? Will I have to spill his innards, Peronnette? Eh?"

"I do not know what kind he is, Marco—except that he can only be your enemy."

"Giles de Sade!" Marco roared, yanking one muscular, richly hosed leg up to slam a foot upon the carpet. "Curse him! Why did he not refuse to bend to his vulture uncle?"

Lamia's head jerked around at the mention of Giles' name, and she glared accusingly across the room at the man who spoke of him so murderously. "I will tell you what kind he is," she called out defensively. "He touched me when the bishop shouted against it. He smiled at me though he knew me to be a witch. He has a gentle touch. He told the bishop a thing or two. You need not be in fear of him."

Marco's mouth was once again open in amazement. "Where in God's name could you have met Giles de Sade?" he snarled at her.

"At the river," she replied simply, as if there were only one river location in the world, everyone as familiar with it as she.

"I do not *fear* any man," he raged, but withdrew from further argument about it. In truth, it could only be called fear. How long past? Twenty years? No, it began long before that.

For many generations two major textile merchants had

flourished without rancor in the city of Florence—the de Sade family and the Cellinis. Then, in 1479, Marco's father, Bernardo Cellini, had discovered the process of extracting a violet dye from certain lichens, and being of a naive character, eagerly shared his development with old Francesco de Sade, who gobbled it up as a hawk consumes a field mouse, naming it his own, denying the Cellini right to process it.

Although never proven, Marco believed that his father was poisoned—murdered—by the de Sades, to insure the rights to the remarkable violet pigment. The elder de Sade passed away, and Cinto, his eldest son, with his purple wools marketing at enormous prices, was able to squeeze the Cellini firm into near bankruptcy—then came smirking, with a purchase offer. Marco accepted the criminally small price and left Florence sick with hatred, determined to build again in France, a land to which so many of his countrymen had migrated recently, to amass great fortune.

Within a few years Marco was able to send a man to England and one to Flanders for superior wool. Cinto de Sade subsequently made an appearance here in Bourges, all smiles and generosity. Would Marco take de Sade goods into his shop? Cinto could give him a more than generous price. Marco threw the man out. But before Cinto de Sade left France that year, he had bestowed his sister, Francesca, and a sizeable dowry upon the widower, Count Jacques de Nevers, who had suffered financial disaster as a result of the king's devaluation of currency.

Count Jacques was penniless when Cinto came to Nevers that year. He was enormously rich in land and castles, but lacked sufficient wherewithal to meet another month's expenditures. He had borrowed heavily from the Duke de Bourbon only weeks before King Charles arbitrarily gifted the people with devaluation, and now he owed expensive gold and was paying with the cheaper. His ready cash seemed to dissolve from the treasury before his eyes, so he happily accepted the sixteen-year-old Florentine wench, despite her peasant blood. His loan from the Duke was paid in full by the de Sades, who possessed not a single castle, nor any land of much value, but whose coffers overflowed with a seemingly unlimited supply of gold.

Within the first year of her marriage to the count, the de

Sade wench coughed out a son and heir, and Marco Cellini saw only too clearly Cinto's intention. The arm of injustice had reached across the continent to be his second ruination. The infant would become Count de Nevers. An entire French province would have been gained by inheritance. Now, taxes on foreign merchandise protected Marco. But tolls on imports would be avoided by Cinto if he established a de Sade woolen works in Nevers; his merchandise would be undeniably French, produced on French land by French hands. De Sade shops would be opened in Bourges, Tours, and Dijon. Marco knew that he would not, even in twenty years, be wealthy enough to compete long against the inexpensive, de Sade-woven merchandise. He would collapse financially within two years of their beginning trade.

Thus far, Marco had prevented Cinto from selling more than a trivial amount of woolens in central France. A works less than fifty miles distant? A shop on this very street? No. Giles de Sade-Nevers would not live to give over Nevers Province to his murdering uncle. All the powers of Satan would be pitted against him, if necessary. Marco had made a pact with Cinto's Devil long ago—long ago. Until the day that the rich and powerful no longer sucked the blood of the defenseless with impunity, the Devil's way was the only way.

"I shall leave her, then, with you," Peronnette said softly, moving to depart.

"Eh? Ah. Yes. Yes, she will remain here. I will make a witch of her, the Devil willing—and we both know, do we not, that he is always willing. Since she is marked witch already by public opinion, she may as well be an accomplished one. And deviousness will be our first instruction, following a transformation from wench to lad." He fingered his short-clipped beard thoughtfully, scrutinizing Lamia from head to toe. "Methinks it advisable to shave her head and cover it with a wig of less striking and suspicious color. A veil of innocence, child. You must wear a mask. Ah, many a trick can Marco Cellini teach you, wait and see. If you are attentive and of a mind, you will one day hold your palm over the fire and *truly* suffer no pain. You may not be Satan's daughter today, but tomorrow you *will* be."

Gracefully, Peronnette moved to stand before Lamia,

whereupon she once more touched the child's face with a caressing hand. "Farewell, ma petite. May Satan protect you from the demons of God. No matter how bad it may seem in this house, remember you that it is far worse outside it. The stake is beyond the far door. Stay. Until you have learned as I know by your bright eye you can." With that she turned and quickly left the room, without a word of goodbye to Marco Cellini, who gazed after her regretfully.

"Where has she gone?" Lamia asked, feeling suddenly uneasy, quite deserted. "Who is she?"

"She is yourself," Marco reflected aloud.

Marco sighed and turned his eyes from the door that had softly closed behind Peronnette, fixing his gaze upon the neat table that displayed many finely appointed books and manuscripts. In a husky voice he began to tell Lamia about the woman who had heard a strange voice telling her to rescue a child from men of God.

Peronnette was from the town of Claire. She had been a clever child, always questioning. She was far too pretty; beauty had been her curse. When she was not quite fifteen years old a tanner's son had chosen her for his wife, and they had gone to the Baron Junot de Claire for permission to wed. She was a delicious sight to the old baron's lecherous eye, and he upped the marriage fee beyond the poor lad's pocket. But he had allowed that they could marry, if the first night was his according to ancient custom. The lad angrily refused, but Peronnette loved him very much and vowed she would bear any punishment to have him and bear his children.

When the priest led Peronnette from the church ceremony to the baron's castle, not only the lord of the manor, but his entire horde of butchers, called knights, awaited her. The priest was given the second place in line, after the baron, out of respect to his position in the community. Peronnette's screams raised the hairs on the heads of the entire countryside—all that night and into the next. Her young husband was run through with a sword, when he attempted to save her.

Marco swallowed hard against a rising emotion. "Now," he said on a sigh, meeting the uncomprehending eyes of the child, "Peronnette weaves cloth which I sell in my shop. No man touches her. No children have ever emerged from her womb. She taught herself to read, has read untold numbers of books, including this detestable product of mental degenerates!"

Marco had clutched up an enormous volume from the table and now threw it at Lamia's feet, informing her that she, too, would learn to read, and this obscenity she would memorize until she could recite it backward. He said it was called the Hammer Against Evil, and it was her death warrant, as well as his own. God was on a rampage. All of Europe was overcast by a reeking cloud of smoke from the stakes of Holy Church. With his help she would beat God, outwit Him, fool that He was to let the Devil live and tempt. No evil on this earth could exist without His almighty consent, this the cherished edict of His Holy Church. If He would take such joy in man's sufferings, then let Him swim in gall, for the multitude was the Devil's breed and none of His.

"Protector of the privileged," Cellini raged, pacing furiously back and forth before the bewildered child. "Let Him keep his paradise. The serfs no longer seek afterlife rewards as payment due for a hell on earth. They seek a rewarding existence here, the Devil take beyond!"

"The king is our man, little witch," Marco shouted, shaking a finger into her startled face. "Remember you this. If they would breathe free of slavery, the people must support the king. All your curses you will direct against the clergy and the noblemen, your *kind* Giles de Sade in particular. Do you comprehend me? Eh? Do you?" He nudged her with an elbow to maintain her waning attention.

Lamia nodded, her eyelids drooping, fairly asleep on her feet. But Marco seemed not to notice, persisting with hand-waving fervor.

"The counts and barons, they allow us to profit but only until our purses are fat. The yearly tournaments come due and they want to hold court for thousands, so they empty our purses to pay for their pleasures, stealing our profits!"

The merchant class commanded no soldiers to protect them against these vultures. Only the king's men served them, but his civil authority did not yet reach into Nevers, Sancerre, or Bourbon. Count Jacques de Nevers, robbed by the Baron de Pevele, took his personal army of knights, called forth all those duty bound to him, and snatched back what was rightfully his. "But when he strides into my shop, demanding I empty my purse into his pocket, who will fight for my rights, eh? Who? These Lords who rape our women and our pockets, they are preaching, praying men of God who pay the clergymen to secure the best seats in Heaven for them. I sit not with them, but choose Hell in preference. Hell, rather than—"

Lamia had abruptly sagged, first to lean on the table, then sliding limply to the floor at Marco's feet.

"Ah . . . poor little red witch." Marco smiled, forgetting his furies. He kneeled down and lifted her into his arms, carrying her out of the room. He laid her upon a bed in the small chamber behind the cookroom, placed a coverlet over her and left her to sleep.

It was merely nonsense, Marco argued with himself, as he lay wakeful upon his own bed—infantile, peasant superstition. It happened after every Sabbat. The child's mother could have dallied with half a dozen men that fortnight and it would have appeared the same. This red-haired waif could not be his child. It was against all probability. Utter nonsense. He fell asleep on that certainty and never questioned himself about it again. It was of no consequence. If so, or if not, the red witch was in his house to stay.

Chapter 4

 MARCO CELLINI CANTERED THE horse across the bridge. Wisps of early morning fog swirled around him. Rising before him loomed a maze of towers, walls, gray and brown battlements, and soaring above it all, a massive great tower, from the summit of which idly trailed the orange-and-black banner of Count Jacques de Nevers. He thought, this is not a man's shelter and comfort, it is a shrine, a monument to brutality and the hereditary megalomania of the select blood.

Young knights in iron suits were hooting and howling on the exercise grounds to Marco's left, testing their armored horsemanship. Passing through the barbican gate, he slowed his mount to watch with petulance two knights charging full speed toward each other in the lists. They would do better, he told himself, to keep their weapons in battle trim, prepared for action. Breaking lances was a child's game and a sinful waste. These cavaliers played infantile games today; tomorrow, when Louis or his successor marched from Paris, they would play with lances once again and then nevermore.

Marco spurred his mount, plunging across the castle drawbridge under which the moat stretched partly filled with slime-covered rainwater. He waved an arm to the porter, who recognized him and did not question his right to enter the bailey.

Peasant women were already baking bread in the count's great oven. The entire bailey was alive with echoing, converging life and sounds; carpenters sawing and hammering; the smith clanking his mallet against the metal of a new breastplate; hawks and falcons screeching as the chief falconer fed them pigeons—and children in various degrees of nakedness and filthiness scampered underfoot everywhere.

Leaving his horse with a stable boy, Marco strode across the cobblestoned courtyard, past the thatch-roofed storehouses, the hovels of the castle servantry and onto a second drawbridge that spanned a second moat. The ancient counts of Nevers surely were ingenious, as well as apprehensive; only a tedious siege could succeed against this monstrous pile of rock upon rock. Even kings hesitated to attack this castle. But if the experimental cannon now occupying King Louis' armorers developed according to expectations, one shot could create a passage and let an army through. Such a weapon could only be the product of the Devil's fertile imagination, and praise him for it.

Before clanging the gate hammer against the gong, to be let in, Marco turned and gazed to his left, then his right. His breath caught, as it always did when he looked upon this panoramic view.

At the triangle formed by the rivers Allier and Loire, where they dashed together, rose this abrupt rocky plateau, upon which the castle was perched, inaccessible from the banks of either river. Standing thus hundreds of feet above the land, it was an inspiring sight—those two streams that seemed forever divided in the distance, snaking through green, rich fields dotted with sheep, tumbling down hills, the Loire cutting a gorge through the forest, each so utterly separate and unique yet destined to become one stream, the waters of one indistinguishable from the other.

Directly below him a heavy chain of iron reached across the Loire, anchored in stone piers sunk at shallow places to force boats to pass close under these ramparts within range of descending missiles. Several barges lolled in a single file line, waiting as the front boatman argued bitterly with the toll taker. Finally a dozen sacks of the grain he was transporting were lifted to the pier as his toll and he was waved on. Those behind him paid, but in the king's coin.

Marco's temper began to boil again, and he prayed that King Louis would march this day upon the Duke de Bourbon—then the roads and waterways would be open again to tradesmen, and France would be one country, not a collection of independent dynasties each of which exacted its toll, until a merchant had little left by the time his boat or wagon reached Paris or Tours. The Devil burn in hell the men he would now kiss on their behinds while yet he must.

Under a carved wooden canopy, Count Jacques sat slumped in his ornate oak chair. He was listening to Rainulf chide his sister Adela about the romantic Italian novels she continuously read. The room was crowded with elegantly dressed people of rank and of relation to him. Logs blazed in the enormous fireplaces, casting grotesque shadows upon the ribbed and vaulted ceiling. Those who spoke above a whisper were bombarded by their own echoes that mingled with the reverberations of others to create a general, hollow din. Tapestries in tints of flat red, yellow, and brown, without artful perspective or fine lines, hung in scattered profusion upon the twelve-foot-thick granite walls. The few windows were closed by small panes of glass set in lead, barely transparent. The room was depressingly dark and musty.

Marco Cellini entered the dank hall unnoticed, automatically bringing up a hand to his nose in defense against the putrid odor. At a far corner of the room he noticed Mabila, the count's obese and spent mistress. Barely visible through the crowd surrounding her, the lady was squatting over a chamber pot while two pages with bored detachment shooed flies away from her exposed backside with long, feathered fans. As he moved closer, in his approach to the count, Marco heard the words Mabila uttered as she evacuated before her company: "I hate and love. You ask, perhaps, how can that be? I know not, but I feel the agony."

Marco choked back contemptuous laughter. Reciting romantic verse while she crouched there so vulgarly was a monstrous paradox. A new age might well be imminent, but this household had grasped only the smallest hint of it. These noble personages were the scurvy refuse descended from men whose world had required no more of them than animal courage proved by a sharp and bloody sword. Birth alone held Count Jacques to his petty throne, and well he knew it; blood alone rendered him "superior." The so-called nobles of this house of Nevers foolishly mimicked men they believed to be lesser than themselves, because it was the fashion to do so. They used words such as *modern* and *civilized* while uncertain of their meanings and paid the priests in gold to keep silent before the rabble as to the curious sympathy the Son of God had expressed for the detestable little men who made up an ominously large proportion of the population. From the "rabble" came the books they were learning to read, the art they were trying to appreciate, and the manners they attempted to imitate. Still barbarians, they sought to refine themselves, by becoming more commonplace.

Jacques de Nevers had so refined himself that he bathed once a year, at which time he attired himself in clean apparel from the skin out. The following year he would remove, to be washed, the undergarments he had worn night and day for twelve months; fresh outer garments were donned of a lighter weight when summer came. It was no small step toward elegance. Jacques was the first Count de Nevers in history ever to wet himself for the purpose of cleanliness, which had heretofore been considered a pointless and sinful act. He had often commented that whenever he passed by the portrait of his father, he thought to hear Count Henri laugh aloud, then groan in disgust. Thus his baths wrought both pride and shame in him. In spite of the women's fascination for the latest court fashions, they were no more certain of the propriety of yearly bathing than their men; it was no longer frowned upon by the clergy, nor was it recommended. They drew up different gowns over the same filthy chemises and petticoats, covering offensive odors as best they could with perfumes.

Marco felt himself immensely superior in his cleanliness, for he bathed himself regularly, every six weeks.

"Sire Cellini, is it?" Count Jacques queried, leaning forward in his chair, his small yellow eyes squinting. "A good day to you, my man."

"Monseignor de Nevers." Marco bowed from the waist,

and as he did so he critically examined the coarse wool of the count's hose, from which fleas fairly bounded. When the count reached a smooth, pale hand into his jerkin, scratching vigorously, Marco laughed politely and said, "In truth, the fleas of Nevers are the size of toads. The physicians should discover a poison, eh? to rid us of such gigantic vermin."

"Ach," the count coughed, "they cannot even prescribe for my ailing lungs, or the infamous plague of Satan that dashes me to the chamber pot a thousand times a day. Worthless pigs! They know nothing; emptyheaded thieves. Worse than witches brews, the stuff I swallow only to puke up immediately thereafter." He forced his eyelids up and stared blindly over Marco's head, seeing only a blur of faces and backs of heads. He brought his attention back to Cellini, rocking forward to finally bring the man's Italian face into clearer focus. "The linens and cottons arrived yesterday, Sire. Fine stuff. Excellent weaving. Mabila was delighted, has her women stitching this moment. But your prices. Good Saint Mary; I am not made of gold, my man."

Before Marco could offer any defense of his prices, the count's ear caught the coarse remark Rainulf had passed to Adela, and he coughed violently on upsurging laughter. Throwing an arm out to slam it against his son's broad chest, he bawled, "The Devil kiss my behind, a good one, Rainulf! Giles is not man enough for wenches, eh? A pewling, mewing pussycat, too gentle to scratch, eh? And too free-minded to wear the soutane. What is our Giles, then? Besides being a delightful source of revenue? One swing of my tail and he sprouted in Francesca. Methinks I was not fully ripe that night—or the *lackey* got to her first. Hmmm?" He giggled delightedly. "God love him, would not Cinto burst every blood vessel, if he thought he had paid all these years to me and—and—" He could not continue, he was so dissolved in appreciation of the joke.

Marco was smiling broadly, had given up any hope of a fair price for his cloth. This was what he had come to learn, exactly how welcome Giles de Sade was in this house, how good the chance was of his becoming Count de Nevers one day. His eyes narrowed to slits as he studied the eldest bastard of the four acknowledged by Count Jacques. The lad was eighteen years old, with the flat face of Mabila. His nose spread wide at the nostrils and was too short, leaving a vast expanse of cleft between nostrils and thin upper lip. His coarse, straight yellow hair frizzed over his ears and stabbed into his high, stiff collar, to his constant irritation. Still, he was a sturdy youth and not entirely unhandsome, nor any less intelligent than the average serf.

Rainulf caught Marco's examining eyes and he frowned peevishly, snapping between clenched, badly decaying teeth, "And what about myself so intrigues you, merchant? If it is the de Sade wool upon my back from which you received no commission, understand that it was a gift. An extremely generous family, the de Sades of Florence. Do you not agree, Sire?"

"You well know my opinion of the de Sades, messire Rainulf," Marco said evasively.

"Uh, refresh my memory."

"Murderers and thieves, the lot of them—"

"Hah! Did you hear that, father?" Rainulf interrupted, before Marco could name Giles as a possible exception. "He of the diminutive lance and glib tongue, your so long-lost heir—he is a murderer and a thief. May God spare us."

Count Jacques turned a far less certain eye to his son, a fluctuating frown pleating and unpleating his forehead. "Do not allow your tongue to become *too* sharp, Rainulf—you might slash your own throat."

"With my tongue alone I could subdue him, one flick of it and he would collapse. It is an enormous jest. Within one week I would have this castle and all the land, have him running squealing in terror back to Florence—if the duke would so much as consider such a meal-mouthed weakling as fit to be lord of Nevers. The duke requires warriors, knights, not—"

"The duke!" Count Jacques roared, deeply injured. Lurching half out of his chair in an attempt to capture a good image of his son's face, he shouted, "*I* say who is heir to Nevers, and whoever *I* say will be lord of Nevers. Child of sin! You are not my son in the eyes of God. You are my folly; my excommunication. Do not presume to edit my will, nor to anticipate my death. I intend to live another forty years; how do you like that? At fifty-eight, you will storm these vast walls against your doddering older brother? Fool! Without monies you will starve to death in this fortress, and then the king will fall heir to my lands. Think; if that is possible. Befriend your brother and you befriend the source of our *livelihood*! Be a clever mouse before the pussycat who threatens you."

Marco was fairly exploding with satisfaction and relief. He did not relish the idea of spilling the blood of an innocent lad who had never harmed a Cellini. The temperature of this house was feverish. Perhaps Giles de Sade would be ousted in good time. He would wait and see.

Adela, standing silently while her brother was verbally chewed and digested by their father, now spoke out in a studiously sugared voice. "Mon père? Now that the de Sade woman is in her grave, why do you not wed our poor mother? Half the de Sade yearly dowry has gone into the bishop's purse to spare us excommunication and hellfire. Is it not the time to make amends to God? Hmmm?"

The count visibly flinched as each word Adela spoke struck him like a knife to his lower region. His mouth convulsed over jagged teeth, and he managed a weak smile for his daughter. "Witch," he muttered affectionately in her direction. "Twice I have stood before the bishop and God. Two women did I tie to me forever. And each remained with me less than two years. Better fortune have I had with your good mother, God love her, who, I swear, is stitched to my flesh and soul, not separated from me nor out of my sight more than a few days or months these twenty-odd years. Methinks it safer to let it remain as is. Sure enough, if I wed her she will vanish, like *that*"—snapping his fingers ominously— "within the year. As it is, my sweet Adela, as it is."

Adela's bright blue eyes showed that she understood her father completely, quite aware that he had long ago wearied of her mother, that he took great satisfaction in frequent, amorous affairs, which he made no effort to keep secret; they spoke of a virility that he was in deathly fear of losing. She offered blandly, "Mother does not appreciate Giles' presence here, any more than Rainulf does. She went into hysterics yesterday and insisted she would poison him."

"Bother and nonsense. Mabila has threatened to poison everyone in this house a thousand times—me, ten thousand times. A childish tantrum. Jealousy. He is Francesca's child."

"Of course, mon père," she agreed sweetly. "For what it is worth, I find my brother Giles quite agreeable, but then, he does not threaten me in any way."

Rainulf could no longer contain his hatred. "And why not, Adela?" he spat out. "The way he sucks your hand when he kisses it fairly sickens me. Frankly, I think he forgets you are his sister, oozing compliments and fluttering his eyes at you like a—a—" He could find no word vile enough and stood mouth open in stuttering confusion. "And you are worse. I swear you will be in his bed before the week is out. I—"

"Charming. What a delightful prospect." Giles' eyes displayed his anger as he stepped around from behind Marco Cellini. He had blended into the crowd, standing behind the merchant long enough to hear his brother's last condemnations. "You are dead wrong, brother. I do indeed, and with bitter regret, remember that Adela is my sister. I remind myself of it each instant she graces my presence. Forgive me. I have disappointed you. Do beg Adela's pardon, Rainulf. You have sorely injured a lovely and virtuous maiden."

Count Jacques cleared his throat and coughed vulgarly into a fist. Then, in a strained voice, he said pleasantly to his eldest son, "Did you find your pitiful orphan, Giles? Your sister Alienor's shoes and dress are gone from under your arm, so I suppose that you offered them and they were accepted. Such charity is commendable, my son, but quite unnecessary. We take care of our people here; you will see. Mabila and the girls give to the needy each morning; those who come to the castle gates and are worthy of God's mercy. It is a sacred part of our religious duty and we fulfill it willingly. Indeed, none of God's children will be neglected while Count Jacques is lord of Nevers."

Marco Cellini gaped at the count for a moment, opened his mouth to speak, then choked on his spit, coughing so violently his eyes began to water, his face reddening dangerously.

Giles leaped to Marco's side and began pounding on the merchant's back with the flat of his hand. "Are you ill, Sire?" he queried sympathetically, ceasing his beating only after the man seemed to have regained control of his breath.

"I—I am quite all right," Marco said hoarsely. "I seem to

have swallowed wrong. I thank you, messire Giles, for rescuing me."

"Your accent . . ." Giles said curiously, as he closely examined the stranger whose bearing was no less than regal. "Are you by any chance Florentine?"

"I am," Marco replied, smiling warmly. "But I am stunned that you detected an accent. I like to consider myself a fluent linguist, French my particular forte."

"Barely discernible," Giles said with a disarming grin. "You are—?"

"Marco Cellini, Sire—textile merchant. Perhaps you have heard of me from your uncle?"

Giles thought upon it, then shook his head. "No, no, I think not. You know my uncle well?"

"I know him."

Giles retreated uncertainly from the mysterious coldness behind the merchant's eyes. Turning back to his father, he said, "No, mon père, I did not find the orphan, though I searched for her all morning. I gave the clothing to your armorer's wife for one of her little girls."

Count Jacques raised his eyebrows, musing, "That is the second child to vanish within the week. The bishop is—to say overwrought would be an understatement—he is livid. His Red Witch took flight in the dead of night seven days past, and none can or will tell of her present whereabouts."

Marco glanced to Giles, noting the cloud of caution that had veiled the lad's eyes.

"Witch, mon père?" Giles asked innocently. "Do we have a witch in these parts who has escaped the justice of God?"

"Not any longer," was his father's equally guarded reply. "As I have said, she vanished in the night."

"A curious title. Why is she known as the *Red* Witch?"

Marco continued to study Giles' face with a cold, thoughtful eye. The lad was unwilling to admit that he had met and been kind to Lamia. He had gone to meet her, as she had said he would. The only way Giles could successfully deceive his father was if the bishop also kept silent about that meeting. Curious. Why would the old fool keep quiet, unless he had in mind some more gruesome fate for this de Sade? An interesting conjecture.

"Because she has hair the color of hellfire," Count Jacques

answered hesitantly, his eyes flicking around the room as if searching for the vanished demon's skulking presence. His voice lowered and he said in a barely audible voice, "I saw her grandmother fly. With my own eyes, I saw it. From the window of my chamber on the night my first wife died. She stood on the far bank of the Allier, and then—then she transformed herself into a bat which flew straight across the river and crashed into my window. And when the glass fell to the floor, my poor wife dropped dead in her tracks, stone dead in her tracks, her throat still holding the potion that—"

"Oh! I have not slept a night," Adela interrupted in a high-pitched voice, "since she vanished. I fear she will fly right through my walls and—and drink my blood." She shivered in dread, wrapping her thin arms tightly around herself, her eyes as roving and fearfully searching as her father's. "I have heard from the village women that she—she lives on blood, that she turns into a cat at night, an enormous red cat that—she is the actual child of Satan, you know, Giles. Blessed Mary, Mother of God, I will not step a foot from this castle until she is found."

Giles made no comment. He studied the inexplicable workings of his sister's face with a detached, inquisitive attitude.

"You appear skeptical, messire," Marco commented, moving to stand directly before the lad. "So recently from the city of enlightenment, perhaps you think us overly awed here by contemplations of satanism and all its variant manifestations?"

"Perhaps," Giles admitted pleasantly, meeting the man's gaze squarely.

"Surely you do not accuse the Church of false premise."

"Oh, indeed not, Sire Cellini. I merely find it difficult to imagine a woman turning herself into a bat. By what impossible process does she alter bone and flesh, which I find to be quite stubbornly inflexible and invariable?"

"May I answer a question with a question? How does a worm become a butterfly, eh, messire Giles?"

Giles laughed delightedly and threw his hands in air. "God only knows, Sire Cellini!"

"It follows, then, that only God knows how a woman can become a bat; only God and the Devil, that is. A little skepticism is healthy for the mind, but too much can lead to heresy. A word of warning from one of good intention."

"Sire Cellini, you intrigue me," Giles said. "Do you sincerely believe that a child with red hair took wings and flew from Nevers? For some reason I do not believe you do. In your eyes I see the look of mental balance and incredulity. I think you are performing for the benefit of myself and this company. You are more skeptical than I, I would wager."

"Sssh," Marco hissed good-humoredly. "Would you have me suspect? I am only a poor merchant with a measure of intelligence and a modest Florentine education. I do not question what the church claims to be irrefutable; that would be an unhealthy indulgence. Extremely unhealthy. But, if you are ever of a mind to discuss witchcraft—academically—my home and shop are at Bourges. You will be welcome and free to probe my mental processes to your mind's content. I am fortunate to have established a rather adequate alchemical laboratory, if you are interested. My experiments are entirely within the range of secular approval, of course, but stimulating nonetheless."

Giles laughed delightedly. He had not been so thoroughly taken with anyone since he had dragged the little witch from the brush. Cellini was magnificently Florentine. He possessed an obviously fluid mind, and a significance of stature that the count with all his thunderings and power could never manage. In truth, this merchant was superior to any of the fifty or so persons surrounding him in this hall, all of whom placed Cellini but one step above the lowest serf, indeed considered him far more contemptible because of his attempt to rival their positions and wealth. The force of his personality was fairly staggering. His eyes cut through one's skull like swords and numbed the senses. "I will most assuredly take advantage of your kind invitation, Sire Cellini, at the earliest possible date. If the Red Witch does not devour me in the between-time, hmmmn?"

"Ooh," Adela squealed, "how can you jest about it? How can you, Giles?"

On the first day of the month of September, Audette d'Archambault arrived at Nevers Castle accompanied by her mother, the Baroness Louise, and a dozen knights. She suffered an increasing trepidation because she was decidedly against her mother's obstinate purpose. Giles de Sade was a derelict Italian without high-born training. He had not served a term as squire, so he could not claim the title of knight or cavalier. Audette felt herself debased by this approach to Count Jacques for the sake of suggesting a betrothal. Divinely exciting to think of herself as a countess, but whispers had it that the duke, without meeting the de Sade, had announced his violent displeasure at the prospect of this upstart as lord of Nevers. To agree to marry such a man would be suicidal. She did not care a whit how rich the de Sades were. What was mere wealth compared to the title of countess and all the benefits accruing from being of the nobility? The Court of Paris would be opened to her, and all of Nevers and Bourbon would kneel and kiss her skirts, if she were mistress of Nevers Castle. The de Sades were merchant peasants, no better than swine in noblemen's cloaks, thinking gold would erase the fact of their low birth. She would prefer to wed Rainulf, despite his illegitimacy, for most assuredly he would not allow this Italian pretender to take possession of Nevers and keep it. But her mother would not hear of it, seemed so certain, with a suspiciously bourgeois reasoning, that the de Sade gold would have its way.

But then, there he was, striding divinely handsome across the count's hall toward her, and Audette instantly chose to forget that he might lose Nevers to Rainulf. Yes, he was half peasant, but she could overlook that, because his eyes were so divinely amber; she would concentrate upon that half of his blood that was untainted. How exquisitely tall he was, and he did *seem* true-blooded, the way his shoulders were set back so proudly, his eyes harboring no lights save those of purest self-esteem.

"Ma mère," Audette whispered aside to the Baroness Louise, as Giles approached slowly toward her with a winning smile, "my mind has altered. You may proceed with all haste."

Her mother acknowledged with a triumphant, thin smile, then purred up to Giles when he stood directly before her, "A most pleasant day to you, messire Giles. So good of you to come to greet us. I am the Baroness d'Archambault, distant cousin to Mabila of this house, whom we have come to visit, as we often do in the autumn." Stepping back and aside, placing a satin-clothed arm round her daughter's waist, "This is my sweet and youngest child, Audette. She pleaded not to come; so desperately dull, you understand, listening to two old women gossip. I do hope we can find some youthful entertainment to make her stay more agreeable? Do you dance, messire Giles? Audette is graceful as a swan. Rainulf is such a clod. Your brother, Conon, tries his very best, but he is too young and unpracticed to take to the ballroom floor.

Giles grinned knowingly upon Audette's deliberately shy countenance, as her mother rambled on with an endless stream of trivialities. The girl's features were so finely drawn as to appear almost sharp. She was no thicker through the waist than his two hands could circle, and the greater portion of her bosom was stuffing and none of her—but she was the only reasonably attractive wench about, save his sister Adela, and he treated her accordingly, lavishing upon her his entire stock of insincere compliments.

Before Giles had kissed Audette's hand thrice and said half his speech, Rainulf was beside him leering like a cat drunk with nip, and the girl's hand did a swift exchange.

Kissing Audette's hand exaggeratedly, Rainulf gushed dramatically, "My eyes are blinded by what appeared from across the room a rare forest bloom and now, before me, is so exceeding fair I am struck dumb."

"Struck *dumb!*" Giles laughed sarcastically. "You run off at the mouth like our father runs off at the bowels, and you say 'struck dumb'?"

Audette allowed Rainulf a modest smile, purring, "You are too generous, messire Rainulf."

"Audette . . ." Rainulf said, deliberately ignoring his brother's words, as well as his presence, "you have grown up since last I saw you."

"I am sixteen," she said demurely, letting her eye drop provocatively. But almost immediately her glance returned to Giles, eyelashes fluttering. "Do you find Nevers pleasing, messire Giles? I do hope we see you often during these days of our visit here. I—"

"Ach!" Giles barked exaggeratedly. "I shall never forgive myself. The loveliest maiden in all France appears not more than hours before I must depart. Curse me! Had I known you were so fair, that my heart would expand thus at the mere turn of your eye, I would not have committed myself to this journey. But . . ." He shrugged helplessly with a wench-destroying smile.

"You leave?" the baroness fairly wailed. "Is it so very urgent?" She recovered herself and said less agitatedly, "We had hoped to get to know you on this visit, messire Giles."

"He consorts with alchemists," Rainulf remarked nastily. "But what else could you expect? Is not Florence noted for its Godlessness?" Then, directly to Giles, "Take care, my brother. Cellini may not be as friendly to you as he makes out."

"Your concern for my welfare touches me deeply," Giles replied with equal rancor.

Rainulf caught Audette's apprehensive eye and said grandly, "May I have the honor, bright flower that illuminates this murky hall, of escorting you while my brother dallies in Bourges with the alchemist? Your humble and adoring servant, always, Audette."

Bitterly hurt by Giles' unwillingness to set aside his plans, Audette, in an attempt to put him in his place, shone a bright smile upon Rainulf. "You overwhelm me, Rainulf. I would be most pleased to have your company. Cousin Mabila's garden is so lovely. Would you accompany me there! Now?"

"Audette!" her mother protested.

"We will return shortly, ma mère," Audette chirped defiantly, and was off with a pale hand on Rainulf's arm without so much as a further glance at Giles.

"I apologize for her—I—" Louise began, blushing under Giles' now severe and penetrating gaze.

"Rest assured, Baroness," Giles said coldly, "that when I decide to marry I will give your daughter due consideration. But know, also, that at this moment I have no intention whatsoever of taking a wife. None. And your daughter is not so endowed as to sweep me off my feet, which are most solidly and contentedly set into the blissful state of bachelorhood. I have sufficient worries; I do not need a wife to further complicate my existence. Good day to you, Baroness. I expect we will meet again one day very soon."

Baroness Louise stared incredulously at his retreating back, but suffered no pangs of defeat. It would merely require an extra trick or two. She twisted her pinched mouth, biting down hard upon her lower lip in grim concentration. The de Sade fortune and the title of Countess de Nevers were a combination impossible to forsake; they spelled a miracle of preeminence. Married to Giles de Sade, Count de Nevers, Audette and her children would enjoy all the benefits accruing from good blood and unlimited wealth. The de Sade pretender would wed her child, so help her God. And to insure that celestial aid, Louise made straight for the castle chapel and there lit a candle to her patron saint, praying for guidance on how best to proceed.

Chapter 5

STARING INTO THE SMALL mirror held in her hand, Lamia twisted her mouth in pouting exasperation. She turned her head sideways, to the other side, then back straight. Slowly she moved the glass away for a broader view, then rested it upon the table and tilted it to lean against the wall. Bending down, she could see her entire head and face. Reaching up with both hands she took hold of her hair and lifted it off her head, to reveal the shining globe of her naked skull.

"Ach," she gasped, dropping the brown, boy-cut wig back on her head but slightly awry.

She vowed to immediately set a curse upon Cellini, but quickly abandoned the idea, without admitting to herself that she did not know how to make her curses work. And damn the Devil, also. Why did he avoid her thus if she truly were his child?

Cautiously she glanced back to the glass. Her head itched unbearably where red bristles were already sprouting. She had understood that she must not be recognized, but she had nevertheless given the pigs a good fight. It had taken three servants to hold her down while a fourth took a razor to her head. This brown nest for vermin that blanketed her skull was a curse. When she itched she could not scratch under the wig without the sire's stick, or the cook's, slashing out to swat her backside. All were brutes in this house, those in the shop as well, and she would bear no more of it.

But Lamia made no move toward the unlocked door. In the back of her mind there lurked a magic fairy of warning and truth, that spoke clearly to her; it had caused her to hold back a step one night as she ran through the woods—an animal trap was there that she could not have seen with her eye. It always knew what was right for her to do and what could only lead her into danger. Now it spoke firmly and said, "You must stay in this miserable house because there is no safe place outside it." She angrily pushed herself away from the table to fall back upon the bed, her eyes examining the ceiling where filtered sunlight and shadows danced like ghouls at the Witches' Sabbat.

Her room was very small, musty and dim, but it was far handsomer and warmer than the cave; that much could be appreciated, at least. She bounced her body on the bed, smiling at its miraculous softness. Then, bored, she whirled over on her stomach to study the coverlet design with a tracing fingertip. Marco Cellini's deep voice hummed in her ears, repeating . . . repeating . . .

"What is your name, lad?"

"Guy," she would reply.

"Where do you come from, Guy?"

"From Dijon, Sire."

"Your parents—?"

"Are dead, God rest their souls."

"Your father was—?"

"A tanner. His name was Guy."

"He died of—?"

"Consumption, six months past."

"Your mother—?"

"Her name was Maria. She died when I was born, Sire."

And on and on, again and again. She was a lad in apprenticeship, a poor orphan adopted by Sire Cellini to work in his textile shop, which she did, lugging enormous bolts of cloth, sweeping the floor of twine and cuttings, each of the fourteen days that she had been in this foul house. Today she was ordered to stay hidden in this room, because Giles de Sade was to visit the merchant.

The pox take him, that Cellini; what a cold-eyed demon he was. Not only was there work to learn and perform backbreakingly, but she had to suffer the pretense of being a brown-haired boy, and worst of all, endure what he called "religious training." After one more month of instruction, she would be forced to attend church regularly, as further proof of her new innocence. Now that, even her mind-fairy would not abide. Sit in the house of God, allow one of his soldiers to touch her? No. She would not do it; never. There were worse things than being burned at the stake and giving God or his bishop quarter was one of them. She would not bend to him, ever, not so long as she lived. And he would *not* burn her as he had Eliza. She would outwit him.

Lamia stiffened and her eye slowly turned to the table where the bishop's shoes lay sprawled—waiting. Her heart began to pound erratically, and she leaped up to clutch them into her hands, biting down hard on her lower lip in her urgency. She curved her hand around an imaginary knife, slashing and brutally stabbing the leather half boots. "Into his head, his throat," she cried dramatically. Down upon the table she threw them, jabbing, pounding, but not so much as a dent did she make in the resilient leather. Furious at her impotence, she grabbed the shoes up and tossed them across the room, where they bounced off the wall and dropped to the floor, out of sight behind her bed.

Sire Cellini could teach her important things, she knew that he could. She would stay until he taught her to truly erase pain—then she would leave this house to stalk the bishop, and kill him.

The sound of a voice seeped into her room from the kitchen. Startled, Lamia whirled around to stare at the locked door. It was the sire ordering his cook to serve the meal in an hour.

Each night, except for those two days when he traveled to Nevers Castle, she had eaten with the merchant at his table, at which time he always talked of pretense and disguise.

"Be what they expect you to be, child. Learn their patterns of speech, of reaction, of thought. On the surface be a duplicate of them, but in the back of your curtained eye let your thoughts be uniquely your own. To be outwardly unique is to commit suicide, for naught nourishes suspicion like individuality, and suspicion is evidence enough to convict you."

Sire Cellini was very good at deception, most different before his customers than when alone with herself and the servants. His dark eyes would veil over in a bewilderingly swift and subtle way just an instant before he lifted them to an outsider. His smile would widen, his manner becoming much less regal and more forebearing.

A thought flashed across Lamia's mind and she smiled wickedly, thinking that Cellini's life was in her hands. All she had to do was lift a finger in accusation, telling of his association with witches, and he would be burned. The man was as vulnerable as she, a fact that eased her temper considerably.

Marco Cellini leaned back into his chair before the blazing fire, lifting his glass to examine the pale Burgundian wine shimmering amber and transparent in the flickering firelight. He brought the crystal to his lips and drew into his mouth a small taste of the tangy liquid, holding it, rolling it around on his tongue investigatively, then swallowing with a satisfied sigh of approval. "A delightful brew," he said admiringly.

Giles stood with one elbow leaning upon the stone mantelpiece, gazing pensively into the fire, in his upraised hand a half-empty glass identical to Cellini's. He did not reply to his host's remark, letting his eyes slide around the comfortable, richly furnished room in sentimental reminiscence.

The de Sade house in Florence, the only home he had ever known, was quite similar to this merchant's palais—many windows allowing in light and air, passageways decorated with delicately carved woods and frescoes and made to seem less extensive by the use of pleasing archways. His father's castle, on the other hand, was a dank seven-hundred-year-old tomb, from which he had run as if from a prison. A thousand people swarmed like bees in a hive through the foul-smelling halls and chambers all the lighted day, and, at night, they sprawled out anywhere—on table tops, floors, window ledges; not even his father was allowed the slightest privacy, with at least ten noble guests sharing his and Mabila's quarter nightly.

The boredom was mind-numbing. Rainulf played with

lances and swords, took the falcons to hunt, but was otherwise, in these warless years, reduced to raising drunken hell, or tormenting the servants and his two sisters. None of these knightly occupations appealed to a man starving for intelligent conversation and good company. He would give his very soul to find a tavern full of rousting students, who until their tongues grew thick on wine and beer turned sharp philosophical swords upon one another in fast-paced mental duels. And then to wenching until the night had vanished with the sunrise. How he missed those student days.

"How forlornly you gaze about the room, young man. Does it displease you?"

"On the contrary, Sire. I find it painfully reminiscent of my home in Florence."

Marco allowed his shrouded eyes to rest a moment upon Giles' face, then said carefully to him, "You remind me of an Andalusian stallion, proud and lithe, stabled amongst clumsy plow horses—stomping your hooves in resentful protest. Why do you not rear and bolt, eh? Return to Florence."

"You have said you know my uncle."

"Hmm," Marco murmured in agreement.

"He has threatened me with impoverishment, which would be very difficult to adjust to, after having enjoyed unlimited resources all my life. He was quite explicit. Either I come to Nevers and claim the heritage he preserved for me, or out upon the streets I would go. I could not choose other than to grind my teeth into this bit and stomp my hooves against my loathing of this land, these people that I must call my *family*."

"I see," Marco said flatly. "How do you fill your time, eh? The nobility suffers the plague of ennui to the point of near madness. When there is no war, often they invent a grievance simply to put their restless bones and wits to some exciting task. A hanging will sometimes pleasantly distract them, or a witch trial. A burning now and then temporarily alleviates their boredom. I doubt that you have come to such a pass as yet, so what have you been doing with your days and nights since arriving from Florence?"

Giles laughed and quipped, "Mostly, I pout and curse my uncle."

Marco amiably laughed with him.

"I tried my hand at painting," Giles said, his expression indicating his total lack of success at it. "I doubt I could occupy myself satisfactorily with anything," he added despairingly, "for I am somehow drained of spirit. I feel quite displaced and unnecessary to the scheme of things."

"The scheme of things? And what is that, eh? Can you define it?"

Giles frowned and reached out his now empty glass to be filled from the flask near Cellini's elbow. "By the scheme of things I mean a river of people flowing rapidly in a not too clearly defined direction, each individual having a role in the accomplishment of an obscure goal. I see myself, today, as a pebble at the bottom of that river, going nowhere, all others surging past me on the surface. Oh, I do not fear that I will fail here. I fight against scrambling toward a goal I do not truly wish to achieve. I will receive the land and title, after perhaps half my life has been spent, only to give it away; I do not want it. Live in that cursed castle the rest of my days? I would prefer an early death. I am no knight, no soldier, nor would I become one. I feel cursed by the blood in my veins."

"Indeed; a trying situation. But there are rivers within rivers. Cross currents."

"Cross currents?" Giles echoed uncertainly.

"I am willing to agree that each individual may indeed have a role to play toward the accomplishment of a society's goals, but there are always those who swim against the current, who have ideas and goals of their own; it is they who are usually the architects of change and progress. Jesus Christ as an example."

Marco sipped at his wine several times, waiting for Giles to digest what he had already said, before he went on to drive his point home. "Your father's scheme of things is not a rushing stream. It is a dry bed in which he and a few like him flounder in blind tradition, while above, in the highlands of progress, a mighty storm is building that will flood the dry bed with a new stream that will drown him and his ilk. If you take a role, as you put it, in the accomplishment of your father's goals, you will go down with him into oblivion."

Bewildered, Giles argued, "But even if the king absorbs Nevers into his domain, if that is the flood of which you speak, the blood of Nevers will continue to hold this land and gain from it. To be part of a nation is not oblivion, not to my mind."

"Ha!" Marco barked. "To your father, obeisance to King Louis would be far worse than death, for he is virtually king of Nevers as things are, with full authority. He would be little more than a poverty-stricken landowner under King Louis, having only a small voice in the governing of the nation. To serve their own ends, both your father and your uncle, Cinto, will aid the Duke de Bourbon in his scheme for war against the king. As long as they live, Cinto, the duke, and your father will own you. But they will not live forever, eh? Cinto has no son. He seeks to establish the de Sade family in France, not only as inordinately wealthy merchants, but as noblemen. Have you not wondered why the Baroness d'Archambault appeared so quickly at Nevers Castle, eh? With her marriageable daughter? Ah! You are surprised that I am so well informed."

"Indeed I am," Giles said uneasily. "Have you set spies on me, Sire?"

"Certainly not," Marco lied, smiling. "Gossip flies fast over the countryside. I try to keep abreast of those I intend to cultivate. Think upon it. Do you truly believe that you will be allowed to return to Florence to cavort your life away in taverns?"

"I do!" Giles exclaimed defensively. "It was a promise made to me; a bargain."

"Cinto is not known as a particularly honorable man. Do you know so little about him?"

"Do you have some grievance against my uncle, Sire? If not, then why do you persist in this—"

"Cinto is also a king," Marco interrupted smoothly. "He is absolute monarch over all those subject to his favors. Frankly, it would appear far more sensible for you to befriend your father for your own sake, and not for Cinto's—to take what by right of birth is yours and be grateful for it. But that is no affair of mine. You would like to inspect my laboratory. Come along, then." He rose to his feet, turned and swiftly strode toward the door.

Giles stared dumbfoundedly at the man's retreating back, then followed the merchant while seriously examining what had been said to him. It had never occurred to him to take his inheritance and refuse to give it over to Cinto. It had always been a choice of refusing it outright or taking it and handing it over to Cinto. But not a particularly appealing prospect; the rest of his life tied irrevocably to this barbaric land.

Giles followed Cellini out of the room, across a dimly lighted passageway and into the cookroom, where two servants turned curious heads to sourly inspect the noble guest. Giles automatically stepped to a door which he supposed his host would enter but was abruptly taken by the arm and drawn aside to where a heavy, folding screen reached from floor to ceiling between the stone fireplace and a standing chopping block. A door was hidden there, which took them down a dark flight of granite steps into a torch-lit cellar. Giles followed the sturdy, purposeful merchant with growing anticipation, the wooden heels of his boots creating an echoing, clacking rhythm in the passageway.

A partition slid back at the touch of Cellini's hand to reveal a cellar room crammed with an astounding array of strangely shaped apparatus, a phantasmagoria of seemingly unrelated debris. Animal skeletons dangled from the ceiling, and bouquets of herbs and plants were hung to dry on walls painted over every inch with weird inscriptions and symbols. Tables were strewn with parchments, skulls, books. Glass jars holding mysterious contents were in such profusion they seemed to spill from the tables to the floor and were spread out upon an hundred shelves. A glass mask, flasks and cupels and porcelain crucibles cluttered the ledges of a brick furnace. Shelves also held flacons, gourds, vials and tripods. And in an alcove behind the furnace an altar had been constructed, upon which a human skull and a Bible rested.

"Fantastic!" Giles exclaimed in admiration, standing open-mouthed in the entrance.

"Enter and look around," Marco said. "This is an alchemist's beau ideal and cost me a small fortune. Worth every penny."

Giles fairly bounded around the room, a rush of excitement whipping his innards into a tension that made him feel almost ill. "What is this?" he asked eagerly, poking at a reddish gold substance at the base of a small crucible.

Marco moved to the table, shoving aside papers and debris to closely examine the substance himself. "I am uncertain," he admitted. "To all appearances, it is Spanish Gold. To make it, I used, according to the directions of Theophilus, red copper, basilisk powder, human blood and salad vinegar." Frowning, he added, "It has the weight and color of gold, but it is not gold."

"Basilisk powder? I have read of it, but never knew what it is, exactly."

"The ashes of lizards," was Marco's quick, matter-of-fact reply. "Triturated with a one-third proportion of blood from a red-haired man; the whole mixed with a sharp vinegar. This mixture is then spread on two faces of thin copper plate, which is then heated white-hot and dipped into the mixture again—and so on, until the copper is thoroughly penetrated. And this is the result. Lift it. Curious, eh?"

"What is the elemental property in a lizard's ashes that can perform such a feat? Have you discovered that, Sire?"

"Damn me, no; not yet. These *absurd* recipes!" He clutched up a handful of wrinkled, frayed parchments, shaking them vigorously. "One enigma after another. I was not trained by an adept. The *tradition* was denied me. So my intelligence has to scramble through this deliberately evasive and obscure Latin in search of the one key phrase. For instance, the basilisk powder: I was instructed to shut up two old cocks in a stone cellar which has barely any light, leaving them an abundant amount of food. They were to couple and lay eggs; can you *imagine?* Toads were to brood on the eggs. And from the eggs would hatch *basilisks*—in the form of chicks with dragon tails. After six months, I should burn the chicks and use the ashes—ridiculous. But from the suggestion of creatures with dragon tails hatching from eggs, I came to lizards, logically enough, and to this red gold. . . . I hope to identify the mutating property within the ashes before I go on to another investigation. To date, I have managed to obtain a substance similar to those produced when metallic oxides are exposed to an acid. But what the metallic element is, I cannot say, as yet."

"Fascinating, Sire Cellini," Giles said, awed. "I find you and this laboratory of discovery an intriguing respite. Do you think to perform the Magnum Opus one day? A man is at least half a god, when the gift of creation is in his hand, his mind. This substance is entirely new, created by a man's intelligence. A small miracle which God cannot claim. I am deeply impressed, Sire."

The veil momentarily dropped from Cellini's eyes and he examined Giles with a sharp intensity. The lad's enthusiasm proposed a solution to the de Sade dilemma. If the count did not eventually reject Giles and if Bishop Geoffroi had no gruesome fate planned for him, then it would be prudent to encourage him in this and let his own hand light the blaze that would consume him. On the subject of alchemy there was a fine line indeed between what the Church accepted as harmless and what it considered demonically inspired.

"The Magnum Opus?" Marco asked blandly, once more guarded. "Solve the earth's mysteries, eh? Yes, that is my goal. But what I will no doubt discover is that the Philosopher's Stone does not exist. However, while I am involved in proving that, I will be examining and observing everything accessible to investigation, using all the resources at my disposal. I will have performed, hopefully, a thousand such creative, small miracles as this peculiar substance along the way. For instance, this root." He lifted a grotesquely twisted object from the table debris, holding it before an enthralled Giles. "This ridiculously insignificant twig, when brewed, can quiet the leaping limbs of those afflicted with the Dance of Death. Why, eh? And this; the digitalis that grows abundantly in every forest—what is its secret power to cure the human heart of disordered beating? If I never perform the sacred magnus and transmute base metal into gold, it will not have been a waste, this marvelous investigation into the marvelous."

Suddenly uneasy, Giles said, "You say the Church allows all this? You are not accused of attempting to rival God, in the creation of miracles?"

Marco offered Giles a radiant, somewhat condescending smile. "I have not been accused of sorcery, yet, Giles. Except by the credulous peasantry, who find it impossible to distinguish between alchemy and sorcery. Remember that Saint Thomas Aquinas said that to devote oneself to the metamorphoses of matter was not at all censurable; even the making of gold. He pondered the question and gave secular sanction to any gold alchemically produced; it was real and could be spent. Alchemy, he claimed, became suspect only when it fell into magical practices, or served as a means of communicating heretical doctrine. So long as I do not *administer* the potions I concoct in my vials, and as long as I do not conjure demons to *aid* me in my work, I am tolerated, though definitely not *admired*, by the clergy."

Giles' eyes swept around the room enviously. "Sire, I would give my soul to work in such a laboratory as this. Neither art nor poetry has captured my imagination as have the mysteries of which you speak. As a student in Florence, I dabbled in alchemy for a time but without notable result, simply imitating the chronicled experiments of others—all the while certain God would strike me down with a bolt of lightning at any moment." He laughed, flushing. "I ask myself the most idiotic questions sometimes. Such as, Why is grass green? Why not red, or blue? Nothing in the world can be taken for granted . . . all things, even to the smallest speck of dust, are miracles—mysteries. I am continually stunned by the degree of my ignorance."

Marco waved an arm to take in the entire laboratory. "Feel free to come here any time. Investigate what you will. At the same time you can aid me in my own experiments, which often require an extra pair of hands; a second intelligence might also help, methinks. Eh?"

"Are you—*serious*?" Giles exclaimed. "I cannot—do not believe this possible. Sire Cellini, you will actually allow me free use of your magnificent facilities?"

Marco laughed, finding it increasingly difficult to maintain his loathing of this de Sade. At this moment Giles was like a small boy before a gigantic toy, with a gleam of pure, innocent delight in his eyes. Ah, to be that young once again, only twenty and totally awed by the wonders of the world.

Marco's forehead creased as he recalled himself at the age of twenty, his father still warm in his grave, the Cellini firm rocking under his feet. He had not been allowed this kind of naiveté, faced as he was with violence and hatred which served to quickly mature a gangly lad barely whiskered. Now forty and one, he looked upon Giles and others as young as he, envying them the gift of youth that he had not been able to enjoy.

"Come," Marco said paternally, taking Giles' arm. "The hour is late. A night's rest, and when the sun rises you can return to this laboratory and fill the morrow with exciting investigations. Eh?"

Chapter 6

 Sprawled naked on the bed, his head resting on back-folded arms, Giles stared up at the rich, dark wood of the bedchamber's ceiling. His mind was afire with a thousand thoughts that made sleep impossible. Here, in Cellini's house, he had a room and a comfortable bed entirely to himself. Not since he'd left Florence had he enjoyed such luxury. As the eldest son of the count, he had been given his due, allowed to share the chamber in which Rainulf, fifteen-year-old Conon, and their several personal servants slept. The snores, grunts, wheezes, the stench of chamber pots—all was enough to cause an unrelieved insomnia.

No bathing facility existed in the hopelessly outdated castle, and he had begun to scratch at an array of flesh eruptions, but had, so far, been spared the festering boils and cankers that plagued the entire household. He had not wished to immediately set himself apart from the family by insisting upon a bath, but had just decided that a swim in the river each month would suffice. He would establish such a habit directly upon his return to Nevers.

Giles' mind wandered to Audette d'Archambault, recalling her elfin features with derision. He supposed she was precisely the kind that he *should* wed. No doubt Cellini was correct; Cinto had put the baroness up to it. But God spare him as inescapable a bond as marriage between this land and himself. No house in Florence would ever satisfy the likes of Audette, no matter how splendid. She was without an ounce of warmth. Put his hands to her flesh and they would ice over. He shivered at the prospect of living an entire lifetime by the side of such a woman.

From contemplations of the ambitious Audette, Giles' mind was brought to consideration of his dead mother. Emotion upsurged and closed his throat. She had been the single light in an otherwise dark and lonely childhood; she had loved him. Cinto always accused his sister of frigidity, suggesting that coldness of the flesh was the reason her marriage to Count Jacques had failed. Giles knew, though she had never spoken to him of his father, that some awful brutality had been inflicted upon her by her husband which had frozen her thus against all men. It had constantly amazed Giles that his heartless uncle could have managed sympathy enough for his sister's plight to wrench her from her husband's grasp, an act of compassion even more peculiar considering Cinto's appetite for these French acres and the title that came with them. But rescue her he did, swiftly and apparently without hesitation. From that day on she had whispered through the years, dressed always in black, a gentle sister to keep order in Cinto's house, the only wife his uncle had ever possessed.

At the thought of Cinto *possessing* his mother, Giles bolted upright on the bed, shaking the vulgar hint from his mind. It was not true. How could he be so mentally deranged as to have this vile suggestion creep into his head again and again, year after year? Cinto had constantly chastised her about the manner in which she lived, vowing he would bring a man into the house to penetrate the ice encrusting her, to share her virtuously empty bed. The murmur of their voices that summer night, her soft, pleading cries. No, he would not think upon it. She was a saint, the sweetest most virtuous creature that had ever graced this earth.

Giles leaped from his bed and reached for his hose and breeches, quickly donning them. Slipping his arms into a white shirt, he did not bother to close the fastenings, moving quickly to the door, intent upon taking a stroll in the clean night air to clear his head and prepare himself for sleep.

Silently, he tiptoed down the long, twisting staircase, feeling his way in the dim light of an overhead lamp. At the bottom, he halted, seeking to establish directions. Cellini's reception room was that door to his right. The cookroom was through the door at the end of the hall and to the left. He was famished and thought to find a morsel or two of the lamb left over from dinner. But when he entered the cookroom, stumbling over an unidentifiable object in the dark entranceway, he found the lamplit room's tables and counters picked clean save for a half loaf of bread.

Humming and chewing at a hunk of the stale bread, Giles lifted the bar of the heavy door and stepped out into a moonlighted alley.

Cellini's house was attached to and behind his business establishment. His storage vaults and shop were on the market square, these personal quarters behind and above. From the square to this alley, the recently constructed building stretched between ramshackle, decaying wood structures like a rose amid weeds. Such an abode as this was extremely unusual for a man less than noble. What was it someone had called this increasing breed of men? The middle class. More power to them, Giles thought, for what man alive would not be rich as a de Sade or a Cellini, if he could? Men like Sire Cellini were plowing a comfortable and powerful place for themselves between the nobility and a desperate multitude.

Giles suddenly halted his step, as the sound of low voices emerged on the breeze to catch his attention. He did not notice the bright face peering down at him from the open window above.

The sounds seemed to be coming from within Cellini's house, but that was impossible; it had been in total darkness as he passed through. From the cellar, of course. But there was no window in the laboratory, no door leading to the outside through which sound could pass . . . or was there? He moved in the direction of the voices until the building against which he pressed his back cornered sharply. He waited with breath held, a woman's voice distinguishable now, but the words indistinct. For an instant he felt idiotic, skulking thus like a spy, for it was likely only the cook or the chambermaid departing for some rendezvous. Still, he clung to the wall. Soft padding steps were swiftly coming closer.

"Ah—ee," Peronnette gasped, as she rushed around the corner and plunged flat into Giles' blocking form. Her eyes rounded in terror and her hand flashed up to her bosom. "Get out of my way, please," she ordered breathlessly, glaring into his equally startled eyes.

"You are not the cook," Giles said with a grin, throwing his weight aside to thwart her effort to pass him. "Nor are you the chambermaid. Pray tell me what a fetching wench like you finds interesting in the cellar of Marco Cellini, hmmm?"

Peronnette's eyes faltered, but only momentarily. She raised herself to full height, which brought the top of her scarfed head level with Giles' chin, and invented a hasty excuse. "I weave cloth for Sire Cellini. I—I came to deliver what I had completed. Now, will you please—"

"Delivering? In the dead of night? By way of the alley and not by the Market Square? Come now, you can do better than that."

Peronnette stepped back and glowered at him. Infuriated, she snapped, "Giles de Sade-Nevers, you are a guest in Sire Cellini's house, and I am his close friend. He is your host. Do not insult him, or myself, with your crude buffoonery. Allow me to pass. I have a long way to travel. I say let me pass, damn you!"

"You know my name. How curious. I think, then, that I should know *yours*."

"Please," she exclaimed, exasperated, pushing against his arm with a trembling hand.

Giles had met many a wench on back streets such as this and all of them had been willing, or they would not prowl the alleys so late. It occurred to him that that was what she and Cellini had been up to, but, by the look of her, somehow he doubted it. Her face was in shadow. He could not see the light of her eye. Because his experience with women was so limited, Giles saw desire where there was only fear. He reached up and caught her hand, pulling her into his enfolding arms.

"Now, that is better," he murmured manfully in her ear, while one hand moved up her back to take hold of the scarf that hid her hair. He jerked the scarf away, loosing a torrent of golden hair that dropped over his holding arm to her waist.

Her face, haloed by gold and closer to his eye, shimmered before Giles more lovely than any artist could conceive or imitate. Her face was heart-shaped; a delicate cleft dimpled her chin. All this Giles noted in an instant, as he sucked in air to relieve the shock of her beauty that had his heart hammering against his ribs. He moved his hands to take her by the arms, holding her off from him to examine her with eyes that saw, beneath her ragged shawl, bodice, and skirts, a body as lovely as her face. He had felt the fullness of her bosom against him when he held her close.

"To hide such exquisite hair in an ugly scarf," Giles whispered huskily, "is a criminal offense against all men. You are, beyond doubt, the most beautiful woman in France. What is your name? Please. I will not harm you, I swear. You are not a streetwalker; that is very clear to me now."

Peronnette met his awestruck gaze, her body trembling so violently she thought to lose her balance. "Please," she pleaded helplessly. "Please let loose of me. I cannot—bear—" She lost her voice and could only plead with enormous eyes that announced her terror.

Regretfully, Giles loosened his grip, dropping his hands to his sides, moving aside to lean his shoulder against the wall. Her path was clear, but she did not seem able to move. She stood with her doe eyes focused straight ahead, still shaking uncontrollably.

"Forgive me," Giles said sincerely. "I did not mean to frighten you so. I—I only thought to—"

Her face turned up to him then, and for long moments she dumbly searched his eyes, her dry lips moving as if in speech she could not bring forth from her throat.

"What is it?" Giles asked, concerned, stepping before her once again but keeping his hands from her.

Her eyes dropped from his, down to his mouth, lingering there an instant, then to his chest that was bare between the lengths of his open shirt. "You are so very young. You remind me of someone that . . . that . . ." She could not go on.

Giles was thrown into confusion; not at all what he had expected her to say. There was a strangeness about her that he could not identify; it whispered at the back of his consciousness and had since his first close sight of her. She was perhaps thirty, though no line or shadow spoke of her age. There was a virginal quality about her. Not merely something he sensed, but evident in her bearing and features, as if she were a physically matured fifteen-year-old; a quality sometimes captured by artists in their portrayals of the Virgin Mother, a divine essence of otherworldliness, a soul and body untouched by any of the ravages of living.

"I am indeed young, but man enough," Giles said pointedly.

Her eyes lost their wistfulness, her mouth tightened, and she said bitingly, "You are indeed a *man*, messire."

"You say the word *man* as if it were an obscenity," he complained with amusement.

"Did I?"

"You did. Must I call you *woman*, for the love of God, or will you tell me your name and where I might look to see you again?"

"Sire Cellini tells me he has offered you the use of his laboratory."

"He has."

"Then you will see me; I fear it is unavoidable. I come often to this house. Each fortnight I deliver my goods. My name is Peronnette. A good night to you, messire, until we meet again."

Giles opened his mouth to protest, then closed it and stood aside to watch her move into the shadows and disappear. Immediately it seemed to him it had all been a dream. He turned to walk in the direction she had taken, but his eye was caught by the scarf at his feet that she had forgotten. Entranced, he kneeled to lift it into his hands, holding it while he enjoyed a rush of romantic daydreams.

Romance was the soul of Giles' generation, expounded endlessly in songs, novels, and lengthy verse, and Giles was by no means immune to its influence. Not noble, she, but such a woman a man could love with limitless passion for all the days of his life and after. He would throw himself at her feet, be her absolute slave, if he could be rewarded with but a tender glance from those magnificent eyes! It would not be necessary to possess her carnally, to love her throughout eternity. He felt himself akin to Dante, this mysterious Peronnette his Beatrice. He would compose splendid poems and dedicate them all to her; he would sigh, weep, and pray for the tiniest favor from her.

But Giles found himself at the mercy of a nagging, decidedly earthy side of his nature, and his aspiration vacillated in quick reversals between the romantic ideals of the times and quite ordinary lust for a beautiful woman—to his bitter disgust. He was deeply enamored with the notion of a chaste and grandiose love, which was known to be impossible between married couples, and he was impatient to experience the phenomenon. Already he was twenty. Life was escaping him so swiftly. To see her but once again! He prayed it would be soon. Then that magic would occur and transcend the flesh. He would be raised to the heights of emotion that Petrarch and Dante had reached in their platonic affairs so admired and imitated.

Giles chose to ignore the fact that Petrarch's adored Laura bore her husband eleven children, while he dallied with the pen immortalizing her, not once even dreaming of an intimacy that he believed could only contaminate the purity of his devotion to her.

Impulsively, Giles began to dance about the alley, sweeping the scarf around his head in dramatic arcs, singing, "I stand in my lady's sight in deep devotion. Approach her with folded hands in sweet emotion. Dumbly adoring her humbly imploring her—"

"Idiot!" someone said mockingly from above Giles, followed by coarse laughter. "You are ridiculous."

Giles stumbled to a surprised and embarrassed halt, snapping his head around to meet a strange lad's gaze. "Oh, you think so, do you? Well, what is it—you have nothing better to do than poke your nose into another man's business? Why are you not asleep? And who the Devil are you, I might add, who leans from a window of Cellini's house, another total stranger to me? I swear, people are coming out of the planking tonight! Is he a magician that he can hide so many from my eye?"

"My name is Guy, Sire—apprentice to Cellini. I was ill and confined to my bed."

"I see. And to entertain yourself, you have been spying upon me."

"Oui," accompanied by further laughter.

"I am as amusing as all that, eh?"

"Oui."

"Guy, my good lad, do you know your way about the cookroom? I am about to expire of hunger."

"Come," was the enthusiastic response, and his tousled brown head vanished in an instant.

Giles whipped the scarf around his neck, tied a quick knot, then bounded down the alley, plunging through the cookroom door just as Guy leaned to poke into a cupboard to extract a bowl of fruit, sweet cakes, and a bottle of wine.

"Will this satisfy you, Sire?"

"No lamb left over?"

"The cook and I consumed it all, I fear."

"You did! I thought you were ill." Giles grinned at the lad, as he stuffed a cake into his mouth, chewing and swallowing it ravenously.

"I was. But I am not, now."

"Is it the itch you suffer?" The lad was viciously jabbing at his scalp with a forefinger.

"Vermin, Sire," was his confidential reply.

"Ach. Nothing we can do about them, boy. They are with us eternally, creeping into our diapers and calling us 'home' for as long as we live."

The lad smiled and sat himself down. He placed folded arms on the table and let his chin drop to rest upon them, turning his green eyes upon Giles in amused, secretive silence.

Giles ate two more cakes and an apple, washing them down with a glass of wine, uncomfortable all the while. The cursed lad kept staring at him as if he expected something, or was greatly satisfied with himself about something.

"Look, you," Giles finally threatened with a pretense at extreme annoyance, "end this silence, or be gone. I dislike being stared at."

"You are very pretty."

"Pretty!" Giles choked on a swallow of wine. "What kind of remark is that for one man to make to another?"

"Handsome, then. Is that the word? Most beards look as if

they belong at the other end of a man, but yours is best where it is. Your hair is the same color as your eyes. You are very handsome."

Giles laughed delightedly. "Handsome I well may be, but should not be to *you*, methinks. Boys do not appeal to me, so go back to your quarter. You are annoying me."

"Am I not a very pretty boy?" said with all the instinctive coquetry of a courtesan.

Giles scowled severely at the wretch, finally taking a close look at him. Indeed he was fair of face, with slightly catlike green eyes, and a gracefully fine nose. He had lashes and brows of a deep auburn, while his brown hair showed no lights of red. Curious, but he thought he had seen this lad somewhere before. Passed him on the street, perhaps, upon approaching this house.

"Oui, you are a pretty boy. Now go to your bed before I lay a blow across your backside."

"I am not tired."

"You are not tired . . ."

"No."

Giles reached for a second apple and poured himself another glass of wine, pondering what possible delight the ancient Greeks could have found in the fondling of young men. Small-boned, fair ones such as this lad before him; well, it was almost conceivable. There was a distinctly feminine grace about him and a sensuality around the mouth amazing for his tender years. Those eyes. Damn him, there was a light behind them so familiar, but out of reach.

"Have I seen you before, Guy? Now speak the truth."

"Me, Sire? I think not. I have not left this house since I came into it. From Dijon. Sire Cellini found me orphaned and adopted me. My mother died when I was born, you see, and my poor father, his name was also Guy, he was a tanner, and he died of consumption six months past." He ended with a satisfied smirk.

Giles glared at the boy suspiciously. "That sounded as if you had memorized it, much as I memorized the catechism."

"Cate—? Oh. Oui. The catechism."

"You *do* know what I am talking about," Giles barked, amused by the lad's confusion. "The *catechism*, lad!"

"Certainly!"

"Explain it to me. Proceed."

"I find that I am tired, after all, Sire. I think I shall go to my bed." Lamia lunged to her feet, sending her chair clattering to the floor.

Giles reached out and easily captured her arm, holding her back. "Wait, now. Just one moment."

"Please, Sire," she pleaded, bravado having escaped her in the dilemma of a single unknown or forgotten word. Her disguise had gone so well until now; it had been such sport to pretend, to fool him. But if Sire Cellini discovered she had allowed herself to be cornered thus, he would beat her soundly.

"You do not know the catechism; am I right?" Giles persisted. When the lad refused to reply, only trying to loosen his grip on him, Giles suggested "You are a Jew, perhaps?"

"A—a Jew," she dumbly echoed, then fairly shouted in relief, "Oui! I am a *Jew*!" She did not know what a Jew was either, but he seemed to think it reasonable that a Jew would not know that strange word.

"Ha! You clutched at that straw quickly. We shall see if you speak the truth. A glance at you will tell me."

Before Lamia knew what was happening, Giles was on his feet, his hands flying out to yank down her hose, which entirely bared her lower region.

"For the love of Christ! They circumcised you *close*, lad!"

Giles roared with laughter, as the lad—no, the *wench*—stumbled from his grasp and hopped away, tripping over the lowered hose, her small backside ludicrous in the lamplight and shadows. As she plunged through the doorway of her quarter, he saw her frantically trying to lift the hose as she ran knees knocking together. The door to her chamber slammed shut, and Giles exploded into weeping hysteria. How could he have known? Not in all his life had anything so funny happened. The expression on her face! He beat the table with his fists, tears streaming down his cheeks.

Finally drawing himself up, he wiped the tears from his eyes, swallowed giggles, then sobered to a broad grin. By Jesus Christ, he felt alive again for the first time since Cinto had called him to task, cut off his allowance and sent him forth to France. Tonight he had met an exquisite woman to woo, and he had discovered a mystery to unravel. Why would Cellini adopt a girl and disguise her as a boy, and hide her from his guest's eyes? That magnificent laboratory at his disposal. Life in France was going to be fair interesting.

"In sweet emotion," Giles began to sing softly, so as not to wake the whole house. Moving out of the cookroom and up the stairs toward his bedchamber, he chirped, "Dumbly adoring her. Humbly imploring her."

Having been rousting half the night, Giles slept until the sun reached its zenith, while below him in the house, Lamia confessed her escapade to Cellini, describing in full detail how Giles had discovered that she was a wench and not a boy. She quickly added that he did not guess *who* she was, hoping to avoid the lash of that stick being lazily twirled in Marco's hands.

"Not *who* you are, eh?" Marco growled. "But must he not be curious as to why you are disguised, and will not one speculation lead to another, until he does realize? Eh? Fool! You are still an impossible little fool. Now lay your wretched self across that bed and take your whipping."

Lamia stiffened, her lower jaw jutting out in defiance. "If you wish to beat me, you will have to catch me! Or get Etienne to hold me down. I will not lie down and *let* you!"

Marco's arm slashed out so swiftly she had no time to leap aside, and the stick caught her sharply on the thigh. But before he could swing again she was out of reach, standing with both feet planted full center of the bed, hunched over, prepared to lunge in either direction, whichever side of the bed he attacked from. "The Devil curse you and fry you where you stand!" she shrieked down at him.

Marco turned a fiery eye upon her, but it was all he could do to keep from laughing out loud. Wild, undisciplined little cat, how could he ever be certain what she would do next? Corporal punishment was no good, that was now quite obvious. An appeal to her reason, then. And if that failed, she was hopeless and he would have to dispose of her.

"You win, daughter of Satan, plague of my middle years," he shouted in exaggerated dismay, throwing the stick into a far corner of the room. "Step down from there. You look ridiculous all ruffed up like a squalling cat. Your wig is askew. Straighten it."

Lamia hesitated, twisting her mouth doubtfully, suspecting a trick. But she quickly grinned. Smugly thinking herself triumphant over the brute, she jumped to the floor with a thud. Reaching up, she set her wig backwards on her head, splitting the hair open to leer foolishly at Marco, with no attempt at humor out of pure, cursed defiance.

Marco raged, "The stake looms before me, and you play games! Listen close to me, child." He leaned to put his dark eyes directly before hers, that still peered through straggly hair. "The blisters on your hand only recently healed were but the slightest hint of the pain suffered by those who are burned at the stake. Think. Think of all your flesh roasting thus, but you are not dead, nor unconscious. You are alive yet—aware—there is no escape. Pain. Pain so agonizing you go mad before you die. If you take this disguise so lightly, if Giles recognizes you and announces your presence here to the bishop, then you and I *both* will burn. All you do is destroy us both with this blasted willfulness. You are twelve years old. It is time for you to think like a *woman*. You cannot be a child any longer. If you are old enough to burn, then you are old enough to have the sense to *avoid* it. Now, shall we laugh further, or will you straighten your wig and use the intelligence God gave you? Eh?"

Lamia scowled up at him, while she listened to the equally stern commands of her mind-fairy. Slowly she raised her hands and set the wig properly on her head. Smiling disarmingly at Marco, she asked, "What shall I tell Giles?"

"Damn me; how should I know! A wench disguised as a boy. What would he think probable?"

She smiled slyly, "That you are so vile, so loathsome and brutal a man as to work a girl in your shop, but you would not have your customers know how cruel you can be."

"Bless the devil! You do indeed have an inventive mind. Excellent. I could think of no more logical medicine to cure his doubts, or anyone else's. For this display of growing good sense, two copper coins to spend as you please in the Market Square. Go out and mix with the citizens of Bourges. I know I can trust you from here on. Good girl. We will get on, you and I. Tomorrow, when Giles has departed, I will give you your first lesson in reading, and begin your instruction in control—of the mind and of the flesh. As a man thinketh, ma petite. In this phrase there is a miraculous power."

"Oui, Sire Cellini," Lamia said obediently. She moved to the door, intent upon returning to the shop and her unfinished tasks. With her hand upon the latch, she turned half around and said wistfully, "I wish that Giles would not leave. This house was like an empty cave until he came."

Chapter 7

 " 'DELIVER ME, O LORD, from the fear of Hell. Let not the demons destroy my soul when I shall raise them from the deep pit, when I shall command them to do my—my will.' "

"Continue. Continue!" Marco insisted, with an exasperated thrash of a fist in air. "May the day . . ."

Lamia sucked in a breath, grimly putting herself to the task in a monotonous, drawling voice, " 'May the day be bright. May the sun and moon shine forth, when I shall call upon them. Terrible of aspect are they, deformed and horrible to sight; but do Thou restore unto them their angelic shapes when I shall impose my will upon them. O Lord, deliver me from those of the dread visage, and grant that they shall be obedient when I shall raise them from Hell, when I shall impose my will upon them. . . .' Damn you to Hell, Marco! I am tired. I will not say it again. I refuse!"

"You will do as I tell you, stubborn wretch! I swear, if you managed to actually conjure a demon with that chant, it would look once upon your mean visage and wither at your feet! Why must I badger you this way? Do you not possess one cooperative drop of blood in your veins?"

Lamia rolled her lower lip into a pout and refused to answer. She dropped her aching body into a chair before the fire and gazed sadly into the flames. The night was chill and the house was very drafty. Absentmindedly, she pressed a hand to her abdomen, where pain swelled and retreated in vicious spasms. A low groan escaped her drawn lips, as another strong wave began at her navel and worked down like a knife slicing her innards apart.

"What ails you?" Marco snapped, striding around the chair to face her. "Too much mutton at dinner, I wager. You *would* gorge yourself, blasted little glutton. Moderation. Will you never learn it? I say; what ails you, eh? Answer me."

"Nothing ails me," she answered sourly, avoiding his eyes.

Marco examined her suspiciously, then reached for the decanter and poured a glass of wine, which he held out to her. "Drink this. It might relieve the mysterious ailment you deny you suffer."

Lamia shook her head in refusal. A heat had come to flush her face, as if she leaned too close to the fire, and it spread all over her body, wetting her clothing and terrifying her. The Devil had come to her at last. While she slept last night, he had crawled inside her. Now he was hacking his way out, tearing her flesh apart. The same as he had tortured Eliza month after month, tearing her innards so that she groaned and bled. But she was his child; why did he treat her with such brutality? She turned frantic eyes up to Marco and wailed, "The Devil is inside me, Sire. I am bleeding to death, I fear. He cuts me to pieces."

"Uh?" Marco muttered, bewildered. "Have you gone mad, eh?"

"The pain. Here. I am bleeding—here. It is leaking out of me slowly. Sire Cellini, I think that my father is angry with me, that he intends to kill me."

"Oh, good Lord!" Marco exclaimed, throwing his hands in the air. "Eleven months ago you entered my house a flat-chested infant. When I said, almost a year ago, that you must be a woman—did you have to take me so literally? Out in front you have sprouted breasts the size of melons. And now this—this death you suffer. Ignorant wretch. This bleeding is not Devil-inspired, but God-inspired, a part of His almighty plot against the inheritors of Eve. Go to Maria and tell her of your trouble. She will instruct you."

"I do not die?"

"Ah no, ma petite. You are beginning to live. Today you are truly a woman. Go. Go now. No more lessons for a day or two."

Lamia got to her feet, hesitating before Cellini long enough for him to note how tall she had grown, her eyes now above the level of his own, her bosom fairly bursting the fastenings of the boy's jerkin she wore. But a month past, it seemed, she was believably a boy. Now, in clinging leg-hose, her limbs stretched exquisitely long and shapely, and her rump was provocatively rounded and firm. Under her wig eight or nine inches of flaming hair curled in stubborn refusal to be denied. He no longer shaved her head, having admitted to himself that it was cruel, and really not necessary. A wig was sufficient disguise, now that she was agreeable to wearing one.

As Lamia put a hand to the door latch across the room from him, Marco said to her, "Tell Maria, also, to give you something more—more feminine to wear. You have played the boy for one year, for as long as you can. Hose and jerkins do not disguise your femaleness now; nothing could, I fear. It is time for the brutish Cellini to admit he has worked a girl in his shop all these months."

"But what of Giles?" she asked worriedly. "He visits again soon. Will he not recognize me?"

Marco did not reply, but waved his hand and nodded for her to go. When the door closed behind her, he moved to the fireplace and sipped the wine from the glass Lamia had refused, thinking about Giles de Sade, whom he had not seen again after that first visit. But letters came regularly, addressed to Peronnette.

When the first letter arrived, Marco could not believe what his eyes proved to be fact; *Peronnette* written in a flourishing script, under which was printed *Sire Cellini. Please to deliver into her cherished hands.* Quickly enough he had prodded the story of their alley meeting from Lamia, who had thought the episode hugely amusing and of no consequence. Peronnette was equally as blasé about the matter, until he showed the letter to her. She recoiled from it and refused to open it, ordering that it, and all subsequent communiqués, be swiftly returned to the foolish youth.

Marco did not return that first letter, nor any of the ten

others. Carefully he had broken the seals, reading each one, then put them into a strongbox for future reference. Romantic letters to a witch. The Devil was uncommonly cooperative these days. Giles de Sade did seem positively bent upon destroying himself.

All of central and south France still talked about how the eldest son of Count Jacques de Nevers had confronted Charles Duke de Bourbon for the first time, in dire need of his approval and affection, and proceeded, before the interview was over, to call the duke a liar to his face. Some remark had been passed about Francesca de Sade's indiscretion with a castle lackey. Purportedly, the lad's mother had been caught in the very act of adultery by her husband, who was so enraged that he beat her severely and demanded that she leave his house. All this was common knowledge. What Marco had heard at the time, however, from his informants at Nevers Castle, was that the so-called indiscretion was a falsehood deliberately spread throughout the court, to cover the fact that the woman had been brutally raped by her husband when she refused him any further access to her bed, the real explanation for the bruises that had confined her within her chambers for a fortnight.

Count Jacques was said to have enjoyed the duke's remark immensely, adding a few jibes of his own—to the violent objection of his son and proposed heir. It was the considered opinion of all those who speculated upon it, and they were numerous, that Giles de Sade-Nevers would dig the grave of his uncle Cinto's ambition with his tongue, and that he had best return to Florence while he could yet save his neck. Already he had alienated half the local nobility. The Baroness d'Archambault was his single, avid defender. He did not attend church nor to any other of his religious duties, which caused Father Jean de Nevers to become heatedly suspicious. But Bishop Geoffroi continued to ignore the lad, as if he did not exist, appearing to suffer a deep-seated, curious loathing for the young man that no one quite understood but about which every court gossip chattered at length. As collector of half the de Sade annual dower, the bishop would certainly be reluctant to destroy such a lucrative source of revenue as young Giles de Sade.

After his bout with Charles de Bourbon, Giles was said to

have gone into a depressed state from which he seemed of no mind to emerge. He sat upon the riverbanks entire days simply staring at nothing or reading a book.

Marco's mind wandered thus for half of an hour. Then the door opened softly behind him and he heard the faint rustle of skirts. He turned to see who it was and gasped in surprise before an astounding transformation. Lamia stood there hesitantly, leaning back against the closed door, looking as though she expected him to yowl in rage and disapproval.

"Come here, child," Marco said huskily, "and let me look at you."

Standing there with her fingers fluttering over her bodice, her skirts, then up to her naked red hair, Lamia came as close to humility as she would ever come. She felt herself enlarged out of all proportion, the entire world scrutinizing her with Sire Cellini's dark eyes. She was so painfully aware of herself it required severe concentration to lift one foot and put it before the other. As she walked toward Marco, once again a foreign image appeared in the mirror, a head of waving, short-cropped red hair, enormous, thickly lashed eyes, a thin, white throat, and then a voluptuous bosom rounding up from the low-cut edge of her bodice. She felt so entirely and suddenly altered. Again it was impossible to recognize herself. So used had she become to the wig, she had not removed it even to sleep in recent months. A rise of panic turned her stomach inside out, as she stared anxiously at that broad hint of the woman she was to become.

"Marco—I—I feel so—so nothing," she whispered to his image in the glass. "My life and person are altering so swiftly I cannot recognize myself from day to day, nor know what I am, nor why, nor where I go." She whipped around to Cellini and cried, "Is this—this ... I cannot find the word to describe it. Is this what it is to be a woman? If so, I do not like it, I think."

Marco smiled and stepped close to take her cold hands in his. "You merely suffer the pangs of metamorphosis, that is all; much as the caterpillar must sense a loss of reality while it is in between what it once was and what it is to become. You are not a child, nor yet a woman. Each day you alter slightly—miraculously—toward an intention hidden somewhere in the depths of your being. God only knows how our bodies determine what to do in pattern to all other human creatures. But do not fret. From a forest weed you are magically transforming into a red, red rose. You will be very beautiful, ma petite. Look again into the glass, and swell with pride. God may not love you for it, but you will love *yourself* better, and self-love is the best love we can ever know, for it is never fickle but constant all the days of our lives."

"I care nothing about God's love," Lamia said sharply, once again inspecting that mysterious, lovely face in the glass. "Before I was born he condemned me to Hell. If, as you insist, the Devil is not my father, then I have none at all; certainly not him in Heaven."

Marco shrugged, smiled, and said, "How do you feel now? The pain, has it subsided?"

"Oui. But I am so swollen. As if I swallowed a goat and it is lodged right here." She pressed a hand against her abdomen. "Maria says that this will happen every twenty-eight days, the same with all women. Is this *true?*"

"Completely true."

"Bother!" she spat out furiously, certain God had only her personal agony in mind when he conceived such a curse of the flesh. She dropped into a chair and said up to Cellini, "May we continue the lessons? I do not feel like being alone in my room and I cannot work in the shop."

Marco studied her for long moments, the veil slipping from his eyes to briefly reveal an affection for her that he would have denied vehemently had it been suggested to him. All that he would admit to himself was that if he could have had a daughter, this ornery plague of a child was exactly what he would have ordered in his prayers to the Devil. "All right," he said softly. "Shall we go on with the memorization? Or return to the Malleus?"

"Let us discuss the book," she replied, settling back into her chair.

"Bon. It is stated in the Malleus that for witchcraft to exist, three things must occur. Do you recall the three?"

"The Devil, the witch, and the permission of God."

"Precisely. Witchcraft, according to Church doctrine, depends upon a pact with Satan, and four pursuant factors: the renunciation of the Faith; the devotion and homage to the Devil; the offering up to him of unbaptised children;

and the indulgence of carnal lust with incubi and succubi. These are the four activities declared by the Malleus to be generally necessary to damnation."

"The definition of 'incubi' and 'succubi'? I do not understand these words, nor the meaning of that last activity—'carnal lust with.' "

"Good. It is very important to question. In that way you learn more quickly and thoroughly. The Malleus contends that evil spirits, acting within their allowed limits, can create a kind of semi-body, first taking shape in and of the air—they gather into this body such gross vapors as they can in order to become visible and tangible. They do not speak, however, nor do they see, nor hear. When they want to speak, they cause a disturbance of the air, producing sounds not unlike voices. Generally, they communicate their meaning directly to the mind. Incubi and succubi convey seed from one living being to another, the succubus receiving, the incubus delivering. But there is one thing they cannot do; they cannot themselves beget. In this way it is claimed the seed of a sorceror or a witch can be delivered into the womb of any vulnerable, lustful woman; the child that emerges is the issue of a man whose seed has been *transferred*, but is never the issue of the Devil himself. . . . This discussion has led directly to yourself, has it not, Lamia?"

She glared at him a moment, then snapped, "Are you asking me to believe that one of these spirits, an incubus, entered Eliza's body?"

Marco raised his brows and cleared his throat against a fist. "I am not teaching you what *I* believe, but what the Malleus teaches. But I understand your mother was the priestess at the Sabbat, and—."

"No," Lamia interrupted wearily. "It was the Devil himself, not succubus or incubus, who went into Eliza, so I am the Devil's issue."

"My dear child, I have never seen the Devil, and I have called him with a thousand different chants and incantations for fifteen years. A man, Lamia. A man playing the role of Devil for a credulous mob."

Lamia met his eyes, her mind wrestling with a logic she did not wish to accept. Someone was her father. If not the Devil, then who? Forcing that unpleasant subject from her mind, she blurted out the first question to pop into her head. "What is the purpose of killing children, and why unbaptised?"

"Ah, yes. If all the infants slain by witches and sorcerers as a sacrifice to their god were baptised and eligible for Heaven, that place on high would fill up with elect and the Kingdom would come. The witches do not want *that*, eh?" He laughed to indicate that the reasoning was absolutely ridiculous. "As to the purpose: The bodies are cooked in a caldron until the flesh comes away from the bones. The solid matter is made into an ointment for transportation—flying, that is—or simply eaten. The liquid is poured into a flask, and whoever drinks from it is supposed to immediately acquire much knowledge. Certain spells must be evoked over an eviscerated infant. The uses of newborn flesh are infinite, including a potion for longevity."

A long silence ensued, as Lamia thought over all that he had said to her. She frowned at last, and said incredulously, "Do you say that this book speaks the *truth?* To me it sounds like the ravings of Eliza when she lost her senses entirely. I am very stupid, as you tell me every day a thousand times, but I cannot believe this book of God's. I think He has allowed the monk, Jacob Sprenger, to write it for him just so he can condemn more women and burn them alive. This I believe. The book is all a lie. Eliza was a witch, but she did not cook children. She knew that the Devil required no—no *incubi*, because he went into her *himself!*"

"What you are being told are not exactly lies, Lamia. They are misconceptions, the delusions of deranged minds, but they are, nonetheless, the truths of Holy Church, which is what you are attempting to learn here. The Malleus Maleficarum is a vile travesty of Christianity, and much of it is absurd, but certain facts cannot be denied. I have personally witnessed the slaughter of children. Witches and sorcerors indulge themselves in every horror that can be conceived by man. This book proposes to outdo the witches, eh? It is far more insanely murderous and evil than any witch operative or ever burned."

"Do *you* boil children, Marco?" she asked. She suffered no violent distaste for the idea, nor did the practice appeal to her. It was rather like the wine she did not enjoy drinking herself, but objected not if others enjoyed it. Having seen her mother burn alive, it was difficult for her to sicken at lesser extremes of human depravity. Actually, she took such things as cannibalism—widely practiced by the witches—child murder and the Inquisition quite for granted as the state in which men had always lived and always would.

"I have never boiled a child," Cellini answered with a patient smile.

"But you are a sorcerer."

"Oui. But I am not a sadistic cannibal! As I have said, Satan does not heed my calls. I made a pact with him by renunciation of the Faith, by vow, by intent, without once seeing his face. I am not a *good* man. I have done many evil things. But I stop at making soup of infants! This life I do not so adore as to drink the warm blood of a freshly killed child to prolong it. I avoid the stake, being particular how I depart this world, but death, for me, offers a blissful release from earthly harassments."

"You do not fear Hell? Maria turns ashen whenever I say the word. I suppose Hell is like being burned at the stake without dying, just burning and screaming forever and ever. I do not think I would like to die."

"But you will die, Lamia. Every living thing does."

Lamia's mind staggered and she shivered violently. God killed everyone. It seemed she had always known this truth, but that he could kill her self was beyond comprehension. Gone was her protective delusion of immunity. If she had to dismiss the Devil as her father, she must also reject the idea of being immortal. God's image appeared, vast and threatening, before her mind's eye. In his hand he held a sword that dripped human blood—her own. She shivered again and swallowed down a coldness that closed her throat. "I will fight him off as long as I can," she whispered.

"Oui, ma petite," Marco said gently. "Ah, it is a neverending battle, the flesh against annihilation, man against God's will."

"As a witch, shall I learn to boil children?"

"You will *not!* What you will learn is a science of mind. How to pit your will against men, beasts, the elements, and prevail. And how to salve some of the ills of men that doctors are too ignorant and superstitious to even investigate.

Most importantly, you will lead the people into Satan's stall, with your hideous insinuations of personal league with him. Utilize the methods of Holy Church, and rule with fear and cunning. Perform for the multitude until their tongues flick out like that of a reptile in search of blood, until they lust for all the evils you suggest to them—and then watch the brutes turn upon their masters and devour the nobility and the clergy like starving cannibals."

As she listened, Lamia's eyes had widened in surprise and confusion. She thought a moment, then asked, "Are you now saying that witchcraft is only *pretense?* Eliza did not pretend. She truly was a witch. At night while I slept, she flew about the forest upon a tree branch, and—"

Marco interrupted her with, "For the most part it *is* pretense, child; when we speak of those witches sane enough to keep a grasp on reason. The intelligent witch soon comes to realize that the powers she enjoys seem to emerge not so much from a supernatural entity as from deep within herself, from within her own mind and soul. Peronnette has an amazing ability to see into the future, predicting events there with miraculous accuracy. To accomplish this, she at first tried to conjure demons, but soon attempted the feat without seeking their aid, and was successful. One can only conclude that the essence of Satan is innate in the human being, more pronounced in some, waiting only to be called upon and put to use, a natural resource, to put it another way. Do you comprehend me?"

Lamia shoved her body out of the chair. She stood before Marco in profound confusion, her expression writhing with the concentration she was applying to all he had said to her. What was irrefutable fact, through logic became delusion? What could only be considered delusion, could, perhaps, be fact? What was life? What good? What evil? What was truth and what a lie? "Am I to believe that not only is the Devil not my father, but that he does not exist at *all?* You stir up my mind until I cannot think straight. No, I do not understand you; not at all!"

"Oh, yes! The Devil does indeed exist. Forgive me, if I implied otherwise. When man fell from Grace, the angel, Lucifer, fell with him. If man exists, then Satan also exists; the two are synonomous. Until men become angels, the Devil will never be vanquished but will roam the earth drinking the blood of our souls. But why is it only madmen or fanatics see his face, eh? Why is it I offer him my soul without qualification, yet he does not appear to me? When God is called, he does not show himself, nor does his nemesis. The intelligent mind is staggered by contemplations of all sorts of possibilities, the least alarming of which is the question of Satan's actual existence. Far more disturbing is the *logic* drawn from the premise that he does *not* exist; it would follow that if *this* doctrine of the Church is false, so might all others be, including the nature and existence of God, of Heaven, of Hell—and then where are we? Suspended in space, emerging from nowhere and destined to return there. Horrid! It freezes the mind. Any sane man would prefer to believe himself doomed to a hell rather than to absolute oblivion. When God becomes reprehensible to us, we can only seek out the Devil—out of our terror of oblivion; and, perhaps, therein lies the seed of Hell's invention, and Heaven's also."

Lamia rocked on her feet, staring blankly into his earnest face. "Forgive me. I am indeed stupid. Your words have washed over me like the river over rocks. I am hopelessly ignorant. I—"

"Ah no," Marco protested. "No. I only insincerely scold when I accuse you of stupidity. That you are extraordinarily intelligent is an incontestable fact which you can cling to in your confusion. What you have learned in one short year is miraculous. One day very soon you will understand, when you are fully a woman. Do not worry upon it. Be patient. Listen closely. Absorb what you can."

"I am very tired," she sighed. "I think that I will take to my bed."

"You must return the wig to your head, you know, eh? I will purchase one of longer lengths. Guy, whom all within five miles know to be a wench disguised as a boy—as we so carefully spread about after Giles returned to Nevers—must now be revealed for what she is by this vile merchant. But Guy cannot also become red-haired."

"Have they not forgotten me by now? I am so weary of hiding my hair."

"The Red Witch of Nevers will never be forgotten, Lamia.

Since she vanished, her evils have swelled into a horror legend. Every child is stilled from crying by the threat, 'Hush, or the Red Witch will get you.' No one goes near the cave where she was born and lived, though the bishop set a massive blaze within it to capture and destroy her clinging aura, leaving a cross above the entrance to keep out the evil spirits. The peasantry is certain the Red Witch lives, and stalks Nevers nightly. Every child that dies at birth has been somehow touched by her putrid breath. Every insane hysteria is laid to her possession of that pour soul's mind. You stand here before me in all your innocence, and fifty miles away your crimes multiply daily. You see how difficult it is to distinguish truth from delusion? You are very real to me, and equally real to the people of Nevers. Which eye sees the truth? Cover your hair. A red-haired wench would not live in this house a fortnight without the finger of accusation pointing at her."

"And Giles?"

"Nonsense. In the brown wig, yourself so altered since that day a year past, when he looked briefly into the eyes of a filthy urchin, he could not possibly recognize you. Now go to bed. Practice your reading a bit, then sleep. Tomorrow we will return to the laboratory and review the poisons and their potentials for cure, as well as for quick death. A good night to you, ma petite, so evil a witch, eh?"

Lamia made no move to leave the room. She gazed down upon her clenched hands for a moment, then lifted hot eyes to Cellini. "The Devil *has* to exist!" she cried. "I need him to aid me in a curse against the fiend who burned Eliza. I must kill him! I must!"

"The bishop," Marco remarked, annoyed.

"Yes! The bishop!"

"Your capacity for hate is unsettling." He laughed humorlessly. "I would not relish the thought that you despised *me* so much. I would not sleep a single night until you were dead in your grave, and then I doubt I would sleep soundly, for your spirit would, no doubt, return to haunt me." He paused and looked at her meaningfully. "You are quite capable of murder, Lamia. What need have you of the Devil?"

"I? But—"

"Tomorrow. Tomorrow we will study the poisons, eh? And perhaps the puppets into which long pins are stabbed that reach across space and plunge into the heart of the intended victim? I say again: what need do you have of the Devil? We humans are capable of every wickedness. Supernatural assistance is quite unnecessary. Now go."

Lamia thought upon Marco's final remarks, and, this time, clearly understood him. No power outside herself but entirely within herself. She met his eyes, smiled, and in that moment the ties between them tightened to unbreakable bonds. "I think I am beginning to like you, Marco," she said, then turned and left him gaping in surprised pleasure.

Chapter 8

 THE WIND RAGED, HOWLING from the north, whipping the woodlands into a frenzy of bending, cracking, and groaning trees. The torrential rain had flooded the forest floor and turned the roads into stretches of impassable muck.

Giles bent his head low as he rode, his mantle raised over his head. The horse stumbled, unsure of its step in the midday darkness. The road was visible only a few feet ahead.

He reined in sharply. He had come upon a crossroad and was uncertain which direction to take. He strained his eyes to see through the sheeting rain, but no signpost was in evidence, probably blown down by the wind. Because of this cursed storm, he had taken the highroad from Nevers that led to the monastery of Saint Aliquis, hoping to turn west at a better road than that low trail following the river, which threatened to flood at any moment.

He sat his mount for some time, cursing the weather and his own stubborn refusal to cancel this journey; he had simply had to get away. Finally, he decided on the left turn and brought the horse around with a sharp yank at the reins.

Instantly Giles drew his mount in again as a chilling wail rose above the screams of the wind to freeze him in his tracks. He whirled around in the saddle, his mantle falling back over his shoulders. God in Heaven, what a monstrous, high-pitched, gasping utterance that had been!

Giles slid from the saddle, intent upon discovering the source of the cry; someone might need his assistance. Wet and muck oozed over the ankles of his riding boots as he stumbled into the wind, making his way to the center of the crossroad, where he stood slowly turning in circles, his eyes searching the undulating brush and trees. He saw a flash of movement and ran across the road, plunging into the brush.

Again Giles froze in his tracks. He had come upon a grotesque hag who was bent over a deep ground-hollow. She reared backward, gasping in surprise at his unexpected appearance. When she saw who it was, her foul mouth slashed open in a toothless grin. She screamed curses at him that were caught by the wind and thrown away from his hearing, then pushed herself to her feet and stood hunched over, backing away from him with a hideous leer. Suddenly, and with astonishing agility, the hag turned and vanished into the woods, leaving Giles open-mouthed and chilled to the bone.

Only then did Giles drop his gaze into the hollow she had been leaning over. He sucked in air and recoiled. It was a shallow grave and in it was the monstrously decomposed corpse of a young man. Its entrails had been removed and spread over the entire trunk. A live frog sat immobile on the cavity where once a nose had been, blinking up hideously at the horrified intruder.

Giles' arms flew up to hide his eyes and his heart seemed to miss several beats. He staggered away, tripping over a fallen tree to fall flat on his back. Rain slashed against his face. Numbly he rolled over and raised himself to his feet. He ran back to his mount. When he was again in the saddle, prepared to swiftly take that left road away from this nest for demons, his eye fell upon the fallen signpost and his memory was nudged. A witch. The hag had been a witch. The ancient saying went, *The witch's curse will best proceed when employed where the four roads meet.* Monstrous!

Giles spurred the horse viciously, dropping the reins and leaning to clutch the animal around the neck. Every scream of the wind emerged from a witch's throat. Death lurked around every curve, behind every shadow.

It was six hours before Giles reached Bourges. The rain had not subsided; rather it was more torrential than before. Soaked to the skin and shivering, he jumped from his horse before Cellini's shop and left the animal to fend for himself, rushing head bent against the wind toward the merchant's door. He beat on the door soundly with both fists, then lifted the knocker and hammered it against the plate again and again.

"Giles!" Marco exclaimed, as he opened the door wide. "Hurry in. Great God, you are drenched. I did not think you would come, the weather so inclement."

Giles gasped for air, trying to smile in greeting, his chest heaving as if he had run all the way from Nevers without benefit of horse. He could not speak, only throw his hands up in a gesture that said, "But I did come."

Marco took Giles by the arm and led him to his reception room and the blazing fire there. He left him shivering before the fire, returning minutes later with a warm robe and cloths with which to dry himself.

When Giles had stripped, dried himself and wrapped the woolen robe around him, Cellini offered him a mug of heated, spiced wine, which he drank in gulps, still quaking, though he sat close enough to the fire to scorch his flesh.

Standing near Giles' chair, sipping at his wine, Marco said blandly, "I am most flattered that you would come on such a day. It has been all of a year since you graced this room. You discovered there were engrossing pursuits, after all, in your father's castle?"

"My esteemed father forbade my coming here," Giles said peevishly, staring into the fire.

"So? But why, eh?"

"You are a merchant. A species so inferior in his eyes that my noble person would be contaminated by prolonged association that transcended the ordering of woolens. And he does not hold with Saint Thomas Aquinas, but rather considers alchemy no less than necromancy."

"Not surprising. What *does* surprise me is that you are here despite his disapproval."

"I *spit* upon him!"

"Ah, Giles. You have changed since we last met. The carefree lad is gone, eh? The bitterness of living does not allow us the luxury of lightheartedness for long."

"My heart would lighten considerably, Sire Cellini, if my weary bones could find that bed so enjoyed months past."

"Ah! Of course. How rude of me to chatter on. I will have the chambermaid warm the bed immediately."

As Lamia busied herself removing hot stones from Giles' bed with long pincers, he stood with an arm around the bedpost, sourly examining her.

"My friend Guy, is it not?"

"Oui," she murmured under her breath, refusing to meet his glance, her heart fluttering inexplicably. She reached the pincers far under the quilts for the last stone, drew it out carefully and placed it in the metal-lined basket.

"If you were to try and trick me now, as you did in the kitchen that night, I would never be fooled." His eyes were fixed pointedly on her bosom.

"I am too old now to play games, Sire," she said haughtily, lifting the basket and dragging its weight across the room toward the door.

"And so am I. What is your true name?"

"Sire Cellini still calls me Guy; it became a habit." At the door she dropped the basket with an outrush of breath, reaching for the latch.

"That was not an answer to my question."

"Nor will you get one. A good night to you, Sire." She snatched up the basket and started through the door.

"And if I said I *know* who you are—and where I had seen you before. . . ."

Lamia froze in the open doorway. She whipped around, stunned, glaring at him accusingly. "Seen me before? Whatever do you mean?"

"Come back. And close the door behind you."

"No."

"Do as I say, damn you!"

She hesitated, listening to her conscience, the name Marco had given to her mind-fairy; it recalled to her Marco's warning that if Giles reported her whereabouts to the bishop they both would burn. Since she had discovered she was not immortal, fear often tightened around her heart like this. She lifted her gaze to Giles, furious with him for threatening her thus, but unable to suppress a love for him that had begun and grown from the first touch of his hand that day by the river. It was not a romantic kind of till-death-do-us-part love. It was more the kind of worship a puppy offers to the master with a kind eye and gentle hand. She sighed, stepped inside, closed the door and leaned back against it, meeting Giles' cold eye with an equally icy stare.

Scowling, Giles fell back to sit on the bed. "Come here to me, girl," he ordered. When she obediently did so, standing close enough that her skirts brushed his knees, he said, "You have grown even prettier, my friend."

Her eyes closed to slits, as she continued to stare unblinkingly into his disrobing eyes. He was bluffing. He had not suspected a thing, had believed the story she and Marco had concocted to stem his curiosity about a girl disguised as a boy. When she ran from him a year ago, her mind-fairy assured her he did not suspect who she truly was. But now—she smiled uneasily and said, "I thank you for the compliment, Sire."

"Freckles across your nose—just a faint patch. And your brows and lashes are red. Nature was fair confused when she designed you; one would expect your hair to be red, not brown."

Lamia stiffened and fell back a step, but could not avoid the arm that shot out, the hand that wrenched the brown wig from her head.

"Ah, ha!" Giles exclaimed exaggeratedly. "You see. I was not toying with you. The name is Fiametta, is it not?"

"Give it to me," she cried, trying to grab the wig from his hand, but he held it higher than her reach. She became so infuriated when he laughed at her futile struggle that she struck him soundly across the face, slicing her fingernails down his cheek. "May you burn in Hell! Give it here to me, I say!"

Giles threw the wig to the floor and lunged for her. Catching her in his arms he tossed her flat upon her stomach on the bed. He proceeded to spank her on the behind, while she wailed vile curses upon him. Then he took her by the shoulders, yanked her to a sitting position, shaking her until her teeth clacked together. "Wildcat! Never strike me again. Understand? Never!"

"How did you guess?" she wailed, eyes rounding under his fury.

"I did not believe your story, though it was well enough told. At dawn, as I prepared to leave, I entered your room to say a goodbye. You were not wearing the wig. Your head glowed red as fire and I recognized you."

Lamia sat thus held by his hands, his face but inches from her own, feeling his angry breath kissing her nose in warm gusts. His chest expanded and collapsed with his heavy breathing, and she found herself compelled to smile at him, felt her body leaning toward him. The strangest sensations plagued her, centering around her lower region and in the area of her breasts.

Startled by the suddenly obvious lust in her eyes, Giles recoiled from her, shoving her roughly away from him. "You are an *infant*," he complained.

"I am not! I am a *woman*. Each month I bleed. My breasts are like melons. Sire Cellini said so. And—"

"For the love of Christ!" he yowled, disgusted. "You have the manners of a—of a harlot. Have you no pride, or shame?"

Lamia pouted. "What has pride to do with it?"

"Pride is a virtue that prevents a woman from discussing such facts of life that are unmentionable and distasteful."

"You find my breasts distasteful?" she asked, hurt.

Giles leaped from the bed and turned his back upon her. "Get yourself off my bed," he ordered roughly, "and stand before me as demurely as possible. I want to speak with you. I am a man who does not relish the deflowering of infants. Do as I say, now!"

Fury again ignited within Lamia and she slid off the bed to bolt across the room for the door. Giles did not catch hold of her until she was out the door and at the head of the staircase. He grabbed her arm and wrenched her around to face him.

"Do not tell Cellini that I know you," Giles insisted.

"I *will!*" she snapped at him.

"I was kind to you once, have you forgotten? Do this, then, for me. Do not tell him I know you."

Inexplicably, she was smiling at him again, stepping so close to him her bosom pressed against him hard, but yielding.

"If you kiss me, I will not tell him," she offered coyly. "I have seen how young men kiss girls and I would enjoy it very much, I think."

Giles could not help laughing at her. Her eyes held all the purity of a curious child, while her flesh quivered with the lust of a seasoned harlot. He had not laughed in months and it seemed to cleanse him, even if only briefly, of the bitterness he had suffered of late. With a conspiratorial grin, he nodded his head toward the door of his room and whispered, "Come back to my room and I will treat you to your first kiss, then. Anyway, you left your wig behind."

"Ahh—!" she gasped, her hands flying to her naked head in pretended dismay. She ran back into the room, tripping over her skirts in her eagerness.

When Giles entered with an easy stride, closing the door behind him, Lamia stood in the center of the room with the wig set neatly in place on her head. Smiling, he moved toward her, warning himself not to lose control. Her bosom was certainly not in the least distasteful, rising and falling in tempting rhythm. Not a single wench had he taken in all these long months. Not that none were willing, but that no privacy whatsoever was possible whenever one became available. On a pile of hay in the stable was for stable boys. The stench of manure and the prick of straw would quickly put out the fire of his passion. A bed, candlelight, whispered words of love, even if insincere, time to woo, to build the fire within her to raging—time to rest and then begin again. The prospect of Rainult and Conon looking on was hardly a pleasing one. Everyone in the castle took the lack of privacy quite for granted, eyes looking on their most intimate occupations had to be expected. During long sieges hundreds of people would be locked into the tower room together, for months at a time—few functions were denied simply because someone might see. No wench had been willing to ride into the country, where a meadow by the river might serve as a charming trysting place. She would prefer to be seen, which was incomprehensible, considering the magnitude of the sin she was willing to commit. Sin was easily washed away by confession, he supposed. A romantic episode that she could boast about for years was what she wanted—and not to be called a lie, because so-and-so saw it with her own eyes.

As he approached her, Lamia seemed to suffer a small apprehension, her eyes rounding, a retreating light shining there. He stood close a moment, then put a hand on each side of her face.

"Do not give me a baby," she whispered, helpless against a flood of emotion that was drowning her reason.

Giles threw his head back and laughed, then sobered himself and leaned to lightly press his tight-closed lips against her mouth in a brief kiss. "There now," he said. "Fiametta, you have been kissed."

But Lamia was not satisfied with so cold a touch. She threw her arms up, fastened them around his neck in a vise grip and planted her mouth on his with ecstatic groans rumbling in her throat. He tried to loose himself, stumbled over her leg that had caught between his and dropped to his knees, carrying her with him, while her moist mouth clung, slid over his, devoured him with an animal passion he had never before encountered. He could have thrown her off, but he did not. His arms swung around her and he returned the kiss with equal fervor until the light in the room seemed to dim behind his closed eyelids. Her breath hissed in and out through her nose, a hot wind against his cheeks.

Lamia at last fell away from him, gasping, her eyes afire. She lay on her back below him, smiling, inordinately pleased. "I *knew* I would like it," she said on an outrush of breath, smirking.

Giles knelt over her, breathing heavily, the weight of her kisses still lingering on his mouth. He ran the back of his hand over his lips, never taking his eyes from her. "You stand up on your two feet, Fiametta, or a baby is precisely what I shall give you."

"Then I *am* a woman."

"I concede it; how can I deny it?"

"I have a very bad pain—here," she complained dreamily.

"It will pass."

She closed her eyes, smiling secretively. "Giles? When I decide to have a baby, will you give it to me?"

"Perhaps *before* you are ready, if you do not now rise to your feet."

"Swear it!"

"When you are ready, you will have forgotten me entirely, ma petite."

"Ah no! I will have no baby but yours. Never!"

Resigned to the fact that she was not going to get to her feet, Giles moved to lie on his back beside her, resting his head against his back-folded arms, the heat within him slowly ebbing. He turned his head to study her profile. She was staring wistfully up at the ceiling. His heart constricted, recalling the fate designed for her. Why had he not come sooner? Cellini had not cared so much for his own life that he refused to take in and protect this tragic child.

Commendable, Giles had thought at first, to show such mercy; he would have done the same himself. But suspicion had quickly grown in him. Why, he asked himself, would a man like Cellini, who had worked long and hard for his wealth and position, risk accusation and death for a hapless waif? Why, indeed, unless the stake already threatened, unless the merchant was already in league with Satan. For all his high-blown scientific investigations, Cellini was a Satanist! Then whoever stood in the merchant's shadow stood in the shadow of the stake. The realization that he had put himself in jeopardy had sent shivers of dread through Giles, but by the time he had closed the door on Fiametta's chamber that dawn, he had convinced himself that he was being absurd. That impish child asleep in that room was no witch and Cellini would not be fool enough to risk his life for her if she were.

Giles had not been at Nevers Castle more than a day after his return from that visit to Cellini before he was forced to listen to a horror story about the Red Witch. She had returned to Nevers, Adela had assured him almost hysterically, to yowl and hiss outside the window of her chamber through an entire night; not possible that it was only the storm wind whining through cracks in the windowpane. If a woman miscarried, it was the Red Witch who caused it. When a cat screeched in the night, all within earshot trembled, certain it was her. A red-haired infant was born in the village in the month of May and was smothered to death by Father Jean, who insisted that the mother had been carnally possessed by incubi carrying the seed of the Red Witch. The tales being spread from village to village, from church, to bailey, to castle, became increasingly morbid as the days and weeks passed. Giles began to realize that far more than mere superstition and foolishness was involved. It was a kind of insanity. An entire society had simply gone mad. Made uneasy by the slight possibility that Cellini might indeed be a Satanist, Giles could not bring himself to go again to the merchant's house. He cursed himself endlessly for his cowardice, which seemed to lend credence to the delusions of the credulous.

Weeks passed. He penned a letter to Peronnette, her image shimmering upon the throne of his fancy in golden splendor, begging her to reply with information as to her whereabouts. He explained that he could not seek her out at this time because of commitments impossible to set aside, but soon as he knew where to find her he would fly to her on wings of adoration. Vaccilating between a desperate compulsion to warn her against Cellini and contempt for his own foolish suspicions, he finally decided not to speak to her of the possibility that the merchant was a heretic.

Giles' mind then wandered to his audience with Charles Duke de Bourbon, a foul, licentious man bent upon a full-scale war with the king. He was a breathing anachronism, a duke from out of antiquity risen from the grave to kill, ravage, steal and play God. Loathsome liar, he would be an age in Hell before he would hear an apology from the lips of Giles de Sade. Francesca de Sade caught with a castle lackey? "Liar!" he had shouted in the man's face, and a liar he was. She had been a saint, a blessed angel. Damn the duke to Hell, and his mother's vile, snickering husband also, who thought to name himself father to a de Sade and to wield the power accruing therefrom.

A lie it might well have been, but Giles' youthful image of his mother as divine had begun to crumble; doubt had dethroned her. Women were of only two sorts, saint and slut. To for one moment admit that his mother was less than virtuous would force Giles to concede that she was a harlot; there was no in-between for him. The purely divine image of Peronnette now rested on the pedestal formerly occupied by his mother. Not once did it occur to him that, like Fiametta, Peronnette might also enjoy the protection of Marco Cellini. To Giles she was an innocent in danger of accusation through association.

Giles wrote to Peronnette again and again, each letter more insistent and emotional than the last, some written in verse that pitiably revealed his desperate yearning to love and be loved in return.

Cinto de Sade's communications from Florence to his nephew became more and more insistent. Giles was to agree to wed Audette d'Archambault without further delay. And he was to apologize to the duke immediately. Following these commands, Cinto always added a dozen separate threats, including the usual, disinheritance.

The Duke de Bourbon had received gold enough from Cinto de Sade to build an army for his war against the Crown, and Giles was expected to support that cause, as vassal and soldier to the duke.

A war was imminent, but Giles fought his own battles; against his conscience, and against boredom which drove him to the depths of depression, against his fear of death, and his loathing of the family who despised him with equal enthusiasm. And temptation, that intriguing laboratory of the merchant calling him as the sirens beckoned to Ulysses.

For eleven months he suffered the pressures being vented upon him by his father, his uncle, the duke, and the Baroness d'Archambault. Then he awoke one morning, after a night of anguished tossing, with a deep sense of resignation and inevitability; he agreed that day to wed Audette. He also penned a letter to Cellini, informing the merchant that he would at long last pay another visit. Fourteen days later, against the wheezing objections of his father, he departed for Bourges in a raging storm.

Scientist or sorcerer, what did it matter? His life at Nevers was a hell in itself, and an eternity with Audette loomed an abyss of emptiness out of which there was no escape. He would never return to Florence, to those days of laughter, comfort, and irresponsibility. Under the lordship of a crazed duke he would grow old and wretched in a gigantic tomb, with the ghosts of Nevers giggling at his plight that was so exactly as theirs once had been. Before he entirely resigned himself to his dreary fate, he would find the woman of his heart, and he would soothe the hunger of his mind in the pursuit of knowledge. Each of these salves were only to be found in the house of Marco Cellini, wherein also dwelt the arch demon.

It was with a conscious sense of giving in to Satan that Giles had made his way to this house today. He lay now beside a girl who was a witch by God's pronouncement. He had stepped out of the stream of Grace, into the tide of damnation, aligned now with Satan's disciple against Church and nobility, and he knew no emotion save that of satisfaction.

Giles turned his head to once again study Lamia's profile. In the shadows her face appeared carved of ivory; a miniature to be framed. She felt his gaze and turned her face to him.

"You should not come here, I think," she said anxiously. "It is dark in this house until you come into it, but Marco hates you and would have you dead."

"What?" Giles sat up, looking at her in astonishment. "What are you saying? I thought to visit a friend in a friendless world. Why should he loathe me? I have done him no harm."

"I do not know, but it is true. He said that I should center my curses upon the clergy and the nobility, yourself in particular."

"Good Lord," Giles groaned, dropping his face into his hands in utter frustration. "I am beset on all sides."

"How you pity yourself."

"Uh?" Giles muttered uncertainly, taking away his hands to glare at her.

"Only *one* man hopes to see *you* dead. While every man, woman, and child in Nevers hopes to see me burn. I cannot be seen as myself, have no home at all, nor can I hope for one in the future. But I am not pitying myself." She leaned forward in her earnestness, emphasizing by shaking her fist at Giles. "I say I will disappoint them all—and live. I say I will kill, first, anyone who seeks to kill me. Can you not do the same?" She did not ridicule, nor intend to insult him, but had spoken out of a simple curiosity and a remarkably mature patience.

"You think that I have wallowed long enough in self pity?"

"Oui. I wish that I could walk safely through my woodland once again, touch a new-flowered bloom cuddled into a blanket of tall, spring grass, or stand naked in summer moonlight in a world that is all my own. But I cannot, and weep not about it. When I am full grown and have learned all that Marco can teach me, I will do all those things again, because I must. I *must!* No event, no person, not God or the Devil will stop me."

"Ah, Fiametta," Giles said to her admiringly, "you are indeed wise and womanly. I humbly beg your pardon for calling you an infant."

Grinning delightedly, Lamia leaped to her feet. "I must leave you now. Do not worry upon Marco. He acts as though deep down he regrets despising you. Perhaps you might win his affection, as I have. He is very good to me now. . . . And, Giles, if you would find Peronnette, she dwells in the village of Claire, in a small house near the convent of Saint Genevieve. When she has grown old, I will be quite the right age for you, will I not?"

Giles smiled in response to her charm as he searched her face, her eyes, for knowledge of a soul so complicated as to defy comprehension. No doubt she was capable of ruthless, conscienceless murder, but also of the tenderest sympathy and devotion, possessed of all the cunning and paradoxes of a jungle tigress. "Fiametta," he said apologetically, "I am to wed Audette d'Archambault within the year."

"Oui, I know. But I care not of her. It is Peronnette who pleases you. It is she who stirs in your mind so pretty, whispering to you, calling. One day I will call, and you will come. You will see me, hear me, even if I am a great distance away, and nothing will halt your steps toward me." With that, she turned with a rustle of skirts and fled from the room.

Chapter 9

"I HAVE NEVER BEEN SO unnerved in all my life, Sire Cellini. The woman was a hideous embodiment of the Medusa. I thought for certain to see her stringing hair begin to writhe like a thousand serpents."

"A madwoman, Giles," Marco commented dryly, as he carefully measured an ounce of acid into the vial he held upraised to the lamp over his head. "Witchcraft is the last resource of the lunatic."

Giles leaned to expand and contract the bellows, the wind from which stirred the fire under Cellini's brew of lizard's ashes to a white heat. The basilisk powder continued to defy the stubborn scientist. But Giles was not thinking about the experiment, nor about the hag he had seen in the forest yesterday. He was struggling with an impulse to have it out with Cellini. He had to know if Lamia spoke the truth.

"Sire," Giles began, straightening himself to full height beside the merchant. "I have guessed that you are in league with Satan here, and . . ."

"Eh? What is that?" Marco laughed, his hands dropping in surprise to the table. He expertly hid how fully taken aback he was. "Giles! And I thought us friends," he complained amiably.

"I—I wish to be your friend, Sire, but I do not think that you truly have friendship in mind."

"Ah, so? Pray explain yourself, while I continue with this." He turned his attention back to his concoction that bubbled noisily and sent up stenchful steam to fog the laboratory.

"I do not intend to accuse you, Sire," Giles assured him uncertainly, frustrated by the man's aplomb.

"No? Well, that is a relief."

"What I mean to say is, that I think—*know* that you are a sorcerer, but that I wish us to be friends in spite of the fact."

Marco glanced sideways at Giles with a fixed smile. "You are weary of living, eh? Is that it? You consider association with me as some grand manner of suicide. May I say that if you wish to have done with this life, there are simpler, uh—less *uncomfortable*—methods than placing yourself in the path of the Inquisition."

Giles scowled in confusion, then slammed a fist down upon the table, causing implements and glassware to shiver and dance crazily. "Damn me! You are a cold, inscrutable—"

"—demon?" Marco offered helpfully.

"Not the word I had in mind, but it will do!"

"Giles," Marco soothed, "calm yourself. It is I who should be unnerved, eh? I stand accused of heresy by the eldest son of Count Jacques de Nevers, an impossible witness to refute. But I am calm—you see? Eh? At your ease, young man."

"You have nothing more than that to say?" Giles protested.

"Should I confess? How foolish a man I would be to do that, without a whit of intelligence or caution. You are obviously entirely convinced of my guilt, so a confession would appear pointless."

"Sire!" Giles shouted, leaning to place both hands flat on the table in his urgency. "I came here fully aware of the risk. I placed myself in jeopardy, to—"

"Well! How flattering." Marco carefully poured the acid into the boiling kettle, stirring with a long, wooden spoon. "Forgive me if I am unimpressed, but if any man on earth has no reason to turn to Satan, it is you. A comfortable nest in Heaven awaits you, following an extremely luxurious existence. I cannot weep over your lot that clothes you richly, feeds you sumptuously and houses you in a castle on top of a mountain that overlooks tens of thousands of desperate, God-forgotten souls. God did not forget you, as he did the monstrous hag who so turned your delicate stomach yesterday. Self-righteous, opinionated, the world owes you better than all the comforts and none of the billion afflictions, eh? Please, do not expect me to fall to my knees grateful for an offered friendship that took an entire year to reluctantly flower. Have I made myself clear?"

"You *do* loathe me!" Giles exclaimed. "But why? Tell me."

Marco ceased his busy movements and turned murderous eyes upon Giles. "I despise the de Sade blood in you. If you propose to give over Nevers to Cinto, I will *kill* you. Sufficiently explicit?"

Giles rocked back as if struck a blow. "And if I do *not* give Nevers over to Cinto?" he asked in a numbed voice.

"Then we might become quite good friends; one never knows." He again turned to the kettle. "Your uncle proposes to establish himself in Nevers, thereby putting me out of business. I propose that he will not. Simple, actually. Either you see it my way, or . . ." He shrugged pointedly.

"What is it you want from Nevers when it is mine?"

"Absolutely nothing, my lad. Duke, or count, or nephew, any friend of Cinto de Sade's is an enemy of mine. If you are compelled to give away your inheritance, give it over to King Louis."

"Perhaps I *will* accuse you," Giles threatened impulsively.

"No. You will not."

"You are very sure of yourself. Do not be, Sire. I—"

"Ah! I was correct. You are indeed weary of this life."

"And what do you mean by that remark?"

"Accuse me, Giles de Sade—and reap the whirlwind. Burn with me."

Giles stuttered in confused fury, his mind spinning toward comprehension but twirling all around the edges of it. "Then friendship between us is impossible," he said roughly. "I admit to self-pity and that it is unjustified. But for this failing I am to be *murdered?* Pray, what is your own excuse, Sire, for turning to Satan? God does not seem to have neglected you, either. Tell me of the weary load you bear. I would be fascinated."

Marco's head snapped around and his mouth curled into a thin smile. "You have me there, lad. Self-pity is not your exclusive pleasure. I enjoy it immensely, and have for many years. The pot calling the kettle black, admitted. Admitted, also, I would not relish killing you. Damn you, Giles! If you were a *man* I could befriend you. But what are you? The whining pawn of two degenerate dynasties. As I said to you once before—Nevers is yours by right of birth. Why do you not seek it for yourself? Take it, and tell Cinto to go hang himself? What need have you of wool and woolens, with three hundred square miles of France to cultivate and profit from? You could build a modern, small palais by the river, raise a fine family and be a proud aristocrat under a monarch who makes all the decisions and carries all the blame, fights the wars and collects the taxes. But no taxes from yourself; the nobles will be exempt from taxation under the Regime. A truly blissful existence would be yours. And my life would not be ruined. Do I ask you to give up Nevers? I ask only that you cease being a fool, that you grow up and be a man, a Frenchman. Go from here. Do as I ask. Do not injure your golden future by association with *me*. Then we can be friends, if only from a distance."

Giles shook his head hard. His mind swam and his stomach had begun to feel queasy. Cellini's words repeated over and over in his head: *Tell Cinto to go hang himself*, a tempting suggestion. Yet he still felt so much the little boy in mortal fear of Cinto's lashing arm and tongue. "But my father is still relatively young," he said questioningly to Cellini.

"A drop or two of deadly nightshade could cure him of that inconsideration easily enough."

"No!" Giles exclaimed, horrified.

"As you like."

"How can you so lightly speak of—"

"It is different, eh? When the death is the result of a friendly brawl in a tavern gone out of control? Or when men line up on two sides, charge and butcher one another? Or when your father and the bishop burn a young woman for giving birth to a red-haired infant? I know much about you, Giles. You killed a man in a tavern when you were seventeen. You did not cringe at killing that man; you felt justified. You wear a dagger at your belt at all times. I do not cringe at killing, either. That we have different ideas to who deserves killing and who does not is of no consequence—the result is the same, a life taken, a murder committed. I, at least, admit my evil intentions, but you righteously deny your guilt with justifications. Hypocrisy."

"My own *father!* That is—is a monstrous—"

"Oh, by all means, murder only strangers. The logic of your code of ethics escapes me. Who would you rather see dead of all those you know in this world? Your father. If you are of a mind to put that dagger to use, then stab it not into a stranger, but make the murder worth the doing. If God can forgive you the death of a stranger, why not that of your father?" The merchant paused, then added sarcastically, "If you confess it meaningfully enough."

Giles shivered under the chilling weight of Cellini's obscene logic. "Sire Cellini, I have no intention of hurrying my father to his grave. Shall we change the subject?"

"Certainly." Marco fell silent, moodily peering into the kettle, then leaning to sniff at the jelling, hissing stuff, to all appearances having forgotten Giles' presence completely.

"I—I will depart from your house this day, then," Giles said questioningly.

"As you wish, my boy."

"Then you have withdrawn the invitation?"

"Invitation?"

"The use of this laboratory!"

"No. Of course not."

"But, I—"

"I see no reason to withdraw my offer to you. If you come here and work closely with me, the stake is a possibility. But at the same time, your coming here would mean you had agreed to take my advice, so I would no longer be a threat to you. It will be very much like choosing between the hives and the itch, eh? Ah, life is that uncertain and perilous. You say you will ride to Claire this day. Then go. Give me your decision when you return. Peronnette may well influence you one way or the other."

"I will certainly warn her about you," Giles threatened emotionally.

"By all means, lad. . . . Damn me! Could the element be . . ."

Giles heard no more, had turned heel to rush from the laboratory in a state of tumultuous determination and rage. But he must return to this house, could not leave Fiametta utterly alone under Cellini's influence.

Furious as he was about the merchant's threats against him, Giles still could not stir within himself any deep hatred for the man. Taking Nevers for himself certainly was not an altogether unreasonable alternative. The castle and its lands could indeed, with ingenuity and modern improvements, serve a man well, and his sons also. Giles de Sade-Nevers, the first Count of Nevers not a soldier; an aristocrat deserving of the title in this new age. That Cinto should presume to dictate to the Count of Nevers, that the punisher of his childhood should rule him throughout his life, would be a fate worse than the death Cellini threatened. Suddenly the idea of living in Florence subject to Cinto's favors, with his hand outstretched begging for the coins his uncle had promised, while Nevers Province became a vast woolen works, appeared no less than insane. He would have to be a lunatic to give so much to Cinto for the sake of a life of ease.

Giles took himself to the shop before he departed for Claire, saying a quick goodbye to Fiametta, where she, in her new capacity, took scissors to bolts, arranging small samples in stacks upon the polished wood counter.

"Will you return?" she asked softly, her hands ceasing their busy movement.

"I will," he replied, smiling at her reassuringly. "Cellini and I have had it out, and I think we are both better for it. I would not leave you alone here without a true friend. I will return in two days, Fiametta. We will ride one afternoon. You have learned to sit a horse, have you not?"

"Oui."

Giles looked upon her winsome face and shivered at the memory of that loathsome old witch bending over an eviscerated corpse at the crossroad. Lamia was not now a witch, nor would she be turned into one. Impossible to believe that that hag had ever been a naive thirteen-year-old bent upon womanhood, perhaps rapturously kissing a young man in trembling eagerness. The comparison shook him violently.

God help her, he would not let Cellini do such a thing to her. Somehow he would find a way to prevent it; God only knew how.

"Do not fly away," Giles said lightly, not wishing to alarm her with his concerns.

Lamia laughed delightedly. But when the door closed behind him, she frowned, wondering why she had laughed so automatically at the suggestion of flying. Only a year past she would have considered it no jest, but the most natural thing in the world to say to a witch. How often she had begged Eliza not to fly away in the night, when she was very little and in fear of the forest creatures and sounds. It was so difficult for her to adjust to the idea that Eliza had never flown through the trees with the night birds, for this was the clearest image she carried from the past. How she herself had yearned to fly! As high as the stars on a clear, black night.

Lamia's eyes slid sideways to focus upon the immobile broom leaning into the corner of the shop, a wry smile twisting her mouth. Indeed, how could such a stick raise a woman from the earth? How foolish—ridiculous. But her feet impulsively moved toward the witch's vehicle and her hand reached out uncertainly for it. She put the stick between her legs, pressing her skirts into a deep V, and let her weight sink down upon it. She felt no power whatsoever, only a heavier object pushing down the lighter. With a disappointed sigh, she put the broom back into its place and returned to her tasks.

The village of Claire straddled the border of Sancerre and Nevers Provinces, sprawling obliquely between towering mountains and an overshadowing gray castle. Baron Junot de Claire paid equal homage to Count Jacques de Nevers and Count Francis de Sancerre, but the parish of Claire was indisputably within the diocese of Bishop Geoffroi.

Giles arrived at Claire soon after sunset. The clouds were still mauve to the west of him, the sky above him purple-black and starlit. Peasants straggled back into the village from steep hillsides, along a dozen trails. Grapevines newly green were visible in the dusk light, stepping up the walls of earth surrounding the squalid village.

A pox-scarred old man limped into view from an overgrown path, and Giles called out to him, "The house of Peronnette, the weaver of cloth. In which direction might I find it?"

The man did not halt his dragging step, but turned up dull eyes to Giles in a slow appraisal. Giles' horse shied, near back-ending the man; he fought back on the reins, waiting for an answer.

"Peronnette," Giles repeated, more impatiently. "Have you never heard the name?"

The man kept walking, while he continuously studied Giles from cap to boots with utter contempt.

"The convent of Saint Genevieve, then," Giles snapped.

"The number of convents in Claire is one," the brute grumbled sourly, "and he asks me where 'tis." Then loudly and sarcastically, "You could ride you through Claire in a hundred countings and if you did you would find it soon enough, methinks."

Infuriated, Giles spurred his mount, yanking on the reins. The horse sprang left along the street that was still amuck from that late spring storm of two days past. Planks had been laid over puddles that relflected the flames of torches held in grimy hands. Merchants were banging shutters closed over the faces of their shops. A silence was beginning, as the night deepened, violet sky beginning to reveal stars. There was no moon. Giles began to grumble, but quickly had to admit the surly peasant was right, the convent could not possibly be missed, looming before him already, a gray mass under sprawling trees where the main road ended abruptly.

As he approached the convent, a nun in flowing black robes pulled diligently upon a long rope that slowly brought the creaking iron gate closed. He tipped his cap to her, and respectfully asked where Peronnette the weaver of cloth dwelt.

The nun's sallow face broke into a smile, but she did not speak, gesturing with graceful hands a pantomime of directions that clearly said, "Around the wall, under the trees, the third house as you ride up the hillside."

Excitement stirred Giles' blood as he thanked her. He galloped his horse toward that house wherein dwelt a vision, a bright dream, the fulfillment of all his hopes of love.

* * *

A pale light gleamed behind the one small window that faced the road. The house was so small and humble that it was barely visible, set back into the trees as it was. Tall grass grew up around it, hiding the stones once set for a clear path. A few bright flowers gleamed in the darkness, speaking of a once cherished garden that had bloomed around this home. With his heartbeat throbbing in his throat, Giles tethered the horse to a broken, rotted post, all that remained of a fence and gate, and moved swiftly through the grass toward the door.

He was ten feet from the door, when an odd sound halted him. He strained his eyes to see in the dark. Again it came, now discernible as giggling from the throats of small children. He thought to ignore it and stepped toward the door again but impulsively altered his direction, running around the house as silently as he could.

"Yah—ee," two small boys of about eight years squealed, when Giles came around the corner of the house. They stared at him an instant, round-eyed, then scampered away laughing delightedly, saying, " 'Tis her familiar, her familiar."

Giles grinned, thinking boys will be boys, letting his eye rest upon the window they had been peeking into. He turned away, halted, stood immobile for a few seconds, then whipped back to look through the cloudy glass. His heart leaped, as he caught his first sight of Peronnette since that sacred night in the alley. She was more lovely than he recalled, than all his wildest dreams. She stood beside a loom half occupied by a gray cloth, talking animatedly to someone out of sight. He cursed under his breath. She had company, and he had so hoped to find her alone. He wondered what best to do, never taking his worshiping eyes from her divine face.

A withered arm appeared from behind the screen that hid Peronnette's companion, followed by a bent form that hobbled into view, her back to the window. An aged countenance with matted gray hair. Watching, Giles frowned uneasily, swallowing hard against an inexplicable apprehension.

"Dear—*God!*" Giles gasped, horrified. When the old woman turned and showed her face to him, he had recognized that same toothless hag from the crossroads—it could be no other.

He leaped away from the window and ran around to the door, exploding into the house. He stood trembling before the two women, whose faces simultaneously snapped around to him in fearful shock at his unexpected entrance.

"Giles!" Peronnette exclaimed, a hand flying up to cover her mouth, while the old woman stood beside her gaping at him, recognition as clear in her colorless eyes as in his.

Choking on fury and revulsion, Giles waved an arm in the air, shouting, "This—this vile heathen—get her out of your house, Peronnette. She is the Devil's own mistress. I swear it is true!"

Peronnette's wide eyes turned helplessly to the old woman. "I am so sorry—I—"

"I go," the old woman interrupted, shaking a gnarled hand at Peronnette. "But first, give to me the cloth I have paid for. Eh, my child?"

Numbly Peronnette obeyed the command, reaching around to lift a yellow wool from the table behind her loom, giving it silently into the woman's hand.

As the hag moved smoothly toward the door, Giles cringed away from her, and in a tone of voice stating his loathing, said, "Never enter this house again, old woman, or I will see you dead."

"Giles!" Peronnette protested.

"That woman," he exclaimed, jerking his head toward the now closed door, "I saw her with a *corpse*. It was—"

"Never mind about her! Giles de Sade, you are not welcome here. Now leave my house at once." She backed away from him until she was against the brick wall. The fire warmed one side of her while the other goose-fleshed in dread. A cauldron hung over the blaze, her evening meal bubbling gently, sending up a thin mist of fish-scented steam. "Leave, I say," she insisted hoarsely.

Giles forgot about the hag as his eyes filled with the sight of Peronnette. He smiled gently. "I cannot leave. I cannot. I rode seven hours, and have no place to sleep."

"To the castle. The baron welcomes noble guests. Well you know it. Go. Go to the castle."

He moved to bring a wooden chair around, sitting on it

with stubborn patience. "Why did you not answer my letters?"

"I read not one of them. Will you go! Please!" She whirled around to put her hot forehead against the wall. "I do not want you here."

Giles noted that her hair had just been washed, for it was still damp, hanging straight to her hip like golden, Persian satin. His hands ached to touch it, to grasp it with his fingers, then put it to his lips, to taste, to smell, to drown in it. Her blue dress was of the finest weave, a delicate pink design artfully embroidered across the bodice, with her own sweet hand, he imagined.

"Peronnette," he said emotionally. "I am tired. And hungry. I have ridden half a day, longed for this moment an entire year. I will not leave. Resign yourself and turn to greet me cheerfully, if not adoringly."

After long suspenseful moments Peronnette rigidly turned to face Giles. She said icily, "I adore no man."

"But how sad," he said gently to her, his eyes saying much more.

"*Life* is sad," she responded wearily.

"Indeed. But love can lighten the burden of it as nothing else."

"Love."

"You have never loved?"

She did not reply with words; the light in her eyes spoke of all that she had once possessed and lost so brutally. Swallowing hard, she steeled herself and moved to take a bowl down from a shelf over the fireplace. She walked across the room and laid it down before Giles on the small, age-scarred table.

"I have a fish soup," she said in a tight voice. "And bread. That is all I—"

"Fine," he answered, keeping his gaze fixed upon her face.

"—and wine."

"Anything, Peronnette," saying her name as if it were an endearment.

It was a silent meal. Giles ate ravenously, while she but tasted her soup at intervals, keeping her eyes away from his.

"I see that you read," Giles commented when he had finished his meal, motioning his head toward the shelves of books in the far corner of the one room house.

"Oui."

"Novels?"

"No. No, I do not like that sort of, of . . ."

"What, then?"

"Anything else."

"Poetry?"

"Oui, Some. If it is not—"

"Romantic?"

She did not reply, again bringing up her spoon to wet her lips with the soup.

"How old are you, Peronnette?" he asked, affection sweet on his tongue.

"Far too old; sometimes I think one hundred and two."

Giles' hand flashed across the table and clasped hold of hers. Tightening his grip to prevent her pulling away, he said, "Look at me, please. Peronnette, I am not a fiend come into your house to ravage you. I love—"

"Get out!" She sprang to her feet, wrenching her hands loose from his. "Why do you torment me so? Why can you not see that I loathe you? You are a boy. And I am one hundred and two. Love! I have had thirty men in me. Did you hear? Thirty!" Her voice broke and tears spilled down her cheeks. "Thirty men and all in one night, one beautiful, moonlit, *romantic* night! That was enough romance to last me a lifetime—two lifetimes. I sicken at the sight of your lecherous face, your pantings, your pawing hands, your sly glances."

Giles exploded to his feet, sending his chair spinning behind him, pitying tears in his eyes. Revulsion had turned his stomach and his mind's eye envisioned thirty men with beastlike faces, each of whom he delightedly stabbed through the heart with his dagger, the pile of them dead at his feet, whereupon he set fire to them, one that would burn for an eternity, but still his rage was unsatisfied.

He reached out and clasped her into his arms, holding her to his breast, saying not a word, stroking her hair as she wept. When she fell silent, exhausted, Giles reached down a hand and lifted her chin so that he could meet her eyes, but they were closed against him. "Look at me," he whispered. "Let me tell you about true love."

"No. I—"

"Just *look* at me!"

Her eyelids fluttered as if it required superhuman strength to lift them. She met his eyes fleetingly, then cast her glance down to his shoulder.

"I will not touch you lustfully," he swore earnestly. "I love you. For your beauty which makes my heart dance to look upon it; for the purity in your eye; for the sweetness of your voice; the graceful movements of your body as you walk; for all the joy you have given me these past months by your miraculous presence in this sad world—dreams of beauty through long months of despair. To me you are un-touched, pure, divine. Possession of the moon is not neces-sary to take rapturous delight in its far-distant splendor. You need not love me in return, but do not treat me as the thirty-first beast come to blaspheme your soul. I love you. Let me hold you close to my heart, thus, and no more will I ever re-quire of you to love you through all eternity."

Tears again welled into her eyes and she smiled a little. She had heard such words before, so long ago. He was twenty, tall as Giles and as handsome. But he was only a tan-ner, a humble, sweet . . . "They killed him!" she cried. "And they killed me with him! The same priest who—who stabbed me half to death with his lust, said pious words over my Edmond's grave, over my dead heart buried with him. . . . But there are better reasons for you not to love me." She raised her head and her eyes filled with concern for him. "Go away from me and never see me again. I am not pure, not di-vine. I . . ."

Giles was fascinated by her lips as she spoke, hypnotized by them, his own mouth compulsively leaning toward hers.

"You must not remain here," she persisted. "You are in danger. Giles! I beg you, please—no."

His lips covered hers lightly, shutting off her pleas. He drew his mouth back an inch, his adoring eyes capturing hers that widened so close under him. "My sweet, sweet love," he whispered against her mouth, sliding his lips over hers, barely touching, his breath mingling with hers, moving along her cheek to her ear, to her eyelids that quivered under his touch. He groaned, his arms tightening around her, as emotion exploded within him, a fire swelling, his will pitted against his love for her that threatened to erupt into lust.

"Giles," Peronnette said in a new voice, reaching up to place her hands upon his face. "It is impossible for you to love as they do in the romances. How young you are! How intent. You cannot deny what is most natural to you." Much as she loathed life, she understood it and this she knew to be true if naught else, that carnal lust is as early with us as the day we are born and dies not until our hearts have ceased to beat. To her constant shame, the truth was that in her burned that Eden fire unquenched. Detest it as she did, deny it as she had, at night her hand relieved the agony which might have been salved by a lustful union with a man. When Giles touched her, she quaked in recollection, screams from the past echoing in her soul. But now—now she was not trembling as severely. Her mind and heart spun in confusion, battling one another fiercely.

"Giles. Treat me gently and with patience, while I try to be fifteen once again."

Giles' mouth fell against hers with bruising force now. He warned himself to be more gentle with her. She did not respond until his hand moved along her back, his fingers pressing into her spine, then sliding down to push against her buttocks urgently, drawing her groin against his, which strained to reach into her.

A cry escaped her throat and her arms flew around his neck and tightened. She sobbed, "Edmond . . . Edmond," over and over again in his ear.

Giles cared not who she thought him to be, or wished him to be, only that he needed her, loved her. He was now beyond stepping away from her with reserve. He moved a hand and held her around the throat, then with his other hand caught hold of her hair. He kissed her until she collapsed against him. Then he lifted her into his arms, carried her to her bed, laid her down and kneeled on the floor beside her. His vision was blurred and his hands shook as he untied the strings of her bodice. For an instant his eye focused on the window above him and he recalled the little boys, so he moved around to blow out the lamp that burned beside the bed.

"Beloved," he whispered in her ear, as his mouth sought hers in the dark, pressing instead into her pulsating throat, then down to a rounding, hard-tipped miracle of warm flesh.

But when he clumsily broke away from her to hurriedly remove his clothing that separated her flesh from his own, she suddenly lurched erect, stark terror in her eyes. He lunged forward and caught her tight, pleading with her, soothing, but she would not be calmed, her very bones quaking under his hands.

"Giles!" she screamed. "Giles, I am going to die!"

"My dear God, do not say such a thing!"

She stiffened in his arms and was silent for a few moments. Then she moved to take his face gently in her two hands. "Oh, Giles," she said emotionally. "You are not my Edmond. They killed him. Not once, nor twice, but thirty times take me, Giles, for those thirty filthy times."

Peronnette wept no more, her trembling now that of desire and straining release. Then they rested, began again, whispering words of passion, lust and love, until the sun lighted the sky. And then they slept.

Giles departed from her three days later, in a state of irrational elation, swearing to her that he would return within a month, begging her to consider accepting monies from him to ease her poverty.

Peronnette kissed him, closed the door, and whispered a goodbye she knew to be the first and the last between them. She would be dead within the month. Of this she could not be more certain, nor did she dread it now. When Giles discovered what she was he would despise her. It was better so.

Chapter 10

 LAMIA PULLED UP THE leather leggings, expertly and swiftly knotting the bindings, then with straining throat-growls shoved her feet into knee-length riding boots. Cellini stood grimly silent by her bed, twirling a thin whip in his hands.

"It could wait until Etienne returns from Boigny," Marco said uncertainly.

"No," Lamia insisted heatedly. "I wish to go."

"Take the black mare."

"Oui. She is sweet for me and does exactly as I wish."

"You sit well enough, but you are carelessly fond of speed. Ride easy, Fiametta. It will serve no purpose to crack your head."

When he spoke Giles' name for her, Lamia's eyes darted up to him in surprise. "Fiametta?" she asked.

He smiled. "It is a better name than Lamia, or Guy, and suits you well. Little happens in my house, or outside it, that I do not observe in one way or another, sooner or later. Fiametta and Giles de Sade have at last renewed the friendship begun at the heath, eh?"

She laughed appreciatively, then frowned. Peronnette had not delivered her cloth. It was three days past the day she had been expected. And Giles had said that he would stop here in Bourges before returning to Nevers.

"Think you Giles has met with an accident?" Lamia asked Marco anxiously. "It has been almost seven days since he left."

"We will not speculate. You ride to Claire for answers to our questions. Supposition only leads to worsened anxiety. Remember you the roads? From the inn, turn left and directly north to—"

"Six times have I ridden to Claire with Etienne. *Once* would have been sufficient for me to know the way."

"Bon. But if the scene is black, do not interfere, or allow your emotions to stampede. Question whom you can, and return swiftly. . . . Damn me! A dozen women do I have in that area and not one word from any of them. Methinks I smell that rank smoke in the air, God's vengeful breath on the wind. When you speak to Peronnette, warn her of my intuition, say that I order her not to make an illicit move nor take too deep a breath. Eh? Go now, and take care."

Lamia reined in sharply before the convent of Saint Genevieve. A noisy crowd of villagers blocked her passage along the road. The horse danced spiritedly and she fought with the reins to control the mare, finally calming her. Swiping an arm across her forehead, she sucked in air to relieve the pressure of heavy breathing against her lungs. The sun was not yet full in the sky. If she had walked, it would have taken two days. What a magnificent beast, the horse. She leaned to wrap an arm around the mare's neck in affectionate praise and admiration.

"They come," a woman cried out excitedly.

Lamia's head turned to follow the glance of the crowd. Down the hill road moved a solemn parade of men and scampering, wide-eyed children. Bishop Geoffroi, surrounded by twelve knights of his ecclesiastical court, strode iron-jawed through the dividing, awed crowd. At the rear, four priests in black soutanes, gold amulets hanging from chains around their necks, carried a large wicker basket, each clasping a corner handle.

When she recognized the bishop, Lamia's breath caught and her heart hammered in her breast. The mare shied, sensing her alarm. But Lamia instantly recovered herself, easily reining the horse aside to allow the procession by.

The richly attired bishop nodded his head and motioned the benediction with his miter from side to side as he passed. When his eyes briefly raised to inspect the countenance of the young woman astride a horse, the lass smiled piously down at him, dropping her chin in humble reverence. Pleased, he felt compelled to murmur up to her, "Bless you, my child."

Not since the great fire that burned Eliza had Lamia seen the bishop so elegantly robed and flanked by so large a guard. That ghastly day, he had stepped up the mountainous pyre to stand at Eliza's feet, reading from a golden Bible held in his hands, and he did not cease his mumblings and wailings to God until the flames threatened to light his luxurious skirts. Austerity had been the man's vow. Only on occasions where ecclesiastical protocol demanded did he garb himself thus in such glittering robes of office.

Marco had taught Lamia a great deal about her enemy: his habits, his nature, the laws and codes that governed his every movement and his responsibilities as lord of his diocese. Austerity was his usual outward appearance, but no wealthier man lived under the suzerainty of Charles Duke de Bourbon, and none whose power was more incalculable. Even the duke hesitated to force a quarrel with so great a spiritual and worldly lord, whose most fearful weapons were arbitrary excommunication and the stake.

The priests were now moving close before her. Lamia's eyes fell upon the basket they carried, noting with sudden apprehension the white cross painted on its top from edge to edge. Viciously she jabbed her heels into the mare, racing up the now clear road. The crowd turned to follow the procession.

Peronnette's house squatted against its backdrop of trees with the door wide open like the gaping mouth of a corpse. Lamia leaped down and ran toward that empty door, rushing inside to abruptly halt before a tall, lanky man with a red, pointed beard, who had been rummaging with a prying finger into a stack of finished cloth.

"Ay, now ye be too late," the man said in a language foreign to Lamia. He raised to full height, which brought his head near to the ceiling. Lifting a hand to jab a toothpick of straw between his lips, he spat out a small piece of mouth debris to Peronnette's spotlessly clean floor.

"Who are you?" Lamia asked suspiciously, praying he would say what had happened here.

"I think," he began in guttural, clumsy French, "to be the single man more fancied by her house than by her burning."

"Burning!"

"Ay. God rest 'er soul." He was speaking in English again. "The poor lass 'as been fingered. Away in a basket they took 'er, and a shame it 'tis—a rare fetchin' dame."

The man's tone of voice had been enough for Lamia to comprehend the situation. She bolted from the house and was upon her mare within seconds, whipping the horse to a full plummeting run down the hill road.

When she caught up to the procession the crowd was just moving into a small whitewashed building constructed between the wall of the convent and that of the rising, spired church. People pressed around the door, silently filing in behind the priests.

Lamia slid from the mare and ran forward to jam through the villagers, elbowing and shouldering herself to a position in a far back corner of the hall. The floor was tilted so that all who stood might see.

The bishop said a solemn prayer over the audience, blessed each witness, and warned all present to beware, for there lurked within this house Satan himself and no one could presume to guess how many of his demons. "Hold thy crosses before thee all the while, good folk, and pray without ceasing for thy protection and salvation."

The bishop now moved to sit in the center position on the dais, on an enormous, ornate throne that was flanked on each side by six lesser chairs, for the twelve lesser notables who then took their places. A side door opened and eight women shuffled in to stand around the still closed basket at the prelate's feet, which he ordered the oldest and most grotesque of the eight to open.

When the hag had unclasped the four corners, the top rose slowly and Lamia bent forward with her heart in her throat, hoping it was not Peronnette, whom she had grown to love as she had loved Eliza. Each fortnight the woman had come to

Cellini's house, remaining two days, and it was this golden creature now emerging as some beast from a cage, who had taught her how to ride on chill winter afternoons, and how to weave and embroider on quiet nights by the fire.

For tense moments Bishop Geoffroi stared at the woman standing proudly erect in the basket, noting that she was damnably pretty, an accusation in itself. She was holding his gaze arrogantly. "Tell me, mistress," he said down to her in a loud voice, "do you believe in witches?"

Not a person in the room seemed to breathe, the hush so deep that the sound of the wind in the trees beyond the open door sang an ominous dirge through the hall.

"I ask you again! Do you believe in witches?"

"I do not," Peronnette said clearly, her shoulders slumping, a hand reaching out unsteadily to support her weight on the edge of the sturdy basket.

The bishop struck like a cobra. "Then you believe that Holy Church burns *innocent* people? That is heresy!"

"I—I did not mean that," her voice breaking in confusion. "I have been accused out of common greed. If I am burned, the Englishman will claim my father's house under Canon Law which authorizes that the property of the burned accused might be divided between the judge and the accuser."

"*I* am your judge! Do you accuse me before this company of baiting hypocrisy? Who but a witch would dare to speak thus against the justice of Holy Church? You touched the child of Jean the smithy and that child immediately afterward fell sick and died—"

"No! That is not true. I—"

"You did *not* touch the child?"

"I did, of course. But he was already deathly ill, suffering so, could not live more than a few hours. I relieved his pain, and—"

"That is all we need to know. Tell us, now, why you persist in a state of concubinage?" The bishop was following the explicit directions of the Malleus, which prescribed, "Again let her be asked why she persists in a state of adultery or concubinage, for although this is beside the point, yet such questions engender more suspicion than would be the case with a chaste and honest woman who stood accused."

Peronnette's hand flew to her mouth and a sharp cry

emerged from her throat. Her face drained, giving weight to the accusation, though her fear was for Giles. She thought they might have him incarcerated for carnal association with a witch, an offense punishable by the stake.

Bishop Geoffroi rose to his feet before her and cleared his throat, then in his most judicious voice announced, "Whereupon that the truth may be known from your own lips, and that henceforth you may not offend the ears of these judges, we declare, judge and sentence, that on the present day at the hour of vespers you be placed under the question and torture both ordinary and extraordinary." He smiled with confidence, for this pronouncement inevitably drew a full, screeching confession from the accused. But the woman uttered a cry and no more. She did not fall at his feet begging for mercy, nor did she confess. On her beautiful face glowed the signs of a puerile obstinancy. He reflected with a shrug that the torture would certainly break her and he waved an arm to the guards, crying out, "To the torture, ordinary and extraordinary!"

Two guards took up long poles from where they had been resting against the wall, wielding them as prods to direct the movements of the witch toward a side door, jabbing at her as if she were a leper, their faces mirroring the horror and fear she wrought in them. Only yesterday they had smiled upon her in friendly greeting, speaking manfully afterward to each other about her beauty and pityingly about her tragic past that had frozen her to all men. Today they dared not breathe in her presence lest they find themselves in her place, accused and condemned. Their necks were weighted down with amulets and charms to ward off her evil powers.

Lamia slid along the wall behind the peasants who craned their necks to see the witch being removed to the torture. At last she stood full center of the door through which they would take Peronnette. Over the door was written THOU SHALT NOT SUFFER A WITCH TO LIVE, words from God's own book.

As she moved close, Peronnette met Lamia's eyes. The intensity of their emotions and thoughts passed in a profound, silent speech between them. Peronnette warned Lamia to be cautious, said goodbye, and transmitted an affection and hope for the child she had saved that brought tears to the eyes of one who bragged she never wept. Lamia said with her eyes a thank you and with a nod of her head a promise to comfort and love Giles de Sade in the days of pain to follow this grim circumstance.

"Move aside there, girl," the bishop called out warningly to Lamia. "Do not allow her to touch you. I cannot say how terrible your suffering would be as a consequence of such a touch."

Lamia continued to block the doorway, pressed on each side by cringing spectators. She clung to a frail hope that she could somehow rescue this blessed woman as she had been rescued. Peronnette nodded her head slightly in a severe command, and Lamia dramatically recoiled from her, raising the cross that hung around her neck in a gesture the bishop had once used against herself. She stumbled aside as if in mortal terror, and to the amusement of the audience ran wild-eyed from the hall, just as the bishop called forth the bent hag to answer the accusation that she had stolen an infant from the cemetery, taking it to the house of that witch just departed for the purpose of consumption, witnessed by two children who would now stand forward and give evidence to what their eyes had beheld.

Outside the building, Lamia stood tear-blinded, breathing heavily, numbly listening to innocent, high-pitched voices asserting that Peronnette was a cannibal, that the two women had danced naked together in the house, rubbed the fat from the boiled infant on their skins, then took brooms and flew up the chimney, to streak across the night sky. When the two witches returned some hours later, they were in the form of goats, with horns jutting from their hideous skulls. Soon as they returned to the house they once again became human. Then the Devil in a man's form approached the house and tried to frighten off the watching children, but they returned to the window to see him kissing the young witch and chewing upon her. He looked like a man, until they saw that his feet were not feet but rather cloven hooves, like those of a goat. The entire audience gasped at this, a loud, rasping pronouncement of doom upon the hag and the lovely weaver of cloth.

Lamia stood on tiptoe so that she could see inside through the open doorway, over the heads of the crowd to the bishop's pallid, triumphant face. Her hands clenched into such tight fists that her long nails stabbed into her palms. "Now you must pay for *two* deaths," she whispered, "so two deaths will you die!"

Once she would have called upon the Devil to bring lightning, screamed invective upon the bishop, would have spat upon him, all to no avail. The power was within herself but she had not yet found it; when she did, in two years, no more than five, she would see him suffer as no man had ever suffered, taking as much pleasure in his torture and his death as he was enjoying now as judge of these women.

"To the torture, ordinary and extraordinary," Lamia heard him say once again. She ran to her mount, leaped into the saddle of the waiting mare and raced tear-blinded toward the safe haven of Marco Cellini's house.

Within six hours Lamia was standing exhausted before Marco Cellini. She had found him in quiet conversation with Giles de Sade. Dropping into a chair, she let her head fall back. Her hands were blistered from the reins and her backside was sore from the saddle. Her mind was in a tumult of conflicting reactions; a morbid loathing of the bishop, pity for Peronnette, grief—and enormous relief that Giles was in good health.

"I have told Sire Cellini that I know you," Giles offered cheerfully. "Forgive my causing you this hazardous and wearisome journey, Fiametta, but I left Peronnette in the late afternoon and was of so enchanted a disposition that I halted beside the Loire and spent these past several nights under the stars, arriving but two hours after you had departed. I—" His words broke off. Lamia's eyes were moving over his face, carefully guarded, but signifying some terrible knowledge she did not know how to reveal. "What is it? Did you see Peronnette? Why did you return so swiftly? She would have welcomed your company. . . ."

Cellini also read sorrow on Lamia's face. He strode over to stand close to her chair, putting a hand on her shoulder. "Tell us. How is Peronnette, eh?"

"When I have rested I will tell you all about it," she said evasively, desperate to avoid hurting Giles, whose face when

she had entered the room shone with the radiance of his ful-
filled desire and joyful hope for tomorrow.

"You will speak now, damn you!" Giles cried, striding
across the space that divided them, an ice forming around
his heart. "Speak now, before I think my love dead, or worse.
For the love of God, speak!"

Lamia met his eyes squarely, took in a breath and forced
herself to speak of it. "Oui," she said gently, "by now she is
most likely dead."

"What are you saying? Impossible." He was shaking his
head in denial.

"Be still," Marco snapped at Giles, his heart breaking.
"Lamia, are you certain? Was my instinct true? Has she been
taken?"

"Oui," she said emotionally. "I saw her stand before the
bishop, listened while he questioned her, heard him pronounce the sentence of torture upon her. She stood there so
proudly, Marco. Refused to confess."

"Ah, no," Marco groaned, whipping around to hide his
tears from Giles and Lamia. He had known Peronnette since
she was eleven years old, when her father became one of his
first weavers in France. He had healed her wounds after that
ghastly night, forced her to live when she prayed to die,
buried her father who was unable to survive the rape of his
beloved child. And he had loved her with as deep a devotion
as any man who ever loved a woman.

Bewildered and frightened, Giles said, "Torture? Are you
playing some kind of game with me? Who in this world
would . . . Damn you!" He fell to his knees before Lamia
where she sat, reaching out to take her arms in his shaking
hands. "Curse you, will you sit silent while I die inside with
anxiety? Tell me—what has happened?"

"Two small boys said that she flew on a broom, made love
with the Devil, and—"

"A *witch*! They said that my—that she is a witch? Preposterous. I do not believe you!"

Lamia then told the entire story, as clearly as her numbed
mind and emotions allowed. Before her, kneeling on the
floor, Giles rocked back, his face twisting in agony at each
further description of Peronnette's suffering.

"A man with a red, pointed beard, you say?" Marco asked,

whirling around to glare at her with a coldness of eye that unsettled Lamia. "Poking about her house, eh?"

"Oui. Peronnette said before the court that some *English-man* had accused her just to take her house."

"A professional," Marco said, his right hand folding into a fist as if he clasped a knife. "Such a man would have put the children up to it, nosing around to obtain what witness he could to substantiate his claims. Swine! Describe the other women, if you can."

"One was very old and ugly. The children said that she was with Peronnette five nights past."

"The hag—the hag," Giles exclaimed to Marco, waving an arm wildly in air, "the same one I saw in the storm." Then his face drained and he leaped to his feet in sudden comprehension, speechless against the inexplicable workings of his own mind that suggested a possibility too hideous—"The witch was there when I arrived." His face dropped into his hands.

"Old Nan. It had to be," Marco said stiffly. "It could not have been Hortense, she was here in my laboratory last night. Poor old Nan."

"I cannot say what the others were like," Lamia said, "for I had eyes only for Peronnette. The old one was forced to open the basket."

"Was—*is* she a witch? Cold demon that you are, Cellini, you brought Peronnette to this—this."

"A witch, a witch," Marco raged, his face reddening. "Damned fool! Can you love a woman one night and the next night name her foul? She is a precious, unique individual, with ordinary sentiments, hates, desires—and a nightmare to avenge. Name her what you will, the judges also, to me she is an angel about to suffer as no one of us in this room can imagine, she who has suffered so inordinately already. My inclination is murderous this moment, so do not press me even a little, Giles de Sade, or I swear—"

"If you care about her so deeply, then *save* her!" Giles shouted at the man. "For the love of God, we must save her!"

"*How?* Name an action we can perform that will serve a purpose other than suicide, and I will this instant begin with it. Shall I call up the demons of Hell, eh? and send them to

Claire in a mighty force? If it were within my power, know that I would brave God's own wrath to save her life."

"You can go to Claire and vouch for her, as I will do. I do not care if I might die in the—"

"*Might* die? Will die. Speak one word in her defense and the finger will swing around to yourself, then to me. A woman was accused of mutilating her own child. She confessed under torture. Her husband pleaded for her, swore she was innocent. So they exhumed the little corpse, only to discover the infant had died of natural causes, was not mutilated at all. But they burned her anyway, saying the Devil, clever as he is, had made it *appear* that she was innocent. Needless to say, the husband burned with her, the Devil having taken possession of him to work this subterfuge. Peronnette is dead, Giles. Oh God! She is dead and there is nothing we can do here now but weep for her!"

"No!" Giles sobbed. "No—no! I will not let it happen. God will not allow it to happen."

"God!" Lamia cried. "Giles, it was *God* who sentenced her, God who will tear out her fingernails, pull her bones from their sockets, and enjoy every minute of it!"

"Stop it!" His hands flew up to cover his ears. Then in hysterical grief and frustration, he said ominously to Marco, "Give money to the bishop, and your word, along with mine, that she is innocent, Cellini, or I will accuse you and see *you* burn!"

Marco stiffened. He stepped toward Giles, but held back the fist that longed to smash into the lad's face. "No, my lad. We will say we do not know her save in a casual way. We will be stunned to learn that she was a witch. We will, if approached by the bishop, be deeply concerned about the menace he is so willing to brave and destroy—a veritable Saint Michael, he. To behave otherwise would be a sacrilege against Peronnette's affection for us. What think you would be her own words to you, eh? How great her further pain to know that you, also, will die, merely for loving her?"

"Damn you!" Giles cried, tears rising to blind him. "Oh God, I—I am going to Claire and I will die if need be. I must try. I cannot remain here and—and . . ."

"You will remain exactly where you stand," Marco said menacingly.

"Do not threaten me!" Giles swept tears from his eyes with a trembling hand and stepped toward Marco in a clumsy fighting posture.

Marco's arm lashed out so swiftly Giles had no time to guard his chin.

"Oh, Giles!" Lamia screeched, leaping from her chair. He had fallen unconscious to the floor. She kneeled to cradle his head in her hands, glaring up at Marco.

"It was necessary," Marco insisted. "Would you have him burn as Eliza did, eh? As Peronnette will?"

"Ah, no!"

"Then go quickly to the laboratory and bring me the vial labeled SOLANACEAE. Quickly."

"You will drug him?" she asked uncertainly.

"Oui. To calm him for a few days, lest he foolishly throw his precious life away."

"But . . . I thought you intended to see him dead."

"Damn me, can I kill the single man my Peronnette has loved in all these years? To do so would blaspheme the love I have always had for her. Now go. Do not sit thus clacking your jaws at me. He will awake, and I will be forced to fell him once again."

Two days later, as Giles lay in a state of numbed consciousness on his bed, a tall, red-bearded Englishman stepped confidently into Cellini's shop. He smiled upon Etienne, asking politely for the master, while his eyes roved avariciously up to the richly stocked shelves, his tongue sliding out over his thin lips.

Cellini graciously offered hospitality to the man, taking him into his house and opening a bottle of his choicest wine for his guest, who sat with his coarsely hosed, long legs outstretched and entwined before the fire.

"You have come from Claire, you say?" Cellini said conversationally in almost perfect English and in his smoothest tone, his eyes devoid of expression.

"Ay, and pleased I am to find ye speak me language, Sire." He smirked over the edge of his wine glass and said carefully, "A nasty business in those parts. You've heard a it, I dare say."

"Yes. And praise God for the bishop's quick hand of justice, else the plague of witches might have spread this far. Nine altogether, was it not?"

"Ay, ay, nine it was. . . . So certain are ye, Sire, that ye have no witches hereabouts, eh?"

"Ah, I should pray not, but one never knows for certain, does one?"

"True enough. One a them at Claire was a weaver a the cloth. Sold 'er stuff to yerself, me informants tell me."

"Indeed? Which of the nine was that, eh?"

"One Peronnette. A rare, fetchin' lass, I do say—God fergive me, 'er bein' a witch an' all."

"The woman is dead?" Marco asked unconcernedly.

" 'Ave ye not heard? Coo, a cold one, she was. They says, them that done the stretchin' an' tore 'er flesh with the hot pincers, that she never felt a thing, not a blarsted thing—just smiled kind a loose at 'em while they done all save killin' 'er. I'd say she was a *real* one, an' well they knew it, scared 'em silly, she did. Imagine. They stuck the long pins into 'er an' still she makes not a peep. Then she went an' took 'er witch's teeth to 'er own wrists, bled 'erself to death in 'er cell. Well now, the bishop 'e went wild at that, an' who'd blame 'im—so 'e 'ung 'er dead body, 'e did, then 'e quartered it, an' then 'e burned the pieces, figurin' to be blarsted sure she don't come back in that fetchin' body o' 'ers."

"She felt no pain, you say. How curious. Indeed, a nasty business." Marco smiled amiably and sipped at his wine, eyeing the man with pleasant interest.

"A fine 'ouse ye 'ave 'ere, Sire."

"Thank you."

"A frustratin' thing, this business a bein' accused. Fair impossible to prove yer innocent?"

"Very true."

"I 'ave this friend, 'owever, back in England 'e is, got 'isself fingered. Now, 'e's got money to burn an 'e buys off the rotter 'at pointed to 'im. Didn't cost 'im more than—"

"How interesting," Marco interrupted, "but, if he had the opportunity to put money into his accuser's hand, why did he not simply murder the man? Certainly that would be a far surer method of closing the man's lying mouth, and permanently. Do you not agree that that would have been a wiser move?"

The man rose uneasily to his feet and said in a small voice, "I 'ave this friend waiting at the inn. Me bones are creaking from the long ride. A good night to ye. Per'aps we'll meet again one a these—"

"A man like you has no friends," Marco said, still smiling up at him.

" 'ere, now, 'ow can ye say that? The bishop a Nevers' right-'and man I am—"

"Do not further trouble yourself. You will never convince me. The truth is that you have met your match in me and your career is at an end. Ironic how many innocent men and women must have died at the point of your finger, and the first time you meet face to face with the genuine article—you will die before that finger can lift in accusation. But then, you should have expected this one day, treading in Satan's path as you must in your work. The powers of the Devil are fearsome indeed, when wielded by the adept sorcerer who has been schooled in all his evil ways."

"I say!" the man exclaimed. "Are ye threat'nin' me? I came 'ere as a friend!"

"You are no friend of mine, Sir—nor of the Devil's. You did not believe there to be such a thing as a true sorcerer, did you? You were wrong, Sir. You will not leave this house alive."

The man laughed loudly, rising to his full six feet and two to tower over the short merchant like Goliath before David. "Is it yer puny self that's plannin' on stoppin' me?"

"Bless me, no. But the mandragora you swallowed along with your wine most assuredly will."

The man's mouth gaped open in dumb disbelief, his throat closing on a terrified gasp.

"And when you are dead, be assured, your body will be hanged, quartered, and then burned. Tell me, Sir, how much gold you received for the performance of your religious duty at the village of Claire?"

"Blarsted fiend!" the brute choked, lunging with his hands open toward Cellini's throat.

Marco swung from the chair, easily avoiding the weakening lout. "If you were not so overlarge, you would already be writhing at my feet! Accuse me, would you? Or take my money for your silence. A handful of gold for nine lives! May the Devil take you into Hell and fry you for two eternities!"

The Englishman collapsed to his knees, wailing and sniveling to Cellini for an antidote to the poison that was now beginning to jab at his innards in sharp little pains.

It took over two hours for the accuser to die. Cellini sat all the while sipping his wine, tears wet upon his face, sliding down into his graying beard.

When it was done, Marco knew well that the entire sum of the Englishman's agony, his screams and terror, had not avenged a single wound upon Peronnette's beloved flesh. He dropped his head into his hands, sobbing uncontrollably, weeping until he was drained of hate and the need for retribution. Then he arose with swollen, red eyes, stepped over the grotesquely twisted body without looking at it, and made his way to his bed.

Giles de Sade rode away from Cellini's house within the week, no longer a boy, no longer capable of dreams; love had died with Peronnette. There was not a single illusion, no hope left to him. He rode toward a future that he already despised, certain he would merely exist from this day until his death. He enjoyed no pity for himself, as had been his habit since leaving Florence, for he no longer loved himself enough to bring forth any emotion in his own behalf except contempt.

"But how sad," he heard himself say in a whisper, to a vision.

"*Life* is sad," the vision replied, a voice from whom the flesh had been divided, but which lived inside him and would forever.

Chapter 11

"Etienne, it is almost dark," Lamia complained, stubbornly maintaining her watch at the shop window. The street outside was crowded with an hundred persons of no consequence. "Are you absolutely certain that this is the day?"

The stout, aggravated clerk kept his eyes on the open ledger before him, scribbling busily with his quill pen. "I am quite certain the master will arrive this day," he said flatly. "Why do you not return to the house and pass the time profitably? Sire Cellini will be annoyed at your laxity these months that he has been away. You have read not one of the books that he left for—"

"Bother!" she snapped at him. "Dull; absolutely mind-drugging. I despise poetry. And the kind I hate most is the nauseating drivel written by lovesick Italians, which is all he left for me. When *will* he come?"

"When he *comes!*"

"Very amusing," she said bitingly, but her mouth twisted into a fleeting smile. She turned away from the window and strode across the darkening shop, standing before the clerk's table to watch Etienne's swiftly moving pen. "Etienne?" She waited for him to glance up to her.

"Oui?" he replied impatiently, letting his hand cease its work, eyeing her with a guarded affection.

"Have you heard—heard any more gossip about—"

"Giles de Nevers again!" shaking his head irritatedly, his sagging jowls swinging to and fro around his cherubic mouth. "How much can I hear, unless I tag at his heels every one of his waking hours? He is wed to the Baron d'Archambault's daughter, who will soon give birth to—"

"I know all *that*," she protested angrily.

"And I know that you know it!" he shouted back at her in despair, throwing up his obese arms. "Go to your books and leave me in peace to finish my work. For five endless months you have plagued me with—"

"His uncle presented him with a villa," she interrupted stubbornly. "Imagine Giles a baron. The Duke de Bourbon must have grown quite fond of him."

"He *loathes* the lad," Etienne disagreed. "The duke *allows* him to play the role of baron, but will only do so as long as the friendship of Cinto de Sade is necessary to his schemes. The entire province is laughing, if you must know."

"Laughing!" she cried. "Why?"

"La Ville de la Fleur it is to be called when construction is completed. The noblemen laugh because the new baron expects to dwell therein without a single moat or battlement to protect him, not a single soldier to do battle in his name. With a few men any one of his enemies could sack him and burn him out. The man is a fool. A *married* fool, at that. Why do you waste your thoughts on him?"

Lamia subdued a compulsion to strike the man for insulting Giles. She had not seen Giles in eighteen months. He had forgotten her, but she would never forget him. She opened her mouth to defend him to Etienne, but the door behind her was thrown open and a blast of cold October wind slapped her skirts about her legs. She whipped around with a flashing smile.

"Marco!" Lamia squealed, rushing across the shop to fall against his chest, sending him stumbling backward. She fastened her arms around his neck and exclaimed, "Oh, I am so happy to see you!"

Marco laughed and reached to unwind her arms from about him, then held her off so that he could examine her.

"My Little Flame," he said warmly, "will you never stop growing? You are taller than I by at least two inches. Now is the time to stop; you are tall enough."

"Did you have a successful journey?" she asked, beaming. "And did you bring me the Persian silk you promised?"

"Indeed, I brought the silk, the likes of which a queen would give her soul to wear next to her royal hide."

"Ah," she sighed excitedly, slapping her hands together. Then her happy eyes caught sight of a dark, personable face hovering behind Cellini's shoulder, and she stepped curiously around the merchant to stare at the stranger. "Who is *this?*" she asked, pointing rudely in the direction of the lad's serene face.

With a curious solicitude, Marco turned around and reached for the young man's hand, as if he were leading a blind person. But the youth's eyes were alight with intelligence and a bewildering array of unreadable attitudes and perceptions.

"I have brought you this gift as well, Fiametta—a friend to brighten your days." He kept his hand lightly on the lad's arm.

Lamia gave the person a thorough inspection, from the tips of his black riding boots, to the top of his head. His flesh was the color of chestnuts, his eyes as densely black as his hair that waved to his wide shoulders. His features were fine and he had wide-set, exotically slanted eyes, a thin, long nose, a full and sensuous mouth; a black Adonis. "He is very pretty," she concluded at last, "but what is he? I have never seen a man of his color before. Did you buy him in Africa?" She backed away from the creature uneasily, because he was following her head movements with darting thrashes of his own head and eyes. "What ails him? Why does he do that?"

"Because he wants to know what you are saying about him," Marco replied. "He cannot hear you, and—"

"He is *deaf?* Oh, how terrible for him." She turned a new and kinder eye upon the poor lad.

"How I came to bring him here is a long story. To be brief. I did not *buy* him. Before the purge of the Moslems in 1492, his father was a Moorish physician in Cordova, Spain. His mother was a Jewess, the daughter of a merchant friend of my father's. She was butchered by the queen's soldiers before the child's eyes; he was only two. Ghanim's father escaped with him to Africa. The terror of the purge seemed to destroy the boy's capacity for hearing and speech."

"He does not speak, either?" The more tender elements of her nature reached out to the Moor, who gazed at her with a disturbing intensity, seeming to know what Cellini was telling her.

"Somehow his father accomplished a fantastic feat, teaching Ghanim to know words by the way a mouth shapes them. Ah . . . Ghanim is very remarkable in many ways, you shall see."

"Why is he with you and not with his father?"

"The physician died while I was a guest in his house. After his father took to his bed, critically ill, Ghanim spent most of his nights prowling the squalid taverns and back alleys of the Casbah. He became impossible to handle; no one had ever understood him but his father. Seventeen years old and a man, he made a choice—to come to France with me. Let us say, he is here in somewhat the same capacity as yourself, eh? and leave it at that for now."

Lamia examined Ghanim's face. Frowning, she said carefully to him, exaggerating her lip movements, "I am pleased to meet you, Ghanim. My name is Fiametta."

The youth's mouth cracked into a pleased smile and he nodded slightly in acknowledgment.

"He understands French!" she exclaimed in amazement.

"And Italian, Greek, Latin, English—as well as Arabic, of course. You name the language and he can probably speak it, or read it—from a book or from a speaking mouth. He writes fluently in French, Latin, and Arabic."

"Is he Christian, a Jew—or Moslem?"

Ghanim threw his head back in a soundless laugh and Cellini grinned with him. As the two men's eyes met a veritable flood of silent conversation seemed to pass between them.

"You are birds of a feather, that is obvious," Lamia commented with a smile. "But where is the silk—the silk? I have waited five months for you to return with it."

"Typical female," Cellini scolded good-naturedly. "If you are not careful, I will find it impossible to distinguish you from the common herd, ma petite. You must wait another fortnight, I fear, my purchases having been sent from Nantes by flat-boat."

"Ah," she pouted.

"But this night will be full. We will eat, and then I will have Ghanim perform for you a thousand and one miracles. I stand in awe before him and you will also. With him I am not so much the teacher as the student. He and I will pass on our new learning to our associates, eh? I want to see them all, in groups of five or six, as soon as possible." He turned to Etienne, who had been silently keeping at his ledgers but missing nothing of the conversation. "You heard, Etienne. Six, two nights hence. Get the word to them. Six the next night. Understood?"

"Oui, monsieur," Etienne replied dryly, rising to meticulously place all the tools of his clerk's trade in their proper nooks and cupboards, six names and faces already clearly itemized on the ledger page of his ordered mind.

"How exciting!" Lamia cried. "Oh, Marco! I am so glad that you have come home."

A frail young woman entered the textile shop of Marco Cellini carrying a basket overflowing with carded fleece. She did not return to the street. Hortense, her bent grandmother, entered Cellini's house with a folded length of newly woven cloth under an arm. Hours later, another woman entered by the street door, for she was of moderately high estate and completely warranted in paying the merchant a social call. One by one the six entered, gathering below in Cellini's laboratory.

As usual, the merchant's shutters were closed over his shop windows at dusk. Etienne sat at his table, a flickering candle before him. He was working late at his books, which was consistent with the pattern he had set. No one could enter the main house without his hearing or seeing the intruder.

In the laboratory, the six women sat in various moods upon their chairs, their expressions ranging from contempt to absolute adoration, all eyes fastened upon Cellini as he imposingly paced before them.

Leaning against the wall near the cold furnace, Lamia stood close beside Ghanim, her eyes scanning the faces of the witches with a hard scrutiny. This was the first time she had been allowed to attend such a meeting, these the first true practitioners of witchcraft that she had ever confronted—except Peronnette, but she had not been the same kind of witch as these. These six were corpse stealers who hovered over steaming cauldrons of loathsome brews concocted of boiled frogs, wolf's hair, and human infants. She felt a certain affinity with them, but was uneasy in their presence because of Marco's constant references to them as *lunatic*.

Marco began to speak in a low, intense voice. First, he designated the time and place of the coming Sabbat. The women listened closely, asked questions occasionally in hushed voices, and accepted without question his statement that he would not preside over the Black Mass this year, or ever again. He considered himself to have reached the age of physical moderation, the rigors of the Sabbat demanding an energy that he might still possess, but disinclination rendered him a poor candidate for the role of Satan.

"Do you expect a marked decline in attendance this year?" the woman of estate queried in a melodious voice, "due to the slaughter at Claire eighteen months ago?"

"No. Rather, the opposite," Cellini replied firmly. "Nothing so intrigues the multitude, or draws them quicker to us, than a resurgence of clerical fury. The human inclination toward disobedience and vulgarity, a delicious sense of sin and derring-do—these things will bring an hundred more at the least. Plan accordingly in your arrangements for food and drink."

Ghanim and Lamia faced Cellini where he stood under a smoking lamp, neither of them missing a word. In the two days that the young man had been in the house, they had become fast friends, many sheets of paper filled by Ghanim in their rapid-fire conversations and arguments. As Cellini talked, Ghanim jabbed Lamia in the ribs with an elbow, nodding his head to the hag, Hortense, who sat closest to Marco. Lamia carefully examined the old woman, then met Ghanim's eyes questioningly. He made an expression that stated his opinion that she was pitiful. She nodded in agreement. Their eyes clung for long moments; then each turned back to Cellini, where he stood now beside the long table in the center of the room, reaching to pick up several ancient manuscripts in his two hands.

"You call yourselves witches," Marco said accusingly to the six, "and these are what can be termed your handbooks. All of you can read, are intelligent, or you would not be in this room with me now. My hope has always been to enlighten you, to convince you of the merits of scientific application of your skills, as against haphazard experimentation and necrotic indulgence of your baser instincts."

"Huh," Hortense commented, swinging around in her chair to stare at the cluttered wall shelves, by way of pronouncing Cellini's accusations completely unacceptable to her.

"I swear, you take pleasure in dissecting corpses, Hortense," Marco said sharply. "You call up the Devil or his demons with ridiculous incantations and atrocities, when, in truth, the powers are your own, and this night I mean to prove that to you. This night I will demonstrate to you the powers that you all possess."

"Philosophical opinion, Marco," Hortense's granddaughter, Nicolette, put in. *"Impossible* to prove. After another lengthy debate we will leave here still—"

"Not by debate; not this time," Marco interrupted enthusiastically. "When I say proof, I mean exactly that."

"Huh," Hortense snorted again, with her back still to Cellini.

"In these manuscripts," Marco persisted, waving the books in front of them for emphasis, "there is a mass of unintelligible nonsense which it is a waste of time to seriously consider. The blood of a hare to be killed the twenty-fifth day of June before sunrise; the skin of a goat newly slain; the fat of a man who has died in the month of July. All redolent of a witchcraft of a base and foolish sort."

With increasing contempt, he continued to name the ancient and traditional ingredients of witches' brews and incantations, insisting that the dark tower upon the height of which they thought to one day meet the Devil on an equal footing was delusory. Futility mocked them around every curve of the road. But there were a few profound compensations to be had along the road of ceremonial magic, the seeker refreshed by an occasional oasis of beauty and discovery in a wasteland of otherwise nonsensical and evil rites. Two sublime truths emerged from these intellectual misadventures, that the secrets of the universe were discoverable, that the mind of man was the key to all the mysteries.

"The long strings of formidable words which roar and moan through your incantations have only one worthwhile effect, other than being an entertainment and lure for the credulous, that of exalting the consciousness to the proper pitch for genuine intuition and the manifestation of your innate powers."

Hortense threw her gnarled hands in air, another wordless condemnation of Cellini's stubborn ridicule. Then she nudged the finely dressed lady beside her and snarled, "Next he will say we are *angels*, eh? Eh? Blessed angels with pretty wings, not witches at all."

Cellini ignored her, moving with heightened intensity toward his demonstration. "Consider these to be the necessary mental conditions for true success in magical operations; an invincible obstinacy—"

A laugh exploded simultaneously from each witch's throat, even Hortense admitting by a cackling giggle that Cellini had hit upon truth.

"A conscience at once hardened to crime."

"Oui, oui," old Hortense said, smirking up at him now, no longer in disagreement.

"Blind faith in all that is incredible; a refusal to accept impossibilities as such. An utterly sincere denial of Holy Church's concept of God. And last but not least, a propensity for perversity. Hortense, you possess more than your share of this final, dubious virtue."

"Perverse. That I am," she said, grinning. "Opposite, opposite; everything in reverse—'tis the Devil's own way and has led to the fruits of our trade, eh? With deadly poisons we cure the sick. Perverse, that I am. But where is your proof? Your *proof*, Cellini! And what exactly did you plan to prove, eh?"

"I will get to it." Marco looked at Hortense with the kind of exasperation a father might express in response to a stubbornly bratty child. "First, look upon this print." He brought up from the table a masterpiece of the painters' and printers' art. "This is an artist's conception, in complete harmony with the contentions of his faith and the concepts of the masses—a representation of the persons in this room at this moment. Here—we have a sorcerer, eh? Hideous, is he not?" He laughed in genuine amusement. "See how my teeth are like fangs. Ah, and a skull beside my elbow with a dagger plunged into it. And near the hearth, here, are three naked witches mounting broom handles in preparation for a flight; you see, this one is disappearing under the mantel of the chimney. Flying is the method by which all witches go forth to the Sabbats; no clergyman, artist, peasant, or *witch* would argue this fact of your occupation. Why is it that you always *walk* to the Sabbat, Hortense? Never have I seen you arrive except on your two well-worn feet."

"Huh," was her reply, her small eyes glistening with a fierce, mocking light.

"Your silence answers my question," he said with a sarcastic bow to her from the waist. "Here—to the far right of the picture, we see an old witch rubbing the legendary unguent on the back of a naked, younger witch." He laid the print down carefully and lifted up a jar of gray paste, holding it up to a lamp and studying it with exaggerated interest. "The unguent," he said meaningfully, bringing the open jar down and moving it under the nose of each woman. "Let us be scientific. Which of you will strip down so that I may rub her with this potent paste, eh? Which of you will demonstrate her flying prowess? Please be careful of my contraptions that hang so profusely from the ceiling. Well?"

His suggestion was met with a chill silence, each woman looking questioningly to the others. Hortense was sputtering indignantly.

"Ah. I see. You cannot fly. A pity. But you continue to boil the infants to make this foul paste. Why? Still you do not answer. Then, here—" He lifted a dark vial from the table. "Here is the fluid of all knowledge, the broth from an infant stew. Drink from this vial, Hortense, and render us thunderstruck by your newly acquired knowledge." He pressed the vial into her gnarled hand. "Go on, drink. Prove the potency of your own brew. Or will you admit here and now that you are a *fraud!*"

"A fraud?" Hortense screeched, rising awkwardly to her feet.

"Precisely," Cellini roared back at her.

"Then what are *you?*" she shouted, shaking a bent finger in his face, "who playacts the Devil for the benefit of the credulous, eh?"

"But I do not delude myself into believing I am the creature I *pretend* to be. That is exactly my point. I do not find it necessary to murder children in my plot against the Church, eh? Fight the battle, yes, but contribute something to the world along this foul path we take. Hortense, your knowledge of the drugs and the poisons, your talents for surgery and diagnosis rival the greatest physicians in Europe, who in hidebound ignorance and tradition stupidly and helplessly prescribe bloodletting and the swallowing of nails and eggshells as cures. What little knowledge I possess, I owe to you; you were my teacher, but—"

"And well you know it!" she exclaimed, enraged. "I taught you all you know and—"

"For god's sake, because you are accused of being vile, must you *justify* the accusation?" He faltered a moment, studying the wretched face of Hortense. He wondered how else she might have learned so much about the human anatomy, without the corpses she had been exhuming and slicing up these past fifty years. To satisfy her unquenchable curiosity and her stubborn belief in a corporeal Devil, she performed autopsies which God and Church had denied the legitimate physician for centuries. His eyes flashed across the room to Ghanim. He signaled the young man with a lifted eyebrow and received a quick nod of acknowledgment. "Again and again each of you has tried to accomplish the feats promised to you in the Keys of Solomon, according to the teachings of your mothers and grandmothers, but without success. I will now demonstrate to you the—"

"Marco!" Lamia cried out. Ghanim had slumped to the floor beside her.

The six women swung around, mildly curious, to gaze upon the apparently unconscious Moor. Cellini strode swiftly to Ghanim and kneeled down to put a hand to his throat.

Lamia dropped to her knees, her eyes frantic, waiting for Marco to say something. "Marco! What is it?"

"Dear God, he is *dead!*" Marco exclaimed in disbelief. He

rose to his feet, his eyes wide with shock. "The poor lad has dropped dead. I cannot believe it!"

"I do not believe it, either," Hortense remarked knowingly. She hobbled over to glare down at Ghanim with an intuitive suspicion of trickery. "Dead, you say, eh? Step aside, Marco Cellini."

All the women were now surrounding the body. Lamia was stunned and overwhelmed by sadness. "Oh, Marco—no!" she cried.

"The demons of Hell as my witnesses," Hortense proclaimed, "he is, in fact, dead. Going cold as stone."

"Here, you two," Marco commanded, indicating Hortense's granddaughter and the lady of quality, "help me lift him to the table."

When the awkward task was done, Ghanim limp and outstretched before them, Marco said to Hortense, "Since he is dead, why do you not perform surgery upon him, eh? Show us those bones and muscles of which you always brag knowledge."

Hortense was startled by the suggestion and hesitated. Then she hoarsely agreed. "I will—I will. Give me a knife. This, at least, I can prove beyond any doubt."

Marco placed a long blade on the table beside the corpse. Hortense roughly set about removing the body's layers of clothing, tearing, twisting, for he would have no further use for them. When the body was fully naked, the shreds of his clothes all around him like rags, Hortense determinedly took up the blade and raised it over his abdomen. All five women were gaping over her shoulder, Lamia hovered back uncertainly.

"*Ah—ee!*" Hortense shrieked, recoiling from the grinning corpse that had suddenly bolted upright to grab hold of her knife-wielding hand.

The women leaped back from him, falling over chairs in their fright, their throats emitting prayers and squealing exclamations.

"A *trick!*" Lamia raged. "A foul, mean trick!" Then it suddenly occurred to her just how successful and clever a trick it had been and she threw her head back in a riotous laugh. "Oh, Marco, I believed it. I really thought him dead." When he only grinned at her, she sobered and frowned thoughtfully. "Marco," she said, reaching to grasp his arm, "could I learn such a trick? Could I? If I could make them think me dead . . . *could* I?"

"I do not know," Marco admitted with a helpless gesture. "If one human being can, surely another can. But how? How does he accomplish such a feat? Even Ghanim cannot tell you."

"He is Satan incarnate," one of the witches observed. "That is how he does such a thing."

Ghanim sat with his legs nonchalantly dangling over the table edge, casual in his nakedness, his black eyes soberly examining the faces of the women, who looked upon him as if he were a demon they had finally managed to conjure, regretting that they had ever set upon the conjuration.

"No," Cellini said firmly. "Ghanim is not Satan, nor is he possessed by demons. You will recall that he instantly dropped into that lifeless state. No incantations, for he cannot speak the powerful words. No skin from a freshly killed goat. No dead body at his disposal. His mind, his magnificent brain, commanded his flesh and it obeyed."

"Huh," Hortense snorted skeptically, but curiosity and her innate fearlessness had gotten the better of her. She hobbled up close to Ghanim, giving him a careful examination, poking a finger into his flat belly as if he were a porker on exhibit for her approval and eventual consumption. "What other miracles can this mind of his perform, eh?"

Marco triumphantly rushed to Ghanim's side, quickly taking up a length of torn shirt, tightly binding it in three thicknesses around the lad's eyes, knotting the cloth behind his head.

"Fiametta!" Marco called, motioning her to him. When she was directly before Ghanim, he indicated a glass vial on the table, silently telling her to smash it on the floor.

The glass shattered when Lamia threw it down with a loud crash that made everyone in the room flinch except Ghanim.

"You see that he is deaf."

"Or craftily pretends to be," a woman put in bitingly.

Again and again Cellini ordered jarring noises to be made behind Ghanim, until the women were convinced.

"Now, watch him closely. At a touch from me, he will

step down and move around this room without once stumbling over an object, or bumping into one of you—without the aid of sight or sound. Do not move away as he approaches you; that will not be necessary."

At the touch of Marco's hand on his arm, Ghanim slid off the table and slowly began to walk toward the far wall, never once faltering or placing his arms out in front of him. He stepped over a fallen chair, eased around Lamia where she stood, flashing her a quick smile as if he knew it was her he passed. When he leaned to carefully move aside another chair that stood in his path, the women gasped. And when he kicked aside the basket of flowers, as a man would who saw it as he approached, his foot swinging back just previous to reaching it, they gasped again.

"What I do, ye also may do, the Christ said in reference to the miracles he performed," Cellini said excitedly. "Believe your own eyes, and see the power. Not supernatural, or God-withheld and hoarded, but *human!*"

"Is there more?" Hortense asked eagerly, hobbling after Ghanim as he continued his easy stroll back to the table. "What a dear, dear boy. And I thought there was no more to learn, eh? Cellini, you old fool, where did you find this dear boy, eh?"

Cellini laughed delightedly, whipping the binding from Ghanim's eyes, slapping the lad pridefully on the back. "One more performance; one more miracle. Then you will forever be convinced. The lad has taught me this technique for rendering others subject to my will, which his Moorish father taught to him. It is supposedly an ancient secret; indeed, I had heard of it but thought it to be fancy."

He took from the table a gold amulet on a chain and moved to stand before Nicolette. "In this amulet there lurks a supreme power which you cannot pit your will against. Watch it closely. See how it spins, now blurs before your eyes. The amulet is causing you to become weak. Your will is leaving you and you cannot keep your eyes open. You are so very tired. When you sink into a trance, which will be very soon, you will continue to hear my voice, and only mine, and will do anything I tell you to do."

Nicolette's credulous eyes blurred almost immediately, for she was most susceptible to suggestion, as were the majority of her cohorts. She believed with a blind faith that she had on several occasions flown, when she was only drugged and told of it when she awoke. Her consciousness soon retreated and she stood in a deep trance before Cellini, absolutely convinced of the power of Ghanim's amulet.

"Speak to her, Hortense," Marco said.

"Nicolette?" the hag said doubtfully, leaning to peer into her granddaughter's dumb face. She took hold of Nicolette's arm and shook it, but there was no reaction. "What ails her?" she complained to Cellini.

"She is *controlled*, Hortense. Her mind is mine to do with as I please."

"Ridiculous!"

Marco smiled smugly and said to Nicolette, "You are a witch. You can fly. Fly!"

Nicolette immediately leaped up and forward, floundering around the room with her arms wildly flapping.

Lamia choked on amused laughter at the ludicrous dance. "Marco, does she truly believe she is flying?" she whispered aside to him, fascinated.

"I think she must. . . . Nicolette, that is enough. Come back and stand before me. Ah, that is good. All right, Hortense. Tell her to fly."

In a wavering voice Hortense ordered her granddaughter to fly, but, to the amazement of all, Nicolette merely stood there as if deaf.

Finally, Marco suggested to Nicolette that her right arm could not feel pain. He then brought a long needle from inside his shirt front and moved to stab the needle into her arm.

"Cellini!" Hortense protested, staying his hand. "She is my living grandchild. Not a corpse!"

He hushed the old woman and proceeded to stab the needle deep into the flesh of Nicolette's arm. No reaction from Nicolette, not so much as a flinch.

"She felt *nothing*, Hortense," he said wonderingly. "Peronnette could control her senses, as you and I can occasionally, but to control someone *else's* mind and body to this extent—miraculous!"

He then began to awaken Nicolette, but Ghanim took hold of his arm, shaking his head in a warning that Cellini did not understand. Quickly the lad scribbled an explanation on paper.

"Nicolette, your arm is normal now. Your arm is normally sensitive to pain, all feeling. Now you will awake. *Awake*, Nicolette."

The girl opened her eyes slowly, her expression blank. She frowned when she saw that everyone in the room was staring at her. "Well, what is the trick, Marco?" she asked curiously. "What is your amulet supposed to do?"

"Marco!" Lamia cried, bouncing in front of him. "Control *me*. Demonstrate with me. Then Nicolette can witness the power. I must have this power. I must learn to be insensitive to pain."

"Not now," Marco said, turning away from her.

"But you must," she insisted. "Please! Stab the needle into *me*." She stubbornly moved as he turned from her so that she remained facing him. "Marco . . ." she pressed.

"Huh. It was a magician's trick, no more," Hortense commented accusingly. "You cannot do it again, eh?" She turned to her bewildered granddaughter and said angrily, "Did you rehearse your part with Marco, eh? Did you? Speak, daughter of an obscene goat. Did you?"

"No," Nicolette wailed. "I rehearsed nothing. I do not know what you are talking about!"

"Please, Marco!" Lamia pleaded, taking hold of his arm in her urgency. "One day I might desperately need such a power."

Cellini threw up his hands in defeat. "Enough! Enough!" He brought the amulet up to impatiently swing it before Lamia's eyes. "Relax now," he insisted. "Do not try so hard. Allow the amulet to do its work. Think of nothing but the light glittering upon the disk. Soon you will feel very drowsy and will be unable to keep your eyes open."

Lamia leaned intently forward, glaring zealously at the twirling gold disk. She blinked several times, as Marco's voice droned on monotonously, repeating the same phrases over and over again. She heard Nicolette whisper behind her, "Whatever is he doing?" and Ghanim's interested black eyes were clearly visible to her over Marco's shoulder.

"Very tired. So very tired," Marco persisted patiently. His legs soon went stiff and he shifted his position as casually as he could, stepping sideways a little to be closer to Lamia. "The amulet swings and your vision blurs. You cannot hold your eyes—"

"Damn you, Marco!" Lamia barked suddenly, "you are standing on my *toe!*"

Marco leaped back, startled, his face flushing.

At the dismayed expression on his face, Lamia exploded into giggles. "I am so sorry. I tried, but . . . you looked so—so foolish, standing there on my toe. So forbiddingly serious."

When a woman behind him laughed raucously, Marco whirled around. He saw Ghanim leaning on the woman's shoulder, quaking in hysterical, silent amusement, tears streaming down his face. If he could have managed expressive sound, it would have emerged a bawling hee-haw.

"A village fair is it? Myself a jester come to entertain you all?" Marco's tone was so thunderous it silenced and sobered all save Ghanim, who had not been watching his mouth. The young man continued with his contortions, and since he made no noise to disturb Cellini, the merchant finished his tyrannical reprimand. "Fiametta is only fourteen. I might expect a lack of solemnity from her. But you, all of you, what do you think me—a fool? Obviously, the control does not take hold the same way with everyone. Cease your smirking this instant!"

"Forgive me, Marco," Lamia said, swallowing a rising giggle. She had long since learned how to handle him. "I should not have pushed you into it. It is my fault."

By this time Ghanim had gotten hold of himself. With a wide grin he moved to Cellini, touching the man's arm for attention. He shook his head to express sympathy and understanding. On paper he scribbled with a charcoal piece, "It often happens. Fiametta was distracted. However, my father mentioned several cases where the person resisted his control and never succumbed to his will. Another day, perhaps."

Before he had finished the writing, every one of the witches was peering over his shoulders trying to read the words.

"Hmm," Hortense commented appreciatively. "To cast such a spell upon a certain vile monk who stalks our village like a daily plague, eh?"

"Or on those inclined to *accuse,*" the lady of quality sweetly put in, her blue eyes gleaming with a sinister fire.

"We could bring many more people to our cause, with such a weapon against the will," another exclaimed enthusiastically.

"Well and good," Marco said warningly, his temper cooling. "But you have seen both a success and a failure here. Practice upon each other. I would hesitate to suggest any attempt to seduce the will of an outsider; if you failed you might find yourself in a torture chamber, eh? in desperate need of a power you did not give yourself time enough to perfect."

"True enough," Hortense agreed cheerfully.

"One night of each month you six will come here as you did tonight, and we will learn together."

Hortense shook a fist at him and cried, "I will not come, if I am to be lectured endlessly. My methods are my own. Be damned your personal objections, Marco Cellini."

"No lecture," he said on a sigh. "I agree that your methods are your own affair and none of mine."

"Huh," she snorted. On her way to the door, she hesitated and leaned close to Cellini, a sadistic leer on her face and said tauntingly, "Like the scarce banana, very ripe, they taste, the little ones. A delicacy I would be loathe to omit from my meager diet, eh?" She laughed raucously and hobbled to the open door, vanishing into the dark cellar.

Cellini stared at the empty doorway, an expression of utter defeat on his face. "To think," he said to no one in particular, "her father was a Dominican monk, her mother a noblewoman. In Hortense there are small proportions indeed of piety and nobility."

Ghanim hastily scribbled on paper, "In Cordova, when Andalusia was at its zenith, before we were driven from our land, the hag would have been accepted as a physician, lecturing at university to students from all over the world. One becomes what one's society allows. France in the sixteenth century was unprepared for her and she has become an outcast. Still, she is what she was born to be. To be pitied rather than loathed."

"Oui," Marco agreed, "to be pitied."

"God pity us all," Nicolette said in an unsteady voice.

"Not one of us in this room is any less pitiable than my grandmother!"

Lamia glared at Nicolette and snapped, "Speak for yourself, girl, and not for me. I deny any similarity to your grandmother."

"Today, perhaps. But when you are her age what will you say in defense of your soul? When you glance into your eyes in a glass, what will you see *then?* If you looked closely into a glass, even now, would you not see a grotesque hag of a face lingering behind a still youthful mask? When you are a little older, you might think Hell to be too charitable a fate. You might wish God had devised worse for you, so intense will be your loathing of yourself. Dear God! I wish that they would come, take me and *burn* me!" She collapsed into a sobbing hysteria, her hands rising to cover her face.

It was not a new experience for Marco. He could not count how many women he had known and heard of who had deliberately placed themselves in jeopardy, were caught, and eagerly confessed their unbearable guilt, burning gratefully. He went to Nicolette and placed a comforting arm about her shoulders, damning the world and every human being stalking the face of it, himself most vehemently.

PART TWO

THE WITCH

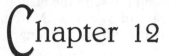

Chapter 12

"BANE OF MY LIFE! Have I taught you *nothing?* Kill him, yes. Poison or stab the man. But you cannot see him burned by Holy Church!"

"He will die on the stake, burn as Eliza burned," Lamia insisted stubbornly.

Marco stared at her, exasperated, and let himself fall into a brief silence. Ghoulish shadows, created by the lamps hanging from the rafters over their heads, danced about them where they sat on stools in his laboratory. He had been teaching Lamia the theories of Paracelsus, the young and famous Swiss physician who was a friend of the witch and the sorcerer. Paracelsus had recently said, openly, before his students, his Church, and his God, "I have learned everything I know from the witches. Outside the official seats of learning, a wilder and secret university has been established. This is the school of nature. If you want to learn science, study nature! Enough of the ancients, enough of the clerics, enough of idiocy!"

" 'The devil incarnate!' his students bellow," Marco had told Lamia heatedly. " 'He has been seized by an evil spirit!' the fools insist. Under pressure from Holy Church, the medical faculty is threatening to drive him out, strip him of his position, his honor. . . . Damn you! Are you listening to me?"

Lamia's wandering mind had jumped back to reality when he raised his voice in anger, startling her. "Not exactly," she replied, yawning.

"Ah, the witch is *tired*. Or are you merely bored, eh?"

"I cannot see how all this . . . those words about a physician in Basle can help me send the bishop to the stake. I am nearly sixteen years of age now, Marco. I *must* see him burned! He is growing old while I linger here, doing nothing!"

That was when Cellini had exploded. Lately he had begun to hope that she had learned enough to know that she could not achieve the kind of vengeance she now longed for, not against a bishop. "You cannot see that man *burned*! He is a bishop of Holy Church, a hawk, and you, thorn in my backside, are an *ant*. He will squash you, thus"—Marco swept an arm in an arc that ended with his thumb flattened on the surface of the table that stood between them; then he wobbled his hand back and forth with force to indicate just how thoroughly squashed she would be. "Squashed! A bow and arrow from a hiding place. A poisoned dart. There are a thousand ways to kill a man. You made more sense when you were *wild*! When did you come to *this*—this—" He lost the sense of what he was saying and threw up his arms in defeat.

Lamia writhed where she sat, anger rising to heat her face. "When I was a child I only wanted him dead," she explained. "Now I know that he must suffer. Suffer! I realize that I could easily enough kill him. I *know* that! Using one of your poisons, here." She waved an arm toward a shelf to her right. "But there would be no satisfaction in that, none at all. I want him to live in terror, to . . . to hear me laugh as the fat starts to boil under his skin. . . ." She struggled for words to describe what was mostly thoughtless imperative. "Should there be no Hell, should God spare him because he is holy and take him into His Heaven, I must make him suffer his deserved portion of hellfire while yet he lives!"

"Fool! Tell me how you will accomplish such a feat. Will you rise and face the court with your red hair and your marvelous reputation and accuse him of—of what, pray? Hmm? Of what will you accuse him, eh?" He hesitated, expecting a response from her, but she merely glared at him, waiting for him to go on with his tirade. "A better question would be, will they *believe* you? Methinks they would be building the fire around a stake with *your* name on it, not his. Speak up! I asked you how, how you would accomplish—"

"I don't *know* how!" she raged at him. I thought that you would *teach* me how! Instead of . . . of just . . . shouting at me."

"If I thought it was possible to see the bishop burned, I would not have left it to you. I would have seen him roasted before you were even *born!*"

"I will find a way," she said vehemently.

He stared at her, then whirled on his heel to begin pacing around and around her where she sat. Confronting her again, he dipped his chin to almost touch his chest, glaring at her from under his brow. "There is nothing I can do to stop you. Is that right?"

She took a breath, met his eyes squarely and replied, "Nothing. I think that I should leave your house and begin—"

"So be it, then," he interrupted icily. "Following the next meeting of the witches in this room, you will leave my house . . . for good." When her eyes widened in surprise, then revealed no little self-satisfaction, he waved his arms at her and shouted, "Do not draw conclusions! In the name of the Devil just *listen* you to me! This day I will arrange for your disappearance from my house and this town. I have long had this plan in mind, but hoped you would . . . never mind. You will be instructed from here on by Hortense and—"

"What?" Lamia jumped to her feet, appalled. "You cannot be *serious*, Marco! She is—Hortense is a stealer of corpses, an eater of infants, a—"

"Do not pompously describe to me a woman who has been my friend for a quarter of a century! There is one thing you obviously have overlooked about Hortense. She is *old*. Old, Fiametta! She has survived to the age of seventy out there! How long do you think *you* will survive, eh? You, who have lived in a cave, or sheltered in this house, all your life. Eh? You will destroy a bishop out there, not even knowing which road to take to Nevers? Do you know the witches' paths that change weekly, that lead from this road to that, this village to that town? You want to be the Red Witch; then you shall be exactly that, and Hortense will teach you how."

"I will not eat *babies!*" Lamia exclaimed. "Is that what I must learn from Hortense, in order to be a witch?"

"I will not dignify that question with an answer! You have three days during which to prepare yourself for departure. You will steal from me and flee from my house in the night. I will scour the town for you, enraged."

"I am old enough to take care of *myself!* I do not need Hortense or anyone *else!*" As she threw the words at him her mind-fairy laughed and told her she was being very stupid. She had to admit it; she had no idea which road to take to Nevers.

"Ghanim will be our link with each other. Should you ever need me, you have but to . . ." Marco was suddenly embarrassed by a surge of emotion into his throat. Tears burned behind his eyes. He had never in his life felt more powerless. The only way he could save Lamia from herself would be to drug her as he had drugged Giles when he was determined to destroy himself in an effort to save Peronnette. He could not keep her in such a state forever and that is what it would require to deter her from this suicidal course. "I will miss you, ma petite witch . . . very much," he said huskily, then strode away from her and out the door, quickly so that she could not see his tears.

On the thirtieth day of the month of October, Baroness Audette gave birth to her second child, a son, whom she named Jacques, to please his paternal grandfather, carving for herself the next step in a ladder to the exalted height of Countess de Nevers.

Baron Giles spent every sunlight hour in his fields with his leaseholders, turning the earth and planting it, his mind full of grand schemes for molding his one hundred square miles of land into the richest farm in the Loire valley. Florence, the city of his youth, was lost to him, along with his hopes of love and all other of his boyish illusions. This plot of earth was his by right of deed, a gift from his father. The river wound close around, a tranquil moat. His home, La Ville de la Fleur, rose august and beloved on a rise overlooking the Allier. If he did not sleep many a night for haunting memories that strained his nerves, it was not so grim a life at la Fleur as to cause him any deep despair. He moved through the days at peace with all save himself.

For many months Giles had seethed about Cellini's cold-hearted sacrifice of Peronnette, which had served only to sicken his soul. Nothing he might do or suffer would bring her back to color the world that rose hue again. Frequently, at first, he had thought of Fiametta, suffering a bitter guilt for abandoning her. She soon began to fade from his thoughts as he turned more and more to the soil, and to the bankers, in his indomitable efforts to become financially secure in an otherwise totally precarious existence. Investments and his land, the two would make him rich enough to name his own fate. Be damned his uncle Cinto, the duke, and his father's title. What else could he strive for in this life now, except for Cinto's idolized gold?

As for his wife, Giles loathed her with an increasing intensity as the months passed. An incessant war raged between them that one day would reach explosive proportions. They had lived at peace together only until la Fleur was completed. Audette preferred to live in a castle.

Early in the morning, the day after the birth of his son, Giles moved as soundlessly as possible along his own well-worn footpath through a wooded area of his land that followed the Allier. He enjoyed hunting with the crossbow so did not leave the task of providing la Fleur with rabbit and fish to his gamekeeper. The air was sharply cold and a brisk wind picked up fallen leaves and sent them spinning around his feet. The trees were almost entirely barren of leaves already. He thought that it would be an early winter.

At a sudden scampering sound, Giles instantly swung around and aimed his bow, finger on the trigger. He remained motionless, waiting, braced for the shot. At first he had thought it a rabbit, but now, more like a—

The arrow whirred from the bow. Lamia shrieked in surprise and dismay as the missile sliced into the earth only a hair's breadth from her left foot. For a moment she was completely bewildered, uncertain whom she had stumbled upon so carelessly. "Giles!" she exclaimed.

He gaped at her in disbelief, the bow dropping from his hands to the earth at his feet. For a long time he could only stare at her, as his mind adjusted itself to accept what should have been impossible but was unquestionably a reality.

"Stupid of me!" Lamia laughed, relieved that it was only Giles and not one of the bishop's guards. "I am *lost!* I cannot believe that I could be so stupid! Hortense will skin me for this!"

"What in the name of Christ are *you* doing here? Are you mad? Where is Marco? He has *abandoned* you!"

Taking in great breaths of the cold October air, she tried to calm her heart that had begun to leap in her chest when she stumbled upon someone so unexpectedly and was almost shot through with an arrow. "No, Giles," she said softly. "Marco did not abandon me. Rather it was I who abandoned him. I *must* go."

When she turned on her heel to depart, without further explanation for her presence here, Giles protested. "No! Stay. A moment, Fiametta. Why are you here . . . on my land? I—"

Lamia came to a halt, turned and smiled sadly upon him. "Rest assured, it was by mistake that I trespassed here and it will not happen again. I am learning the witches' paths and somehow missed the markings today, became completely turned around."

"Witches' paths? Across *my* land?"

She thought upon it, then carefully said, "I am a novice, Giles, only learning the paths. I must be miles beyond the last marker I noticed. I cannot remain in your presence like this, placing you in danger of—"

"Nonsense! This early in the day, there cannot be another person within an hour's ride of us in any direction." Startled by a truant thought, Giles considered the logic that since he would not even have dreamed of stumbling upon Lamia this morning, there could as well be a dozen more so-called *witches* lurking out of sight, but within earshot. What tragic figures these women were, forced to protect themselves from the brutal thrusts of God's sword, wielded by Holy Church, half-starved, desperate, surviving the only way they knew how. They were not witches, but victims.

In Italy praises of women were trumpeted in songs and books that were sung and read across Europe, and men's minds were turning toward a new rationalism and joyousness. But at the same time, Holy Church was reviling women as weak, inferior creatures afflicted with insatiable carnal lust which made them easy prey to the advances of the Devil. The Pope himself was known to be an admirer of the character and intellect of the women of his court, yet he believed that in Central Europe and France, tens of thousands of women had copulated with the Devil and, as witches, were producing stillbirths, killing calves, destroying crops, causing disease and impotence. This was a society in the throes of a nightmare.

As he studied Lamia's innocent countenance, for a moment the features of her face seemed to alter and Giles was seeing Peronnette's lovely face, smiling at him. He thought to hear her say, *Men will seize her, men of God; the child must be saved.* "You have not told me what you are doing here, Fiametta," Giles said warmly, smiling upon her.

Deliberately avoiding his question, she asked, "How are you, Giles? Had you forgotten me?"

He let his eyes rove from the top of her head, that was wrapped in a brown scarf, to her bare, sandaled feet. She hugged a ragged woolen shawl around her against the wind and the chill in the air. Twigs and bits of fall-browned leaves clung to her skirts and to the shawl. Her face was flushed with exertion and smudged at the tip of her nose and her chin. She looked for all the world like an unnaturally tall street urchin. "No," he replied, "I had not forgotten you."

"I can promise you I will not put you in jeopardy. Never. Whatever I do it will not be done on your land, nor will I endanger you by association. I am too fond of you to ever put you at risk."

"But—surely, there is some way that I can *help* you. I have connections with important persons in Florence and could, I am certain, see you safely—"

"No. I belong in this place. I have an important purpose here."

He eyed her uncertainly, a strange sense of destiny disturbing his mind; it was as if this moment in time, this meeting, had been preordained . . . and whatever this magnificent child's purpose was, it could not be deterred. He could not shake the sense that Peronnette was present and pleading with him to save "the Red Witch of Nevers." He said impulsively, "If you refuse to leave France because you have a purpose here, I must refuse to play the stranger to you with the argument that I can, as your friend, be of assistance to you at some *future* time."

Lamia shrugged off his protestation; it was no time for arguing.

"There is sadness in your eyes," she said, wishing she could move close enough to touch him, but Marco's warnings could not be ignored. If she wove Giles into the web of her existence here it could destroy him and she could not bear the thought of that. "Yesterday your wife gave birth to a male child. Does that not make you happy?"

"I am happy to have a son," he said unconvincingly. "You are in touch with the events of my life, I see."

"Indeed, I am."

He stepped closer to her and was distressed to see her back away from him. He halted his step and said, "You may as well tell me where we can meet, and when, because I will search you out until I find you. I can easily provide you with food and clothing, without causing any suspicions."

Lamia smiled knowingly. Hortense stole his sheep for meat, his grain for bread, ate his rabbits, fished from his river, and sold potions to his wife to be put into his wine to cure his impotence, or, depending on the point of view, his disinterest in lying with her. "I will think upon it. Now, tell me where I am, exactly. Better yet, direct me to that heath where we first encountered each other. From there I will find my way."

"Your way to . . . to *where*, for God's sake?"

"To where I live, Giles."

"But . . . there is only woodland and—"

"Yes, woods. The wild is once again my home."

Studying her, Giles noted how composed she was, expertly keeping him at a distance. Sighing in defeat, he said pointedly, "I know that there is to be a Sabbat this night." At a hint of surprise in her expression, he added, "I hear the whispered messages passing between my villains. I am no fool. Half of Nevers will attend, I'm sure, including members of the clergy, and yourself, I have no doubt."

"Direct me, please. I must leave."

"Face the sun, Fiametta, and keep it before you."

She nodded and was gone within a moment, vanishing

into the brush from whence she had come, leaving him more deeply sad than he had been for months.

"To be cured of his affliction, his inability to get his member to rise to the occasion," Hortense explained to Lamia in a high-pitched, amused tone of voice, "I instructed him to urinate through his wife's wedding ring." She doubled over with shrieking laughter.

Lamia frowned, bewildered because she had learned that Hortense's advice and her cures were renowned as astonishingly effective. "But I do not understand how something as absurd as urinating through a ring could cure a person of *anything*."

Hortense attempted to stifle the laughter that erupted from deep within her bent frame. "Imagine it, if you can . . . just *imagine* it!" Once again she was seized by convulsive laughter, tears filling her eyes that she wiped away with a gnarled fist. "Oh dear me, I cannot think of a more entertaining thought than that of the Duke de Bourbon urinating through his wife's wedding ring. Eh? Eh?"

Lamia had to laugh, but was still confused. "But would you not be concerned that when such advice was ineffective, he would be so angry as to—"

"No no!" Hortense shrieked on a laugh. "A success. Did he not come to me and *thank* me . . . reward me . . . recommend me to a friend? Methinks Marco Cellini may be right when he claims that our minds are more powerful than we can conceive. The duke's member *rose* to the occasion! From that fact, what do you deduce, eh?"

"That the skill of a man's own mind is more powerful than the skills of the witch?"

"Sometimes. Or the skill of the witch is in knowing which one of those who come to her for cures she can give a brew that *can* cure, and which one she must merely beguile. Your grandmother, Jeanne, did not heed my warnings and foolishly gave the potion in too strong a dose to the count's wife, when she should not have given her a potion at all. The woman was an hysteric who could easily have been beguiled into believing she was cured, by being given a swallow of sugar and water said to be blessed by Satan himself."

The old woman worked diligently at her spinning wheel as

she spoke, squinting her eyes to see in the dim light of the hovel that she had constructed with her own hands decades ago out of gathered stones and thatch. Lamia sat on the earth floor near the open door, listening attentively. She had come to respect Hortense in the months since she was brought here, if not to like the woman. There was little about her to like. What she admired most about her was her vast knowledge of miraculous things that Lamia had never dreamed of. Hortense had a name for every plant in the woods, understood all the elements of their leaves, their roots and their flowers, that had the power to soothe or excite, sicken or cure, to relieve or irritate the afflicted.

Lamia had been stunned, early in this relationship of teacher and student, to learn that Hortense was selling a potion to a servant of the bishop's court, to cure the irregular beating of the bishop's aging heart.

"Stupid wench," Hortense had snapped contemptuously, at Lamia's suggestion that she was God-inspired if she cured such a man of his afflictions. "How do you suppose I have survived to this age, eh? Do you think the bishop would put to the stake the physician who keeps him alive, eh? I keep *him* alive so that he will keep *me* alive. Eh? Eh?" Then a sly expression had crossed her face and she said, "It is my understanding that you wish to see the bishop cook slowly at the stake. I cannot think how you could accomplish such a feat, if I poisoned him before you grew wise enough."

The logic was sound, but every time the bishop's servant knocked upon the door, eyes bulging with terror, hands trembling, to give Hortense a small gold coin for a tiny bottle of elixer of digitalis, Lamia suffered an overwhelming urge to lace the brew with hemlock.

"When I became lost this morning," Lamia began carefully, uncertain whether she should speak to Hortense of her meeting with Giles, or not, "I stumbled upon—"

"Giles de Sade," Hortense said flatly.

"How could you know that?"

Hortense merely shrugged, her expression indicating that Lamia should only have been surprised if she had *not* known. "You need not fear that man. He has an enlightened mind, does not deeply believe in God, or Devil, takes no sides."

"Oh no, I do not fear Giles. He is my friend. I love him very much."

Hortense's hands went still and she looked up from the spinning wheel to study Lamia coldly. Giles de la Fleur was a powerful man with powerful connections who would be Count of Nevers one day. She would be most pleased to have knowledge of him that could be used to her advantage. Loved him . . . did she?

Misunderstanding Hortense's stare, Lamia quickly added, "I understand that by associating with him I could harm him, so I will not meet him as he—"

"When the moon is full, in dead of night, with friendly, watchful eyes all about, there would be no real danger to him, eh?" Hortense smiled thinly, thinking how enraged Marco Cellini would be should he learn of such meetings. Had he not emphatically set down the rules of this association of hers with his precious daughter, knowing full well she would do as she pleased? The first demand had been that she not allow Lamia within miles of Giles de Sade which had struck her as curious at the time. The second was that there were to be no eviscerations of infants. "Such meetings could be instructive for you," Hortense began slyly, "in how to speak with those from whom you must gain information, without being apprehended."

"He knows about the Sabbat."

"Of course he knows about the Sabbat!"

With that, Hortense returned to her spinning. "Remember, do not eat or drink. You will be there only to observe. Marco Cellini has sent word that he will make himself known to you when he can safely do so. You are not to leave until you have spoken to him."

Lamia's mood instantly brightened at the thought of seeing Marco again. It had been more than two months since she had left his house. Surprisingly, she had sorely missed his constant shouting and lecturing. Hortense would not attend the Sabbat. She said that she was too old now for such ribaldry. The truth was, she found such occasions now bored her to distraction. "One need only watch such goings on for a few moments to fully understand the nature of mankind, an abscess on the face of the earth. That young fool, Paracelsus, attended our Sabbat a year past, observing as I expect you to observe this night. Then what did he do but return to Basle to shout from the rafters what he had learned, that disease of the mind has nothing to do with evil spirits or devils. He said, 'The experienced physician should not study how to exorcise the devil but how to cure the *disease.*' How a man could be so profoundly intelligent and at the same time so stupid astonishes me! He dares the Church to still his voice, which it will do . . . oh, it will, eventually. Know what you know, Daughter of Satan, and do not concern yourself with the ignorance of others."

Lamia touched Ghanim on the shoulder to attract his attention, then motioned for him to follow her. She shouldered her way through the hysterical crowd of revelers, ducking swinging arms and kicking legs, stepping over fornicating couples, disgusted by the spectacle and concerned that Marco had not made himself known to her as yet.

When they had made their way up a slope, to a rise where they could overlook the proceedings but not be a part of them, she came to a halt and turned to study the incredible scene they had left behind. It was a lake of writhing, shrieking creatures from the nightmares of Holy Church . . . a madness created by a doctrine that insisted that this life was not worth the living; only in death, in Heaven, could they ever find a moment of pain-free, joyous existence. Thus had Holy Church turned the people over to the Devil, who kept his promises and gave them while they lived at least this much release from their miseries.

Ghanim stepped closer to Lamia and put a hand lightly on her shoulder, then moved to brush her cheek with his fingertips. She was strikingly beautiful where she stood with firelight fluttering like the shadows of great butterflies upon her face. He wished that she did not have to wear the head scarf, but completely understood the need of it.

Suddenly a masked figure seemed to magically appear below the rise they stood upon, moving toward them, firelight glinting off the metallic death's head mask he wore. "Marco?" Lamia said uncertainly, leaning to watch the man more closely as he approached. "Marco?"

"Why do you not announce my name one more time, to be certain everyone within a mile knows who hides behind this mask? I cannot imagine why I bothered to mask myself!" He whipped the mask from his face and fiercely scowled up at Lamia; he was slightly below her on the rise and she had grown half a head taller than he. "And where is *your* mask, eh? Where? Amidst that mob of maniacs behind me there are those who watch and report."

Lamia smiled defeatedly as Marco's harangue continued. When he paused for a breath, she said, "I am as pleased to see you as you obviously are to see me. I am very well, thank you. And you?"

"Well enough so as not to complain. Hortense tells me you are a diligent student, that you are learning quickly. She agrees with me that you should travel to my house with her for the next meeting and that you should attend all meetings from here on. I asked you, where is your mask?"

"It became uncomfortable, so I—"

"You took it off, threw it away. Fool! Never cease wearing some kind of alteration of your face and figure, so that you are one person today, another tomorrow, never allowing your enemies to have a clear picture of your combined features." Suddenly he shot an arm out and yanked the scarf from Lamia's head. "In the name of the Devil, are you mad? You have not shaved your head. Any one of a dozen starving witches, spying that red hair, *would* hand you over to the Inquisition for a full meal."

"The Red Witch is called that because she has red hair. When I make myself known, I shall have volumes of red hair. Do you understand, Marco? Volumes of long, red hair!" She had so looked forward to seeing him again, but now she was enraged by his badgering. She leaned over and swept the scarf up from the ground, then wound it carelessly around her head. "Is there anything else you want to shout at me about? If not, I shall—" She raised her eyebrows questioningly and waited for his response.

Marco glared at her a moment, then, with a gesture, indicated she was to follow him. He moved past her, striding onto a wide path that led into the woods. When Lamia hesitated, considering simply walking in the opposite direction, to Hell with Marco, Ghanim took her elbow and gently guided her to the path. Marco had vanished into the dark, but she could hear his footfall. Irritated, she shook Ghanim's hand from her elbow and walked swiftly, almost at a run, to catch up with Marco.

The path ended at the entrance to a heath that was not instantly recognizable to Lamia because of the darkness. The sky was lightening in the east, birds singing their morning songs. Marco had come to a halt, breathing heavily due to his swift pace and the length of the walk. The river moved languidly behind him, beginning to reflect the light from the sky.

"I suppose that you will tell me why you have brought me to this heath?" Lamia said sharply, standing before Marco with her fists on the bones of her hips, elbows extended. "I have come here often, since—"

"Have you been to the cave?" Marco asked, interrupting her.

She was startled by the question. Suddenly she was less belligerent, as emotions and memories swept over her mind and soul, causing her heart to beat a little faster. "No. No one goes near my cave. It is forbidden, on penalty of the stake."

Marco nodded, his eyes hidden from her by tree shadows. "Take me there. Can you find it from here?"

She turned her head to study the now achingly familiar scene. A memory flashed into her mind, of Giles pulling her from the briars at the river's edge, very close to where Marco was now standing. Heat attacked her stomach and turned it over, as she recalled the bishop's presence here that same day. "I am not sure. The paths have vanished with the years."

"Try."

Ghanim stepped back, watching Marco and Lamia closely, reading their thoughts and emotions with some accuracy. Marco was unable to express his more tender feelings toward his child, and she misunderstood him, unaware that she was his daughter. Fate was taking a strange course here, most intriguingly.

Lamia cautiously moved away from the river into the brush, calling upon the mind-fairy of her childhood to guide her. Bramble and twigs caught at her skirts, scratched her arms and face, but she pressed on, becoming more confident as the moments passed. She could hear Marco muttering and cursing behind her. Ghanim was following, too, but he was as air, making no sounds.

It was fully light when Lamia stumbled upon the cave, now almost completely hidden by brush and bramble. She stood still, trembling in the throes of overwhelming recollections . . . Eliza sweetly singing to her in the moonlight . . . holding her close and telling her stories about the fairies in the flames. Flames. Eliza on fire, the popping sound of her bursting flesh. "Damn me," she cried chokingly, whirling around to escape.

Marco seized her, stopping her flight. He held her tight to his chest, wordlessly telling her that he understood her pain, but this holding was the only comfort he could offer her.

Ghanim moved past them, pushing aside bramble to put himself closer to the cave. He halted abruptly, turned and signaled Marco to come to where he stood. When Marco curiously approached him, he pointed to the ground a few feet away, then swept his hand to indicate a disturbance of the undergrowth ahead that indicated someone else had recently been to this place, probably no more than a day past. Marco nodded worriedly, acknowledging that he understood.

Marco turned to say to Lamia, "Do not disturb the undergrowth any more than necessary. Step carefully now."

Lamia numbly obeyed, sliding past low-growing bare branches, trying not to disturb the carpet of leaves at her feet. Then, there it was, the cave opening, boarded over. A lopsided, rotting sign was visible behind spreading vine, the words coming into focus as she moved closer . . . a quote from God's book, THOU SHALT NOT SUFFER A WITCH TO LIVE. A coldness raised the hair at the back of her neck and goosefleshed her arms.

"In Christ's name," Marco suddenly exclaimed, "what is this?"

Lamia moved around him where he stood blocking whatever it was that had caught his attention. She was amazed to see, carefully hung from a thick tree branch, a linen dress. Below the dress, on a cushion of leaves, had been placed a pair of leather shoes. Instantly Giles' face bloomed in her mind and she heard him say again, "In seven days I will return to this heath, Fiametta. If you will meet me on that day, I will have new clothing for you; shoes perhaps." She was overwhelmed by the kind gesture, but could not imagine how he had known she would come to the cave.

Marco whirled on Lamia, enraged. "What is this, eh?" He yanked the dress off the branch and waved it before her face. "As if I do not know. Giles de Sade! It would be difficult to judge which of you is the bigger fool."

"If you had not brought me here I would never have seen this dress," she shouted at him. "Are you planning to tell me why we are here?"

"I thought it the safest place for you to hide, since no soul on earth is brave enough to approach it. Except the fool of all fools who hung this dress from that branch!"

Chapter 13

 LAMIA BROKE OUT OF the wood at a run, then stood, awed, gazing across the river at La Ville de la Fleur, moved by the grace and beauty of the house, its windows catching the rays of the sun to send them in lightninglike flashes of light into her eyes.

Ghanim caught up and came to a halt beside her. Marco had left them at the cave several hours ago, after bombastic instructions as to how she was to set about establishing the cave as her hideaway. She could not permanently remain under Hortense's roof. Too many people came to the old witch from near and far for Lamia to be safe there any longer. She must live alone, keep her own counsel, create her own paths. The cave would be as safe a place as she could find, short of leaving France, but she must not disturb the outward appearance of neglect. It seemed to Marco, and Ghanim had agreed, that an entrance could be dug from above, which, if carefully constructed, could act as a window to allow in light and extra air. There was ample room for a table and chair, and a bed. She could not risk having a fire, so Marco would provide her with warm coverlets and Hortense would see that she had food each day; no, not boiled *infants.*

Lamia's heart quickened when she saw Giles in the distance, moving at a brisk pace toward a horse tethered to a post. He leaped upon the stallion's back and sped across a field browned by autumn frosts, vanishing into the woods. She smiled, recalling how she had told Giles that she would have no child but his. She wondered, now, how long she could wait, how long she could bear the unquenched fires that had been burning in her lower regions this past year or two. A perfect stranger of the male sex sometimes appeared to her hungry eye as some rare, delicious stew which she felt compelled to devour completely, or die of starvation. But Cellini kept her under tight observation at all times.

Ghanim, since the day he had arrived from Africa, had taken upon himself the occupation of being her personal guard. No opportunity for experimentation had been available to her here with the witches, since Hortense had a thousand eyes. This night she felt particularly fretful. The orgiastic rituals of the Sabbat, disgusting as they had been, produced a throbbing and heat between her legs that still burned and set her mind to all sorts of fancies and considerations.

Now, she suffered an almost overwhelming compulsion to chase after Giles, to clasp her arms around his neck and kiss him as once she had in the past, so deliciously. Then she was suddenly plunged into sadness, because what she wished for with Giles could never be.

Ghanim, instantly aware of Lamia's altered mood, took her by the shoulders from behind and turned her to look at him. She threw her arms around his waist, pushed her face into his shoulder, and hugged him tightly for a moment. Comforted, she pushed back from him a bit and looked into his eyes. A strange force seemed to fuse their minds. They could not, per se, read each other's thoughts, but neither for an instant doubted what the other was thinking.

Lamia raised her eyes to the cloudless sky, wondering if the now-hidden stars truly were the maps of individual destinies, as Ghanim believed. It was difficult for her to see how she could find any comfort in the fact that future events were written in the stars, thus were unavoidable. It did seem as if she were being helplessly drawn by some invisible force toward a predetermined, inescapable conclusion. She sometimes felt that if she did not execute the bishop, the man would somehow live forever, that she had been born to be his executioner. Yet she also believed unfalteringly in the power of her own will. Marco had taught her that no force outside herself was, or could be, the master of her soul or her fate.

Surely, she could take a different path, quiet this vindictiveness, this murderous inclination, if she willed it? But, in so doing, she would be saying to Eliza and to Peronnette, "What do I care how you suffered, or how many more the man will torture and burn?"

A flash thought struck her mind: *You cannot alter what is written.* She scowled at Ghanim, who still held her firmly by the shoulders. Sometimes she found it extremely annoying when he knew her thoughts and interrupted with his own. His smile seemed a bit smug, but no, Ghanim was never smug. Familiar as she was with the superficial workings of his mind, she did not know him well. Ghanim was another of those ten thousand mysteries that Marco so urgently sought to unriddle. As she returned his smile, her mind wandered away from this place in the sun, to a winter night soon after Ghanim arrived from Africa.

They sat on the carpeted floor before a warm fire. Marco was slumped in his chair, reading. Lamia gazed silently into the flames, her mind at rest. Suddenly Ghanim put a hand on her knee and she looked around to see him scribbling words on paper.

What do I hold? the paper said and he waved a balled fist in front of her nose. His eyes were smiling, but behind them there was a strange urgency.

"How would I know that?" She laughed, frowning at him.

Speculate, he insisted with charcoal.

"A . . . a *button?*" she asked, shrugging.

He let his fist fall open and a tiny shard of broken red glass lay in his palm.

"So? It is glass." She made a face that indicated she thought the game pointless.

Ghanim became extremely serious. Moving closer to her on his knees, he sat back on his heels and stared into her eyes. From around his neck he took the gold amulet that had the power to control others. He held it, swinging it in a slow arc before her startled eyes.

"You will try to *control* me?" she exclaimed. "But you cannot speak the charm!"

Earnestly, as if his handicaps suddenly infuriated him, he scrawled on paper, *Words are the power. As potent when seen as when heard.*

She faltered an instant, refusing to let her eyes rest upon the amulet, but his eyes seemed to burn into her forehead, drawing her gaze with a powerful magnetism that forced her to concentrate on the swinging, glittering disk. She heard Marco move in his chair, felt his attention upon her. The fire crackled. Then all sound began to seem hollow and she felt as if her body were falling backward into a deep, black pit.

She fought against the pulling force, but knew that she could not win the battle, nor did she truly wish to; she wanted to be controlled so that she could avoid pain. The amulet vanished. Ghanim's eyes seemed to flow into her like a river into a sea.

You are controlled. She saw the words and believed them.

You can see through my hand. What do you see in my palm?

"A key," Lamia responded instantly, seeing it quite clearly, though he held the hand behind his back.

When Ghanim opened his fist, to show Marco that it was indeed a small, brass key, Cellini was delighted, moving to sit himself on the floor beside Ghanim, as fascinated as a child.

Ghanim wrote a Roman numeral and gave it to Marco to hold. *What number is Sire Cellini thinking upon?*

She hesitated, then guessed, "Four?"

She had transposed the number. It was six.

Ghanim had not pressed her that first time, quickly releasing her from his control, promising future experiments. The real test, he argued, was not in what she could accomplish under his control but through her own endowments, so he refused to help her establish an immunity to physical pain.

What purpose would it serve to stick her with a long pin? He could assure her that if he stipulated it, she would not feel it. But if she were in dire need of such insensitivity, he probably would not be there to administer the control. It was a power within herself that she would have to discover for herself.

Within two months Ghanim and the power of his amulet were no longer necessary. Lamia could tell him what object he held or was thinking about, while in a normal state of consciousness. Accuracy was not one hundred percent, but sufficient to render Marco thunderstruck and to encourage further practice.

Ghanim rarely exhibited his own skills. He refused to treat his abilities as a bizarre kind of entertainment for the rabble. He had agreed to be a party to Marco's demonstration before the witches only because it was an honest effort to draw the women away from demonism and all its vileness. If Lamia thought him so wise and clever, he wanted her to know that his ignorance and ineptitude rendered him a blundering novice compared to his father, who had taught him. He told her in flowing prose about all the wonders performed by true adepts. He had seen a man buried alive, who rose from the grave thirty days later, as prearranged. He had watched as a slave was nailed to a cross, then saw him step down without a wound upon wrist or abdomen. His physician father, with an ancient Egyptian manuscript at hand, had opened the skull of a man to reveal his brain and from the brain he removed a tumor. The skull was closed and within seven days the man walked away, grateful and cured of what other physicians had diagnosed as madness.

To accomplish the artificial death that Ghanim had demonstrated required no profound, secret knowledge, only a simple conviction, an absolute faith. When he was fifteen years of age he had shut his eyes, closing off that only connection with the world other than his sense of touch, and in the silence and the darkness the conviction became the reality; he appeared to have died, but maintained awareness. It was a trick the lowly silk worm could perform and with far more noteworthy result. If he could become a butterfly, or a soaring hawk, or hold off the real death, rid the world of madness and disease . . . ah, but he could not. He was only an ineffectual man stumbling on the brink of true knowledge. He believed that Lamia was akin to himself in these endowments, such as they were, and had taken over her lessons almost completely, for he knew the drugs and poisons as well as Cellini and was nearly as well read.

Ghanim did not, however, share Cellini's loathing of the

feudal system, which he considered, as he believed all things to be, the will of Allah. *If you took all the gold and power away from the noble man,* he wrote, *and divided it equally amongst the populace, within a year it would again be in the same tyrannical hands.* Still, he did not argue vehemently against Cellini's methods of altering the minds of the wretched, for if the merchant felt compelled to it, that too must be written and the will of Allah. When Lamia asked him why he had come to France with Marco, for he seemed to know more than the merchant and was independently wealthy, Ghanim simply looked deep into her eyes and she knew that he believed that Marco's visit to Africa had been fated, that he and she were meant to meet in this place at this time. He had come because he could do naught else.

Standing beside Ghanim, still gazing solemnly upon La Ville de la Fleur, Lamia thought upon Peronnette, who had dreamed of a red witch and had followed that vision as if led by Ghanim's mysterious hand of fate, then died, her purpose apparently ended, but not before she had given love to a man and received his love in return.

With a sigh, Lamia turned to once again meet Ghanim's eyes. He smiled. She put a finger to her forehead, raising her brows questioningly, in that way asking him to guess her thoughts.

His smile faded and he shook his head, *no.*

"But you chase after every harlot in Bourges," she complained. "For years I have been a woman, but I am virgin still. Giles refused to take me, but I was still a child then. Shall I have to become a harlot, offer myself on the streets, to get what I must have or sicken to death?"

Ghanim showed her ten fingers, then six, to indicate she was that old and should not concern herself with such matters, that the time for passion would come soon enough.

"With *you?*" she shot at him, her eyes brightening under his stern gaze.

For a moment his eyes were filled with sadness. Then he shrugged noncommittally, turning and striding toward the path that had led them to this place.

Lamia rushed after him and took hold of his arm, bringing him to a halt. "Oh, Ghanim," she exclaimed, "I care not that you are mute! Why should I? I can read your thoughts and feelings. I adore you!"

He reached out and touched her cheek lightly, smiling thinly. Taking her arm, he firmly led her along the path and into the wood. It had been a very long day and night and they were both exhausted. He must return her to Hortense, then ride to Bourges.

As they moved swiftly along the path, Lamia thought upon the hysteria that would follow should Bishop Geoffroi discover that such a man as Ghanim dwelt within this diocese, a man who could die at will and return from the dead, who could see without need of his eyes. Ghanim would be accused of sorcery, his powers called demonic and obscene. The Church would burn him.

Lamia thought, too, that no man on earth could be more fair to look upon than he who strode beside her through the wood this morning. Indeed, he looked not so much like a delicious stew, but more like a stuffed, roasted peacock, and she had never in her life been so hungry. Her desire was a distinct pain now and her knees were weakening, hands trembling. Damn him, she would take him lustfully if she had to control *him*—which was a very interesting idea. Was Ghanim susceptible to control? He had never said. She smiled impishly, glancing at his solemn profile with a determined eye.

The moon was full, its cold November light veiled and then unveiled by passing, threatening clouds. Though it was near midnight, Giles did not leave la Fleur unobserved but was followed by his personal manservant who was in the pay of Father Jean. The priest did not trust a man who had little faith in either God or Devil. If he could not wield the power of excommunication against the Baron de la Fleur, the threat of the stake might suffice to assure his obedience. Father Jean hoped the baron could be caught in the act of seeking the ministrations of witches for some ailment, as nearly every soul in the diocese did at one time or another.

Giles had not ridden more than a mile before the man following him at a discreet distance was thrown from his horse by an invisible obstacle that crossed the road from tree to tree.

Lamia remained well hidden at the heath, until she was certain it was Giles who approached. When he dropped to the rain-soaked ground beside his horse, moving to tether the animal to a small tree trunk, she moved into the open and said with a smile, "I thank you for this dress, and these shoes. Tell me, how could you know that I would find them there?"

Giles whirled around at the sound of her voice, his heart seeming to miss a beat at the sight of her. She appeared frail and vulnerable, only her face and shoulders illuminated by the moonlight. "It seemed to me to be the only place where you would be truly safe, but I was bitterly disappointed to see that no one had been there for many years. I left the dress and shoes simply because I did not know where else to leave them for you."

A silence fell between them, neither able to find words to say to the other.

Lamia broke the silence with, "Your manservant who was following you has broken his arm in a fall from his horse. Nicolette discovered him lying wounded on the road and rousted the shoemaker to see the wounded fellow to la Fleur in a wagon." Nicolette herself had, only moments before Giles entered the heath, given Lamia this information.

Giles stared at her, thinking she might be toying with him, as she had in Cellini's cookroom years ago. Perhaps his man had been following him, but she could not have knowledge of such an accident. He shivered as an icy wind suddenly hissed across the heath like a demon's breath.

"Come," Lamia said, smiling, turning to lead him into the wood, where, after a short walk, they came upon the hovel of Nicolette. "We can put ourselves out of the cold, here," she said, quickly ducking her head to enter the dwelling through a doorway no more than four feet high.

Giles stood outside uncertainly, studying the dwelling that had been ingeniously constructed, three sides against a sheer, seven foot high rock face, stolen bricks and scavenged stones serving as the walls, thatching covering the roof beams that were sturdy saplings. A window was glazed with the afterbirth of a cow, to keep out the cold.

Warmth washed over Giles when he entered the hovel. A fire burned against the rock face, the smoke rising on a good draft to escape up a teetering, brick chimney. He stood just inside the door, disapprovingly examining the beggarly interior that, as Peronnette's cottage had been, was astonishingly clean. The floor was merely earth, but clean straw was thick upon it, cushioning one's step. He said to Lamia, where she stood by the fire watching him closely, "How could you leave Cellini's house for *this!*" With a sweep of an arm he took in the small room. "What is it you think to accomplish by submitting yourself to poverty and association with so-called *witches!*"

"I am the daughter of a daughter of a witch."

"Nonsense!" he exclaimed, shaking his head in exasperation. "Pathetic, deluded wretches! God knows, I pity them. I cannot think how they would survive without their brews and magic shows that beguile the credulous. But cohorts of the Devil they are not, nor do they possess magical powers."

"Magical," Lamia echoed, smiling across the space that divided them. He was so intense, rigid in his disapproval. "I have seen such *marvels,* here, in the company of women that you name *wretches,* as would truly amaze even you, Giles."

"Ah, Fiametta, no. You are a naive child. Everything is magical to someone as young as you. Magicians create illusions, fool our perceptions of things. You must not remain in such company that can only lead you to destruction."

"How can you be so smug?" she exclaimed, frowning at him. "First, live among them, observe them. Know them, before you attempt to judge them." When his expression reflected his frustration and dismay, she sighed. "Oh, Giles, sit yourself down, anywhere. Sit."

Saddened, because he knew now that he could never convince her to escape, to save herself before it was too late, Giles moved closer to the fire and sat down on the floor. He brought his knees up and hugged his legs to his chest with his arms. When she sat down close-away from him, he was once again moved by how young and vulnerable she looked. Though she had grown tall, her facial features had remained tender so that she appeared, at this moment, in the deep shadows, little older than the day he had first stumbled upon her. Truly, in spite of her bravado and the brutal experiences of her early childhood, she was extraordinarily naive and inexperienced.

Studiously subduing her affection for Giles—it must not show in her eyes—Lamia said, "Let me tell you of the marvels I have seen." When he did not seem to hear her, she reached out and touched his hand. "Giles, I have seen the most miraculous things! Truly, I have."

"Tell me," he said, smiling tolerantly.

"An infant snuggled in a sack within its mother's womb! Fully formed! Head down. I could not believe my eyes! I had always thought that . . . I am not sure what I thought. That by some instantaneous process, the wave of a wand, something, what was merely a great swelling of the belly became, on entry into this world, an *infant*. But no. You should have seen it, growing in there, so perfect, so—" Her words broke off at the horrified expression on Giles' face. He was gaping at her in disbelief. "What? What is it?"

"For the love of Christ! What are you telling me? Where did you see this—this infant you speak of?"

She frowned in bewilderment, having forgotten for a moment that sometimes one had to pass through the grotesque to view the marvelous. "Alienor de Sancerre. She—"

"The woman who died under torture? How in God's name . . ."

"Her body was tossed into the— They were dead, Giles, and no one, not even her husband, was allowed to touch her . . . bury her."

He stared at her, trying not to believe what she was telling him. "Good Christ!"

"It was truly *marvelous* to see!" she insisted. "I also saw how the heart is attached to vessels through which it pushes the blood, with each beat, through the entire body. There are simply *miles* of intestines! One cannot imagine, once they are removed and spread about, how they could have been confined in so small a space!"

"Are you telling me that you participated in the evisceration of a human body? That is *ghoulish*, Fiametta!"

"No! What was done to that poor woman in the torture chamber was ghoulish, Giles! She had no fingernails or toenails, every joint in her body had been disconnected. They had burned her, stabbed long needles into her, and—"

"That is enough. I'll hear no more of such things. Dear God, you are hell bent."

"Yes, I am hell bent. But truly, even if I had a choice, I would live in my world, rather than yours. I have learned so much in the months since I returned to Nevers. My brilliant teacher has observed that clean wounds heal more surely and faster than dirty wounds and I have seen her experiments that prove the argument. She tells me that the witches only rarely die of the plague, but it is not, she thinks, because they have magic powers or are protected by the Devil. She believes that it is filth and people living too closely together that cause the disease, evidenced by the fact that entire cities have been depopulated while the witches in their forest homes went unscathed. She says that Hippocrates—he was a Greek physician—"

"I *know* who Hippocrates was," Giles said impatiently, her enthusiasm beginning to charm him. Her eyes shone with intelligence, now, and a rampant curiosity.

"Oh. Yes. Of course you do. Hippocrates said, 'Our natures are the physicians of our diseases,' and my teacher practices on that principle. A proper diet and fresh air, he said—"

"Fiametta," Giles interrupted kindly, reaching out to put a hand lightly on her cheek, "are you saying that your teacher is a physician? Rather than a witch?"

When he touched her face, her hand instinctively rushed upward to cover his hand with hers, a warmth flushing her face. "Oh yes! Paracelsus has come to study under her, three times now. He has said that everything he knows—"

"He learned from witches," Giles said for her, skeptically. He had thought Paracelsus quite stupid, to plead for an end to superstition and in the same breath speak seriously of witches. Her flesh against his was hot to the touch, as if she were slightly fevered. "Oh my dear child, what will become of you?"

Lamia leaped to her feet, trembling, shaken by his touch and the sweetness of his tone of voice. "I will survive," she exclaimed, avoiding his eyes. "Indeed I will! When my purpose is ended, I think that I will study to become a great physician, like Hippocrates, or Galen."

"What purpose, eh? Tell me why you are here . . . like this," once again sweeping an arm to indicate the dreary room. "You would be admired in Italy, not reviled. You must allow me to—"

"I cannot speak to you of my purpose," she interrupted. "You must remain ignorant of my comings and goings, my intentions. I should not be here with you like this. Should they suspect you know me they would—"

"They will not suspect. I will be exceedingly cautious. I would not want to be responsible for harm coming to you. Send a message with Nicolette, as you did on this occasion, whenever you think it safe."

"Such meetings can never be considered truly safe."

"No."

"We should never meet like this again."

"I know."

"You cannot change my mind."

"I accept that now. Would you like me to give you books, Fiametta? Paracelsus has recently published a new volume of—"

"Yes!" she exclaimed. "Oh, Giles, yes. The books of Hippocrates, as well. And Galen! Marco says that if I should be discovered in possession of such books, it would be the death of me, so he refuses to provide me with them."

"You shall have books, then. You will have to steal them, of course, after I have walked away from my favorite reading location by the river, leaving them behind, one after the other."

She laughed delightedly. Then silence fell between them once again. Finally, she said, "Now you will not need to search for me until you find me, true?"

"True," he said solemnly, slowly taking his hand away from her face.

"It would be very dangerous for you to make a search of this forest."

"I understand that, Fiametta."

Reluctant to say goodbye to him, she laughed self-consciously and said, "Nicolette thinks you quite mad to pay her to wash your clothing in the river. She believes in her grandmother's teaching about cleanliness, but thinks you take it to the extreme. She tells me you must change your apparel from the skin out every other week or so. She thinks you swim not for pleasure at all, but . . ."

Giles stopped her rambling speech with the soft touch of his lips against hers, in a kiss goodbye, the same kind of kiss that he would give to his year-old daughter.

She leaned into that kiss as if controlled, but the strength of her character was such that it was impossible for her to give in to temptations that might harm her or someone she cared for. She was more or less well-schooled on the subject of love now. Women beguiled men, drove them almost mad with desire, to the extent that some men died of the emotion. It began with but a glance, or a touch, perhaps a gentle kiss like this . . . and burned for an eternity. Love was truest, it was said, when physical connection was piously shunned, which was some comfort. She would not do anything to make Giles lose his senses, as he lost them when Peronnette was taken. He had lost one great love in his life. How cruel it would be to give love back to him, only to break his heart all over again. It was possible that the bishop would kill her before she could reap her vengeance.

Lamia whirled away from Giles, the fire in her burning so hotly she thought to faint. "I must leave you. Do not forget the books." With that she ran from the hovel and vanished into the dark within moments.

Two full moons later, in the month of January, when the sun had just begun to spread a mauve, cold light across the eastern sky, Lamia crawled out from under a hiding pile of rags and leaped from the wagon that had brought her from Nevers. Swiftly she entered Marco Cellini's house from the alley. When she entered the laboratory, only moments later, Hortense and Nicolette were already there, and two others. Only the cobbler's wife had not yet arrived for the meeting.

Ghanim stood leaning a shoulder against the brick wall near where Marco sat scowling over a voluminous and crumbling manuscript. He nodded his head, by way of greeting, smiling invitingly. At the last meeting she had confronted him in his quarters, forcing her way in when he tried to close the door against her entry.

She did not need to tell him why she was there, necessary only to meet his eyes. He had impatiently moved to his writing table, where he scrawled, *When you have learned to con-*

trol the flesh and its demands, then will you have turned the first key to unlocking your mind.

"Of *course,*" she had responded sarcastically. "In the brothels you control the *flesh,* yes? While you are with your favorite streetwalkers you do not allow your passions sway, but contemplate the night away. Damn you, I am not ugly. Is it that I am unappealing to you for some reason that has escaped me?"

He threw his hands up in despair, then began to pace the room, his hands clenching and unclenching, indicating the effort he was putting to the control of his desires. With ease did he play dead, but chastity was simply impossible for him to achieve, he could find no merit whatsoever in it. He could abstain, if he willed it with the same faith in accomplishment he exercised with catalepsy, but what man in his right mind would choose impotency, intellectually castrate himself for *any* purpose? He met Lamia's eyes with a studied detachment, his mouth twisted into a tight smile.

"You could say that it is *written,*" she suggested with a teasing glint in her eye. He was weakening before her lust— she knew it.

He returned to the writing desk, to say on paper, *My father's people instruct young adults in the way of the flesh, so that they can well please the opposite sex, as well as themselves. You seek only relief, Fiametta. What can I hope to receive from an innocent such as yourself?*

"What? A man gives *nothing?*"

In response, Ghanim wrote, *I cannot give a pleasure you do not know how to receive.*

"But who *will* teach me, then?"

He was silent for long moments, then sighed in defeat. *I will teach you . . . make the sacrifice,* grinning broadly at that. *But not now. I must first have Sire Cellini's approval.*

"Marco?" she exclaimed, but he was not looking at her. She roughly grabbed his shoulder and forced him around to look at her. "What in the Devil's name does Marco have to do with it?"

I am a guest in his house. Would I deflower his daughter while—

"Daughter?" She stayed his hand, again forcing him to

look at her. "I am not Marco's daughter. Whatever made you say such a thing?"

Ghanim threw his eyes to the ceiling, irritated with himself for having forgotten that she did not know. *Forgive me. I assumed wrongly. But I will not destroy the friendship he and I enjoy, for the sake of satisfying your lust for me.*

"Oh!" She was enraged. Her arm sliced out to slam her hand against the side of his face. "I can well manage without you! You are not the only man in the world." She could barely catch her breath, her anger was so intense. He was laughing at her. "Damn you!" she cried, but before her arm could swing again, he caught her in his arms and held her fast.

Ghanim covered her mouth with his in a brutal kiss that set her senses reeling. She felt as if she were dissolving. Her legs had become so weak she would have fallen over in a faint if he had not been holding her so tightly to him. When Ghanim abruptly released her, Lamia staggered back, unbalanced both in the body and in the mind. She blinked, swallowed hard, then said on an outrush of breath, "If Marco says no, I shall kill him!"

"What?" Marco exclaimed, laughing in disbelief. The lad stood matter-of-factly sipping wine before the fire, as if totally unaware of the absurdity of this request for permission to *instruct* his ward, waiting for Marco to read the entire, lengthy argument. "You have thought of every objection I might put to you—except one." He twisted his mouth into a mocking smile. "I could insist that you marry her."

Ghanim had met the suggestion calmly, shaking his head to indicate that he was well aware of the foolishness of such an idea. The Catholic sacrament was the only legal ceremony. There was no civil rite. No Catholic could wed a heathen blackamoor. And Fiametta was certainly *not* a Catholic.

On the pages that Ghanim had prepared in his quarters for Cellini, he had argued the merits of proper sexual training in the eastern manner. Fiametta was as the bud of a flower, straining to bloom. If not himself, it would soon be another. The question was, did Marco approve of him as the man who would instruct her. He begged Marco to remember that if she took to the streets he would have no voice at all in the mat-

ter; she might well be hurt by a man or men who were as ignorant as she about the finer aspects of intercourse.

Marco smiled at the idea of Lamia taking to the streets;
she was simply incapable of such self-demeaning behavior.
He looked up from the paper to meet Ghanim's eyes with a
bemused smile. "At the age of twenty years, you are so wise
in these matters, eh?"

Ghanim returned Marco's smile unfalteringly, showing the
man seven fingers to indicate that many years of conscien-
tious research.

"This art your extraordinary father also tutored you in, I
suppose?" At Ghanim's quick nod, Marco shook his head to
indicate his irritation. "Blast you! Why must you be so con-
scientious?"

Ghanim lifted his glass and drained the wine, his expression that of complete confidence.

"If you promise coitus interruptus, I will agree," Marco
said with great reluctance.

Ghanim gaped at him in disbelief, then rushed to the table
near Cellini to scratch furiously on the pad there. *No child*,
he wrote intently. *There is a method of avoidance that is determined by the moon's course in conjunction with a woman's menstrual pattern, which my father swore to be
infallible.*

"The truth you speak?" Marco exclaimed, his scientist's
mind caught in the net of another mystery waxing solvable.
"We must talk of this. Tell me—"

Ghanim shook his head and tapped a finger against the paper of arguments, demanding a decision.

"I agree, I agree, young fool! But be gentle with her. Hurt
her, either the flesh or the soul of her, and I will draw and
quarter you, fond as I am of your impossible self. The rose-
bud will open its petals, eh? How sad and old I suddenly feel.
I . . ."

Marco's final, paternal regrets were lost to Ghanim, as he
fairly lunged from the room, his face alight with anticipation.

Lamia was not listening to Marco's lecture, her eyes fixed
upon Ghanim, who had made no move, as yet, to slip out the
door according to the plan he had devised a month past. He

had informed her that Marco had agreed, that at the next meeting he would signal her when to slip away. He would instruct her, most willingly, he had assured her, and sealed the promise with a lingering kiss.

Her heart was beating at twice its natural pace. It was all she could do to breathe without gasping for air. She was beginning to be irritated by the fact that he had apparently forgotten all about his promise to her, when a gentle touch at her sleeve caught her attention. She turned to see Maria smiling at her knowingly. The servant woman indicated that Lamia was to follow her.

Marco watched Lamia leave with Maria from the corner of his eye, never faltering in his speech to the witches. An ache formed under his ribs and remained with him for several hours.

Lamia entered Ghanim's quarters transformed. Her red hair fell loose to her shoulders and her body was sheathed in an Indian sari of blue Persian silk. The sari was Ghanim's favorite style of dress for a woman, which Lamia could wear only within these sheltering walls. On her arms, bracelets. Around her throat, a necklace of amber stones. Her flesh glowed pale as autumn moonlight, scented by a perfumed bath. She felt like a queen from some tale of fancy. She also felt extremely uneasy. Trying to think about it calmly, the act of intercourse was really quite silly; she had lived without it this long, what was another year or so? She had no idea what she was supposed to do. And what had Ghanim meant when he said she did not know how to *receive?* Was it as complicated as all that?

Ghanim stood across the room, dressed in a floor-length, green robe. His back was to her. A single candle burned on his small table, the only light. He was pouring red wine into two crystal glasses. She was certain that he knew she was there, only pretending he did not. Refusing to move from where she stood, just inside the door, she waited for him to acknowledge her presence.

Ghanim slowly turned, a glass of wine in each hand, wearing an inviting smile. His eyes rounded in pleasure at the sight of her so beautifully attired. If there was any feature of hers that he most adored, it was her flaming hair.

Lamia moved stiffly toward him. He thought that she was afraid. A natural reaction. Even the humblest female creatures feared and balked in a mysterious reluctance and rejection of the first male. An element of rape clouded every deflowering. He expected little pleasure for himself, but trembled at the prospect of the next time, and the time after that.

With a trembling hand, Lamia took the glass of wine from Ghanim, smiling uneasily. She sighed, straightened her shoulders, and looked at him expectantly. Still, he did not touch her, only smiled knowingly, exasperatingly, moving away from her a little to lean his shoulders against the wall. The flickering candlelight softened his features and the beauty of his face stirred a renewed heat in her. His slender, brown fingers around the glass he held, his lean, smooth chest showing a little where his robe had fallen open, his eyes so deeply black and filled with tender invitation. It was as if he swung the amulet before her eyes, taking her under his complete control. She felt herself moving involuntarily toward him, until she was close enough to taste his breath upon her tongue.

Ghanim removed the glass from her hand and set it upon the table, placing his own beside it. Then with a delicate touch he unclasped her necklace and let it slide to the floor at her feet. He deliberately and with agonizing slowness removed each bracelet from her arms, holding her eyes all the while. The complicated wrappings of her sari he managed with knowledgeable finesse, allowing the silk to fall to the floor, carefully bringing the blouse over her head. He stood back, then, gazing upon her body, the perfection of which brought a flush of pleasure to his face. But he could not subdue a simultaneous sense of guilt, as if he were about to ravage her, rather than love her.

Lamia smiled pridefully now, all reservations vanished in her eagerness. She reached out to untie the knot of his sash, so that his robe might be removed. But she could not wait and impulsively threw herself against him, desperate to feel the flesh of him against her, a whirlwind of emotions sweeping her up and carrying her to near unconsciousness. His hands caught into her hair and his mouth fell to her neck, lingered there, then to her earlobe, around to capture her mouth.

Lamia's reaction was explosive, not a little violent. She drove him back against the wall with the weight of her urgency, as if she were ravaging him rather than the opposite.

None of the lessons Ghanim had been taught regarding the deflowering of a maiden was he given opportunity to perform. Lamia's reluctance had been short-lived indeed. Tenderness she did not want from him, nor long-suffering patience. She forced the issue, uninterested in how she was to receive the pleasure, certain that this, if it was all, was ecstasy enough.

They fell gasping upon the bed. She ignored the slight pain, biting him on the shoulder. When he fell rigid against her, she winced in surprise and brought his face up with her two hands, to read his eyes. He smiled helplessly, then caught her mouth in a kiss. Then she allowed him to explain with his roving, caressing hands and lips, how this flesh of hers was made, and it was better. And better yet, when the moon's light crept through the window curtains to lie like an ivory coverlet over them.

Chapter 14

Count Jacques' astigmatic eyes futilely scanned the tiltyard. Mabila scolded from his right, "All is in readiness; speak, blind fool," jabbing an elbow into his ribs. He obediently raised the white baton, commanding over the din, "Bring in the jousters!"

Instantly a great blare of trumpets deafened all who sat in the loges near the trumpeteers. Four gorgeously arrayed heralds led the procession on foot; behind them, a jongleur on horseback again and again tossed his sword high in the air to catch it as it hissed downward. Next came the contestants, eighty knights riding two by two. They rode down one side of the lists and back the other. The cheering thousands flung them gages of admiration and encouragement: bright ribbons, flowers, medals, a sleeve, stockings, gloves, and girdles.

Audette sat sullenly beside Count Jacques, refusing to so much as glance at her husband, who was leaning back in his wooden seat with a contemptuous scowl on his face. Her nodulus bosom rose and fell with her seething fury and humiliation. When Rainulf rode close below her, near the rear of the procession, with a gaunt-faced disregard for convention she abruptly rose to her feet. Wrenching the long yellow ribbon from her hair, she flung it down to be caught in Rainulf's hand. His startled eye fleetingly met hers.

"Caution, my wife," Giles muttered under his breath for her ear alone, "lest you announce to this company, like a sound of trumpets, what now is only suspicion."

Audette dropped onto her seat and coldly turned her back to Giles. "As *you* announce, by warming that seat, that you are a useless coward, my baron?"

"Oh, but this night I will still possess my teeth; all my limbs will be intact. Granted, it would be a surgical blessing if Rainulf lost the majority of his teeth, but let us pray he holds onto his life, breaking only a few lances and teeth, not his precious neck, hmmm?"

A herald drowned out Audette's biting retort, with a loud, "Let him come to joust who wishes to do battle." Immediately two grotesquely dressed pursuivants began to hop about the yard, caterwauling, "Here is the good cavalier and baron, Rainulf of Saint Potentin, a brave knight of a valorous house. He will teach a lesson to his enemies!" And the other yowled, "Here is the good cavalier, Raoul, eldest son of the most honorable Count de Sancerre. Watch now his deeds, all you who love brave actions."

The two knights, rigid as statues on their steeds, were led by their squires to opposite ends of the lists. When they faced each other, the marshall waved his baton, calling out hoarsely, "In the name of God and Saint Michael, do your battle!"

All the dames, nobles, and base-born rose in the loges and shouted together when suddenly the two knights and their mighty horses sprang to life. The earth quaked and the sod flew as they rushed toward each other, each bending low in the saddle. Only Baron Giles de la Fleur sat with arms folded indifferently across his chest. The splintering of wood rose above the din, and one and all cried out excitedly in unison, "Fairly broken! Fairly broken!"

Audette was choking on elation, squealing and dancing on her feet with prideful delight.

Giles eyed her sourly. "Sit down," he ordered impatiently. "This barbaric nonsense cannot possibly warrant such a tasteless display of unbridled emotion."

She fell into her seat, whipping eyes filled with rage around to meet his. "Not in half a year have I been out of that prison you call a villa! Allow me an ounce of pleasure, if you please—or is that simply too much to ask? A moment to forget my shame. Allow me to for one moment forget that my husband is a villain, a common farmer with earth under his nails and hayseed falling from his beard."

The muscles in Giles' jaw fluttered spasmodically and his eyes closed to slits. His hand ached to strike her. Slowly he rose to his feet, stood unsteadily over her, then whirled around and stormed past his father. He stumbled over Mabila's obese, outstretched legs, then took the stairs three at a time, disappearing behind the loges to the accompaniment of furious whisperings. He thought bitterly, "Yes, he has done it again, gentle men and women; the Baron de la Fleur has once again shown his colors."

Amid the expectant hush, two squires lugged into the banquet hall an enormous pastry, a fitting climax to a goodly and triumphant tourney, the most lavish wedding feast ever held at Nevers Castle.

Count Jacques raised his dagger high, then decided to make a speech, grinning drunkenly into a blur of faces. "My good company," he began with the flourish of an arm to indicate the pastry, "is this not a—a magnificent concoction, this pastry? For my youngest son, Conon, on his wedding day, a fitting finale, eh?"

Two hounds suddenly exploded into a snarling battle over the carcass of a swan, bones and debris flying all around them. Their racket, plus the delighted howls of the tipsy feasters, drowned out the remainder of the count's meandering speech. He finally gave it up and fell forward to stab his dagger into the pastry, releasing a score of little birds which dashed about the room in a frantic flurry of wings and peeps. The falconers standing in the entranceways removed the hoods from their hunters and, in a twinkling, to the jubilant shouts of the guests, the hawks pounced upon the little birds and killed them.

Everyone was now talking at once. The appearance of the hawks had suggested innumerable hunting stories. The Duke de Bourbon impressed his loyal lieges with how he slew a bear, and as she listened attentively, Mabila was upset from her chair by the still brawling hounds; she landed flat on her backside with the most startled expression on her flaccid, excessively greased features.

A jongleur stood upon the table, reciting to a gaping, small audience the tale of Tristan and Isolde. A tame bear entertained the castle servantry and miscellaneous riffraff before one of the stone fireplaces. Where Giles sat, in a corner of the hall as far from Audette as possible, a minstrel sang in a sweet tenor, to his great pleasure.

Giles stiffened where he sat when he saw Marco Cellini enter the hall. Coming to a halt, the merchant gazed around him, inspecting the crowd somewhat distastefully. Finally, he stepped to a cluster of robed clerics, engaging them in amiable conversation.

"Baron?"

Giles started and looked up to see the duke, Charles de Bourbon, standing over him. He hesitated an instant, then rose to his feet in proper homage. "Monseignor Duke," he said, bending his head in a polite manner.

The duke's close-set eyes scrutinized Giles with a sobriety that belied the tankards of wine he had swallowed. "You suffered illness during the tourney, did you?" he asked coldly.

"No, monseignor—boredom."

The duke laughed goodnaturedly. "How refreshingly frank you can be, Baron Giles. When you have attended as many such tournaments as I, then you will know how monotonously boring they can be. Now, in my great grandfather's day, when as many as sixty men spilled their blood on the field—then a man could, with some real anticipation, ride two hundred miles to witness the melee and return home well rewarded. All the fire is gone. Dull. I agree, quite dull these days."

Giles nodded a polite thank you for the generosity, meeting the man's eyes squarely.

"And how are you faring, Baron, at La Ville de la Fleur? You offer me only a pittance tax and a most reluctant homage, but, out of curiosity, I would like to know how well you are managing to increase the profits on your vulnerable lands. Four years now you have been lord of la Fleur, and no enemy has attacked you. Amazing, for you are a man with few friends."

Giles noted the gleam of suppressed amusement behind

the duke's eyes and accepted it philosophically, as natural and expected as the cat's disdain for the pitiable mouse under its crushing paw. Admittedly, the duke held every advantage. He was Baron de la Fleur by this man's permission and indulgence alone. Frail King Louis lay stricken with grief at the loss of his beloved Queen Anne and of old and lingering ailments. Count Francis d'Angouleme would soon be king. The duke's war was once again postponed, in hopes the dashing young pretender would be more sympathetic than was his royal father-in-law. For the moment Charles de Bourbon did not wish to discourage the de Sades of Florence, so he suffered Giles to hold his meager section of Nevers and to name himself lord thereover. Giles hoped for a miracle, namely that this overgrown, pretentious anarchist would expire by some means, fair or foul, all Bourbon thereupon falling to the monarchy.

"I have few friends, that is true, monseignor," Giles said carefully. "But I do not possess any mortal enemies. My distasteful qualities tend to stir a mocking contempt for me, rather than a vengeful wrath."

"Indeed," the duke laughed. "A rare gift, I would say. My mortal enemies have all my days so far outnumbered those deeply loyal to me that—but what is this I hear about your strange relationship with the villains of la Fleur? From what gossip tells me, I gather you have adopted the lot of them, the clergy's concept of brotherhood taken by you most literally."

"There is nothing strange about it, Duke. The practice has been accepted in Florence for many years. I have abolished a few of the outdated customs, nothing more."

"Such as the death tax."

"Oui. It is cruel and unnecessary to tax a family when a useful member dies. I need their devotion, not their undying hatred."

The duke's wide mouth curved into a ridiculing "imagine that" sneer. "And what is this about purchasing their leases?"

Giles patiently stood his ground, meeting the question and the man's mocking attitude head-on. "Those who wish to do so may give over to me the leases they hold, for which I pay a fair sum. They continue to work the land, but the risk has become all mine. They receive a wage, as a clerk receives a salary. In addition, they may receive an unstipulated sum at the end of each harvest, if my profit is extraordinary."

"You *pay* the brutes for what is yours by right of deed? Are you quite sane, Baron? Do excuse my rudeness." His eyes darted to left and right, meeting the glances of those now milling close to listen. He had the de Sade on display and meant to make the most of the man's failings. "Pray continue. I am fascinated. What do you call these persons—your flock?" He laughed at his own wit and his audience happily joined in.

"My workers," Giles replied with a tight smile.

"And if I should agree to your father's present inclination and name you Count de Nevers, will I one day discover all of Nevers to be under so revolutionary a system? All the happy *workers* receiving your wages, my barons, in obedient homage to their liege lord, freeing their own men and women in Christian charity—the hangmen and tax collectors unemployed, the noose ropes rotting from lack of use—the dungeons empty—the knights' armor set aside? Blast me, that is quite a prospect, fairly staggering in its portent. Will you, then, as Count de Nevers, refuse your responsibilities to me, hmmm? Shall I be required to storm these walls and hang you from the donjon? Speak up, Baron. As your suzerain, I this moment demand a renewal of your vows to me, made the day you were named baron under my sovereignty."

Giles faltered, glancing uneasily around him at the grinning faces of his peers. "As long as you are Duke de Bourbon, I will pay you homage as is your due. All except riding to your battles, which you agreed to delete from my vows, since I was not trained as a knight. I pay my taxes, honor your name and title, and lend not aid to your enemies. My father is young still. I do not covet his title so much as to wish him dead. No more can I say to you, monseignor."

The duke opened his mouth to argue further, but a loud confusion along the far wall caught his attention. Within moments the entire assemblage began to surge toward the windows, and anxious, excited cries emerged from throats just previously filled with giggles and bawdy jests.

Giles found himself alone. The duke had walked off, curious to discover the source of the new amusement. Relieved, he quickly bolted across the hall, where he pushed open a door that took him into a fetid, lantern-lit passageway. He halted his step, uncertain which direction to take, whether to his bed or out into the fresh air. A young couple lay straining and gasping in a vulgar entanglement of skirts and breeches, either unaware of or unconcerned about his presence.

Following an impulse, Giles placed a well-aimed boot into the lad's backside. "Take yourself to the kennel, tail-wagging cur!" The lad continued, ignoring Giles' repeated boots in the rear. Cursing under his breath, "Common swine," he strode down the passageway to another iron-faced door, which he flung open. Stepping out into a blissful solitude under a million brilliant stars and a full, bemused moon, he sucked in a breath of the clean air and then another.

Where Giles stood in the night air, he was surrounded by rising, sheer walls of granite. The donjon tower rose one hundred and ten feet behind him, its walls over twelve feet thick. Before him, across the narrow outer passageway that completely circled the donjon, rose a rampart tower, its wall jutting out to form a battlement square. He walked lazily past the tower and to the far wall, then leaned to stare down upon the river that was bejeweled by the moon's light, creating a shimmering path across the water that looked as traversable as the nearby bridge. He let his chin fall to his chest as his thoughts wandered aimlessly. He thought it a pity Adela could not have come from Trabey for the wedding, but she would give birth soon, the journey impossible for her. Imagine, little Conon wed.

Shouts echoed from behind him and Giles turned around, curious. The iron door swung open to pour out a flood of open-mouthed, walleyed men and women. They spilled toward the wall to lean over the rampart, frantically pointing across the river, crying, "There! There she is! The saints protect us, there she is!"

"Good Christ!" Giles gasped, falling forward to balance his weight against the rampart, straining to see more clearly what had to be an illusion. But several hundred others were seeing the apparition. How could he deny that she was there?

"The Red Witch!" a woman shrieked behind him and

promptly fainted, dropping in a crumpled heap of lace and satin at Giles' feet.

Suddenly Giles was overwhelmed by the realization that the magnificent, red-haired nude far below at the river's edge, bathed in moonlight, defying man and God, was Fiametta. No, it was not possible. The image he was seeing was entirely contrary to the image he held of Fiametta, but try as he might, he could not convince himself the woman was a total stranger to him.

In the nearly two years that he had been meeting her, only occasionally, sometimes several months passing before he would receive a signal from Nicolette, Giles had never seen this persona, this *woman*. In his presence, she had somehow managed to remain the urchin, the wide-eyed student of nature, and his devoted friend. How she had hidden this voluptuous maturity from him he could not imagine.

"What do they see? Tell me . . . tell me!" Count Jacques had suddenly stumbled against Giles, in his rush to the rampart to view the spectacle, but his eyes saw only blackness and the pale illumination of the moon.

"A young woman, mon père," Giles responded emotionally, "standing naked across the river, directly in the moon's path."

"The Red Witch!" Count Jacques wailed. "Is it . . . is it . . . think you it is she?"

Giles threw his eyes to Heaven impatiently, trying to get control of his heart that seemed to be beating at twice its normal pace, and of his tongue. If it was Fiametta, he must not say or do anything to increase the danger to her. The willingness of the crowd encircling him to believe the illusion being staged for them boggled the mind. In a strained voice he said to his father, "She has red hair, mon père, flowing over her shoulders to her waist. She is tall. A black cat winds around her feet."

Count Jacques gasped at the mention of a black cat. "Like her grandmother!" he cried. "One of us will die this night. Holy Mary Mother of God, we are doomed. The Devil has returned to Nevers."

"It is only a woman," Giles protested weakly, his mind spinning now with a thousand conflicting thoughts and emotions.

"Only a woman!" Count Jacques echoed. "Naked, you say. A black cat, you say. Is she a woman still, pray, or now a bat? Curse me! If I could but see more clearly. Damn these rotting eyes of mine. Is she yet a woman? Speak!"

"Of *course*," Giles began, more sharply than he meant to. "Of course she is still a woman."

Turning his back upon his father and the hysterical crowd, Giles leaned over the rampart, once again searching for justification to believe it was not Fiametta. She was moving, now, gracefully to and fro along the riverbank, the enormous black cat ever at her heels. He let a defeated outrush of breath escape his lungs, and accepted the fact that it could be no one else. Grasping hold of the rampart ledge, he sent his thoughts across the space that divided them. *No, Fiametta. Do not do this thing. Go. Return to obscurity. In the name of God, do not do this!*

The young minstrel, in a gay orange, red, and black costume, less impressed by the vision's occupation than by her beauty, leaped to stand teetering on the rampart ledge. He cupped his hands around his mouth, shouting down to the witch, "You are magnificent! Diana, the night huntress! Or Helen. Ah, Helen were not worth comparison . . . Gardens no such beauty show!"

Count Jacques rejected entirely the minstrel's suggestion that the apparition could be anything less than monstrous. "I think that I am blessed by blindness. Look away, Giles, or like your Greek . . . what was his name?"

"Ulysses?"

"Oui, oui. Like him, you will be hauled into her spell. Curse him, where is Father Jean? Fetch him, Giles. We must take some action against—the bishop must be informed at Pevele. Listen you to the holler. The Saints protect us, my household has gone mad!"

"I will not ride after her in the dead of night," a quivering voice announced.

"Nor I," another proclaimed.

"That cat! 'Tis the Devil sure, pacing at her heels thus, waiting for one of us to risk chasing after her. Let the bishop himself order it, I shall refuse."

"Giles," Count Jacques exclaimed, "you must find Father Jean and bring him here to me."

"I am beside you," Father Jean said softly from the count's left.

"Is it herself, Father? The Red Witch?"

"Oui. There can be no doubt. Satan's forces have descended upon us. May God have mercy upon—"

"My amulet!" the count suddenly wailed, grasping at his throat in search of the missing chain.

"Ah! You had grown complacent," the priest scolded. "Perhaps this is the reason why God has allowed Satan to return this night, as a warning to you. A warning, Sire."

"The bishop. He must be—"

"I have already dispatched a courier. Another will follow him in one hour, in case the first lad is caught and devoured by the lamia." This was said in such matter-of-fact tones as to drain the faces about him. "A long and fearful night it will be. Let us pray, Count, for our salvation and God's mercy."

Count Jacques obediently fell to his knees before the priest, his shaking hands folded under his thin beard, while all nearby did the same. Giles listened for a few uncertain moments to the priest's skillful manipulation of the faithful, then moved hurriedly through the praying crowd to the door that opened upon the long, shadowed passageway and the stairs.

As he took the steps down two and three at a time, an anger began to grow in him. This distasteful, idiotic display of Fiametta's for the benefit of the credulous and the stupid was insane, no less than suicidal. As he entered the Great Hall, he heard Audette's wailing voice call his name, and he stiffened, but did not falter.

"Giles!" she shrieked, obvious by her tone that she could see that he was deliberately moving away from her, rather than to her. "Giles! How *dare* you! Giles!"

Few of the guests had remained in the Great Hall; most of them were out upon the ramparts enjoying the spectacle. Marco Cellini sat upon the raised stone hearth of one of the enormous fireplaces, a solitary figure, looking almost miniature in stature, surrounded as he was by such a vastness of space. With a brooding intensity, he was gazing into the flames that rose from enormous, burning logs.

"Sire Cellini!" Giles called sharply from across the empty hall. His words echoed back to him from the rafters.

Marco slowly turned his head, fixing his eyes upon Giles, who stood near the entrance to the hall, feet planted wide apart, fists against his hips, indignation and defiance clearly visible in his stance.

"Greetings, Baron," Marco called out. "If you would speak with me, perhaps it would be best if you stepped a little closer?" He braced himself for the confrontation, knowing without having to be told what was on the lad's mind. Not too far from what was on his own mind, he wagered. She had picked a fine time for this, the foolish wretch. She might have warned him to stay away from this wedding celebration. It had only been fourteen days since she had attended a meeting, at which time she gave him not so much as a hint of this. As Giles strode defiantly toward him, he said testily, "Calm yourself, lad. Witches only eat those who believe in them." He laughed insincerely and got to his feet, a hand lifting to lay against the dagger at his hip.

Giles came to a halt a few feet from Cellini. He was still breathing heavily from his dash down the stairs. Cellini stared hard at him with cold eyes, waiting. Hauling in a breath, forcing himself calm, Giles said in hushed tones, so that only Cellini would hear him, "It would be foolhardy of me to ask that you do something about this . . . this spectacle, of course?"

"Of course," Marco echoed sternly, holding the lad's eyes. Damned fool, he thought, young fool.

"Of course. Your kind never put themselves at risk. How can you sit here like this, making no move to—"

"To what?" Marco interrupted. "What would you have me do, eh?"

"Giles!" It was Audette screeching at him from across the hall. His name echoed, Giles! Giles! Giles! off the walls.

Giles whirled around and shouted, "Go home, woman! The children! You must see that the children are safe. Go!"

"But . . . no, I cannot. Dear God, are you mad?" She gaped at him in disbelief, then ran from the hall, turning to take herself up the stairs to where she could seek the comfort of Father Jean's blessing.

"Take your own advice," Marco said softly, "and go home, Giles. Tend to your children."

It was all Giles could do to contain his rage, to control the need to smash his fists into the man's face. "I will find her and talk sense into her head," he swore, knowing the vow was foolish even as he spoke. If Fiametta did not wish to be found, he would not find her.

"Tell me. What would you suggest to her, eh?" When Giles refused to respond, merely glaring at him, Marco said, "Believe me, she is more than capable of fending for herself. You chasing after her strikes me as ridiculous, like the mouse attempting to rescue the cat, eh? All you could possibly achieve is to indict yourself and burn with her if she burns. Stay out of it. Leave her be. If you built a fire under me I would not tell you where to find her, even if I knew, which I do not. . . . It has been good seeing you again, Baron." With that, he moved quickly past Giles and strode, with a clacking of heels, across the hall, vanishing into the passageway that would lead him to his quarters for the night.

Giles watched the man until he vanished from his sight, thinking Cellini would, no doubt, sleep like a lamb this night, giving no thought whatsoever to Fiametta. He turned and gazed into the crackling fire, his mind wandering back to the last time he'd seen her, about three months past. She had taken him from Nicolette's little house to the cave, to prove to him at last that she had turned the dark space into an adequate shelter.

He had given her about a dozen books which stood in a neat line on a small table near a quite elegant chair that he recalled seeing in Cellini's drawing room. A small Persian carpet covered the earth floor. A brightly colored mattress had been tossed upon the carpet and was piled high with quilts and needlework pillows.

"Now are you convinced that it is amazing?" Lamia had asked excitedly. "I am most comfortable and enjoy my own company." She looked around the snug space and sighed deeply. "I was born here, you know. I am told Eliza was quite mad, but she was very kind to me, so loving."

"Yes, Fiametta, it truly is quite amazing," he had said sincerely. He had been so certain that she was living in abject squalor, unable to conceive of a cave being habitable. Carpets had even been hung, somehow, over the walls, closing her into a warm and colorful cocoon. "So, tell me. What have you learned since last we met, hmm? Did you finish the Aristotle?"

"No, I did not," she said with some annoyance. "He stated that a woman is only the incubator for the child she carries, has nothing whatsoever to do with creating the child. The man implants the infant and she incubates it. Do you believe that, Giles?" Before he could think on it and say a word, she flounced over to her books and picked up the Aristotle. "Utter nonsense!" she exclaimed, waving the book at him. "I have examined the sperm of cats and dogs and almost every creature in this forest and I have yet to see anything in the sperm resembling a kitten or a puppy. It makes more sense to believe that the *female* produces the fetus, which needs the sperm to ... to *come alive*; one only has to observe the male fish pouring sperm over the female's eggs to see the sense of this."

Giles smiled at her intensity. "I have often thought the same thing, particularly when I see a man or woman who is almost a twin of the mother in appearance. If only the father created the child, then all children would look like the father, never like the mother."

"Hortense grows roses for rose water, which she sells. She says that if the male rose is red and the female is white, the offspring will be both red and white, seeming to be as much a part of one parent as the other. If that is so for roses, then it could as well be so for human beings. Or dogs."

"Logical enough," he said, smiling.

She had abruptly fallen into a somber mood and seemed uneasy with him. He had the sense that she was concerned that he might read thoughts she wished to keep hidden from him. She dropped down upon her mattress and grabbed up a pillow, hugging it to her chest. Picking at the pillow's fringe, not looking up at Giles, she said, "I wish to exact a promise from you, Giles."

When she said no more, waiting for a response from him, Giles said, "Of course, Fiametta. Anything. What is it?"

Now she glanced up at him, meeting his eyes rather warily. "If something should happen—" She glanced away from him again and cleared her throat. "Should word reach you that I am in great difficulty ... some kind of danger ... you understand . . . promise me that you will not openly acknowledge that you knew me, that we were friends."

Giles flinched at her use of the word *were*. It seemed as if she had resigned herself to some terrible fate. "Oh, no. No, I cannot make such a promise. I would confront the Devil at his door to—"

"You must," she insisted. "For the sake of your children, if not for yourself."

"But you seem safe now. Rarely does anyone speak of the Red Witch these days."

"They will speak of me," she said emphatically, with a secretive smile.

Giles studied her where she lay curled up on the mattress, looking no older than thirteen years, lost within a dress several sizes too big for her over which was thrown a ragged wool shawl. As always, her hair was covered with a scarf, this one gray and motheaten. He let out his breath on a sigh. "Why? Why must I make you such a promise? I sincerely hope that you are not going to do anything foolish."

"Please. Your promise." She sat up and brought her knees to her chest, hugging them with arms invisible under the voluminous shawl.

A large spark snapped out of the fire with a loud, crackling sound, startling Giles out of his reverie. He had finally made her the promise, that he would never acknowledge that they were friends. Now he understood why she had been so insistent. This farce, this show of witchery for the credulous had been her plan, even then. She had put herself into a cauldron, to be boiled by Holy Church. Tears of frustration filled his eyes. He whirled around to walk across the hall to the exit. He must take himself to la Fleur, where he would wait for a message from Nicolette, in the event that Fiametta needed him.

Just after dawn, Giles brought his mare to a halt, listening while four mounted guards of his father's court questioned a woman of indeterminant age, who carried a basket of wilted flowers. She said in a listless monotone that she was walking to Nevers Town to sell her flowers there. No unusual sight had she seen, nor had any of the nearby villagers spoken of seeing the Red Witch that was reported stalking the count's fiefdom, God save her from such a sight. Her thin mouth twisted into a crooked, weary grimace, a frail hand wiping across her pocked forehead to push aside long strings of graying hair.

Giles listened, looked full and long upon her face, but he did not recognize her. When the guards grimly rode off, he also spurred his horse to a gallop, not giving the common peasant a further glance. A thousand exactly like her could be seen in any village, as on this, his own land, anywhere in Europe . . . a ragged woman aged before her time, scarred by disease, tired, spiritless, a shell of bones and flesh within which dwelt a depleted soul. The woman made no deep impression upon Giles. His mind was fixed upon that magnificent nude . . . there in the moonlight, slapping the face of Holy Church with a flamboyant audacity.

When Giles and the guards were out of sight over the hill's crest, Lamia's shoulders straightened. She cast her eyes up, examining the sun to determine the time of day. Breaking into a run, she crossed the road and dashed to the crest of a rise. To the north lay her destination, where she would await her prey. There was much preparation before her, perhaps days of patient waiting.

When she finally moved into the heath, Ghanim was there, according to plan. From a wooden casket he withdrew a grotesque sheath of scales, a sealed bottle of blood, another bottle full of live, wriggling creatures. A small wicker basket contained a long snake which Ghanim caught up and held high for her inspection, grinning wide at her.

Gently Ghanim reached to lift the wig from Lamia's head. Then he one by one carefully removed the pins from her hair, each move of his hands an endearment, adoration warm behind his dark eyes. His fine nose quivered at the scent of her flesh, as she loosened the fastenings of the ragged dress and dropped it to the earth at her feet.

Lamia reached up a hand to touch Ghanim's cheek, to assure his attention, then carefully said, "Use your talents well. Render me fierce as you can. I can perform this act but once."

She laughed delightedly, as Ghanim, with a dramatic

flourish, reached into the bottle to remove a long, wriggling worm, which he fastened into her hair by her ear, as if it were a rose.

When her costume was complete, Lamia stood tensely in the warm, midday sun, her hands clenched into fists. She whispered to the earth at her feet, "Satan! If you exist, one ounce of aid give to me now. I can do this without you, but, damn you, I could use a little help."

Chapter 15

 Bishop Geoffroi halted his ass and dismounted, moving sourly to the river's edge. He leaned and splashed up the cool water to his flushed brow. Dropping with a creaking and snapping of joints to the bank, he lifted his skirts, removed his soft leather shoes and placed his burning feet into the water. Every motion was in the unaltered pattern of twenty-seven years going and coming along this route. The heath was unusually quiet this midday. No cry of the falcon reached his ear from the wood. But it was a certainty that Nevers Town was not quiet this day, he thought contemptuously.

If he dropped everything every time someone claimed they had seen a manifestation of the Red Witch in these parts, charging down from the mountains with his army, he would spend his entire existence indulging such fancies. Hysterical nonsense. Satan had been vanquished at Claire. The power of the Almighty surrounded this diocese like an impenetrable wall. In the four years since the purge at Claire, the demons had slowly, one by one, perished for want of sustenance—the people shunned them, fought off their enticements with pious fortitude. Glory be to God, not a witch had been burned since the purge. A drunken assemblage, bewitched by the hallucinations of one or two, had gone emotionally aground upon the rocks of delusion. The one who sparked the hysteria might well be possessed and should be dealt with, but that was as serious as he wished to consider the situation at the present time. He had refused to make a special visit, had waited three days after being informed of the so-called sighting at Nevers Castle, until it was the scheduled week for his appearance at Nevers parish. He sighed resignedly. Contemplating the task of calming the frantic mob at that castle wearied him to his very soul.

Since the extermination at Claire, he had suffered an ever-increasing doubt as to God's purpose in allowing Satan so wholesale a consumption of already wretched souls, and this questioning had wrought a guilt in him that was so intense as to defy absolution. If he could only capture the Devil himself, burn *him*, render that arch fiend nonexistent, thus ridding the world of evil temptations. But man could redeem himself only individually through belief in Him, through contrition, virtue, and the sacraments . . . these were the only weapons against damnation, the only steps to beatitude.

God pity him, he must continue the endless bloodletting, steeling his mind against the screams of agony that had begun to haunt him when he was yet a lad, increasing, blending one into another, until the shrieks of the nine women of Claire had transformed the tumult into a nightmare that was with him night and day, awake or asleep. In his dreams wild-eyed faces appeared, scorched fingers pointed, shrill voices cried out "Thou shalt not kill . . . thou shalt not kill!" It was the Devil plaguing him in retribution, of course. The man most despised by Satan, tormented most viciously by the fiend, was the judge of the fiend's accomplices. A few judges had even been burned, falling beneath a demonic onslaught so terrible as to defy the purest soul's stamina.

The bishop abruptly struggled to his feet, panic catching in his throat. Satan's daughter was dead. Her aura could not have survived the fire he had set in the cave years ago. She could not have eluded the thousands of eyes searching her out for weeks after she vanished. God dwelt singly and without rival in Nevers diocese, Satan's strength weakened to a degree that would make it impossible for him to manifest himself in the flesh. Impossible. He would not even consider such a possibility. Father Jean must be made to understand that—

"*Ai—eee!*"

It crushed the stillness of the afternoon: a sustained, paralyzing screech. The bishop gasped, his eyes rounding, his heart slamming against his ribs. The donkey whinnied, terrified, reared up its back legs, and bolted across the heath to race out of sight into the woods.

Bishop Geoffroi stood frozen in his tracks, not daring to turn around or glance either right or left. The cry of a wounded beast, no more. He must get hold of himself. But he shook with a rising apprehension, then a certainty; he could delude himself no longer. Satan had invaded his peaceful kingdom, was this instant prepared to attack his person in a final, pitched battle. All the demon's evil temptations and threats would be pitted against what little strength of piety was left within him.

Something fell with a soft thud behind him, and the bishop numbly turned his head, dropping his gaze to stare bewilderedly at a leather shoe exactly like the ones now resting on the riverbank where he had minutes before laid them, but blood was smeared on this one, and a long needle had been stabbed through the sole of it.

"Holy Jesus—*At Verbum Caro factum est*," he cried on an outrush of breath, and his eye shot upward into the branches of a large oak that overhung the heath.

"No," he whispered, a hand wildly reaching for the iron cross around his neck. He fell backward, away from an apparition so hideous as to defy belief. A fleeting blackness shrouded his pure eye from such diabolism.

In the tree's top, as if she had only just landed there, crouched the Red Witch of Nevers, a broom caught between her scaled and bloodied thighs. Her naked body was entirely scaled, scabbed as if she had once been slowly roasted over a fire. Her red hair fell to her waist, wriggling with worms and insect vermin, while a bull snake curled around her throat, its vile tongue flicking out, its beady eyes fixed upon the man of God below. A frog was caught in her teeth and its legs waggled hideously.

"*Ya—eeee!*" she screeched again, then flew straight down to swoop back and forth across the heath, while the bishop ran hysterically before her and behind her, his blurred eyes catching only glimpses of her as she hissed past him—now behind him—now out of sight. Where was she? He whirled around, maddened, his breath coming in painful gasps.

"Death!" the lamia howled. "Death to Satan's enemy. I am come to judge thee. I am come to sentence thee. To the torture, ordinary and extraordinary!"

The fiend now stood upon the ground. She moved menacingly toward him, the frog held up and out in her vile hand, as he would have held the cross against Satan, but his hand was disconnected from his reason, his cross dangling beyond his ability to reach it. He could do no more than whimper and cringe back—back. He stumbled into the river, whirled around, fell face first into the water, then reared up in a geyser of white spray to run clumsily and breathlessly down the stream, his wet skirts dragging a terrible weight against his weakening, aged limbs. A piercing, riotous laugh followed him, echoed from all sides of him.

"Not one death, nor two, but a *thousand* shall you die! And then you shall burn. Burn!" the fiend shrieked.

He fell into a sinkhole, slipped on slick stones, but did not leave the water that was the sacred fluid of the baptism—running he knew not where. Each step increased his terror of the chasm into which he could fall in the next instant, to wail in eternal agony beside all the victims of his justice.

"*Et Verbum Caro factum est,*" the bishop moaned again and again, until he collapsed upon the riverbank, dropping first into a black delirium and then into unconsciousness, his fingers fastened with a vice grip to the decayed solidity of a fallen, dead tree.

The bishop was discovered at sunset by the forester of la Fleur, who irreverently threw the soaked, unconscious priest over the saddle of his horse and carried him to the villa of Baron Giles.

Word swiftly reached every ear in Nevers, and great was the ensuing furor. It was said that the bishop, when he regained consciousness, had spoken of being attacked by the Red Witch. Bloodied and bruised he was, as evidence. No one except Father Jean thought to doubt the veracity of the powerful prelate.

Father Jean's ambitions had always been singular and unfaltering. Bishop Geoffroi was old and senile. The path should be made clear for a more capable man. The coadjutor would accede. The chancellor to coadjutor. Jean, himself, was in line for chancellor.

Geoffroi had been thirty-three years old when he was investitured in Rome as bishop, only two years older than Father Jean. After twenty-seven years, Father Jean was still a parish priest. He loathed Geoffroi for being the son of a cardinal, the nephew of an archbishop, and for his pious conviction, his naive presumption.

Father Jean might be only two years younger than the bishop, but his faculties were intact; he was not senile. Flying red witches, indeed. The bishop had lost his mind completely, that was the truth of it, and bless the Devil for it. A stealthy practitioner of the Devil's magic for many years, Father Jean harbored a heretic's skepticism, which did much to maintain his mental balance on the subject of witches. An occasional accusation and burning served to emphasize his pious diligence and to cloak his secret indulgence in a veil of sanctity. He now affected a careful watchfulness, coiled like a snake prepared to strike. With cautious insinuation he would lead Bishop Geoffroi like a lamb to the slaughter. Father Jean could not have known how judiciously he aided the scheme of that lurking Red Witch.

Critically ill, Bishop Geoffroi was quickly surrounded by a small army of knights and loyal nobles, and, as soon as he was well enough, was whisked away from la Fleur to his castle at Saint Aliquis, where he slowly recovered from the lung congestion following his five-hour immersion in the river Allier. But the wounds upon his soul did not heal. With hysterical fury he ordered a search of Nevers that was not to be forsaken until the fiend was taken. Fortunately, no red-haired woman of the right age lived in Nevers to suffer in Lamia's name. The search was fruitless, since Lamia and Ghanim were forty miles away, having had a full day to escape while the bishop lay unconscious and delirious.

They lived in idyllic unconcern within the shelter of an ancient, burned-out, and abandoned inn off a seldom-used, overgrown road that followed a tributary of the Loire River from Nevers Castle to Moulin. The part of the inn's roof that had not been burned away sheltered them from the rain and from the sun when it became too hot. Often at night, when the sky was clear and filled with stars, they lay on straw-filled mattresses in the open, rediscovering their passion for each other in the moon's light.

Ghanim felled woodland animals for their meals, while Lamia crouched endless hours over the stream, retraining her hand to the swiftness of her childhood, until she could snatch a fish up from the water just as easily as she had in the past. But in deference to her new refinements, she dashed their heads against a rock to kill them, and cooked them before devouring them.

Lamia waited for the bishop to once again make himself vulnerable. Her plan was clearly defined, if decidedly more risky than an overt act of murder, which would not serve to even partially appease her rancor. Her goal was to see the diocesan indicted through irrefutable evidence of possession. Then he would burn as Eliza had. A fitting end. A noble triumph in irony.

Cellini had taught her that hysteria was the first ingredient in the brew for conjuring mass delusion. First you created the illusion, which you allowed to simmer long enough to firmly jell—you could then create any reality you chose and all the mob would see is the illusion. Men saw what they expected to see. Thus the broom between her legs as she perched in the tree's top had suggested flying to the credulous bishop; he had not seen the thin rope about her waist because he *knew* that she could fly, expected her to fly about him as she had.

Lamia laughed at the man's terror in smug amusement. Her performance had been a triumph of staging and theatrics—*beau mélodrame*. His terror and his ultimate face-first plunge into the river had been far more rewarding to see than merely poisoning him, or stabbing him, might have been. She could not possibly have been more confident in the ultimate success of her plot.

After two months at the inn, Ghanim, his chin now fully bearded, left Lamia alone and returned to Bourges, where it was believed he had been to Flanders as purchasing agent for Sire Cellini. He remained in the merchant's house seven days, then departed again, this time supposedly to Dijon. In actual fact, Ghanim rode into Nevers to ask, observe, and learn. He visited Cellini's several weavers there as a further cloak for his real purpose.

Ghanim returned to the inn with news that Bishop Geoffroi had recovered, but that he still would not venture from Saint Aliquis Castle. However, Father Jean had so stirred the clergy to suspicion of the bishop's inability to continue in his office that the prelate would soon be forced to show himself in denial, to set upon a renewed meeting of his ecclesiastical duties and habits.

On Ghanim's next venture into Nevers, he was rewarded with more than gossip. He was treated to a close view of Bishop Geoffroi riding bent and emaciated in the saddle of his weary little donkey—the ass, the friar's robe, each emblematic of the humble image he had created many years ago. He rode in tremulous dread along the familiar paths. The single alteration in pattern was the new road he took between Pevele and the Nevers Town, so that he could avoid that heath where he had been attacked.

Bishop Geoffroi was helpless before the forces being pitted against him. The enemy was supernatural, rather than of this world, thus he could not with impunity demand a guard of his person, for what man in Nevers wielded more holy and immutable a God-ordained power than he? His individual sanctity and indestructible will had to be considered sufficient protection against the wiles of the Prince of Darkness.

The bishop's cross and his holy eminence were all he possessed with which to fight the Devil. There was no arguing with his superiors or subordinates on this dogmatic principle. Even as Saint Anthony had fought off the furies of a thousand demons on the desert, must he meet and do battle against the fiend that had besieged his diocese. He did not think in terms of multiple demons now, but in the singular—she, red and terrible, the Devil incarnate, the Red Witch, one unique and hideous monster that he must destroy or be destroyed. To suddenly, following upon that brutal test of his will on the heath, surround himself with soldiers as he moved along these roads, would have announced like a herald's cry the fact of his shattered confidence. He knew, also, that all his enemies were not otherworldly. Some were certainly of this earth, but he was as impotent in opposition to them as he was versus the lamia. To cry false accusation before any explicit accusations had been made against him would lend credence to the suspicions Father Jean had so slyly planted.

Suddenly the entire world had turned a bitter face to the bishop. God had withdrawn His mercy, and he was lost and bewildered, ill and embattled in a maze of inexplicable happenings.

Lamia allowed the illusion to brew for three more months. The Red Witch grew more enormous, more loathsome, more real every day, while weary, impatient soldiers of the bishop's court combed the provinces, storming into villages, examining every scalp of every young woman for signs of red hair that might have been dyed to black or brown.

Though the bishop insisted the lamia was inhuman, of a half-animal, half-woman shape, the men who beat the brush for her confined themselves to a search for a human being, partly out of an unconscious incredulity, partly out of terror. What pale weapon did they possess that would be sufficiently potent against an ogress such as His Holiness had described? But by their very tenacity, the illusion grew to the proportions Lamia had hoped for. The entire province was now fully conditioned to believe anything they saw or heard about the Red Witch and her sinister familiar, the great black cat.

Rumor had it that Bishop Geoffroi, in desperation, finally wrote to his Eminence, Jacob Sprenger, in Cologne, asking for aid in the battle with the fiend of Nevers. But the Inquisitor General, it was said, replied with decided coolness. Since, just as the bishop had admitted, the demon was single and unaccompanied, except for the familiar, he felt certain the might of an entire diocese could manage to control the diminutive plague. No aid would be forthcoming.

Lamia departed from the inn two days following her eighteenth birthday, her highly trained black cat in a wicker basket that was fastened to the horn of her saddle, her peasant disguise expertly administered. She had deliberately decreased her intake of food, so that her countenance was realistically emaciated.

On the fifth day of August, Lamia moved unnoticed through the streets of Nevers Town. Her dark dress was soiled and worn, her wig caked with dust, tangled and briar-ridden. On her feet she wore crude wooden shoes. Over her arm she carried a basket of flowers. She called out in a dull voice, "Buy my pretty flowers. Buy my pretty flowers."

Lamia entered the church of Father Jean at midday, briefly kneeling in prayer before the crucifix. Listlessly fingering her beads in filthy hands, she moved to the rear of the house, to await the mass. A few parishioners entered the high-ceilinged, ornate church, most choosing to sit close to the dais, thus far from where Lamia sat at the back in deep shadow.

Bishop Geoffroi entered in full regalia, to sit behind Father Jean throughout the mass. Lamia was careful not to once allow her eyes to show any light save despair, her lips never once forgetting to droop in bitterness; no air of confidence or lack of humility was visible to the eye.

When mass was concluded, Lamia hurried out and placed herself at the corner of the building with her basket, that she might see the bishop as he entered the alley that cut between the church and the rectory. Within moments he appeared beside Father Jean and they walked silently across the alley to enter the stone building.

Lamia's eyes cast up along the walls of the rectory, noting the thick intertwining vines that hid most of the stone, and the sharp outcroppings forming ledges where extra window spaces had been cut out of the ancient construction in an effort to modernize it. The main entrance was from the street, but she was certain the bishop's quarters overlooked the church. No investigation had furnished this information; she simply knew it to be a fact. Quickly enough her certainty was vindicated, as the bishop's gaunt countenance flashed by a window on the second level directly over her head. A strong ladder of tangled vines led straight up to a wide balcony, the window dropping out of her view, probably descending to the floor. Heavy wooden shutters lay open to each side of the window, held fast by metal hooks. A servant boy appeared and threw open the windows, which were in two sections, opening like doors. It was a close, hot day, and the night would likely be stifling—those windows remaining open.

Lamia knocked upon the cookroom door of the rectory. When the sullen woman who opened the door spat out her disdain for the wilted weeds in her basket, Lamia fell weakly against the doorjamb, sighing in apology, saying that she was very hungry, had not eaten in two days. She received a pitying charity: soup and bread. While she ate, she sought the information she required.

"Pasque dieu! You say the bishop dares to sleep alone, with the Red Witch about?"

"The Lord protect us," the cook sarcastically replied, "he does. As he always has. The man is daft. Believe me, woman, he is plain daft, says his faith is plenty. Plenty for the likes of him, but not for me, I tell you."

"Not a single guard? I should say he is very *brave*, not daft. Myself, I keep my man on the door side of the bed, you understand—between me and *it*, if it comes."

"He keeps no one 'tween him and the door. Says the Devil, if he wants to enter, could come through the walls. Says no door or window would keep out the fiend, and no guards could keep him away. The houseboy sleeps at the outside of the door, but half the time he sneaks off. Can you expect otherwise from the runt of a hangman's litter?"

Having all the information she required, Lamia quickly finished her soup, while discussing hangmen with the cook, agreeing that they were indeed a scurvy lot, without exception. But if they did not do the vile work, someone else would have to, as long as there were gallows and the thieves to hang from them. She escaped as quickly as possible, after finishing her meal.

When it was dead of night, the streets silent and empty except for roving, scavenger dogs and stealthy cats in search of rampant rats and mice, Ghanim appeared according to plan, on foot and with the large wicker basket in arm. Lamia saw him from where she hid in the alley shadows and moved hastily toward him, her heart in her throat. There was no room for the slightest error, and no possibility of escape if they were detected. The entire scheme rested upon the strength of that earlier created illusion; if it failed, the prospects were grim. Their horses were tethered a good distance beyond earshot of the rectory. The sound of running horses would destroy the inference they hoped to create; thus they would have to melt into the darkness on foot, as inconspicuously as they had come.

Ghanim took Lamia's face in his two hands and leaned to lightly kiss her mouth. He strained to read her lips in the dark, then nodded solemnly and turned his eyes to the rising wall. Then he reached down for the basket and put himself directly to the task at hand. Lamia slipped out of her wooden shoes, climbing expertly up the vines behind him.

They had chosen a moonless night. On the balcony, they saw the bishop on his bed, tossing in a restless sleep, his cross held tight in a skeletal hand.

The hangman's son was awakened by a terrible screech coming from within the bishop's quarter. For a moment he lay inert on the floor outside the prelate's door, his feeble brain slow to comprehend the meaning of such a racket. He heard glass shatter and a heavy object crashed against the other side of the door. Finally, the brute rose sluggishly to his feet, his tongue sliding out over his thick lower lip. He cautiously reached for the latch, then pushed open the heavy door.

"Huh!" The boy gasped when his eye fell upon an enormous black cat crouched full center of his Holiness' bed, illuminated terrifyingly by the light of a nearby lamp. The beast hissed at him, its fur ruffled, its back arched, its green eyes like the Devil's own. The cat wore the bishop's cross and insignia of office around its neck. The hangman's son stood leaning forward, eyes widening, his mouth falling open and drooling. Finally the implication of what his eyes beheld penetrated and from his throat escaped a cry of terror.

The lad stumbled backward and ran down the hallway, shouting, "Into a cat. He turned into a cat!" waking the entire household with his ravings.

The cook, sleeping on the first floor, had been awakened by the original racket, but God himself could not have dragged her from her bed to investigate.

When Father Jean and two clerics in white, flowing nightshirts entered the sleeping quarter at a running pace, they pulled up short before a glass-eyed, seemingly delirious bishop, who sat in the middle of his bed looking as if he had just been dropped there, his cross and insignia of office around his neck, his pale lips moving in soundless speech.

The hangman's son gaped, disbelieving. "I *saw* him!" he protested. "A cat, he was. Right there on the bed, 'fore my very eyes, the cross around its neck. A big—big black cat, with horrible green eyes."

Father Jean's reactions wavered between astonishment and knavish delight. A practiced opportunist, he grasped the boy by the arm and commanded him to repeat what he had seen for these two clerics, which the lad did, not once but three times.

"A hand clasped over my mouth," the bishop choked out at last, too shaken to move from the bed. "Held me on the balcony—my face pressed into the shutters. The cat must have—have been. As God is my witness, I swear, I—"

"Can you describe the culprit?" Father Jean asked doubtfully, giving his clerks a knowing side glance.

"I can not! But if you would chase after the fiends, instead of standing here gaping at— Take after them, you fools. Fools!"

Father Jean hesitated, giving deep thought to this rather miraculous occurrence. The Lord was being very accommodating, sending such a clever culprit to lay the foundation this way. It would seem a good idea to make at least an effort to apprehend the prankster, whoever he was. "You did say that it was a man, or men, did you not, your Holiness?"

"As strong as one," the bishop replied uncertainly.

"You are uncertain. I see—"

"It was a man who held me!"

"But you did not see his face, or that of his accomplice? How many cohorts were there?"

"I did not see his face, and I do not know how many there were!"

Father Jean nudged one of the clerics and motioned the young man with a nod of his head to the task. "No one in particular. Anyone will do; the bishop has said it was a man. One should be about somewhere, would you not think so?"

"Father Jean!"

"Your Holiness?"

"Disregard my command—for a search."

"Indeed—"

"Go. Get out of my room, all of you. God have mercy on you, for what you are thinking. Get out!"

"He was a cat," the hangman's son insisted dully, as he retreated in fumbling obedience. "The truth I tell you; he turned himself into a cat."

Father Jean did nothing to still the stupid fellow's wagging tongue, knowing full well that before the week was out the residents of Nevers Town would have added to the lout's tale a multitude of embellishments. The Red Witch had been seen by a thousand persons with a black cat at her heels, her familiar, the Devil in disguise. The priest fairly giggled in his glee. Time. Allow the suspicions to brew into a forceful potion. Then pour it into the minds of the citizenry. To fell a bishop with the accusation of possession demanded a skill far more versatile than that necessary to convict the rabble.

Lamia and Ghanim rode slowly along the highroad through the black night. A furious pace would have suggested a suspicious urgency. At the crossroad where one road led to the inn, and the other to Bourges, they parted. They tried never to be seen on the roads together, so they could never be associated with each other. No one had an inkling that the Red Witch had a confederate. This cautiousness served to assure Lamia of some kind of aid if ever she were apprehended. Ghanim could only be of assistance to her on the outside of a prison.

Ghanim took the road to Bourges, promising to meet her a week hence at the inn, and Lamia continued toward Moulin for another hour; then, when the sun's first rays stretched across a cloudless sky, she halted the mare and dismounted, walking the horse off the road into a cluster of beech trees, stumbling on her feet. She was so exhausted she could barely walk, had not slept in two days. Having tethered the mare to a tree trunk, she moved away from the animal, always sleeping a good distance from her mount for it was a large and easily noticed beast. She found a hollow between two fallen trees, fell into it, and was asleep within moments.

As he rode west, Ghanim became increasingly anxious. He was as weary as Lamia was and thought at first he suffered only physical depletion which was frustrating his usually adroit mental processes. But he found no relief from the mounting pressure over his brows. He felt eyes upon him, distinctly sensed the presence of following riders, yet no horsemen were in sight, before or behind him.

An hour passed, and he approached a small village. Inexplicably, his heart began to slam against his ribs. He was suffering all the elements of terror, but faced no danger.

Abruptly, he drew back on the reins, his white stallion rearing and whimpering, foam thick around its mouth. He had experienced a sufficient number of forewarnings in his life to recognize the symptoms. He would not drive the stallion another step along this road until he had interpreted the danger he sensed.

The horse shied and birds fluttered curiously in the trees. Ghanim leaned forward and dropped his face into his hands, blotting out distracting light, retreating into silence. He cleared his mind of all thought so that it became an empty canvas upon which a vivid picture began to take shape.

Lamia lay curled in sleep between two fallen trees. Four clerics of Father Jean's parish were approaching her, combing the woods in an obedient search for a demon they did not believe existed.

Ghanim reared up in the saddle. Driving his heels into the stallion's sides, he yanked on the reins and turned back, following the map of his peculiar instincts. He knew exactly where she was sleeping. His heart was pounding in reaction to the real danger now. Men had not been stalking him, but Lamia—the eyes had been upon her.

Lamia heard the cracking of brush underfoot, but the sounds were indistinct. She groaned, rolled over, and returned to a deep dream-disturbed sleep. Suddenly a lightning bolt seemed to explode in her head. She saw Ghanim's eyes—urgent warning. "Danger! Danger! Danger!" In an instant, Lamia was on her feet, trembling and confused. Four men in gray robes surrounded her.

The young man closest to Lamia grinned drunkenly, his heavy eyelids blinking spasmodically. He was not looking for the Red Witch—any female would do. He said not a word, moving with a lascivious grin toward her, while his companions closed in from behind.

Lamia's fists whipped up to rub her eyes, in a frantic effort to clear her head and vision. She leaped toward a gap in the wall of men, but was caught by strong arms and thrown back against the trunk of a tree. She whipped around and sank her teeth into one of the arms that held her. The man yowled and fell back. She lunged blindly forward into the brush, not noticing the thick, low-hanging branch; it caught her across the side of the face and wrenched the wig off her head as she sped on.

"Holy Jesus!" one of the men shouted. "Red hair!"

Lamia ran as fast as she could, but in Ghanim's stars it was written that she would be captured. She tripped over a rock and fell sprawling. Eight brutal hands clutched hold of her and held her.

Ghanim found Lamia's mare lazily munching grass, the hollow between the fallen trees empty. In a fury of grief, he beat his palms against his forehead, cursing his mind that had warned him too late. Why? Why had he not sensed this when he left her? Or an hour before that? He had momentarily forgotten what he believed to be a profound truth, that every circumstance is preordained. He could not have prevented her capture if he had known of it, an entire day beforehand.

"Ghanim, no!"

Marco Cellini reached out to take the lad's arms in his hands. "Are you positive? Perhaps—"

Ghanim shook his head violently, speaking of his certainty.

Marco whipped around and slammed both fists against the stone of the fireplace wall. He should not have allowed her to take such risks, but he could not imagine how he might have stopped her, save chaining her in the cellar of this house. She would bear it, could prevail. She must. He had not known how much he loved her, until this moment.

Marco felt Ghanim's trembling hand on his arm and turned to read what the grief-stricken man had written.

She will not be burned. If I have to ascend to the heavens and rewrite the stars, I will do it. She will not die!

Cellini believed him. "She will not die," he agreed huskily, reaching to firmly squeeze the lad's arm in a gesture of affection and confidence. "We are not altogether helpless. Without qualification, I would say that no human being on this earth has a stronger will to survive than Fiametta. They will not prevail against her. Which gives us time. Time, Ghanim."

Chapter 16

 IN THE TOTAL DARKNESS, Lamia calmly sat on the stone floor, her naked thighs and buttocks sinking into three inches of black mold and maggot-ridden human excrement. Heavy chains were clamped around her ankles and bolted to the floor. The bishop was taking no risks; she would not fly away from his ecclesiastical and personal vengeance again.

She did not know how long she had been sitting thus, whether it was night or day. Certainly a guard must be outside that door, a door so low she had had to crawl into this cell on her hands and knees—the jailer likewise, the trembling pig who had dutifully chained her to this floor. She had received no food, but hunger was the least of her concerns and could be ignored for the time being. Water was the prime necessity; her throat was dry and scratching. She knew they would not starve her to death and thereby forsake all the triumph and spectacle of a trial, torture, and the ultimate of agonies, the stake. Prisoners were never so weakened that they might die on the rack, which would spoil all hopes for a spectacular burning. She clung to this knowledge and it gave her a modest peace of mind, some control over the crying demands of her flesh.

Control. It would be her salvation in this ordeal. She spent endless hours practicing, speaking urgently to herself in a whisper. She heard Marco's voice in monotonous repetition, saying, "The conviction directly precedes the reality. Believe with absolute faith." She closed her eyes and whispered, "I will not feel any pain. I am capable of insensibility. I have accomplished it before and I will again," and not the slightest doubt did she suffer.

Lamia was more devastated by the fact that the bishop had defeated her than by the conditions of her imprisonment. Now she could never reap her revenge against him. On her next and final attack she had planned to drug the bishop with masterwort and set him to dancing on the hallowed ground of a cemetery. Before she had begun toward her vengeance, she had already failed. But as bitterly as she regretted the failure, she could not convince herself that the bishop would escape the punishment due him. There had to be a way, a weapon against him, even in this cell, and when she found it she would wield it unrelentingly.

It was no ordinary witch that was about to be tried; it was the Red Witch. Word had reached to the far borders of the four provinces surrounding Nevers, and the curious were riding into town by the hundreds. noblemen, villains, traveling jesters—a rabble intent upon witnessing the trial and the burning, or profiting therefrom.

All the paraphernalia of the yearly fairs had been raised, peddlers hawking their wares, the jesters clowning with their palms open for the coppers tossed to them. A festive excitement raised a hum and holler that did not cease even through the dark hours, drunken brawls, murders and rapes harrying the count's guards and his noble patience.

"Insanity!" Giles shouted at his father, enraged. "Goddamned insanity. And you will allow it?"

"*Allow* it?" Count Jacques protested. "It is God's wrath in—"

"God! What has God to do with murder, save to condemn it with a commandment? Father, I plead with you, do not stand back and let them torture that poor child."

Count Jacques was deeply disturbed by Giles' anger. He had grown quite fond of the boy. This sudden attack sorely wounded him. He did not take particular pleasure in burnings, nor did they disturb his conscience or his appetite. From earliest times it had been an accepted method of clerical punishment. To burn, to hang, or behead, or draw and quarter—he could see little difference—she would be as dead. He could not understand why Giles was so overwrought. But then the lad had always been a queer one. Certainly, Giles was out of his right mind on this Red Witch affair.

Count Jacques cautiously suggested to Giles that he might make a visit to his beloved Florence at this time, remembering how the lad had always longed to return home during his first years in Nevers. "My son, your continued defense of this witch can put you in jeopardy."

"Witch, for Christ's sake! If she is a witch, then I am Satan."

"Giles!" Count Jacques protested, reaching out in his near total blindness for his son, "be careful what you say. What is it? Surely— Giles? Do you know this young witch?"

No answer came. His son was gone—God knew to what place or for what purpose.

That same day the bishop petitioned the count for the use of his great hall for the trial, for the church could not hold the numbers demanding witness to God's justice in this case.

"Here? In my castle? The entire world has gone mad! Absolutely not. I will not have that creature in my house, your Holiness."

"Your son, Giles, has touched the hand of this witch," the bishop said accusingly, in a quivering, threatening voice, and the count's face blanched.

Count Jacques immediately agreed that his great hall would be made available for the trial. He begged the bishop to get to the trial quickly and to get the proceedings over with as soon as possible, before the rabble completely leveled Nevers Town.

On the tenth day of August, Lamia was hauled from her cell, stuffed into a basket that her feet might not touch the earth, from which she gained her power to fly, and carried in traditional parade to face God's wrathful interrogation.

From the church, through the streets, over the bridge, just to the bailey, it was a normal hour's walk, but the procession was constantly stalled by caterwauling, rioting gawkers. Lamia's mind was so unruffled that she slept through almost the entire bobbing journey. It was good to smell clean air again. The basket was a heavenly bed. It would do no good to worry about the questions they would ask; she knew them all. And all the answers, the wrong and the right answers. She knew their laws as well as they did, perhaps better. Peronnette had known of this day and had taken her to Marco Cellini that she might survive.

"If you are captured there is one way and one way only to preserve your life and that is by refusing to confess. It requires superhuman endurance, but the reward is life." These, Marco's familiar words, were the final thoughts Lamia had before dropping into a light sleep.

When Lamia stepped from the basket to face her judges, a hiss of gasps rose from the crowd in the great hall like a wind. Her figure had been draped in a sheath of sackcloth. Her long red hair, her entire body, was thickly coated with a black and stinking filth. But she stood with her head held proudly high; wearing a mask of humility and deference was no longer necessary.

The crowd was hushed. Not a rustle of movement did Lamia hear, though she sensed the great hall to be filled with spectators. She refused to turn and give the audience so much as a glimpse of her face.

She listened patiently to the prayers, the hurried blessings, the justifications, which consumed the better part of an hour, all the while fixing her hate-filled eyes on the bishop's ashen face. The bishop felt the fiend's malicious gaze upon him, but he refused to look at her. His hands shook so that he could barely control them to turn the pages of the Bible. His lack of coherence was announcing his senility and a layman's terror of the fiend he stood in judgment upon. Lamia could almost smell the fear in him, taste it upon her tongue, and it warmed her to the task at hand. Marco's words entered her mind and she listened again. "Calm denial. Never allow them to ruffle you. You are innocent."

The preliminaries dispensed with, the bishop sat down on his throne and leaned to whisper something to his coadjutor, who sat to his right, then to the chancellor at his left.

Lamia suddenly stiffened when a familiar signal flashed across the forefront of her mind. She whipped around and for the first time faced the congregation that instinctively leaned back in a wave from her evil eye. All cringed from her except Ghanim, who stood near the center of the room. Though he was almost lost in the pressing multitude, her eyes had gone in a straight line to meet his. She instantly turned her glance away, her heart leaping over. With strengthened confidence, she swung around to glare at the bishop, who had risen to stand unsteadily before her.

As the bishop's stricken eye at last rested full upon the Red Witch, his mind suddenly floundered in a high sea of opposing sentiments. The power of the invisible malice as outlined by apostolic bull, and the Malleus Maleficarum, against which his offices were directed, was in fact not a new persuasion, but of fifteen centuries' duration. Impossible to be even a little uncertain of his righteousness, yet he wavered thus in a corrupt gloom of doubt.

The faith of the multitude was waning. The power of Holy Church was weakening. Malfeasance abounded. But was the traditional Satan being blamed out of a reluctance to place the responsibility where it belonged—at the foundation of Holy Church itself? His illness, the mental and emotional ordeal of the past months, seemed to have opened a door in his mind that had been closed throughout his devoted life.

The filthy wretch stood before him and the bishop's suddenly heretical eye could see only a young woman. Her feet were not cloven. No scales crusted her flesh. Her eyes were brazen indeed, full of loathing, but he saw not Satan there, no gleaming fire capable of supernatural abominations. Our Lord in His Sacrament was everywhere being subjected to defilement, but was He not also being defiled by these atrocities of trial, torture, and burning?

Toads and cats, judges and torturers; he could not discern a difference between himself and a witch's toad, or a witch's debasement. He felt utterly debased. He was weary of life and living, of the hideous nightmares, these unending trials. He shivered, his wasted body quaking so that he grasped hold of the lectern for support, his eyes caught and held by Lamia's unretreating, chilling gaze.

The Devil. How tenaciously he had chased after the fiend

these long years, like a dying man on the desert stumbling, mad, toward an ever-distant mirage. Virtue, love, and peace, the profound hope for human grace—were these, too, merely illusive mirages on the horizon of man's existence on earth? He had believed. God knew that his had been an unimpeachable faith—that the fires, the tortures, the screams, all the agonies were justified as a means of attaining the noble, promised end—the return of Eden.

A veil had momentarily dropped from the bishop's eye, and even as he had shown Christian mercy to the child Eliza by releasing her from that cell, able to pity her as the Christ most certainly would have, he was now moved by a genuine benevolence, and he smiled charitably upon the accused, in a manner fitting the role of spokesman for Christ on this earth.

He was a dead man and he knew it. The fact that he might soon stand where this witch now stood served to increase his awareness of the vast gap between accusation and the truth of the matter. A part of the pity he outpoured to her was for himself. Still, fifteen centuries and a lifelong conviction could not be erased in a moment's revelation, and the opposing force struck a sharp blow.

The pillars of Heaven rested upon the premise of Hell. If God was in His Heaven, then Satan was in his Hell, or in this hall—the punishment, therefore, must be meted out, God appeased, as he himself could never be appeased again; his pain of doubt and guilt would broil unremitting within him until the day he died.

"And at this house, which is high," the bishop began in a weak voice, "every one that passeth by it shall be astonished, and shall hiss; and they shall say, 'Why hath the Lord done thus unto this land, and to this house?' And they shall answer, 'Because they forsook the Lord their God, and have taken hold upon other gods, and have worshipped them, and served them; therefore hath the Lord brought upon them all this evil.' "

Lamia recognized the biblical quotation. Marco had not neglected that book in his meticulous instruction. Now the interrogation would begin, and she braced herself, drawing her shoulders tensely back.

"Your name, mistress," the bishop demanded, his eyes blank of expression now.

"Lamia, daughter of Eliza, who was the daughter of Jeanne."

Taken aback by her quick, honest reply, Bishop Geoffroi clumsily rummaged his brain for the next question. "Do you confess before this multitude—"

"I confess nothing. I stated a fact."

"Indeed. You—you have stated before God and these witnesses that you are the child of a child of a witch. Will you, then, herewith and now, as quickly confess that you also are of the blood and sect of Satan?"

"Mere circumstances of birth cannot make me a witch. Nor can association be considered evidence. What man in this room has dwelt more in association with witches than yourself, yet you are not possessed?" deliberately raising her voice questioningly.

"I—I did not request an argument, but a confession. Are you prepared to admit your guilt, to repent and receive—"

"I deny all accusations."

"You deny you are a witch, and that you are the flesh, through incubus, of Satan?"

"I am not a witch. As for the circumstances of my conception, how can I say? My memory does not go back that far."

A single, harsh laugh exploded from the audience, and the bishop flinched, startled. "Whosoever in this house," he cried out in threatening tones, "is disposed to laugh during these holy proceedings, can only be assumed in league with the accused and of identical character. Stand and be judged, or beg His forgiveness and pray for your salvation." Satisfied that no further outburst would be forthcoming, he turned back to Lamia, with, "You claim that you are not a witch?"

"I do."

"Do you *believe* in witches?"

Lamia hesitated, to gather her thoughts, then smiled wryly and replied at length. "If I answer 'no,' that would be heresy, a denouncement of Holy Church as the slayer of innocent persons on the stakes. To say 'yes,' would leave your Eminence no alternative but to state the premise that *belief* in witches can only be considered a *faith* in witches, which would imply a sympathy and compliance. Therefore I refrain from answering, on the grounds that the question was designed to incriminate me rather than to reveal the truth."

A flurry of motion and whisperings commenced between the twelve personages on the seats of justice behind the bishop. Father Jean leaned to fill the archbishop's ear with his doubts as to the bishop's ability to manage this peculiar witch, considering the man's health, his increasing senility. But the bishop was not interfered with.

"With Satan's glib tongue do you argue in the face of death. Who but Satan's mistress would stand in such arrogance before God, without humility or remorse? Your very glibness condemns you, names you what you will not admit you are. Tell us who your accomplices are!"

"Accomplices in *what*, your Eminence?"

"In witchcraft!"

"But I have told you—I am not a witch."

"Do you deny before this court that you pranced foully naked for a thousand eyes to see? Do you deny that in a scaled and hideous form you took flight, flew yowling, blood-smeared—my own eyes beholding your diabolic rampage? Do you deny that you are the *Red Witch?*"

"I deny that I am a witch, that I have ever flown, that I can at will become half beast. But I can hardly deny that my hair is red, which it obviously is, through no fault or choice of mine—God given."

"You lie!"

"I am not a witch."

"Where have you dwelt and what persons have sheltered you all these years?"

"I dwelt alone. No one sheltered me." At Bourges a brown-haired chambermaid had vanished. Almost a year past. No one would think to connect the two—she hoped.

"You expect this court to believe that alone and unaided you gained sufficient education to stand so glib of tongue before your judges? A wild thing you were, and today you possess all the power of wit and words attached to gentle breeding. Your lies trap you. Name your cohorts in Satanism, repent, and God will be merciful in His justice."

"Merciful, your Holiness?"

"Oui. I can promise."

"That you will behead me before I am burned?"

"If you reveal the names of those—"

"But if I were what you accuse me of being—Satan's flesh—could I be expected to require assistants? Alone, I would be an autonomous, superhuman, illimitable force. Satan requires no aid. No generous shelter would I have required. My wit would have been placed upon my tongue, magically, by the fiend himself."

"Then you admit—"

"I admit *nothing*. I merely point out the stupidity, the inconsistency of your arguments."

"Why—why do," the bishop stuttered, his bony fingers whitening where they clutched the edge of the lectern, his mind retreating to the Malleus for aid. He recalled that one of the Devil's favorite ruses was to argue with the judge as a logician through the mouth of the witch. The judge must be wise enough to avoid such verbal entanglements, which would only serve to weaken the conviction of those witnessing the trial. Incriminate and insinuate. But what about truth? His head was spinning in the dust of the battle between those two forces, conviction and doubt. He opened his mouth to say the irrelevant, "Why do you persist in a state of concubinage," but the words refused to emerge from his throat. A murmur of voices hummed in his ear. The congregation had become restless, disturbed by his extended hesitation. Panic rose to blur his vision and he fell forward in a half faint. Almost immediately he felt the pressure of his chancellor's hand on his arm, drawing him back to slump into his seat of office.

"Bishop Geoffroi, as you have seen," the booming voice of the archbishop cried resoundingly to the audience, "has swooned in horror before this feculence—for he *knows*, as we all can guess, how many infants this lamia has devoured in her demon feasts, first sucking their blood—the graves she has desecrated—the carnal orgies she has perpetrated and enjoyed in her depravity, mocking God, placing her vile mouth around the phallus of Satan in obscene lust! The Devil has cloaked her in an aura of innocent youth and beauty, to beguile our eyes and bewitch our thoughts, to detour our righteous indignation, toward a mercy any one of us would eagerly show to one who was *innocent*. But she—she—is not—innocent," pointing dramatically at Lamia. "I dare say, we are fortunate indeed that she maintains this lofty disguise, saving us from the furies she could well bring down upon our flesh and upon our vulnerable souls."

"Well spoken," Lamia said softly for his ears alone. "If I were indeed Satan's daughter, you, your *Holi*ness, would be my next victim."

"Heretic!" the round-faced prelate cried melodramatically. "Unless you confess, this court will have no alternative but to pronounce sentence of torture upon you, that the truth might be loosened from your witch's tongue. What was the nature of your pact with Satan? Speak!"

"I have made no pact."

"When was the last time you flew to a Sabbat?"

"I cannot fly."

"Ah! You went by some *other* means."

"No. I have never been to a Sabbat," she replied patiently.

"You say that you have never attended a Sabbat, but you have been *seen* there."

"By *whom?*" she shouted at him. "Yourself?"

The man's mouth dropped open in shock, his expression crumbling. If she confessed now, in her rage she would likely point the finger at him as her cohort, so he quickly uttered a thunderous, "To the torture, ordinary and extraordinary! Let our eyes and ears no longer be offended by the loathsome sound and sight of you, the Devil's whore!"

It was what she had expected, the only alternative to confession, but Lamia's flesh went cold and her throat closed at the sound of those words, *To the torture.* The stake could be imagined, prepared for, but not even Marco knew exactly what she would have to face in the torture chamber. Some said that red-hot pincers were put to the flesh. There were vague descriptions of monstrous machines. But only a few could precisely detail the inventions of the Inquisition for pain, and they either chose not to speak or did not live to tell about it. Death was not the goal, but agony, of the flesh and of the spirit.

Her mind screamed on a rising panic, *Ghanim! Help me.* With the panic entered a seed of doubt as to the invincibility of her spirit. She sensed Ghanim's pain and fury, felt his affection for her wrapping around her heart and mind, a protective shield against despair. He would not let her die. She must not waver in her conviction that she would survive.

Lamia sighed and raised her head in arrogant defiance, allowing herself to be stuffed into the basket for the return trek to her cell. The rabble was raising havoc in a sudden, explosive release of tension. Her last glimpse of the bishop's face was enlightening. His sunken eyes were fastened on her with an almost insane scrutiny, as if he were desperately trying to see cloven hooves, scales, and a broom between her legs. He wanted to believe her Satan's daughter, but he no longer could. An idea hovered out of reach and her mind scrambled for it, tried to catch hold of it, but fruitlessly. If it was written that she would be his executioner, then this circumstance was also predestined; thus the weapon had to be in the torture chamber where she and the bishop would next meet.

No longer calm and unruffled, Lamia was once again chained to the floor of a cell, to await torture.

"Audette! I warn you . . ." Giles raised a threatening hand to his nagging wife.

"*Lydia* was there," she persisted, enraged. "Rainulf allowed *his* wife to travel all the way from Saint Potentin. But *my* husband is some kind of—of— Why? I ask you, why did you keep me from the trial? I could have—"

"Damn you! For the love of Christ, leave me be."

Giles fought to control his loathing of this woman, while at the same time his mind punished him with self-incriminations. He had had every opportunity, almost seven years, to save Lamia from this monstrous circumstance, but his concerns had been centered upon himself alone. Two years past, when he stumbled upon her in the wood and at their first planned meeting, he should have been more forceful, less accepting. He should have bound and gagged her and had her taken to Florence, kept her prisoner there, if necessary. Imprisonment in a suite in Florence would have been a far better fate than *this*. He shivered, as his inner eye saw Fiametta bound to a stake and slowly roasting over a sanctimonious fire. Good Christ! What decent man would stand by and see a *horse* so cruelly abused? In truth, all priests were devils, Holy Church their foul breeding place. Satan's altar was the Holy Cross.

"I tell you, husband," Audette persisted, flouncing around the sparsely furnished bedchamber, "when she is burned I intend to witness it!"

"You could actually *watch* such a thing?"

"She is a witch and deserves to burn. Should I pity her, for God's sake?"

"For God's sake, yes, you might! You are guilty as the priests, as barbaric as they!"

"Oh, please! Spare me another of your sermons. I could not bear another."

"Likewise, spare me your vile tongue, which exhibits the grossness of your mind, the vast cancer that afflicts your soul. I would prefer to think of you as—as merely stupid rather than obscene!"

"Obscene!" she screeched. "That—that filthy *witch* is the obscenity."

"Witch! How do you know that she is a witch? Tell me."

"Well, of course she is, or why would she have been put to the torture?"

"Oh, my dear God. If she committed ten times the crimes stated in the accusations, you, my wife, would still outclass her in every respect." Livid, he lunged from the bed to rush for the door.

"I!" she raged behind him. "I am not a witch. How dare you—"

Giles turned and shouted at her, "You are a *born* witch, Audette, lacking only the refinements of the trade!" With that he wrenched the door open and slammed it closed behind him with a house-quaking blast.

From the witch waiting to be tortured he had received adoration, a selfless, innocent love, and from the unsuspected woman who called herself wife to him, not a single kind word or glance. Audette spent her entire existence pining for his father's death, conniving for the title of countess. Her children were conceived through no choice of her own; were it not for the hold of affection they had upon their grandfather, she would have loathed them utterly. Audette was an immoral, deceitful, cold-souled vampire. He had often suspected her of an inclination to murder. She would certainly poison his father without regret, if she felt certain enough of his will, which he kept a dark secret, claiming he wished to delay dissension between his sons until after his death that he might not have to suffer it. She poisoned this house, polluted it insufferably, and day by day laid waste his soul and his hope in living. The villa was exquisitely beautiful, as was the surrounding countryside. But for Audette's presence, he could forget the ugliness and bestiality of the world beyond the borders of la Fleur and live modestly at peace.

"Baron Giles?"

The manservant's voice halted Giles as he strode down the curved, open staircase. He leaned over the railing to glare down questioningly into the old man's patient face. "Well, what is it?" he snapped.

"A man to see you, Baron," the man said falteringly, "in the court."

"I will see no one. Tell him—"

"But I—I cannot tell him. He does not hear or speak."

"What?" Giles said absentmindedly, his thoughts still raging. "What did you say?"

"He neither speaks nor hears. Handed me a paper which I took to the houseboy who reads and—"

"A *deaf mute?*" Giles exclaimed, prodded by a memory. "Dark of skin?" He had seen Cellini in the company of such a man, several times in the past few years.

"Oui. The paper said he wished to see you on an urgent matter. That is all."

Giles took the remaining steps two and three at a time, racing across the expansive entrance hall to throw open the door to the court. Slowing his step, he moved under the tiled arcade out into the bright August sunshine.

The man stood composed by the pool, his dark eyes fixed on the fountain that spilled water in two graceful falls over a miniature mountainside. The mute turned, as if he had heard the footsteps behind him, meeting Giles' eyes curiously.

Giles stared uncomfortably at the Moor, not knowing quite how to communicate with such an unfortunate.

Ghanim quickly relieved the strain by reaching out a hand in greeting, a tight smile twisting his mouth. He gave Giles a folded message, which he hurriedly broke open, certain it was from Cellini and about Lamia.

The message read: *If you are truly concerned for the welfare of our mutual friend, and possess the courage to act on her behalf, I request that you accompany the bearer of this message to a place where that action can be discussed safely.—MC*

As Giles read Cellini's plea, the mute's eyes fairly burned through his forehead. When he had finished the note, he glanced up to the Moor with a sense that his thoughts were printed across his brow for the man to read. He looked away quickly.

Giles could not quell a surge of triumph. Imagine: Cellini, the cold one, the cautious, the callous—so overwrought now as to plead for aid. Giles' first instinct was to respond to Cellini with a gloating and frigid "Never! Aid her? But how foolish. Incriminate myself? Let her die. We will say we know her only in a casual way." An opportunity for revenge for Cellini's callous indifference to Peronnette's suffering and death. But Fiametta might die horribly as the price. "It says here in this message that you know what I say when I speak. Is this true?" Giles had mouthed the words exaggeratedly. Receiving a nod, yes, he continued with, "I will join you within the hour. Shall I need to be away overnight?" Again a nod in the affirmative. "Please, enter my house and rest, while I prepare."

Ghanim shook his head, his expression and gestures indicating that he preferred to wait here in the garden court. Their eyes met and held for long, mutually distrustful moments; then Giles turned heel and strode back into the house, to make the excuse that his textile supplier was threatening to sue for nonpayment, so he must see his banker in Bourges immediately.

The meeting place chosen by Marco Cellini was a mud hovel near Saint Aliquis, the house of Odelina, an ancient whose familiar, unpleasant countenance chilled Giles to the very bone. He sat on a rickety chair, hunched over, facing Cellini and the silent, watchful Moor. The hag sat close-mouthed on the hearth throughout the discussion.

"Cellini," Giles said in a half whisper, as if he expected

the bishop to be outside the hovel listening, "what can we hope to do? Know that I will do all I *can*; I mean that sincerely. Since Peronnette . . . died, I . . . I have lived in dread of a resurgence of Church atrocities. I hoped . . . not a burning in four years, but—"

Marco eyed Giles severely. "I know how you loathe me, blame me for Peronnette's death. But you were so deeply in love, you never would have believed me if I had told you she did not wish to live. She put to use none of the lessons I had taught her."

"No more!" Giles insisted, swallowing an impulse to attack the man as emotion rose to close his throat and inflame his mind. "We are here to discuss Fiametta!"

"Oui, our Fiametta, eh?" Marco said, quickly looking away from Giles to hide his own high emotions.

"You brought her to this, Cellini!"

"I did, perhaps. But responsibility is not under discussion here."

"What have you in mind?"

Marco sighed, rising from his chair to pace the low-ceilinged hovel like a caged jungle cat. He swung around to Giles and in a deceivingly calm voice began to summarize the situation.

"She knows that any confession gained under torture is worthless, that another has to be obtained after she has recovered sufficiently to be of sound mind. A pitiful recognition—admission—of the baseness of their inhuman methods!"

Marco went on to say that the law of dual confession was defined explicitly in the Malleus Maleficarum and judiciously adhered to. Only a few corrupt judges in Spain indulged themselves in forging confessions or the acceptance of those gained under torture.

The torturers were not as lacking in conscience as it might appear. Actually, they were scrupulously correct regarding the precisely written laws of procedure; this scrupulous attention to the details of the law prevented any sharp deviations. And the limitations upon them were clear.

"Not only must they obtain a second confession after the torture, but only three sessions of torture are allowed. If, after the third ordeal, Fiametta has not confessed, the case would have to be considered *unproven*. Oh, never *innocent*—no. There is no allowance in the *good book* for any verdict of innocence. She would simply have to be released until such time as the case could be *proven*. Needless to say, they are far less *careful* during that third and last session of torture, eh?

"This is the law," Marco reemphasized. "Fiametta is well aware of all the guiding principles. She knows that she can get relief from her agonies by confessing on the rack, but that she must not repeat that confession in her cell afterward; she must deny it flatly and constantly."

"Good Christ!" Giles exclaimed in horror and disbelief. When he could find his tongue, he asked, "How many people could survive three sessions of torture? After the first, what person would be so strong-willed as to stand firm when faced with another session?"

"Fiametta has certain unusual abilities, Giles, of which you are unaware."

Giles stared at him, then let his glance slide over to Ghanim's impassive face. "It was said that Peronnette suffered no pain," he murmured.

"Exactly. That lesson she taught herself—and used it."

"But—how is such a thing possible?"

"That is neither here nor there," Marco replied impatiently. "Only God knows whether Fiametta can maintain her strength, her will, against the fiends in that dungeon. The fact is, we are left with only three possibilities by which to make plans. First, she may be taken to Pevele. And on that trek she would be in the free air, within reach of our intentions. Or, she will break, confess—and be sentenced to the stake."

Giles shivered and hugged himself with both arms, nausea rising in his throat. "Then she would be taken from the dungeon to be burned," he said huskily. "Once again, you would be able to—"

"Indeed," Marco interrupted grimly. "Then Ghanim and I, with our friends, will save her, or burn with her. There will be no time then for plans, or for self-protection. She will be in the free air, even if surrounded by an army. What you would do in that instance would be your own choice. I would suggest that you go to la Fleur, weep your tears for humanity, one or two for Fiametta, one for me, perhaps, then forget us."

"This is a rather glaring reversal, Marco," Giles said bitterly. "Why have you not told yourself to pretend you do not know her—except in a most *casual* way?"

"I wish I knew!" was Marco's honest reply. "But I do not. She is so young, Giles. She wants so much to live."

Giles nodded and said, "There were *three* possibilities, you said."

"Oui. The third possibility is, perhaps, the most likely. I say that because I know Fiametta so well. I think it more than likely that she will withstand the first two sessions of torture, which will force the bishop to retreat to the Malleus out of desperation. Only one more session would be allowed and if she withstood that one he would have to release her." He paused, then began to quote directly from the Malleus. "And finally let the judge come in and promise that he will be merciful, with the mental reservation that he will be merciful to himself or the state; for whatever is done for the security of the state is merciful, and let him say pleasantly that he has decided that, rather than being a witch, she is undoubtedly bewitched, the plaything of some demon that has entered her body." Marco hesitated, to gather his thoughts.

Giles, who had been sitting bolt upright, listening intently, said excitedly, "Go on!"

"The accepted action in such stubborn cases is to send the accused witch to a nearby castle, where she will receive careful treatment of her wounds. Through prayer and fasting, she will regain her health, they would tell her, and the demon would be driven from her body."

This last resort was designed to trap the witch, Marco continued. Almost entirely free, the noble persons of the castle having become her good friends, she would be expected to relax her guard sufficiently to fall prey to a standard ruse. The noblewoman of the house, now her dear friend, would beg for a potion to alleviate some grave infirmity. The poor, unsuspecting witch would be surrounded and taken into custody the moment she put the potion into the hands of her hostess. With so many witnesses having observed her folly, she would immediately confess and that would be an end of it.

"Few indeed are the cases where this action has been taken," Marco said despairingly, "but the bishop is more than desperate to see her burned. I think it could come to that, and only you can aid her then, Giles. Why I called you here."

"My father's castle!" Giles exclaimed.

"Good enough."

"Or my villa?"

"Better still. If you can have her sent to your house without seeming too eager, eh? What I mean to say is, that you would have to appear at least slightly discomfited at the prospect of having a witch lodged in your home. You must connive to make it seem that you continue to want nothing to do with Holy Church and its affairs, giving in with great reluctance."

"I will do it, Cellini! Beginning immediately, I shall reform my position regarding—"

"Do not be too obvious," Marco interrupted urgently. "Make no sharp reversals of character or opinion."

"Of course. I understand. Over the past several years I have followed the line of least resistance, which will now serve me well. My Florentine skepticism has, conveniently, come to be accepted by the Church as indifference rather than heresy. Having no interest whatsoever in Church affairs, I *never* interfere." He paused, swallowing his rising emotions. "Cellini, I beg of you . . . if we do save her, convince her that a witch's life is a base life. She must try to find a haven somewhere . . . somehow."

Marco shook his head despairingly. "In these times what man or woman lives anything but a base existence? Life under the oppression of Holy Church and its Inquisitorial forces, under feudalism, is insufferable. You and I, my young friend, are among the rare exceptions. Tell me, if you can, where our beloved Fiametta can hope to find a true haven. Even if she were released on the basis of an unproven verdict, she would not be safe even in enlightened Florence, because a Holy Church accusation is tantamount to conviction. No other means of survival save witchcraft will be available to her. Holy Church will hound her all her days."

Giles wanted to give Cellini a solution, struggled to think of one, but he could not. Tears came to his eyes and he said huskily, "I will keep a close watch, do my best for her. How shall I keep contact with you?"

"Ghanim, here, will ride to your villa every second day. If a sudden emergency arises, I have other eyes than yours watching. Many pairs of eyes, Giles. If there is serious trouble, we will know it quickly enough, I assure you."

Giles hesitated, then abruptly offered Cellini his hand. "For now, we must be friends, Marco Cellini."

Marco took the offered hand warmly. "Whichever way the wind blows her, we three will be there to catch her. God help her, would that we could protect her from the tortures. Can you not hear Christ moaning in Heaven, as they do these things in his name? Damn them, they will probably bring those machines to Nevers, and we will have no opportunity to snatch her from them."

Chapter 17

 WHILE THE MACHINES WERE being transported from Pevele, Lamia enjoyed comparative luxury. Following the trial, she was returned to the dungeon beneath Nevers' Church of Saint Francis, but was manacled to the wall of a lighter, less unsavory cell. Only heavy iron bars were between her and two pacing, watchful guards. Twice a day half a loaf of hard bread, watery broth, and a wedge of cheese were cautiously shoved through the bars, pushed across the floor to her with a long-handled paddle. She ate every crumb. They wanted her to build her strength, and she was not about to argue with Inquisitorial generosity.

After three days, she began to hear faint hammerings, thumps, and the hollow echoes of men's voices at labor. The machines had arrived and were being raised.

Lamia stabbed her long fingernails into her naked thighs until blood showed, feeling no pain, only the numb sensation of being touched, as if with cotton rather than by something sharp. She must pretend to suffer. She must feel the touch, but not the agony. Only a witch could be insensitive to pain and she was innocent. But how long and how effectively could she maintain a melodramatic, mock suffering? How long did a torture session last? One hour, two—three? Eight hours, perhaps. She desperately wished she knew exactly what to expect.

On the seventh morning after the trial, Lamia awoke to see through the bars of her cell a grim formation of God's representatives—Bishop Geoffroi, Father Jean, Coadjutor Louis, and four clerics who stood with their hands folded into the sleeves of their robes. Several guards stood behind them, holding flaming torches.

"God is merciful—God is just," Father Jean said in reverent tones. "Will you confess, mistress, that your flesh may not suffer the rage of our Lord in His Sacrament, which exacts truth from silent tongues?"

Lamia struggled to her feet, the shackles clanking in the silence. "I have nothing to confess," she said emphatically.

"So be it. Fear thy God, for he is a vengeful God."

The door of her cell was opened by a guard. Her shackles were unlocked and removed from her ankles and wrists. The clergymen moved aside, allowing her to follow the guards toward the chamber of torture. The bishop moved in close behind, the coadjutor next, then Father Jean and his clerics. It was a solemn parade.

The chamber was below the cell block. A long, twisting flight of stone steps led to it, deep under the church. No screams would be heard by the citizenry to disquiet them or stir doubts in them.

It was a large stone room with moldering walls that reeked of death and decay. For centuries dead prisoners had been unceremoniously tossed into this cellar and left to rot. Human skeletons were grotesquely piled along the walls, having been swept from the stone floor in the preparations for raising the machines of torture. The only light was provided by smoking torches set into crevices in the walls. The flickering firelight hideously illuminated leering skulls.

Through the murky haze, Lamia made out several ponderous contraptions; one in particular, which dominated the middle of the chamber, its ropes slack, its wheels freshly oiled. A charcoal brazier glowed with red-hot coals. Irons, wedges, a spiked collar, two beet-shaped iron stoves. But none of these contraptions stirred terror in Lamia. The heat in the pit of her stomach was kindled by the sight of the chief torturer and his three assistants. They were dressed entirely in black, with hoods over their heads in which slits had been cut to reveal bloodthirsty eyes. Their hands were huge and rough, their frames hulking beneath their robes. Around their bull necks they wore amulets of blessed salt and herbs enclosed in wax, to ward off demons.

"God is merciful—God is just," Father Jean's voice intoned again. "Will you confess now, that your flesh—"

"No!" Lamia said urgently. "I have nothing to confess."

At a signal from the bishop—who now sat in his chair of office near the door, an open Bible in his hands—two of the clerics moved around the chamber sprinkling holy water on the machines, singsonging incoherent benedictions. The torturers were blessed by the bishop. Then all those present bowed their heads in a brief prayer to a merciful God and His compassionate Son.

"In Jesus' name, amen," the bishop concluded, giving the signal to his chief torturer to begin.

The four giants quickly seized Lamia and threw her flat upon her back on the long wooden table. One held her shoulders firmly against the table, another held her right ankle and thigh, a third her left leg and thigh, while the fourth, chuckling under his hood, snatched a razor-sharp knife from his belt. He tested the sharpness before her widening eyes by running his thumb across the blade.

"Wider—wider," the brute with the knife demanded, and Lamia's legs were spread fuller apart

She bit down on her lower lip, concentrated, and felt herself floating in a half consciousness. She felt every scrape of the knife on her flesh as her pubic hair was carelessly shaved away. The hair under her arms was scraped off. Then her long, red hair fell in dismal piles to the floor. She had expected this. Shaving was necessary in order to determine that she carried no charms that could be hidden in body hair.

Next, the chief torturer extracted from his robe the long needle, crusted with old blood and filth. Lamia thrashed her head from side to side, groaning and whimpering in genuine terror.

Father Jean said behind her, "The needle is for you, if you refuse to make an honest confession."

She choked out, "I have nothing to confess."

"Beatae Gloriosae Mariae Virginio fuit dulce et suave

Domino Nostro Jesu Christo," Father Jean mumbled, waving his hand over her face in a gesture of blessing.

Lamia withstood a compulsion to spit into his sanctimonious face that hovered over her. Then her eye caught the glint of firelight on the descending needle and she set her mind and flesh for its plunge into her body. She screamed, then screamed again, as the brute drew the needle out of her inner thigh to thrust it into her again, an inch away from the first wound. Fresh blood dripped from the point now, her own blood, and the sight of it sickened her stomach. The needle seemed to have been stabbed into her mind, rather than her leg, increasing her fear. Her very life was in that blood they were spilling.

The Devil's mark. They were searching for the place where Satan had entered her body when she made a pact with him, or when his seed entered her as she was formed in Eliza's womb—the spot would be marked by insensitivity to pain. She thought about *why* they were doing this to her, rather than *what* they were doing to her, in a desperate effort to maintain detachment. But she became confused and forgot to scream when the needle slid deep into the pliant flesh of her vagina.

"Hah! There it is," Father Jean exclaimed triumphantly. "Speak now, witch, for you are proven possessed. The Devil's mark is upon you."

"I—I am not a witch," Lamia cried, frantic, her failure to scream at the proper moment sorely undermining her confidence.

"What was the nature of your pact with Satan?"

"I made no pact."

"To the box," Father Jean commanded.

Lamia was roughly hauled across the room and stuffed into a tall, iron casket. The lid was slammed closed and locked. She stood there tightly enclosed in total blackness. There was not room enough to turn around. She could bend her knees only just a little.

A creaking sound came from over her head, but she could see nothing. Then something brushed the top of her head and her hands flew up to feel spikes, dozens of them, lowering slowly. Frantically, she bent her knees as far as she could, dropping her chin. There was no pain to avoid in these moments of terror through control; the spikes over her were cutting into her mind rather than into her flesh, into her conviction. They would not kill her in the torture chamber. Their aim was *not* to kill her, but to terrify and torture her until she confessed. But how did they know what was happening inside this casket? Accidentally, they might— No. Marco had said they were experts, proficient. It was a new trade, that of professional ghoul. They were maiming fiends, but not murderers.

The spikes pressed against the back of her head. She could bend no further, but she did, just a little, her forehead scraping across the rough metal of the box. The blades descended at a snail's pace, jabbing into her scalp, deeper, deeper.

Lamia's confidence suddenly shattered and pain overwhelmed her, multiplied by the abruptness of its attack. Blood ran into her eyes and her mouth, blending with her salty tears to a mixture that tasted like death on her tongue.

The creaking stopped. The casket flew open and Lamia fell out to sprawl, hysterical, upon the putrid floor at the feet of Father Jean.

"God is merciful—God is just. Will you now make an honest confession?"

"I—have—nothing—to confess," Lamia gasped, remaining face down on the floor, every wound of her flesh throbbing and burning. She weakly brought a hand up to wipe blood from her eyes and mouth. Then she felt herself being lifted, one of the brutes deliberately carrying her with his hands cupped around her breasts. The work was far more enjoyable, when the witch was young and pretty.

"To the rack," Father Jean ordered impatiently.

As they bound her, arms extended, to the ponderous machine, Lamia's eyes were fixed upon the bishop's bent countenance. Near exhaustion of both body and mind, she thought to hear a child's passionate cry, "Satan! Satan, kill him! Put a knot in his—"

"You possess a familiar. A black cat. Well do we know this as the favorite disguise of the demons. Tell us what *other* disguises your familiar affects. Name your cohorts and God will be merciful and just. Does your familiar skulk invisibly near you at this moment, hoping to rescue you? Speak, or I will command the cranks to be turned."

Lamia dropped her chin against her chest, glaring down at Father Jean. Eliza's tormentor. Over and over again Eliza had told her the story of those terrible years in this same church cellar, about her suffering at the hands of this priest.

Suddenly Lamia laughed out loud. The *weapon!* It shone bright before her mind's eye, bright as a star in the heavens. The Devil had not deserted her!

Whether in this chamber, or outside it, the weapon was accusation. Not planning on being captured, she had always thought it would be necessary for someone *else* to point the finger. The bishop would have swallowed the masterwort unbeknownst, would have danced on the graves. The whisperings would have turned to condemnations. But now her own finger could be pointed at him, to multiply the satisfaction of revenge. Here, upon the rack, the weapon was even expanded. Now, it could include Father Jean, who excommunicated and murdered Jeanne and who drove Eliza to insanity, then saw her burned.

She laughed again, startling the men of God who watched and causing extreme discomfort in Father Jean, who stood but a few feet below, looking up at her anxiously. "Have no fear," she whispered down to him, "I will not speak."

"What? Uh—" Father Jean stuttered in confusion.

"Eh? What was that?" the coadjutor called out, striding toward the rack. "What was that the witch said?"

"No!" Lamia cried dramatically. "I will not speak. I cannot. I dare not!"

At the new, more brazen, tone in her voice, the bishop sat forward in his chair. There seemed to be a hint of defeat in her words. Surely, it was *defeat!* Slowly he rose to his feet, an ice forming around his heart. Before his mind's eye he saw Eliza de Nevers burning on the pyre. He knew that the weapon of accusation was within reach of her child, who was now upon the rack. The question was, would she use it? He moved with stiff, reluctant steps toward the machine, his heart beating irregularly.

The pink-cheeked coadjutor said softly up to Lamia, "If you confess, my child, I promise you mercy, in His name. Speak, do. Do not suffer further pain. Confess, my child."

"I cannot—cannot speak."

The cranks were turned rapidly, until the slack in the

heavy cords was taken up, then slowly, in a half circle, until Lamia screamed, her ribs about to snap apart, her ankles, wrists, and arms straining out of their sockets.

"Stop!" she shrieked, sweat running in rivulets along her arched body, dripping through the rack to the floor.

The men let loose of the cranks and she gasped for air in an ecstasy of relief. "I confess," she whispered.

The coadjutor smiled, also relieved. But the bishop's face had blanched, and Father Jean stood frozen below her, barely breathing.

"You must name your cohorts," the coadjutor said with paternal gentility.

"Oui," she whispered. "But, I am so in fear—of—what they will do to me."

"In this house, God will protect you, my child."

"My cat—my familiar is—"

"Turn the cranks!" the bishop cried in a high-pitched voice, his mind suddenly springing to his own defense. "God has spoken to me and told me she will lie. The Devil is on her tongue. Turn the cranks, I say!"

"But—your Holiness," the coadjutor gasped in surprise and pious indignation, "the child has confessed. Torture is no longer—"

"You dare to question my Holy judgment, Louis?"

"No! No, your Holiness. But—"

"You see!" Lamia cried. "You see how he attempts to still my tongue?"

"Turn the cranks," the bishop commanded, rising to his full and holy height before the chief torturer. "Obey, vile lout, or find *yourself* upon this machine!"

"Belial! Belial!" Lamia wailed. "He is Belial, and Father Jean is a sorcerer. They attend every Sabbat." Her words were choked off, as the ropes tightened according to the bishop's hysterical command.

Her ankle and wrist bones snapped out of their sockets— cracking sounds exploded in her ears and she could not utter any further accusations. With a piercing scream, she fell into blessed unconsciousness.

The four torturers loosed the ties on her wrists and ankles, carefully lifting her down to lay her flat upon the wooden table. They looked to each other with knowing glances. Highly experienced at this work, these men had become accustomed to such vengeful accusations. Many a clever witch had taken her judge and accuser with her to the stake. It was the way of this peculiar business and they watched with heightened interest the faces of the holy men she had just accused—and the face of the bewildered coadjutor. The four clerics wore impassive expressions, but it was easy enough to guess what they were thinking and what they would excitedly tell the curious crowd above in the town.

Expertly, the torturers put themselves to the task of resetting Lamia's joints; they had been careful not to break the flesh. One day the physicians of the world would learn invaluable lessons in anatomy and bone-setting from these brutal practitioners of Inquisitorial arts. Surgery was being mastered by these ghouls, in their quartering and continual experiments in search of new ways to create agony without death.

Lamia fought her way out of unconsciousness, forced her eyes open, and saw the blurred image of the coadjutor's face; he was leaning close to her, pale and trembling in his genuine concern.

"Will you now confess that you lied? Admit that Bishop Geoffroi is not Belial, the demon—that your torment can be ended."

"He is Belial—my familiar. Now he wishes to—to kill me. In retaliation." She closed her eyes and prayed for a return of unconsciousness.

"And Father Jean?"

"As—as a goat—he flew with me to the Sab—Sabbat, many Sabbats. Belial—the bishop—he hid—sheltered me all—all these years." She slid into unconsciousness again, but a burning sniff of a traditional witches' medication, a condensation of hog's urine, wrenched her back to Hell. The torches hurt her eyes; she could barely see.

"She lies!" the bishop shouted from behind his coadjutor. "Continue the torture."

"A foul liar," Father Jean raged, his mind unable to accept what was happening to him. Thirty years, and no witch had ever had presence of mind enough to attempt such a retribution.

"Have you no Christian pity?" the coadjutor suddenly

cried, whirling upon his superior. "She is half dead with pain and loss of blood. She has confessed before God and these witnesses. To continue the torture would be—."

"I said—continue the torture!" The bishop cried out.

He could think of nothing but himself, felt himself slipping into an abyss. All the witches he had burned and tortured were reaching skeletal arms up from Hell to drag him under. He must save himself. He did not want to die. "Continue the torture, I say!"

The coadjutor stepped back, appalled, as slivers of wood were driven under the witch's fingernails.

Coadjutor Louis was a sincere and dedicated man. He did not question the *Die gratia* for torture, but he did not like it—it sickened his stomach, if not his soul or conscience. Never had he seen the holy laws so flagrantly perverted and desecrated. She had confessed, and the command for pain had been doubled, rather than called to a halt, constituting unbridled blasphemy, a sinful brutality. With such hysterical efforts to force her, through further punishment, to admit she lied, the bishop announced his own guilt. Her accusations could have been ignored, would have been—by a man calm in sanctified grace and innocence. The bishop was of holy eminence, his sanctity unimpeachable. How could he, as coadjutor, without an order from the Catholic See, hold such a man on accusation of heresy, a man of such power and estate? But, as the Malleus contended, no office was too high or sanctified that the holder was immune to Satan's lust and temptations. Giles de Rais, marshall and peer of France, a man of vast wealth and power, had been accused of sorcery, tried, convicted, then hanged and burned.

Louis' mind began to list the names of bishops and lesser prelates burned in the past fifty years—while the torturers sat Lamia up, placed her feet in iron shoes, then poured hot oil into the shoes.

She thrashed and screamed, moaned and wept, and still the coadjutor floundered in a fearful dilemma. He finally decided that he could not take it upon himself. He must write to the Inquisitor General, Jacob Sprenger, and give him all the evidence at hand, including the witness's written account of the bishop's transformation into a cat, x'd by the hangman's son. He did not interrupt the proceedings again.

For three more hours the torture continued, until Lamia no longer responded to the vapor but remained in a state of shock, her eyelids fluttering, her lips moving in hissing, delirious condemnations.

Two guards were called into the chamber. They carried her up the long flight of steps, blood dripping a trail behind them. She was chained to the wall of her cell and a physician was brought to salve her wounds as best he could. To aid her recovery, he opened a vein in her limp arm and let blood flow forth to fill a cup.

Lamia lay naked and half conscious on the cell floor, her face swollen—a grotesque mask of bruises, open scratches, and crimson welts. Her fingers were twice normal size, her feet broiled red and puffed with enormous, watery blisters; her shaved skull was jagged-cut and bleeding slightly. Her joints were so swollen and painful that she could not lift an arm or move her head from side to side.

For three days the apathetic physician patiently spooned broth between her rejecting lips, keeping her alive to face a second session of torture and eventual burning.

"Will you *tell* me what is happening," Count Jacques raged, while Giles sat tensely across the table from him, not touching his evening meal. "Giles, I do not understand it. Any of it. The *bishop?* Preposterous. I think I should storm that prison and see him released."

"No, mon père," Giles said patiently. "Leave it to the Church. The order came from the Inquisitor General himself."

"Oui. Indeed," the count said uncertainly. Reaching to locate his plate with searching hands, he picked up a chicken part and lifted it to chew off a large mouthful, chewing thoughtfully. "The Red Witch accusing him. Beyond belief!"

Audette dropped her spoon to her plate and snapped, "The bitch lied. I know she did. The bishop would not—would never make a pact with Satan."

"Of *course* not," Giles agreed, but avoided her eyes.

"Pasque dieu; whatever has got into you, Giles?" she sang sweetly, rarely harsh before the count, particularly when he was in her home. "How civil you are this evening. Amazingly agreeable for the past few weeks."

"My Giles?" the count said on a laugh. "Why Giles is *always* agreeable. Once I did not feel kindly toward him, but now, I think to understand him. A man could have far worse an eldest son."

"Indeed," Audette said flatly. "I hear the witch is almost recovered enough to be sent back to the torture chamber. Six weeks it has taken. Her wounds must have been terribly severe. I would adore to watch sometime."

Giles flashed an accusing glance to his wife's profile, then instantly looked away. Expertly hiding his revulsion and shame for her, he turned his attention back to his father, who was not the slightest bit taken aback by her statements; half the people he knew had said the same thing to him.

"You seem less—less *furious*, Giles," the count said around a mouthful of savory rice. "About the witch, I mean. You were fair livid the day she was taken, as I recall."

Giles felt Audette's attention upon him. "Oui. Less furious. I still do not approve of Inquisitorial methods, but a witch is a witch and must be punished."

"Of course, of course. Now you are making sense, my son. Hanged, quartered, burned—they are just as dead."

"Oui, mon père."

"Do you think they will burn the bishop?" Audette asked. "I cannot imagine His Holiness—I mean, it staggers me to think of it. It would be like burning, well—*God!*"

"He will be taken to Cologne for trial," Giles offered, trying not to sound pleased. "They say the poor man sits speechless and staring, touching not a drop of food. The Inquisitor General will be his judge, no less."

"Father Jean was accused, too, but he is *free*," Audette added sourly. "Now *he* is the one I would like to see burn. Do you know what he had the temerity to say to me in the confessional last week? The callous brute, he—"

"Audette," Giles scolded mildly, "the confessional should not be discussed at table, or anywhere else. That is between yourself and the Almighty. Hmm?"

"Yes, well—he is free. Why did they not arrest *him?*"

"Because only a witch's word is not enough. There is the hangman's son, who is supposed to have seen the bishop turn into a cat, and several new witnesses have come forth against the bishop."

"Truly?" she squealed, delighted. "Tell me, Giles."

"Riffraff. I think the gossip turned their feeble brains toward delusion. One old woman swears the bishop turned her daughter into a toad which hopped away never to be seen again; insists she witnessed the transformation as well as the conjuration."

"A *toad!*" Audette laughed, shaking her head contemptuously. "Oh really, that is too amusing. The bishop once tried to avoid setting his foot upon a little frog and sprawled on his face before the entire congregation. Not that he was afraid that he would kill it; he is simply squeamish about crawling, hopping things."

Giles thought bitterly, squeamish about reptiles, but able to burn his fellow humans alive and batter their flesh and bones beforehand. A tragic paradox. "He is likely innocent and will be proven so. . . . But the Red Witch *will* burn."

"I do hope so," Audette said doubtfully. "But they say she steadfastly refuses to repeat her confession."

"She will," he said with studied assurance, glancing aside to his father. "She will never withstand a second session of torture."

"Pray God you are right," the count muttered sourly.

"What is it, mon père? You sound distressed."

"Father Jean roams free, true enough. Straight to my person, he came, with the suggestion that I take that fiend into my house if she should prove inordinately stubborn during the second torture. Can you imagine! He had to show me the words—read them to me—in the holy book before I would believe he was sane. Mabila almost fainted at the mere suggestion."

"In God's name!" Giles exclaimed, feigning complete bewilderment. "Why would they want you to take her in? I do not understand. She is imprisoned and—"

"Oh, Giles," Audette scolded condescendingly, "you can be so—so obtuse sometimes. If you were not forever with your hands in the dirt with your villains, you would have heard, as I did from Lydia, that it is common practice to place a stubborn witch in a fine home under the ruse that she is now believed innocent. Then—"

"I do not believe it. Is this true, mon père? Father Jean

wished you to take her in and to somehow trick her into—into God only knows what? Appalling idea. Monstrous."

"Huh," the count grunted, moving uneasily on his chair. "He expects poor Mabila to befriend the fiend, can you imagine—trick her by asking for a potion. My poor Mabila is in hysterics at the very idea."

"Indeed, I do not blame Mabila. If that witch were in your house, she could be stalking you and you would not be able to *see* her. She could stab you in your sleep, or drop poison in your wine under your very nose!"

Count Jacques' face drained, his eyes widening.

"You would have to leave it entirely to Mabila, since you are almost completely blind."

At this, Audette laughed sharply. "Mabila! She would dissolve, simply dissolve at the sight of the witch. So how, I ask you, can she be expected to become *friends* with the harpy? Ridiculous. Too amusing."

"Amusing?" the count reflected doubtfully. "Not very amusing to *me*. Father Jean will have to find another castle. Oui. Somewhere else. Not my house. No, never."

"The nearest is forty miles away at Pevele," Giles offered, damning his heart that insisted upon thrashing wildly in his chest; he was certain the sound of its thumpings was reaching Audette's ear, or his father's.

"Hmm," Count Jacques growled. "Give me some bread, Giles. I cannot see it to reach for it."

Giles handed him the loaf of bread. "I will speak to Father Jean about this, if you like, mon père."

"About what?" the count asked dazedly.

"Seeking another house."

"Ah. Oui. I would appreciate that, my son. Poison me, eh? You know, she could. I will not have it." He suddenly slammed the flat of a hand on the table. "I will not be subjected to such risks. I? Make friends with a witch? Can you imagine. Insane nonsense."

Giles turned a smile upon Audette. "I would wager *you* could make friends with her, Audette." He then turned quickly back to his father, adding, "My wife is not the skittish kind, mon père. She is strong emotionally and not easily frightened." He hoped his compliments would offset what might have appeared to be an insult. Not many weeks ago he had accused her of being worse than the witch, lacking only the refinements of the trade.

Audette had indeed bristled, but she chose not to object until she was certain how her father-in-law would react to such an idea. She fixed her eyes hard upon the count, watching every twist of his expression, weighing every word he spoke.

"Would you dare?" Count Jacques asked admiringly of Audette. "It would require an enormous amount of courage and piety."

"But you have said it is insane nonsense, mon père," Audette chirped.

"And so it is. But someone must do it, I suppose. I would, if I were not blind. It is only my blindness that makes me reluctant, you understand. For me to attempt such a ruse would indeed be insane."

"Of course I understand," she said sweetly. "I could manage the witch easily enough. She would not frighten me one whit."

Giles smiled upon her bemusedly. "You *are* a cool one, m'amie. What if she bewitched you, hmm? Cast a terrible spell upon you while under your care?"

"Impossible," she snapped confidently. "Those of unwavering faith cannot be influenced by Satan. Those who tremble in fear of witches' spells are guilt-ridden and vulnerable. I, my husband, am invulnerable regarding Satan and his foul handmaidens." As she concluded her argument, she watched the count closely for his reaction.

"Ah," Giles said, grinning, "I think you would change your tune, if we were not just *supposing*. If we were actually—"

"No!" she interrupted quickly, "I am sincere. If Father Jean asked us, I would readily agree. It would be truly exciting."

"Oh, wait a *moment!*" Giles exclaimed, lifting half out of his chair in pretended shock. "We are doing exactly that—supposing, and no more. God forbid that Father Jean should suggest such a thing to me. Let us change the subject, please!"

"There are no ramparts surrounding your villa to hold in the witch," the count reflected.

"True, mon père! Exactly. But from what I have heard of the tortures, she would not be able to fly, to so much as breathe deeply, for many a week."

"Confined to a bed?" Audette interjected, behind her eyes a gleaming temptation. "Giles, it would be so simple, really it would."

"Audette! You cannot be suggesting—suggesting that we take in this witch, be a party to her burning? You well know my thoughts on the subject of burnings. I will have no part in bringing her to such a fate."

"Indeed," she answered absentmindedly.

"I mean it. You will not press the matter."

"Of course not, Giles," she agreed, while her mind considered exactly how she would put the idea to Father Jean.

How very exciting. Lydia would simply perish with envy. All Nevers would speak of the piety, courage, and wit of the Baroness de la Fleur, and the count would see how capable she would be as Countess de Nevers. Lydia would never be countess, never. Strong, Giles had said of her, not easily frightened. He had never paid her compliments and his words warmed her; she deeply longed to see admiration in his eyes, if not undying love—anything save the contempt that always lay cold behind his glance, even while he made love to her. Of course, the witch might confess during the next session of torture, but, if not. . . . She trembled with anticipation, imagining the various, devious methods by which she could win the witch's confidence and affection.

Chapter 18

 AT DAWN, ON THE twenty-fourth day of the month
September, Bishop Geoffroi de la Tremoille,
stripped of office, was removed from Saint
Aliquis prison to begin the long journey to Cologne, Germany, where he would be tried. He was accompanied by a dozen members of his personal staff, a small army
of knights from the court of the Inquisitor General, the
hangman's son, and three other witnesses against him.

Coadjutor Louis, already investitured as bishop, had assumed Bishop Geoffroi's duties. The chancellor would soon
be named coadjutor, and a young Flemish priest was being
considered for chancellor. Father Jean's name did not appear
on any list of candidates for any status other than that of a
suspect.

For the time being the new bishop stomached the parish
priest of Nevers Town, which disturbed his saintly digestion
to a painful degree. He tolerated him because the arrogant
priest had threatened to take half the court of Saint Aliquis
with him to the stake if he were taken to trial, and Bishop
Louis did not for one moment consider that threat an empty
one, nor one impossible to carry out—the present predicament of Geoffroi as evidence. And he had received direct orders from His Holiness, Jacob Sprenger, to cast an obscuring

shadow over any other clerical offenders, the Church suffering disaggrandisement enough in Nevers Parish already.

Father Jean walked a tightrope. Whichever direction he chose to step led to destruction. If he moved backward along the rope, Bishop Louis' ecclesiastical justice awaited like a flaming abyss, and if he moved too far forward along the rope, an aroused citizenry loomed, a grim threat. Thus the aging priest teetered in the middle, maintaining his equilibrium as best he could, placating both sides, before and behind; the rope was his lifeline.

The Red Witch was returned to the torture chamber on the seventeenth day of October. Father Jean wanted to see her accidentally killed, to still her accusing tongue, but he did not dare. He could not take the slightest risk—had been unable to think of any method of destroying her that would not somehow point to himself as suspect. He was entirely and directly responsible for her in the chamber. With damnable resolution and willpower she had recovered almost completely, was as coldly defiant and implacable as ever.

While Bishop Louis observed closely, Father Jean had the thumb screws applied, then the spiked collar, then her fingernails and toenails were pulled out one by one. She was hung from the ceiling by her thumbs, to swing above her tormentors for long hours.

Finally the ashen-faced bishop approached Lamia where she dangled, and he said up to her, "Why did you not repeat your confession in your cell, child? Why do you persist in this? Have mercy upon yourself. Confess and I will cut you down immediately."

"I confess," Lamia hoarsely responded.

"But will you repeat the confession in your cell—sign a written copy with your mark?"

"Probably not, your Holiness," she whispered, "most likely not."

"God damn you to Hell!" Louis shouted up at her. "Who but a witch would persist in the face of such agony? You tax my patience and my pity. You will burn in any case. There is no *point* in refusing to confess!"

Lamia groaned, tried to hoist her weak and battered body up, to relieve the pain and breaking weight upon her thumbs, but she only swung around in a circle, then back the other way, like a lifeless puppet on strings. "Whatever else you must do—do to me. Do it—and have done—have done with it."

"Only the pincers are left," Father Jean offered in his most subservient tone. "The result is usually permanent destruction of the flesh. Sometimes death results, though not often, we are careful to avoid that. If cautiously applied—"

"Reserve the pincers," Louis replied sourly. "Return her to the rack. I will depart to preside over Mass." In actuality, he felt ill to the point of retching and wished to escape the blood and stench for at least an hour or two. "If she confesses and promises to repeat it in her cell, have one of the clerics take it down. Adhere to the laws, Father Jean. The smallest transgression will be dealt with severely. There are nine witnesses in this chamber. At least *one* of them is loyal to me."

Father Jean nodded obediently, to indicate he understood what was being said and what had been left unsaid.

"I will confess!" Lamia cried weakly down to the exasperated bishop. "Do not leave me with this sorcerer. He will kill me!"

Louis turned his head to eye her severely and doubtfully, fully aware that only one more session was available to the Court of Justice. And he was certain that she knew it, too. Perhaps she was filled with confidence, having survived thus far through the second session. If she could bear two, why not one more after that? He wished to have done with this inherited, messy affair, to see this witch burned, to have peace and order restored to Nevers Parish. He certainly had no intention of setting her free to plague his newly gained holdings. She was a witch and had to burn. Her guilt was patently obvious and generally accepted. The very foundations of the Inquisition would be threatened if obstinate *children* could prevail against the might and inculpability of Holy Church. She had weakened once and she would again. There were other ways, within the law, of penetrating a stubborn will, and he would not hesitate to use those devious methods, if it became necessary.

"Cut her down," Louis commanded, swallowing nausea when a splash of her blood splattered upon his sleeve. "One more turn on the rack, as a reminder of its cruelty, then write down her confession." He warned Lamia, "Know that the third session is the worst, child. The red-hot pincers will tear your flesh from your bones. The rack will be allowed to wrench you apart at the joints. The knives in the box will stab deeper into your skull. In one week I will come to your cell to receive your mark upon a written confession. There is no escaping the stake, but a return to this chamber can be avoided."

In the dead of night, on the twenty-fourth day of October, a wagon guarded by six mounted knights in full armor drew up to La Ville de la Fleur. Father Jean gave the command and a swathed, limp body was lifted from under piles of sackcloth and carried into the house.

In a third-floor bedchamber Lamia was laid upon a bed and left alone in the darkness. She did not know where she was, or why, nor did she care. She could not move a muscle, had not eaten in more days than she could recall. She vaguely recalled Father Jean explaining that they believed now that she was innocent, but he could not have said that; she must have been dreaming. Pain wracked her entire body, ever increasing, swelling in brutal spasms.

Below, Giles rushed nervously about the house. The arrival of the witch had been expected, but not so soon. He had a servant woman awake his two small sons, dress them, then sent them off in a carriage to his father's castle for their protection, and as evidence of his belief in the witch's guilt and powers, his reluctance to have her in his house.

Lamia was supposed to think herself now completely free of suspicion, the master and mistress of this house having offered Christian charity to her for the duration of her recovery. Her judges had to stoically accept the risks involved in this release from prison and punishment. She would escape justice in any case, if she survived a third session of torture. In the Malleus Maleficarum this ruse was highly recommended by His Holiness, Jacob Sprenger; thus they had no fear of Inquisitorial reprimand if it somehow failed, the fiend taking flight.

Two young clerics took their places as servants in the house, as guards for Giles and Audette, and as the watchful eyes of Holy Church.

Father Jean paced the house as uneasily as Giles. He finally stormed up the staircase to the chosen third-floor room. There, he inspected the sheer drop from the windows and searched the room again for possible escape hatches, ignoring the shallow-breathing wretch on the bed. She could not walk, thus she could hardly fly—but what witch could fly? God knew he had been to enough Sabbats and never had he seen a demonstration of that particular satanic art. Satisfied she was for the time being safely imprisoned in this room, he returned to the lower level, barking orders to his clerics, instructing Giles meticulously in what was expected of him.

"Win her trust, her affection. Rest assured, no act of pity or charity will be construed as anything save diligence to religious duty. I will expect the baroness to report to me daily. I will visit the witch on Fridays, to encourage her return to Grace and to God's mercy. She must not suspect that she is being watched. This kind of ruse has taken a year and longer to be successful. You must realize it will not be accomplished overnight, Baron."

Giles nodded, listening intently, suffering a genuine apprehension. His nerves were near the breaking point. He had received a message from Cellini not one hour before the wagon and Father Jean arrived, warning him that she would arrive sooner than expected, though Cellini did not know exactly what day. No need to send word, he would know when she had been moved.

For as long as possible the town of Nevers was to think that the witch was still in the prison, though no one hoped to maintain the illusion for long. Giles' servants and villains could not be expected to remain close-mouthed and they, also, had to believe Bishop Louis had released her as innocent—few of the unlettered knew the thousand secret formulas for death and deceit in the Malleus. The main purpose in the secret move was to insure against a rioting of the populace, a spontaneous burning that was not sanctioned yet with a valid confession, Holy Church ever certain that the public was as bloodthirsty as itself.

Giles had stubbornly refused to take the witch in, but gradually weakened under Audette's nagging arguments. He had known from the beginning that she would not be able to resist this barbarous and sensational plot against another. He finally agreed on the premise that obtaining a confession by friendship was a far kinder method than by torture. Since the stake was inevitable, he argued, his conscience could accept it. Father Jean had been heatedly against la Fleur as the place for the witch, recalling Giles' rash impiety during his first year at Nevers Castle. But it was argued that the baron had shown himself to be at least acceptably devout in the past four years. Bishop Louis finally insisted upon la Fleur, considering the lack of ramparts and battlements an advantage rather than a liability. The witch would feel far more free here and would actually be more accessible. When the castle drawbridges were lifted at night, the entire population of that house could be murdered before aid could force its way in.

Audette had been carefully instructed, blessed, and prayed for. She was fully prepared to launch the attack and absolutely certain of her eventual success. The witch would be so unnerved by being tricked, virtually caught in the act, that she would instantly sign the confession.

Father Jean finally admitted that all was as secure as possible, and he departed for Nevers Town.

Giles moved in feigned exhaustion up the long staircase, the two clerics close at his heels. When he reached the third level, he turned and demanded of them, "Do you intend to stand over her bed, for God's sake? How free can she feel, with your eyes constantly upon her?"

"We intend to stand guard outside the door, Baron."

"I see. May I look at the wretch?"

"But of course. You may lie with her, if you like." The man smirked, pleased by his cleverness. "The bishop has said any method you choose that results in her valid confession will be acceptable, will be forgiven, on the basis that the intent is pious, though the act itself is sinful."

"I should think lying with her would be carrying it a bit far," Giles casually joked with the cheerful clerics.

"A bit, perhaps, Baron, but I doubt that you would be interested in any case. She is not a pretty sight, I can tell you."

"The Church does seem rather inconsistent in this case," Giles remarked conversationally, slowly moving toward her door. "First, they carry her in a box so she cannot touch the earth and fly away, they vow her to be capable of the grossest transformations and powers, not a single guard daring to lay a hand upon her—and this night she is free in my home, men's arms having held her to carry her to this room. To be truthful, I am confused. But my sons are safe, and it is my duty. Will it be safe for me to touch her, do you think? Truly?"

The taller of the two clerics smiled reassuringly. "She has no charms, nothing with which to conjure demons. She is drained of strength. For now, she is powerless, I would think."

Giles put his hand to the door latch. For the benefit of the clerics, he crossed himself before opening the door. He entered with his heart hammering. Turning, he put a forefinger to his lips, indicating silence, and easily closed the door in the clerics' faces, with polite apology on his face—they knew they must not be seen by the witch.

He rushed to the bed. He had not seen her when they brought her into the house, wrapped as she was in a friar's robe and hood. When he had lighted a candle beside her bed, he sucked in his breath, a hand flying up to his mouth to hold back an eruption from his objecting stomach.

Open wounds pocked her hairless skull and her lips were scabbed and puffed where her teeth had bitten into them in her agony. He leaned and with a shaking hand drew back the coverlet. She was clothed in a sackcloth sheath, from out of which stretched bloated limbs, scalded, gashed, black-and-blue flesh. The ends of her fingers and toes were horribly enlarged, pustulent abcesses which gave off a carious odor that sent Giles reeling for the chamberpot, into which he emptied his last meal.

Looking upon Lamia where she lay moaning in semi-consciousness, Giles thought of Jesus Christ's plea on the cross, *Father forgive them, for they know not what they do.* Jesus could forgive, but he could not. And surely God would not forgive this blasphemy against his own. Moving close to her, he reached to lightly brush her bruised cheek with a forefinger.

Lamia's eyelids fluttered up, but for a few seconds she did not recognize Giles in the dim light.

"Fiametta," he whispered, choking on emotion. "You are free. You are at my villa."

"Giles? Are . . . you real? Or just . . . a dream?"

"You must not call me Giles, but Baron—or messire. We do not know each other. Do you understand?"

She just perceptibly nodded.

"They hope to trap you. You know the ruse. We managed to get you here, but it will be many weeks and months before you will be strong enough to travel and endure hardships."

"Burned . . . him?" she whispered.

"Hmm?" he asked, leaning to hear her hoarse whisperings.

"Have . . . they burned the . . . bishop?"

"No. No, Fiametta."

"Ach—" Tears filled her eyes; it had all been a waste.

"But he has been stripped of office, and will be tried at Cologne within the month."

She sighed and turned her eyes back to him. "The price one pays—for hatred. Hmm? Eliza . . . can rest? Peronnette, too?"

"Oui, they can rest, ma petite."

"You should not . . . have done this."

"Risky, to be sure," he said, smiling achingly, "but you are definitely worth the risk."

"I—wonder."

She gasped, eyes squeezing closed, her teeth biting into the scabs of her lower lips, as pain hacked at her body in a thousand separate places. "Bring Ghanim—to me?" she said between clenched teeth. "Need him . . . desperately. Cannot—cannot find power to . . . the *pain*."

Giles hesitated, but how could he refuse her? He said, "I will try. I will get word to Cellini first thing in the morning. Rest now. Can I— What can I do to soothe your wounds? Fiametta, I—I am so sorry, but I am totally ignorant of any salve for such infections as—as," nodding helplessly to her toes and fingers.

"Ghanim knows," she hissed. "Will heal me. His father was—was a . . ."

She slipped into unconsciousness and Giles brought the coverlet up to her chin, then softly moved to the door. He stopped, altered the expression on his face as best he could, then opened the door to face the curious clerics.

* * *

"Exquisite!" Audette sang, happily clapping her hands together, as Ghanim, with a flirtatious smile, spread a length of embroidered Indian silk across her lap.

Giles appeared relaxed where he sat in his chair, a glass of white wine in his hand. He watched Ghanim closely.

"Giles," Audette called aside to him, "will you truly buy me any pieces I choose? Any?"

"Any, my love," he replied in a cool voice.

Audette did not question his new attitude toward her, merely moved through the days in a cloud of rapturous triumph. Still, he did not make love to her, but that would come, a hint of it gleaming behind his eyes. How long since he had taken to a separate bedchamber? A year? No, far longer than that. Now he had ceased to bicker with her, giving her her way in every smallest thing. Giles had always been miserly in his spending, but he had suddenly offered to have this Moorish acquaintance of his bring silks and cottons from Bourges for her choosing.

"I must have this silk," she exclaimed, "and the yellow linen, and the blue, designed cotton."

"Speak to *him*," Giles said to her. "The man can read your lips. Tell him what you have chosen."

Audette flashed a coy glance up to the handsome face leaning close, discomfited by his afflictions but stirred by the sensual beauty of his features. His fingers occasionally brushed hers, and, as lowly a personage as he was, the touch burned her flesh. She again named her choices, enunciating carefully, her eyes deliberately speaking of her interest in him as a man, eyelashes fluttering provocatively. After all, Giles neglected her unmercifully, and love dwelt only in the bosom of youth, which was fast escaping her; she was already twenty and one. Rainulf had been her first lover after her marriage; it had continued until he married Lydia. Then the Italian architect who came from Florence to supervise the construction of the villa. This proud Moor would make a delightful third.

"Do ask the merchant to stay the night, Giles," Audette chirped. "It is very late, and I am certain he would prefer not to stay in that beastly inn on the highroad."

"Of course," Giles agreed, rising to his feet. He moved to

touch Ghanim's shoulder for attention, and made the invitation.

Ghanim politely refused. Audette and Giles insisted and he reluctantly agreed. He was given a bedchamber on the second floor.

Later that evening, Giles followed his wife into her bedchamber and purposefully shut the door behind him. Audette's breath caught, as he moved toward her with a bright promise in his eyes.

Ghanim wandered restlessly about the house. The servants had all retired. He finally aroused the interest of one of the clerics who was sprawled out on the floor of the reception room before the fire. With expressive hand and arm motions, he coaxed the man into a game of dice and several glasses of drugged wine. When the cleric was in a stupor, Ghanim moved up the staircase, the bottle in his hand, two glasses in the other hand, the powder up his sleeve—to likewise incapacitate the cleric who guarded Lamia's door.

Ghanim whipped into her room. Kneeling beside the bed, he skillfully hid his emotions. Gently he slipped his arms around her, holding her injured head against his heart, his mind pouring words of love and comfort into her mind.

When he pulled back a little, to meet her eyes, Lamia smiled at him and said huskily, "I lost . . . the power. Give it back to me . . . please. The pain."

He moved the coverlet back and with studied detachment examined her wounds. She had been in Giles' house three days. The festering had increased. Her joints were livid, black, and swollen.

Ghanim jumped to his feet, turned heel, and left the room. After a short interval he returned with a kettle of boiling water, clean cloths, and various bottles and jars from his carrying case. He used henbane, a deadly poison, as a soothing plaster that would relax the tissues and relieve her pain; in addition to having an emollient effect, this treatment often appeased the infection. It was a witch's preparation and treatment, therefore the use of it was punishable by the stake. He applied steaming cloths to her swollen joints, gently massaging between applications. Ghanim forced Lamia to swallow a potion concocted from the snake root that would console her tortured mind. Finally, he bound all her joints and her ribs with long strips of cotton and smeared a thick henbane plaster on each toe and fingertip.

By the time Ghanim had finished, Lamia's awareness had begun to blur under the effects of the drug of solace. She smiled dreamily at Ghanim, unable to utter a word in gratitude. But he knew what she wanted to say. He leaned to brush his lips against hers, put his hand on her salved and bandaged head, nodded in goodbye, and moved quickly out of the room.

Giles left Audette's bed after midnight. He met Ghanim at the head of the staircase. Ghanim gave him the bottle marked SOLANACEAE, instructing him in the proper dosage, also a written message that explained to Giles what he must say, that he heard her weeping in the night, got up, and she instructed him to bandage her—that he complied because he had to demonstrate an honest interest in her recovery. Each day, fresh bandages. If any infection showed signs of putrefaction, Giles was to get word to Ghanim at once.

Giles nodded that he understood, a light of admiration for Ghanim in his eyes. They separated, each going to his own chamber.

In the morning, Giles severely reprimanded the clerics for drunkenness. With Audette, he sent a demand to Father Jean for more dependable guards. His life was at stake here, and that of his wife, as well as the guests in his house, and these stupid louts had drunk themselves into a stupor.

The two clerics shamefacedly admitted to overdrinking, but they could not recall just how much they had swallowed.

Before leaving for Bourges, Ghanim offered his hosts a written apology for encouraging their servants to drink, adding, "Do you take the drinking of your servants so seriously, Baron—as to discharge them?" confirming his ignorance of the clerics' true occupations.

No one else in the house knew as yet exactly who occupied that third-floor bedchamber, but speculation amongst Giles' servants ran high.

The winter wind beating against the shutters and the constant drumming of heavy rain on the villa's roof grated on the nerves of everyone in the house. Three months had passed.

Lamia sat before the blazing fire, wrapped in a blanket of violet wool. Her head was covered now with two inches of softly curling hair, except for one spot above her right eye and another at the center of her forehead, where thin lines of scar tissue prevented the growth of hair. Her face was clear of bruises and scars, but dreadfully thin, her cheeks and eyes sunken and purple-shadowed.

"Are you certain you do not wish to play?" Audette invited pleasantly. "Just one game?"

"No. But thank you, Baroness," Lamia replied listlessly.

Giles left the chess board and his frustrated wife, moving to stand by the fire facing Lamia. "Do your hands pain you?" he asked softly.

"Oui. A little, Baron."

A servant girl entered the room with a tray, giving Lamia a wide berth. She set the tray of cheese and wedges of bread beside Audette.

"Really, Julie," Audette snapped. "You insult our guest again. Make your apology this instant. Go and offer her the tray. She can hardly reach it from where she is sitting. Do as I say!"

"But, Madame, I—" the girl whimpered.

"She has been *released*. Innocent. Does that word have no meaning for you? For shame! God have mercy on you, Julie, for your lack of Christian charity. Now, do as you were told." Audette stood and picked up the pink Venetian glass platter, pushing it unceremoniously into the servant's shaking hands. She then took the girl by the arm and pulled her to where Lamia sat.

"Forgive her," Audette said to Lamia. "These ignorant peasants simply cannot understand. One has to beat any sense at all into them."

"Peu de chose," Lamia smiled up at Audette, ignoring the trembling girl leaning over her with her breath held, eyes squeezed tightly closed.

"But it *does* matter!" Then to Julie, "Your apology. I have not heard it."

"I am not exactly a guest here, Baroness," Lamia said carefully. "Julie and I are of the same station, equals, so she need not apologize for being afraid of me."

"Oh, but you *are* a guest, Lamia. Tell her, Giles. She is here at our invitation. Those *fiends* of the Holy Inquisition! Truly, it warmed our hearts to be able to do this for you, my dear."

Lamia almost laughed out loud. She thought, *Beware, hungry snake; you are trying to swallow an elephant.* She glanced up to Giles and with exaggerated fearfulness, said, "Can it be true, Baron? After my terrible experiences, it is so difficult to again put my trust in *anyone*."

"Believe her, mistress. My wife speaks the truth." Giles' voice was flat, his severe annoyance written on his face. Lamia insisted on badgering him with guileless questions and double entendre.

"I am *so* gratified," Lamia said on an outrush of breath, but letting her glance flutter doubtfully from one to the other, a subtle message to Audette that she was not yet entirely won over.

Julie finally muttered a fearful apology and made a hasty escape. Giles and Audette returned to the chess board, while Lamia gazed moodily into the fire. The storm outside had subsided, the shutters banging less noisily. The clock struck eleven and Lamia clumsily rose from the chair, hanging on to the arm as she shifted her emaciated body around and up to a standing position.

Giles got to his feet and rushed to help her, taking hold of her at one elbow to ease the burden on her ankles and feet that were swathed in wool hose and soft, overlarge leather shoes.

"I hobble like an ancient," Lamia said, laughing dryly.

At the bottom of the staircase, Giles leaned to lift her into his arms, moving quickly with her up the long flight of steps.

"She will not like this," Lamia whispered in his ear, tightening her arms around his neck.

"So?"

"So, you should have called a servant to carry me."

"He is a spy."

"I know."

"Do you want to be carried to your bed by a spy?"

"Satan deliver me, no!"

"Then hush your mouth, witch."

"Sir! I am innocent. You have said so yourself."

"Innocent as a snake in the Garden of Eden."

"Ach! I knew it. You are against me, attempt to trick me. Woe! All is lost."

Giles put her down carefully on the bed, smiling at her. "Be good, Fiametta," he whispered. "After what you have been through, I should think you could take this situation a little more seriously. More—"

"I am *very* serious, Giles. I have no intention of returning to that damned hellhole!"

"Then cease badgering me," he said hoarsely, finding it difficult to keep his voice down. "You are constantly parrying with me, as if you expect me to drop my guard, or *want* me to."

Her eyes swept over his face, not a glint of humor in them now. "I am so utterly dependent upon you, Giles."

"What, you do not trust me? You must have faith in me. I will not fail you. Do you think me so weak and ineffectual as all that? I am insulted."

"Do not be. It is only that I dislike helplessness. My life belongs in my own hands, not in anyone else's." She smiled, and abruptly said, "Come *with* me, Giles."

"What?" He laughed, startled. His mouth tightened as emotion overwhelmed him and he looked away from her. Ah, to escape the ties that bound him, to find that easy life a lost youth had longed for.

"Whenever I go and to wherever; come with me."

"Now, what are you two whispering about, hmm?" Audette suddenly chirped from the doorway, and Giles bolted upright in surprise.

Audette coldly eyed her husband, then let her glance slide down to where Lamia blandly reclined on the bed. *Impossible*, she told herself. The wench might once have been lovely, but she was decidedly unattractive now. Giles could not possibly have become enamored with the likes of her. But he did act strangely sometimes, his performance almost too believable. Why did he bolt up so guiltily just then?

Audette moved purposefully to the bed and with maternal cluckings and scoldings tucked Lamia under the coverlets, fluffing her pillows and solicitously smoothing her hair back from her forehead. "There now; we are ready for a good night's sleep. Come, Giles. Lamia is tired. Do not forget, my dear—a short stroll along the river tomorrow afternoon, weather permitting. A good night to you, m'amie."

Lamia bloomed with the acacia trees in mid May, her joints only a little stiff, her form filled out to proportions that rivaled those of a year past. Her finger and toe ends were scarred and stubbed, but nails had grown back—misshapen, but, by a miracle, there. One foot turned at a slight outward angle as she walked. She had said aside to Giles one day, "I may never swing through the trees again, but I am whole and alive." She covered the scars on her head by sweeping her hair to one side with a brush.

Lamia had been in Giles' house just over six months and was becoming increasingly impatient, constantly pressing him to set a date for her escape. Plans must be made. She could not simply walk away from the villa.

Once every month Ghanim came to be with her, but she saw him only at meals, or from across a chess board. Audette was far too watchful to risk meeting in his or her chamber at night.

Father Jean had been a paragon of unfaltering, patient benevolence. Lamia knew there was a passion to destroy her beneath the surface of his blessings, but she harbored no deep animosity toward him. His fate was of no concern to her. The vendetta was at an end.

On Good Friday, Bishop Geoffroi had been burned at the stake in the city of Cologne, Germany. It was accomplished. Not exactly as Lamia had planned it for so many years, but done. She had had the satisfaction of pointing the finger of accusation that resulted in his trial and execution. A pale substitute for being there to watch his agony, but in Ghanim's stars it had been written this way and no amount of regret or poisonous raving against the unfairness of fate would wash away a line of it. They had beheaded him before burning, to reduce his suffering. If she had been there to witness his punishment, she would have found such compassion toward him intolerable. Enough that he was dead from the pointing of her own finger. Now she could begin to live out her life.

But how? Where? To what place could she run? Was there a haven someplace where God did not attack the multitude with torture and flaming stakes? Millions of women would burn on the pyres of Holy Church before God's thirst for blood was satisfied, and Lamia did not intend to be one of the victims.

Certainly, there was no safe place in all of France for the Red Witch of Nevers. Her heart lay cold as stone in her breast. She could not run far enough or fast enough to escape the wrath of Holy Church. But she *would* run. She must at least try to find a haven.

Chapter 19

 GILES MOVED SWIFTLY DOWN the hallway and slipped into Lamia's room. As soon as she had begun to walk freely about the house, the clerics had stopped standing guard outside the door.

"Giles? What is it?" Lamia whispered, sitting upright in bed. Moonlight spilled in the open window to illuminate his anxious face.

He sat down on the edge of the bed, meeting her eyes with bitter regret in his own.

"What *is* it?" she insisted.

"Audette and Father Jean have decided that on Friday next, following your prayers and his departure, you will be approached for the potion."

"Wonderful!" she exclaimed. "Now, perhaps you will send word to Marco and start plans for my escape. I am perfectly able to travel now."

"How swiftly these ten months have passed," he reflected wistfully. "I will miss you." He rose from the bed to pace restlessly back and forth.

Lamia got out of bed, to stand before him. Her hair curled below her ears in tangled disarray. She wore a flowing cotton nightdress that covered all save her hands and head. "Giles,

I ask you again to come with me. You are not happy with that—that harpy."

"Fiametta, *please!*"

He rarely spoke her name even when they were entirely alone, and it sounded foreign to her. She would never be called Fiametta, or Lamia, again. When she began her new life, there would be a new name for the new woman.

Lamia reached for his hand and held it tight in hers. "You love her so desperately, do you?"

"I loathe her, you know that. She poisons my soul."

"This is not the life you dreamed of when you were twenty, when I first knew you. Where is joy? And love? Oh, you were so enamored with love, looking for it so hungrily."

Giles looked upon her lovely face and suffered a compulsion to shout, "Yes! I *will* escape with you." But he swallowed the impulse and his reluctance tasted bitter upon his tongue. "I cannot," he murmured. "I cannot desert my sons. Nor could I take them with me and subject them to a life of uncertainty and want. Little Jacques will be Count de Nevers one day; just Baron de la Fleur would be enough. My feet have become rooted to this soil, as Cinto knew that they would. This villa was given to me as fertilizer for the roots that hold me to it now."

"And love?"

"Love is lost for me."

Lamia moved closer to him, leaning forward to say with her lips brushing his, "Do you recall that first kiss you gave me?"

"I do," he said roughly, his hands rising to lie restlessly upon her arms. "I do, indeed."

"You said that you were not the kind of man to ravage virgin infants. I am neither of those things now; not infant, not virgin."

Giles stepped back from her, shocked, and at the same time stimulated. Impulsively he strode to the door and slid the bolt across. He turned, standing motionless, inspecting her where she stood in a flood of moonlight. "You are the most artless, instinctively sinful woman I have ever met," he said, the words critical but his tone complimentary, indicating some confusion. He was beginning to suspect that there was indeed an "in-between" in regard to women. He could not think of Lamia as a harlot, or at least perferred not to. Nor was she a saint, by any means. Peronnette had not been a saint, either, nor had his mother, and he had loved each of them desperately. It suddenly occurred to him that he had never known a completely virtuous woman.

"Good and evil are matters of opinion," Lamia offered, laughing at him, "depending upon where you were born and to what religion. Lust is not a sin to me. It is a virtue, a joy, a reward, an entertainment and a gift I can give to a man I love. May I give you my gifts, Sire? Or are you so virtuous and pious a man as to refuse me, hmm?"

"You said—to a man you *love*," he said, stepping uneasily toward her.

"Oui."

"But you did not wait for me, as you vowed you would."

"I could not put you at risk, could not have you when I was in need."

"So you gave yourself to others."

"Admitted. I am unromantic, Giles. My life, as I am forced to live it, simply has no room in it for swooning, flirting, and silly fancies. I am forced to concentrate on *survival*. But my gifts are gold and silver—" She was deliberately flirting with him, drawing him to her with a shining, promising smile. "As long as you are within touch of my hand, I love only you—you alone."

"Stop it!" Giles caught her arms in his hands, shaking her hard. "Those are harlot's words and they offend me! Fiametta, I . . . Good Lord, you set my senses reeling. I suddenly do not know what I think, or what I want." Shaking his head, he tried to steady his mind. He met her eyes then and said low, "We would be continually at odds with one another, if I ran away with you. You and I are of different breeds. It would be like mixing black powder with fire. You stir lust in me, as no other woman has or will after you, I wager, but—"

"Are you going to allow my fire to burn itself out, while you justify and excuse your lust for me? I care not whether your mind can love me, but how your hands will tremble when they touch me, your lips hard on mine, your fire intermingled with mine." She leaned forward until he swung his arms tight around her, his mouth falling upon hers, closing off her teasing flow of words.

Giles had not held a woman in passionate embrace since Peronnette. He had taken Audette coldly, for relief; she stirred but the slightest spark in him.

After but one lingering, gasping kiss, Lamia's heat had burned into his very bones. He felt her teeth playfully bite into his lower lip and he bit her back, his hand catching her hair, yanking her head back so that he could pour himself into her through her blazing eyes. She laughed at him, as if he were a fumbling boy and she a practiced courtesan. In a fury of outraged ego, he wrenched the nightdress over her head, lifted her in his arms, and threw her upon the bed.

"You may give me that baby now, Giles," she whispered in his ear. "I will take that much of you with me—that much."

"I will give you two—three, perhaps," he gasped against her mouth, his hands around her face. "Witch—witch," he accused between quick kisses. "My angel—my gold and silver witch. I am drowning in you. But I would scream in rage if someone tried to rescue me."

At precisely that moment a soft knocking upon the door interrupted Giles' passion and he froze over Lamia. His hand flew out to cover her mouth, to still any remarks she might feel inclined to make.

"Lamia?" Audette's voice called, hollow-sounding from beyond the door. "Are you all right? Lamia?"

The latch rattled ominously. Lamia tried to rise to a sitting position, giggles upsurging in her throat. Giles pulled his hand from her lips and dropped his mouth down on hers in a brutal kiss.

While his wife apprehensively searched the house for him, Giles accepted Lamia's gifts. Caution, virtue, honor—were all empty words. He was alive again. The moonlight was rose-hued. The world outside glowed rose-red. The ghost of love had risen from Peronnette's grave to return and live in him again.

Audette sat stiffly before Father Jean in his rectory chamber. She twisted a lace kerchief into a thin rope with jerking, fluttering fingers.

"Is there trouble with the witch, Baroness?" he asked, leaning intently forward in his chair.

"Ah—" she began; then her mouth sliced closed. Giles was her means to a throne. Without him she would descend, a pale widow, into obscurity. If he vanished, deserted her, as his grieving wife she would be allowed no other husband; she would be buried alive at la Fleur. Rainulf would become Count de Nevers. *Lydia* would be Countess de Nevers.

"My dear Baroness," Father Jean said solicitously, "it is obvious that you are quite disturbed. It cannot be that the witch has escaped, or you would be far more overwrought." He shuddered at the thought. He was certain, now, that it was Lamia who had placed the cat on Geoffroi's bed. God save him from her wrath, if ever she should run free again.

"No! Oh, no," Audette exclaimed. "Of course she has not escaped! What—uh, I was wondering—what attitude would Holy Church take in the case of—I mean, if she cast a spell upon Giles, or myself, rendering us helpless, or—or weakening our minds and wills. Would this constitute punishable possession?"

Father Jean rocked back in his chair, grinding his teeth in tense concentration. "A simple matter of exorcism," he said gravely to Audette. "The Church realizes the probability of just such an occurrence in these cases."

"I see . . ." she said uncertainly.

"Surely, *you* are not bewitched, Baroness."

"No, uh—but I fear the baron has been put under a spell. I—"

"Ah! Excellent. If we can prove that, do you not see this as extra evidence? Tell me of this spell."

"He behaves—how can I put this, Father?—overly solicitous. I believe she has used her returned beauty and satanic ways to lure him into a lustful union with her. I—Father, I beg of you, do not reveal to her even the slightest suspicion, or she might kill my husband, thinking he has *told* me, and he has *not*. The baron is helpless, bewitched by her, and I think it would be wise to approach her immediately, not waiting until Friday next."

Father Jean scowled, his cold eyes carefully fixed upon Audette. All the earmarks of a jealous wife in fear of losing her man to a flame-haired temptress. The baroness was as incredulous as he. Not for one moment did she believe any spell except lust was involved.

So, Baron Giles had been drawn into league with the witch. The question was, would he risk the stake by aiding her in an escape attempt? And how might he aid her, while maintaining a guise of pious innocence?

The cranks turned furiously in Father Jean's agile mind. Putting himself in Giles' place, he speculated from that position. No, he would not dash away with her. What man would turn his back on the de Sade fortune, and a countship? Feign her death, perhaps—substitute a body. Call in her satanic cohorts; probable enough. But how would the baron know whom to call to her aid? His mouth twisted into a bitter sulk. Of course, the witch would tell him who to contact. Ridiculous. The man would not dare. His wife was unreasonably suspicious since the witch had regained her beauty.

"Perhaps you are right, Baroness."

"Yes? About what, Father?"

"Attempting to extract a potion from her before Friday. Tomorrow? Hmm? Shall we try it tomorrow?"

"Oh, Father, I doubt that she truly trusts me. I feel so strongly that she will only laugh at me, when I ask her for it."

"Then laugh with her. You are friends. There will be other days. This will only be the first attempt. Put it to her lightly. Later you may become gravely ill, begging her to help you."

Audette suddenly thought of the bottle from which Giles had poured forth a liquid which kept Lamia in a senseless coma for days and days. She had asked him where it came from and he had said he did not know—the witch had extracted it from under her pillow the night she asked him to bandage her wounds. His new attitude. It was all becoming clear. The change in Giles had been too abrupt. And that deaf-mute, who smiled so suggestively, brushed her fingertips with his own, but who politely refused all her advances, as if he were keeping her on a puppet string of promise, his real intentions far divided from the appearance of romantic interest.

She did not loathe Giles for taking the witch. Wives of her time and station accepted such affairs as inevitable, an affirmation of her husband's virility. Courtly adultery was not only acceptable but expected. Love and marriage did not walk together. But for him to *leave* her; she could not shake this fear from her mind. At least one hundred times in the past he had threatened to send her back to her father, to drive her from his house and his life. If he should take that harlot as his mistress, as the count had done with Mabila . . . dear God, she would kill the witch before she would let that happen, slash her hideous throat and say it was done in pious fury against Satan. If the ruse failed and Lamia survived the last session of torture, she would be freed, and Giles might bring her back to la Fleur—to stay. Or, if he ran away with her . . . no, he would not desert the children.

Audette departed from the rectory in a seething fury of confused intentions. She had heard that from the leaf of the oleander shrub a poison could be extracted that caused the heart to cease beating.

Audette was positive now that Giles had never intended to trick the witch. He had connived, played a cat-and-mouse game to manipulate her toward this scheme. For *this* she loathed him. Cursed him and his effeminate emotions that prompted him to try and save an unknown witch from punishment. So like him, the fool, forever quoting Christ in condemnation of Holy Church, so tender with his revolting villains. And now he was lying with a witch! He would soon see how naive his wife was, just how easy she was to manipulate, would be able to do nothing, lest he admit fraternity with Satan. She would hold his lust for Lamia at his throat like a sword. If he tried to desert her, she would plunge that blade into him and he would die on the stake beside his foul mistress.

"Lamia, we have become dear friends," Audette purred, her needle flashing in and out of the needlework design she was working. "I know of a certainty that you were never a witch, only possessed by that fiendish Bishop Geoffroi. But, I was wondering . . ."

Alerted, Lamia sat forward in her chair and carefully fastened her needle in the needlework cloth. She sat back again, folding her hands in her lap. It was only Monday. What had altered the plan? "Wondering, Baroness?" she asked innocently.

"Oui," Audette said, clearing her throat. "I was wondering whether the bishop, whose vile influence you were under—if he, perhaps, ever revealed to you any of the secret potions for curing ill health. You see, my heart has been fairly bounding from my chest of late, mostly at night as I lie restful. As you know, Giles was forced to send for the physician last night, but, impossible fool, all he could prescribe was hourly doses of hot water and vinegar. I have heard that sorcerers, such as the late Bishop Geoffroi, cherish a secret potion for the heart that is extracted from some forest plant or other."

"Truly?" Lamia asked. "How interesting, Baroness. I have not heard of this before. Tell me more about this strange potion."

"Ach, I wish I could. Then you cannot help me?" Her voice had broken slightly and she had lifted a hand to clutch her breast over her heart in feigned suffering.

Lamia rose to her feet and went to place an arm around the back of Audette's chair. "Perhaps you *could* obtain the potion, Baroness."

Audette whirled around in the chair. She cried, "Tell me! Where? I must have it!"

"I should think one of your servants or villains would know of a true witch hereabouts, that you could go to in your need."

"Oh, I thought of that, m'amie, but none could, or would, tell me. I am distraught. I think to any day drop dead in my tracks."

"I doubt very much that you will die, Baroness," Lamia said with a smile, moving her arm to press a hand against the woman's shoulder comfortingly.

Audette flinched under the touch. Her hand moved into the pocket of her sewing smock and grasped hold of the mysterious bottle she had finally uncovered in Giles' chamber, after hours and hours of searching the entire house. She was not certain it was a witch's brew, that it was something for which Lamia could be proven a witch. She had hoped to obtain something more incriminating. This bottle would simply have to do, along with her own testimony as to how it was to have been used. In her hand she held the fruit of all these long months of subterfuge.

Standing over Audette, her hand on the woman's shoulder,

Lamia suddenly stiffened. Her mind-fairy was warning her. Alert to danger, now, she saw Audette's hand moving a little inside the pocket of her smock. Quickly stepping around the chair, she stood facing the woman, glaring down at her.

"What is it, m'amie?" Audette asked uneasily, her fingers tightening around the bottle. "I pray I have not insulted you, with such a request. If I were not so *desperately* ill, I would not have asked."

Lamia deliberately let her eyes drop slowly down to the pocket. Ghanim's training now served her well. She saw his writing clearly, saying, *What does she hold in her hand?* Not a button, this time, nor a bit of colored glass, or a roman numeral. A bottle marked SOLANACEAE.

"I do wish you would not stare at me like that," Audette complained. "Forgive me, if—"

"Give it to me," Lamia commanded coldly, holding out a hand to Audette.

Audette's confidence began to crumble and a small fear tightened her throat. "How dare you speak to me in that tone of voice!" She tried to get out of the chair, but Lamia stepped closer and blocked her with her body.

"I said, give it to me," Lamia insisted, vigorously shaking the hand held out to Audette. If she allowed this woman to so much as move out of her sight, that bottle would be in the hands of Father Jean's spies. "Daughter of a *toad!*" Lamia shouted at the woman, "I said put it into my hand."

Audette's face twisted into a mask of murderous hatred. With a lunge she was out of the chair and fighting to escape with the evidence. But Lamia caught her wrist in a powerful grip, wrenching her hand free from the pocket of her smock.

Lamia easily pried open Audette's fingers and removed the bottle from her fist. "Thank you, Baroness, m'amie," she snapped sarcastically.

Enraged, Audette opened her mouth to scream for the guards, but Lamia's hand fastened over her mouth. She fought, but could not match the witch's strength. Audette was thrown back into the chair, her head was forced back, and all that remained of the potion was poured down her objecting throat.

Within minutes Audette was sprawled in the chair like a rag doll, babbling incoherently. When Lamia was certain the woman was entirely insensible, she dashed out of the room in search of Giles.

She found him at the stables and approached him running, dramatically shouting that his poor wife had fainted, had collapsed while they were at their stitching.

Giles instantly broke into a run toward her. Together they ran toward the house. He asked breathlessly, "What happened, for Christ's sake?"

"The bitch stepped out of her league!" Lamia raged. "The solanaceae. She found it and was about to—"

"Oh my dear God! You have not *killed* her?" He abruptly halted, and grabbed Lamia by the arm to stop her. "What have you done?"

"No! Of course not!" She was furious that he would think her so stupid as to do such a thing. "I fed her the rest of the drug, which put her to sleep. You must get word to Marco immediately. I cannot remain here another day."

"But—where will you go? I—"

"Giles! We cannot talk about this out here, for all eyes to see us. Take care of your wife. We will discuss this later. Later!"

Giles carried Audette to her bedchamber, unceremoniously dropped her on her bed, left the room, and locked the door behind him. He sent one of his servants for the physician, then rushed to meet Lamia in her chamber, where he found her pacing agitatedly.

"Why did you seize her?" he asked angrily. "You could have let her think you—"

"Because she was about to use the solanaceae! She would have given it to a servant, saying that I *gave* it to her. I could not have escaped. And if you had tried to aid me, your life would have ended."

"How could you have known her intention? Did she speak of it?"

Lamia shook her head exasperatedly. "No, my darling Giles, she did not speak of it. I read her thoughts. Her kind are not all that difficult to read; she has a witch's intellect. I would have done the same in her position, if a wench such as I threatened to steal you from her." She smiled at him provocatively.

"Be serious, for Christ's sake!" he stormed, spinning on his heels to begin pacing the room.

"I *am* being serious!"

"For the love of God, where will you run to? You cannot go alone. Cellini could hide you somewhere, but for how *long?* Fiametta, I cannot let you—"

"Giles," she interrupted somewhat maternally, "Audette knows. Your part in this—everything. I am sure of it. Not only me to consider now, but you as well. I will not leave you to face the stake, after all you have given to me—my very life, in fact. I have been thinking and thinking about it, for weeks now. How could I have thought to just vanish, leaving you to face Holy Church? Send for Marco. We can risk his coming here now; we must. We have only until tomorrow; no longer. Father Jean will be awaiting Audette's report of success or failure. My recuperation is complete. I can travel by any means, to any place."

Giles swung around and caught her in his arms, pulling her tight against him. "Dear God, how I wish my soul was as free as yours, Fiametta—that I could catch on the wind like thistledown and fly away with you. Five years ago, I would have gone anywhere with you."

She kissed his cheek fervently and said, "No. Oh no, Giles. Five years ago you loved Peronnette. You would not have flown away with *her*, either. While you loved her, your plans were to marry Audette."

Tears welled into his eyes and he hugged her tighter. He whispered in her ear, "Some can fly. Most must walk. I am a man who can only walk."

She pulled herself back and kissed him on the mouth. "Find Marco. Bring him here. I will plan my escape while you are gone. How can I make you appear entirely innocent, hmm? and at the same time close the accusing mouth of your treacherous wife. Shall I poison her for you, my darling?"

"Good Christ! No." He pulled away from her, holding her by the arms, not doubting for an instant that she would do it if he agreed.

"I can see her dead," Lamia said soberly. "I have no doubt that someone will poison her someday . . . Well, she is *your* wife; suffer her as you will."

Next morning, the baroness did not arrive at the rectory, nor had she made an appearance when the sun was full in the sky. Father Jean strolled along the street outside the church, nodding sourly to his parishioners, as they greeted him in passing. His eye fell upon an ancient with a flower basket on her arm, talking in whispers to the daughter of the glassmaker. He recognized Hortense, knew her from the Sabbats, but did not immediately think anything of her presence in Nevers Town.

Another hour passed and Father Jean was becoming increasingly ill-at-ease. He saw a goatherd rush headlong down the street, after a quick conversation with the glassmaker's young daughter, who had been the virgin priestess at the last Sabbat, as if he had been given a vital message to relay. Old Hortense had all day been whispering in the ears of persons he knew to be disciples of Satan.

Father Jean had never accused or burned a single member of the sect that had allowed him into their society. It had been Count Henri who had insisted upon the taking and accusing of Jeanne, long ago. Nor did they accuse him; it was an unspoken, unwritten pact. He had received no information about a gathering. What were they up to? Certainly, word was being passed about a gathering of *some* sort.

Father Jean impulsively approached the young woman in the open window of the glass shop. She met his presence with icy withdrawal, a chill loathing for him in her eyes.

"Do you have a message for me, Matilde?" he asked hesitantly.

"Why no, Father. Why do you ask?"

"You would not lie to me."

"Ah no, Father!"

Precarious as his situation was with the rabble, he decided not to press her. Word had only the day before reached Nevers that a north country bishopric had been attacked by an aroused peasantry, the walled castle taken, burned and sacked, the bishop slain. What was the world coming to? This wench knew all about that accusation made against him by the Red Witch under torture. She knew she herself could accuse him now, and probably suffer no consequences.

He dared not stir this simple peasant's wrath. He said low, "God be with thee, my child. A good day."

He returned to the rectory, but Baroness de la Fleur was not there waiting for him.

Just before sunset, an anxious manservant from the home of Henri LeClercq arrived at the rectory with a message from the physician's wife. LeClercq had been called to la Fleur last night to attend the baroness, who had had a fainting spell, and he still had not returned.

"The madame is that sure the witch has him in her power," the servant exclaimed.

Father Jean quickly called for a horse and an escort of twelve knights in full regalia. He set forth for la Fleur, intending to prevent any attempt on the part of the witches to try and rescue the red-haired whore. That had to be what it was all about; it was the only way Baron de la Fleur could be made to look injured and unsullied.

"At the witching hour," Marco said, smiling, "they will swarm over la Fleur like a plague of locusts. They will take you prisoner, Giles, and treat you roughly before your servants. You will manfully attempt to prevent their taking the terrible Red Witch from this house, but to no avail."

"How many?" Giles asked, trying not to let Cellini know how uneasy he was. His knees were quaking.

"More than thirty. Perhaps fifty."

"That many?" Giles asked, genuinely amazed. "Considering how many the Inquisition has burned, how could there be thirty to fifty in this area?"

Marco laughed at his naiveté. "My good man, the Inquisition rarely burns the *true* witch. She is too clever to be caught. It is usually the innocent who burn. It has been estimated that over half the population of Europe indulges itself in satanism to one degree or another. It is a fad, my friend; a particular fancy of the bored nobility. That surprises you, too, eh? Ah, many a fair maiden, dancing white glove to white glove with a dashing young knight at the Court in Paris, is a proficient witch—perhaps her beau is a studying sorcerer. The Black Mass is imitated in splendid salons, such as this one, in castle great halls, the ensuant orgies a delightful respite from the rigors of being rich and bored. Now and

286 ❖

then they even go so far as to butcher an infant, when the orgies no longer satisfy their craving for unusual excitement."

"No wonder the Church—I mean, the Church, then, is not merely deluded, insanely chasing shadows."

"No wonder, you say," Marco interrupted. "The end justifies the means, does it? Fight evil with evil. Hardly a Christian approach. 'Go, and sin no more,' Christ said to Mary Magdalene; he did not enter into her profession and become a male prostitute, eh? An eye for an eye; yes, that is *my* approach, but I am not a Christian. Why do the priests not admit that they are pagan devil worshipers, and do their burning honestly? Ach! They speak and think more about the Devil then they do of Christ, God, and the Virgin Mary combined!"

Giles glanced to the clock over the mantel, nervously wringing his hands together, only half listening to Cellini now.

"At ease, Giles," Marco scolded. "We have hours to wait. Ghanim will ride in with the witches. Lamia must be waiting for him at the stables. If the barge is somehow rendered unusable, they will take horses."

"Where will he take her, Marco?" Giles asked roughly.

"Up to the sky—to rewrite the stars."

"What a hell of a time for jests!"

"I am serious enough. Once she thought to love you. But now it is Ghanim who will take her, love her, and protect her. You know that the Moslems believe our fates are written in the stars?"

"Yes, and I think I believe it. Not since the day I entered Nevers have I felt truly the ruler of my destiny."

"It was written that our Fiametta would survive. The fate designed for her here in Nevers will be rewritten. God love her, I pray she finds happiness and—"

Suddenly they were interrupted by the sound of many horses outside. Cellini leaped to his feet, and Giles lunged for the door, racing up the staircase to warn Lamia.

Father Jean rushed into the salon, halting to glare at Marco Cellini, who stood relaxed by the fire with a glass of wine in his hand. "Sire Cellini! A surprise to find *you* in this house."

"I must say that your presence is a bit of a surprise to *me*, Father Jean."

The priest walked toward the merchant, his hands clenched together behind his back, his black skirt rustling in the evening stillness. He reached around then, to take hold of the chain around his neck, anxiously swinging his cross in wide arcs as he paced. Finding Cellini here had been a great shock to him.

"Have you stretched and maimed any witches lately?" Marco asked matter-of-factly, his eyes cloaking his loathing of the priest.

"I beg your pardon?"

"I said—have you stretched and—"

"I heard you."

"Then why did you ask, eh?"

"What are you looking for from me, Sire Cellini?"

"Ah, defensiveness, perhaps—just a glimmer of guilt behind your Christian facade."

"What is your business in this house?"

"Money, good and holy Father."

"A debt to collect, is that it?"

"Oui. My man, Ghanim, sold cloth to the baroness for which I have not yet been paid. I was passing this way, and—"

"Indeed," Father Jean interrupted uneasily. "Just where *is* your debtor, if I may ask?"

"With the baroness. It seems she has been taken ill."

"Ill, indeed."

"Oui, ill."

Giles entered hurriedly, pretending to be surprised at the sight of the priest. "Father Jean! What brings you to my house at this hour?"

"Where is LeClercq, the physician, Baron?"

"Why, he left here this afternoon. Perhaps he had another patient to see before—"

Lamia entered the room with an exaggerated limp.

"Lamia," Giles exclaimed in a voice too high-pitched, "see who is here. . . . Will you eat with us, Father? I believe it is chicken tonight."

Father Jean's eyes slid from one to the other. In league, the three of them. The baron, on orders from the wretch, had sent for Cellini—but *why;* what interest would the merchant sorcerer have in this accused witch? Cellini was well known as the kind of man who could see his mother burn without a trace of emotion, without making the slightest effort on her behalf. Suave, inscrutable, stepping suddenly out of his ever-elusive role to enter into this foolish scheme. He would not dare directly oppose a man as powerfully aligned with the satanists as Cellini.

"Are you well?" Father Jean said warmly to Lamia. "You look rather pale this evening."

"Still weak, Father," she murmured, "but well enough, thank you."

"Bon. I came to protect you, child. It has been buzzing around Nevers Town today that the witches and demons will prowl tonight. I was in fear for you."

"For *me*, Father? Why would the witches have any interest in me?"

"Ah, they might try to reap vengeance upon you, for your destruction of Geoffroi, who was, as you well know, one of their leaders."

"Alone, unaided, you hope to protect me from Satan?"

"Twelve knights have surrounded this house. We will remain throughout the night."

"Ridiculous!" Giles protested excitedly. "This is really quite absurd. If the witches wanted revenge, why would they wait almost a year? Lamia has been freely moving about my acres for five months, in my house for ten months. Preposterous."

"We shall see, Baron. Your wife is ill. May I see her, please? What did LeClercq say ails her, hmm?"

"Exhaustion," Giles said quickly, "merely nervous exhaustion." He glanced to Cellini's bemused face, then back to the priest. "She is asleep, Father. I do not—"

"Only for a few moments, Baron. She need not be awakened, to receive my blessing."

Marco nodded almost imperceptibly and Giles automatically moved toward the door, saying, "As you wish, Father." He led the way out of the room, up the staircase and to Audette's chamber, where he reached into his pocket for the key to the door.

"You have locked her in, Baron?"

Giles hesitated a moment, then said confidentially, "Oui.

To prevent the witch entering while she is in such a helpless state. You understand."

Father Jean merely nodded and stepped into the room. He quickly noted that the baroness was not asleep, but was sitting upright with several large pillows propping her. The expression on her face was like that of the hangman's son—one of utter stupidity. "What ails her, *actually*, Baron?"

"As I said, Father, nervous exhaustion. LeClercq thought, perhaps, brain fever, but—"

"Father?" Audette said drunkenly, falling forward to rest on her elbows. "I . . . I am ver-ry happy . . . to see you. Something . . . to tell you, but . . . a bottle, oui, a bottle." Her tongue slid out over her lower lip in fierce concentration.

"You can see for yourself," Giles said worriedly, his palms wet with perspiration, his forehead beaded.

"I certainly can, Baron! Your wife has been *drugged!*"

"Drugged," Audette echoed. "That is it. Bottle. Oh, I do feel so . . . queasy."

"Could the witch have done this to her?" Giles asked helplessly.

"Who else, Baron? Who else would do this to your poor wife? Is this not proof enough for you? Will you stand in accusation and describe this brazen act of—"

"Accuse! But I have seen nothing. Except that my wife is ill. There is no bottle, not that I have seen."

"As you will. I will wait here beside her bed until she is in her right mind. God is with me. No more foul potions will be fed her while I stand guard. Then we shall see if we have evidence enough to prove our case. Forgive me, Baron, but you seem unduly reluctant to have done with this ruse."

"As I told you in the beginning, Father Jean, I am revolted by burnings, though I realize they are necessary and God-sanctioned."

"Indeed, I do remember. You may leave. I want to be alone with the baroness, if you do not mind."

In the salon again, Giles paced back and forth across the Persian carpet, then followed its fringed edges in a march around the room. Lamia sat with her hands calmly folded in her lap, while Cellini leaned his shoulder against the wall in deep thought.

"What will be the reaction amongst your villains, Giles?" Marco said, his voice startling Giles so that he sucked in a breath, "when thirty or more witches in ghoulish masks descend, howling, with lighted torches?"

Giles replied uncertainly, "Why, I—I suppose they will run like frightened rabbits, tails between their legs."

"Certainly," Marco agreed, looking pleased with himself. "What is your point?"

"Could you expect anything different from Father Jean's knights, eh? Would they stand, draw their puny bows, and snap arrows at Satan's demons?"

"It is a weak hope, Marco."

"Perhaps, but I will cling to it. I think Father Jean is going to find himself single and unaided in the middle of a hornet's nest in about two hours."

"Poor man," Lamia remarked on a thin smile.

"The Devil take him, he will be repaid for your suffering, Fiametta. I want you to know that."

"Ah no, let the vermin live," she replied, sighing. "God must have had some purpose in mind when he designed the human maggots of this world. For every one you squash, a thousand more are born. Pointless to exterminate one, out of so vast a swarm. Who would do all this *good* work in God's name, if we rid the world of his vermin accomplices, hmm?"

Marco shrugged, unconvinced that he should leave Father Jean to the hands of God.

The clock ticked away the minutes, then chimed the hour. Lamia did not move from her chair. Cellini and Giles paced restlessly. At fifteen minutes before midnight, Lamia finally rose to her feet, and the two men turned sad eyes upon her.

"Perhaps we will meet again someday," she said to both of them. "The north of Africa is not the farthest corner of the world from France. Ghanim's father left him enormously wealthy; I will not want for anything. Moslems do not burn their own in bushel lots, so I will be safe there. I will think of you both—often."

Marco's mind was filled with regret and affection. He wished he could tell her how he felt, but he did not know how; he was not a man of tender phrases.

Lamia stepped to Marco and put a hand on his cheek. "I

will always love you, Marco—and be grateful to you; believe that."

He reached up and put his hand over hers, smiling wanly.

"I must go," she said unemotionally, and moved toward the door.

"Wait!" Giles called out. "I—" He still could not say it. Strongly as he wished it, still he could not fly. He stepped to her and took her two hands in his, putting his lips to her palms in a lingering kiss. "When you reach the sky, Fiametta, rewrite a line or two of *my* fate, also—my red and gold witch."

She kissed him quickly on the cheek and ran from the room, out of the house and through the garden court, slipping past a bored knight who leaned, daydreaming, against a marble column. When she reached the stables, she hid out of sight and waited.

When the clock struck midnight in the salon, a shattering screech broke the silence outside the house, emerging from the surrounding forest. Then a dense, suspended silence.

Lamia heard the guards shouting uneasily to one another, saw three of them meeting together in the moonlight for a hasty conference. Then came another moaning wail, followed by the shriek of a cat.

Father Jean's head popped out of a high window and he shouted down to a young knight below, "Be prepared for anything. That cry was not an animal!"

A young guard spun around at a peculiar rustling sound and saw a brilliant flare of light heading straight for him, a hideous, demon face behind it. He yowled up at Father Jean, "All Hell has broken loose, for certain, Father!" Within seconds he was surrounded by four monstrous hags carrying flaming torches.

Puffs of blue and red smoke, small explosions—demon after demon danced into view, yowling for the Red Witch, shouting that Satan had sent them for his child. Father Jean bellowed commands from the window that no one paid any attention to; the guards that had not been taken had run for their lives and their souls.

Moving like a wave, the witches poured into the house. They dragged a struggling Baron Giles, the merchant, household servants, and, finally, a dazed would-be countess and her parish priest out into the open of the garden court. The servants were held at bay, made to watch the goings-on; they screamed, wept, and prayed, to the delight of the performers. An enormous fire was built and an idol brought forth. A Black Mass was about to ensue.

Ghanim appeared out of the darkness and strode to Lamia's side. He took her in his arms and held her a few moments under stars that blinked knowingly down upon them. He let loose of her and took her arm, starting toward the river, but she put a hand out to stay him. She could not bring herself to leave, not until she could be certain Giles would be safe. From where she stood in the shadows of the stables, she had an unhampered view of the garden court, where a Black Mass had begun. She strained her eyes to find Giles in the melee.

Audette's eyes widened at the sight of a young girl with jet black hair, who was placing her lips upon the buttocks of a hideous demon. She flashed her gaze about her in terror until she caught sight of Giles. He was being held by two monsters, with a knife at his throat. She screamed, wrenched herself loose from the arms that held her, and raced across the courtyard toward her only hope in living, her means to a throne. As she swept close to the fire that had been built near the waterfall, the edges of her nightdress burst into flame.

Many hands grabbed for Audette with the intention of helping her, but in her hysteria she was strong. She ran in wild circles, around and around, wind fanning the flames. Before Giles could reach her, her hair was afire. He fell upon her in an attempt to smother the flames, but his own clothing caught.

Audette's mad screaming and the scent of her burning flesh ignited a powderkeg of mob emotion. The witches' mock frenzy exploded out of control and became only too real. What had been a game had become a terrible reality.

Marco Cellini elbowed and kicked his way through the writhing mob to reach Giles. He hauled him to his feet, dragging him away from his shrieking wife, slapping out the fire that was burning the sleeves and back of his shirt.

Lamia saw Marco stun Giles with a blow to the chin and drag him into the villa. She saw Father Jean being lifted into the air by many hands, saw him thrown bodily into the inferno; he had not known that the Red Witch was a cherished member of that secret sect.

Stumbling on her bad foot, Lamia ran away from the flames, away from Hell. She jumped onto the waiting barge and threw herself down upon the sacks of grain. Close behind her, Ghanim loosed the ropes, ordered the bargeman to pole away from the shore, then knelt beside her where she lay dry-eyed and staring. He touched her hair and she whipped around to fling herself into his arms, her glance casting upward to the pure night sky where a billion stars seemed to blink a promise—a hope.

The Red Witch was never seen again in Nevers.